Juicy Gossip about *ESCORT*

"I LOVE this book!"

Nikki Next XXX - Adult Film Actress, Los Angeles, California

"This was an enthralling story... I loved this book; I couldn't put it down. I'm looking forward to reading other works by these authors."

Jamie Buchanan - Author, Goodreads reviewer

"I can't put this book down. I'm going to be late getting home and my nanny is going to be pissed."

Bella - Anonymous Content Contributor

"I've always thought most men dream of doing this stuff, while you actually lived it to the fullest."

Jacques - Anonymous Content Contributor

"There had better be a sequel to this book, and it better be available right now."

Capri Jennings - Anonymous Content Contributor

Orange County Girls

A Trilogy of Books

by

Sacha Haughtee & Max Spacer

ESCORT - The True Story of an Orange County Call Girl

MILFs - The True Stories of Hot Orange County Mothers

DADDY I'm Your Daughter - The Story of an Orange County Love Child

Published by:

Sacha and Max Publications

ESCORT

The True Story of an Orange County Call Girl

Sacha Haughtee

Max Spacer

Sacha and Max Publications

ESCORT

The True Story of an Orange County Call Girl

by Sacha Haughtee & Max Spacer

Published by:

Sacha and Max Publications

Publisher's name and logo are trademarks of Sacha and Max Publications

Publisher's website: https://sites.google.com/site/sachaandmaxpublications/

Sixth Edition June 17, 2016

ISBN-13: 978-0-9891049-1-3

Library of Congress Registration #: 1855193

ADULT CONTENT: This material may not be suitable for persons under eighteen years of age.

Disclaimer: Any resemblance to actual persons or events is purely coincidental; this work is for entertainment purposes only. All models appearing in this work, and in the related promotional materials, are hired professional models over the legal age; these models are not the subjects of these works. All sexually active characters depicted in this work are over the legal age.

Cover photos, cover and interior design by the authors.

For Lisa, our little super hero

Contents

Introduction

What happens when a high-end call girl visits a well-screened and carefully selected client?

What occurs from the time she knocks at the door of his hotel room, until she leaves?

What are they doing?

What are they saying?

How are they treating each other?

What are they thinking?

How do they feel about each other?

What is their relationship like when they first meet?

How does their relationship change?

What REALLY happens during these encounters?

Under the anonymity of the call girl - client relationship, the participants are liberated to pursue completely uninhibited verbal and sexual intercourse. These strangers are free to engage in otherwise taboo subjects. The parties can explore their secret desires and discuss their curiosity of incest, masturbation, fetishes, bisexuality and so on...

Paradoxically, this unique relationship simultaneously forbids the exchange of knowledge that is otherwise commonly public, such as the girl's real name, or the man's place of employment. The anonymous aspect of the interaction helps to create an unbridled environment that allows these two intimate strangers to share dark secrets with each other that they are unable to disclose to anyone else.

This is the true story of one Southern California call girl and one long-term client. This story is told first-hand, uncensored, and unembellished. Yes, this is what really happened.

Prologue Part One

As I exit the elevator on the tenth floor, I turn and do a quick once-over in the mirrored wall. My hair looks sexy yet demure. My makeup is just the way I want it, girl next store, but not plain Jane. Then there's my outfit. Well, that's not something that I can change now anyway.

I MUST PRESS ON. My stomach is in knots and my mouth is dry, which will NOT be helpful I presume for the task at hand. Luckily, I have a bottle of water with me. Without stopping, since I am already twenty minutes late, I drink nearly half of it in just two sips.

I have a small piece of paper in my hand with the number 1012 written on it. Searching for a hotel room is never easy, and when you're already flustered and panicking as I am, it can be an arduous task. After what seems like an hour and endless direction changes, I finally find my target, room 1012. I am standing at his door. My heart is pounding. I look down and I can see my left breast pulsing. I want to take a second to calm myself down, but I need to get out of this hallway before anyone sees me.

I knock quietly. Nothing. Perhaps in my efforts to be discreet I have knocked too quietly. I knock harder a second time and I hear movement inside. Immediately my mind starts racing with a stream of questions. What am I DOING? What if I am about to be diced up and skinned alive by some complete psycho? Is any amount of money worth risking my safety? While questioning my sanity, my mind is interrupted by the door opening. I quickly draw in my breath and hope for the best.

There he stands, my first client. He is wearing a white terrycloth robe. Immediately his kind eyes put my racing brain somewhat at ease. I make my way around the door. With a quick hug and glance around the room, I feel I have reached the point of no return. I feel at ease knowing that no matter how much I panic now, I am here. I have come this far and now turning back is no longer an option. The rest is up to fate.

If only I knew at the time that this day would be the point of no return, that once a girl crosses certain moral and personal boundaries, there's no going back.

Prologue Part Two

Where are my keys? Oh, dear! Why must I always be so unorganized and flustered? I search for my keys in the freezing cold, by my thin-blooded Southern California standards, and I notice how much junk and inappropriate crap I have in my purse. I make a mental note, 'Clean out your purse you pack rat.' Ah, there they are, at the very bottom of course.

Finally, I am inside my car. I feel myself calm down as I settle into the leather seat of my messy imported luxury sport sedan. I turn on the engine and anticipate the warmth that I'm about to feel. I am too excited to drive right now, so I will just sit here for a while. I want to collect my thoughts, settle down a little, and maybe make a few phone calls.

I recline my seat back and turn my phone on. I've had it turned off for the past two hours. I assume that silencing my phone is simply proper call girl etiquette, right? He's paying me a fortune for my exclusive companionship, not to listen to me chatting away with my friends, or to be annoyed by my phone ringing. Besides that, I was worried I would be tempted to sneak away to the bathroom, if I left my phone on, and text my best friend Stacie. My phone wakes up and the text messages begin popping up. Four of them appear. I'm not even about to read any of them, since I have not yet figured out a proper alibi for my time away from the real world.

First things first. I reach for the white envelope that I had nonchalantly stuffed in my purse on my way out of the room fifteen minutes ago. I exhale a huge sigh of relief as I count the crisp, brand new hundred-dollar bills. I count them again. They are all there. I have been dreading looking in the envelope. I've been afraid that he had been too good to be true. Perhaps he had given me play money or just some pieces of paper in the envelope. Nope, it is all there, the entire amount we agreed on.

With that settled, the excitement that's been pent up finally sets in. This evening's session went so much better than I could have ever imagined. The expression 'easy money' doesn't even begin to explain it. I have just had an amazing time and I got paid as much as I would normally make in a week! There has to be a catch, or else more girls would be doing this. I do a once-over on myself. My self-esteem seems fine, certainly not damaged, and even slightly bolstered. I vow to not over-analyze this, as I often tend to do, and just chalk it up to good luck. I made a new friend, a nice man who if nothing else, was a delightful person to spend an hour with, and now I have this month's rent money and I can pay my phone bill.

As I pull out of the hotel parking lot and drive past the huge pretentious entrance, I notice an empty condom wrapper that I had shoved in my purse earlier! I roll down my window and release it into the night. I smile to myself as I imagine the person who finds it and picture their shock and disgust. I am such a brat.

Chapter 1

Is He a Perv?

I take a deep breath and knock politely but firmly on the door of room number 537. I shouldn't be so nervous. I have done this before. Well, I have done this once before. I hear someone moving around inside and the peephole goes dark. I'm shaking with nerves inside, but I try to appear calm outside. The door should open now, but it doesn't. He's had enough time to see who it is. Why doesn't he open the door? Why is he just staring at me through the stupid peephole? I smile warmly, but I can't help but wonder under my breath, "Is he a perv?"

There's a knock at the door. It's her! It's definitely her. There's no mistaking an escort's urgent, discreet knock. I jump at the sound like Pavlov's dog. I dance across the room and lunge for the door. I stop abruptly to ask myself, "Should I take a quick look through the viewer first?"

"NO!" I scold, "That's what a pervert would do." But what if she's not the girl in the photo? The image on her website isn't all that revealing. It may not be her photo anyway. I take a quick look.

I focus in on her and gasp, "Oh fuck she's cute!" Oh shit! She's so hot. I can't believe how hot she is. What do I do?

I suddenly realize that I need to stop panicking and open the door, or she'll think I'm a perv.

The door finally opens, but only a little. A wide-eyed, silver-haired man peeks out at me. He's not even as tall as I am and I'm wearing my flat shoes! He looks like he's easily twice my age. I like that he's older. He reminds me of a cross between my dad and Albert Einstein. His unassuming appearance helps to put my frayed nerves somewhat at ease. I give him a big smile and ask, "John?" He doesn't move. He just stares at me, wearing a moronic expression. I wonder if he is going to invite me in. I wonder if he's a pervert or something. He doesn't say anything, but he opens the door and stands to one side. I look him over in an attempt to determine his state of mind. He still has the same idiotic expression on his face. I enter anyway. Our eyes meet momentarily, and then I quickly scan the room. He's alone.

I open the door enough to visually validate the data from the viewer. Standing in front of me is a drop-dead-gorgeous young woman. She is too cute to be real. I can't stop looking her up-and-down. She's tall and slender like a runway-model. Her erotic pelvic bones are revealed by her hip huggers and short tank top. She gives me a bedroom-smile and says something. Her eyebrows go up as she looks past me into the room. I invite her in. She enters cautiously. We make eye contact for that long 'moment of truth' that always happens the first time you meet an escort. She slinks quickly past me, like a cat. She smells great, the way sexy girls smell.

I step across the room to the little table and set my

designer purse and my bottle of diet cola down next to a white business-sized envelope. I turn around to size-up my new client, and think it's odd that Mr. John Smith has yet to utter a single word. I peer expectantly at him and he stares back at me in complete silence.

Her pants are so low-cut that her panties make a whale tail. I bend down for a better look and follow her as she confidently strides to the other side of the room. Arriving there, she gracefully pirouettes like a ballerina and is suddenly facing me. She is toned and tanned like the adolescent dolls at the beach. She's got bushy platinum-blond hair that flows down to the middle of her back. I hope I get the opportunity to see if the carpet matches the drapes. She's so beautiful that I can't speak. I'm insecure that she is too cute to have a session with an average schmuck like me. I'm afraid she is going to cancel and leave.

I can sense that it's about to get awkward. I need to make him speak. I decide to introduce myself. I step toward the silent little man. His eyes get big. I smile at him, "Hi, I'm Tina Moore; it's nice to meet you John." I look him in the eye confidently and he stares back at me blankly. I smile hopefully and he blinks at me a few times. No hello? No hug? Not even a handshake? I think he must be high on something.

This man is a little weird, but he doesn't seem to be dangerous or anything like that. He passed the extensive background check that I ran on him and both of his references said he is a complete gentleman and is always nice to them. Maybe he's just nervous. Wait, why should he be nervous? I'm the one taking all the risks here. I decide I'll get things started. I step close to his chest and look him in the eye. I press myself against him. I wrap my arms around him and give him a big hug. The trembling man whimpers and gives me a weak hug back. Either he's hiding a salami in his pants, or he already has a huge erection.

She's smiling at me. She's saying something to me. She's moving toward me. She's reaching for me. I'm reaching for her. She smells great. I pop a major boner as I embrace her tightly.

I decide to challenge myself to see if I can make this goofy little man actually speak. I release him and ask him if I can sit down. He looks confused for a moment, then he snaps out it and blurts a clumsy reply at me.

"Yes. Of course. Please, make yourself at home. Can I get you some ice... and a glass... for your beverage?"

We chat about diet cola for a minute but the strange little man seems distracted and preoccupied. He is scrutinizing every inch of my body like he's some kind of twisted pervert. This behavior does not match the description I got from his references. They said he was nice. They both said he was their favorite client... Why is he looking at me like that? What is he thinking?

The gorgeous girl pries herself out of my arms and gracefully sits down in a chair at the table. I'm trying to act casual and chat, but I can't take my eyes off her. She's much too poised and confident to be a newbie, but at the same time, she's much too fresh and sweet to have any experience. She seems too innocent, too pure. Oh shit! Is she underage? Should I ask her to prove that she's legal? Should I ask to see her ID? I've asked girls before. Oh, and then afterward I was embarrassed when I found out that the girl actually was twenty-two years old, just like she said she was. I only think this girl is too young because I'm so damn old. I decide that I don't want to go through the awkwardness of checking her age. I can determine if she's legal merely by looking at her. I know I can. I

4

carefully examine the titillating temptress with my eyes. She's such a hotty. She glances at my crotch and stifles a grin. I look down and see that my pants are a tent. What was I supposed to be looking for?

How can I make sure that this guy is the same client that I screened last week? It would be awkward to ask to see his ID. I get an idea; I will confirm his knowledge of the references I used to approve him. I make it look as though I am just making conversation, "How long have you known the two escorts that you gave me for references?" Without giving him time to answer I ask, "How did you meet them?" John's reply is slow and deliberate.

"That depends on whom you contacted from the list of references that I gave you."

"I talked with a girl named Alley and I traded messages with a girl named Lisa."

"Those two girls know me pretty well."

John tells me the same story they did and the corroboration relaxes me a little. John explains that he met them both through referrals from other girls. When he confirms that he has known both of them for over five years, I remember being surprised when both girls said they had known him for such a long time. I didn't think a girl would still be escorting after even six months, or at most one year, and no-way after five years. It's just a short-term, one-time thing you might try while you're independent and unattached. Escorting is just a way to make some quick money, that's all. I would never do this for more than a few months. I will quit the moment I have the cash that I need.

John's discussion of his long relationship with his references makes me curious and I ask him how long he's been seeing escorts. John patiently tells me about his long history with the hobby that extends all the way back to about the time when I was born. He tells me how clumsy he was with girls in his youth and that he had to learn many things the hard way.

We are having a pleasant conversation that is open and unguarded. I innocently ask, "Are you married?" John goes quiet and stares blankly at me. He stammers and then blurts out a suspicious retort at me.

"What? Why do you ask? I'd rather not discuss it. I'm not comfortable talking about it. Why does it matter if I'm married?"

Why is he suddenly paranoid? Is he afraid that I'll tell his wife? I need to keep this a secret just as much as he does. I'll try to calm him down. I casually reply, "Oh, it doesn't matter to me at all, I was just wondering. Most of the men that contact me are married and I'm just curious as to why married men would want to see me. That's all."

I don't say it aloud, but I think to myself, "I don't care that you're married." I just drop it. Maybe he is more guarded than I thought.

Wow, this girl must be too green if she is this innocent. Should I reconsider asking to see her ID, to make sure that she's legal?

I glance at the clock and figure that's probably enough chatting, because according to his references, that's not what he's paying for. While John is looking at me, I glance down at the white envelope on the table in front of me. The envelope is open and reveals a stack of hundred-dollar bills within. I got lucky last time that the money was real and that it was all there. From now on, I am going to get the money first-thing, at the beginning and I'll make sure that it's the full amount we agreed upon. I look at the envelope and then up at John. I ask, "Is this for me?" John turns away shyly.

"Yes it is, and please make sure that I counted

correctly."

"I'm going to use the bathroom."

"Please make yourself at home and feel free to use anything that you want to in there."

I think to myself, "That's a strange thing for him to say." That's not the kind of a thing that any boyfriend would ever say to me. Still, it's friendly and considerate. I grab my purse and the envelope, walk into the bathroom, and close the door.

I look around to see if he left any strange items for me to feel free to use. I look in the mirror and try to be serious, but I'm about to burst out laughing. This guy's more than old enough to be my dad, and he's flirting with me like he has to win-me-over in order to get laid. I flush the toilet to cover the sound of my giggles.

The hot newbie politely excuses herself to the bathroom and closes the door. It sounds like she is throwing up. Maybe she is a little more nervous than I thought. I think she's a newbie.

To help me stop my giggling, I lecture myself in the mirror, "Time to get serious now". I pull a Fredrick's bag from my purse and try to calm down my giggling. I bought a brand new teddy yesterday, because I wanted to wear something new for my first appointment with this client. I take it out and hold it in front of myself in the mirror. It is embroidered satin with lace trim. I undress and place my clothes on the counter, in the corner, where they'll be out of the way. I look at the envelope full of C-notes for a second and then shove it into my purse without taking the time to count the contents. The pile is pretty thick and I don't want to be gone too long. Besides, his references said he's generous and that they never had any problems regarding the donation. I put on the teddy and check my look in the mirror. I evaluate my appearance. He's paying a fortune to be with me for the next hour and I want to look like I am worth every penny of it. I grab a condom from my purse, hope for the best, and step out of the bathroom. John looks up at me. I have to catch myself, so that I don't laugh at the ridiculous look on his face.

I am too excited to sit down; I pace beside the bed. The gorgeous girl has been in the bathroom for a week. A cute girl won't leave a mirror until she has everything perfect. How long is she going to be in there?

The door is opening. There she is... Time stands still. The newbie goddess struts from the bathroom wearing only a sly smile and a sexy little bedroom garment from Victoria's Secret. My heart stops. The sensory overload from this hot little beach-bunny sends me way past the 'raging-boner' stage, directly to the brink of spontaneous ejaculation.

I make sure the client is looking at me when I place the condom on the nightstand. That way he knows that everything is going to be covered and safe today. I don't want him to get any ideas otherwise. I also like to have the condom close by where it will be handy in case I need it in a hurry. My experience with boyfriends taught me that a guy can quickly get uncontrollably excited and I'm not having unprotected sex with any guy, especially a client. Shit! What if I were to get pregnant!

I sit down on the edge of the bed and smile up at John invitingly. He seems to have lost his ability to speak again. I ask, "What would you like?" John's jaw drops noticeably. His expression is like a kid-in-a-candy-shop and I have to try as hard as I can to keep myself from laughing out loud. I notice that his erection is about to burst through his pants. I get up and walk over to him. John starts breathing hard. I undo his belt. John gasps. I pull down his zipper and drop his pants. John is trembling. I get down on my knees and I pull down his tighty-whities. John's penis slaps me in the face when it snaps out. John grunts. I grab it and look it over carefully. It has a healthy appearance and it has just been washed. The pre-cum fluid is clear and sticky, the way it should be.

While I'm stroking John's penis in my hand and looking at it, I notice that this is not all that different from the first time I have sex with a new boyfriend. I am extremely picky about which men I will give an uncovered blowjob to. I gave only covered bj to my other client. I see that John's knees are getting weak. I tell him to lie down on the bed. I look over at the condom and then at John's erection. The one I brought is regular sized, and there's no way that it is going to fit on this big dick. I am not sure what to do about this. I kind of like this client so far and I want him to call me again. His penis passed my inspection and he's clean. Well, I know that guys love to come in a girl's mouth, they're such perverts. I start a bareback blowjob, but he comes so quickly that I'm not ready. I spill some and I start giggling. I turn away and run to the bathroom. I am afraid that John will get embarrassed if he sees me laughing.

She looks me in the eye and sees straight through me. I've never been with a girl this hot before. She smiles slyly and moves toward me. I am so turned-on that I can't breathe. Suddenly, I am in heaven. My eyes come into focus. Tina's pretty little blond head is bobbing up-and-down on Mr. Happy. Life is worth living. She is so pretty that I can't believe my eyes. Wait! What's going on? Her pretty little blond head has popped up and she is prancing off to the bathroom wiping her mouth with her hand. Did I come? She is giggling. Apparently, my big load surprised her.

I return from spitting and see that my client is still lying in the exact same position I left him in. He looks up at me with dreamy-eyes.

"That was wonderful."

I'm flattered and feel unexpectedly appreciated. It's nice that he says it like he means it. I don't expect a client to treat me better than a boyfriend does. Why do I feel complimented by what he said? He's just a client after all.

I am not sure if there will be a second round or just some conversation for the remaining time. Most men come only once, but he's paid for my minimum full hour and it's too soon to get dressed and leave. I sit down on the bed and take two big sips of my diet cola. In an attempt to start up a safe conversation, I pick the most innocuous topic I can. I say to John, "You told me on the phone what kind of work you do." John nods and confesses.

"Yes, as I disclosed to you on the phone last week, I'm a nerd."

I am trying to remember what he had told me during the screening process and this isn't much of a hint. I don't want to reveal that I have forgotten. I play along. "Do you often travel for your work?"

"Only occasionally."

Still no help, and now I'm curious about his hobby habits when he's out of town. "Do you see escorts when you travel?" John smiles as he answers.

"Usually I do. That is if I've got a favorite girl in that city."

Now I'm even more curious and ask, "How do you find them?"

"The first step is to pick an experienced girl from the escort review sites for that city. I go through her

screening and make an appointment. When I see her for the first time, I'm especially nice to her. At the end of the appointment, I ask her if she knows any girls that are more 'my type.' My type being younger, thinner, and cuter. Sometimes the girl will refer me to a good-looking, inexperienced friend of hers. This is how I meet a girl that never advertises. Typically this is a shy, superbly formed female that only sees a client after her escort-friend has seen the client, and only if she approves of him. Sometimes after I see one of these off-the-grid girls a few times, she will refer me to a friend of hers that has never escorted before, a true newbie. Often the newbie will only do doubles with her friend that introduced her to it. This is how I met most of my favorites, the ones that I've kept in contact with for years and years. I have met some terrific girls this way."

I find John's stories interesting, but as we are talking, the maid starts vacuuming just outside our room. I suppose that you have to expect that at a business-class hotel in the middle of the afternoon. I want to block out the annoying sound. I look around and suggest, "Let's listen to some music." I turn on the cheap little clock radio on the nightstand only to discover that the stupid thing only makes an irritating static. Then I see that John has a notebook computer on the dresser and I announce the solution to our music problem, "We can listen to music on your computer. Do you have a folder of downloaded songs or a CD that you burned?" John looks at the floor sheepishly and mumbles.

"I don't know how to download songs and burn CD's."

"What?" I scold him in dismay, "You're a nerd and you don't know how to burn CD's?" John seems genuinely embarrassed. To change the subject and return to the task at hand, I ask John leadingly, "Should I

11

get dressed now or..." John looks at the clock and utters a false alarm.

"Yikes! It's getting late."

John smiles mischievously at me.

"Can I lick your pussy?"

"Sure! We still have time." I get into position.

I can tell that Tina likes my idea. She quickly lies down on the bed and props her head up on the pillows. She's one of those girls that like to watch.

John puts his head down between my legs, but instead of getting 'busy', he starts talking. He asks if I like it a certain way, and to tell him how to do it the way I like it. Finally, I bark at him, "Don't worry about it. If you need directions, then I'll tell you what to do. I assure you that I am used to telling a man how to eat my pussy." John gets the message. He shuts up and goes to work. I don't have to say another word.

John has some kind of instinct for how to turn me on. I can feel myself getting hot and wet. He keeps me on the edge of orgasm forever. He keeps going and going, until I come... who-knows-how-many times, and then I have that big orgasm, the kind of orgasm that makes you too sensitive to keep going. I push John's head away from my crotch. I gasp for air. I rest a moment to catch my breath. There are some strands of gray hair in my hand. I think that during climax I may have accidentally pulled out some of John's remaining hair.

Tina has beautifully sculpted abdominals and a neat, closely cropped landing strip of silky-blond fur on her cat. I'm pleased to note that the carpet matches the drapes. I touch my tongue gently down on her belly, just above the top of her labia. I make little flicking excursions down to her clit, her inner lips and back again. Tina moans unconvincingly and heaves her hips. I work my way down and pull back to admire the view of her anus. She is beautiful everywhere. I go to lick her butthole, but I stop when I remember that it's our first date. I decide to leave her cute little butthole alone today. You never know if a girl has had a bad anal experience. I don't want to do anything that might scare this one off. I certainly don't want to strike a sore nerve on our first date. I go back to work on her and she slowly gets genuinely excited. I start sucking her lips into my mouth and she grabs me by my hair and pulls my face forcefully against her crotch. She seems to be experimenting to see how long I can hold my breath. I am committed to the job and I don't stop until I get her to climax. Finally she does. We are both gasping for air.

"That felt so good."

I lift my face up out of her soaked crotch and she looks at me with a sly, delighted smile. Tina's slim firm body is exquisite. She's lifting her head up while lying on her back, making her abs ripple. She is so appealing that I can't resist her. I go to kiss her on the mouth, but I suddenly stop and explain, "My face is covered with pussy juice." Knowing that girls don't like that, I ask, "Give me a second to go clean up first?" To my surprise, Tina grabs me, pulls me toward her and snaps at me.

"No! Don't wash it off; I love the taste of my pussy. Kiss me pussy-face."

Our tongues touch. I'm stunned by the intensity of her sexuality. All I can think is, "She is way too hot to even be real."

I'm cum-drunk, lying in a puddle, catching my breath as John pulls a box of XL sized condoms out of the nightstand drawer. He puts one on and gets on top of me. He asks me to grab his penis and guide it in. It's big and I'm small, but I am dripping wet from the cunnilingus.

I put the tip of the head in me and tell him to "push."

John pushes the head in, stops, and then moves just the tip, slowly in-and-out of me. I am about to ask him what the hell is he doing, when he asks me a stupid question.

"Do you want it gentle, or do you want it hard?"

Well shit, he's barely even penetrating me and it's only frustrating me! I bark at him, "I want it hard!" I prepare for him to pound me but instead, just to piss me off, he continues with his way-too-slow, not-nearly-deep-enough wimp-stroke that's going to make me fall asleep! Now I'm mad. I grab his ass cheeks, spread my legs as wide as I can and I order him, "Fuck me hard!" Well, this time he responds like one of those bulls at the rodeo and he fucks the living shit out of me. I come hard. I come again, and then again. I don't know how long we go at it, but I know that it's a lot longer than I have with any boyfriend my age.

John eventually comes with a loud grunt and rolls off of me. At least I think he came. I can't be sure. A girl can't feel anything down there when the guy's wearing a condom, so who knows? John is breathing fast and hard. I hope that he isn't having a heart attack. Can you imagine how embarrassing that would be? I can see it now, "Oh housekeeping, you know your guest in 537? Well, I fucked him to death. Sorry about the mess, I'll leave a nice tip." I check John's pulse, then I check the clock and announce that the hour's gone and I'm going to get dressed. I go into the bathroom and close the door.

Tina is cooing from the pussy appetizer. She is ready for the main course. I am so hard that I can feel my pulse in my penis. I grab a condom and get positioned to mount this gorgeous ride. I cover up in preparation for entry, but it seems like I am forgetting something. What could it

14

possibly be? This is the first time I'm going to enter this hot girl. There's an opportunity to do something, but what is it? I suddenly remember the old 'Do you want it gentle?' routine.   Appreciating that this trick only works on the first penetration, I decide to try it on Tina.

Tina falls for it. I screw her silly. I think she might have even come for real. Who knows? A guy can't feel anything down there with a condom on. The moment I roll off of her, Tina pops up out of bed. She flies to the bathroom as if that was just another one of her exercise workouts.

I'm looking at my pile of clothes and then at my sweaty body in the bathroom mirror. I need to think this through. I am going straight home from here. I'd rather wait and take a shower at home. Good, that's settled, I'm not going to take a shower right now but I reek of sex. I still smell like sex even after using a wet towel. I didn't bring any perfume with me, what am I going to do?

I look around and see a stick of ladies deodorant on the counter. It has a pleasant scent and it is brand new. I think to myself, "That seems freakishly convenient." I ask John if I can use it. I almost ask him why he has ladies deodorant, but at the last second, I decide not to. Maybe I don't want to know why he has ladies deodorant. I finish dressing and go back into the room. I see that John hasn't moved an inch. I try not to laugh. I decide that I will interpret his exhaustion as a compliment.

Tina emerges from the bathroom fully clothed and heads straight for the door. I want to make sure she knows that I want to see her again soon.

I have a long drive ahead and I want to get going. I thank John for seeing me and tell him, "It's time for me to go." He quickly gets up, thanks me for coming, and gives me a quick hug. Then he offers to write some review thing for me on some website that I have never heard of. I say, "Oh sure," but I'm thinking, "What-ever."

"I had a wonderful time. When can I see you again?"

I'm not sure what the proper call girl etiquette is for that question. I don't want to see him again too soon, but at the same time, I want to keep a good client. After all, I'm looking for a 'regular' not a 'stalker'. I decide to say, "You can call me in two weeks."

Tina is not prepared for my request to see her again, but she remains composed, and handles it well. She's an exceptionally poised young woman.

I would love to see John again, he's a nice client, and it's not like he's a pervert or anything. I tell John, "My pussy is going to be sore for the rest of the day." He looks concerned, so I add, "But it's worth it. You know how sometimes, you just want to get the shit fucked out of you." John smiles warmly at me. For some strange reason, I feel affectionate towards him. Maybe it's just a high from the good sex. I give John a tight hug, a big wet kiss and I leave.

Tina is in a hurry to leave, so I get the door for her. She pauses to give me a kiss on the lips and a nice compliment. As I close the door behind her, I sneak what I know could be my last peek at her hot little butt. I stand at the closed door and look out the peephole at her. She pauses outside the door and looks down the hallway in both directions undecidedly. Then she starts walking confidently down the hallway in the wrong direction and out of my sight. I stand there quietly looking out the peephole, feeling like a complete pervert.

I think aloud, "She's so hot. I can't wait to see her again. I hope I get to see her again, I hope she'll still be

available."

The simple fact is that the good ones like her aren't usually around for long. They either find a few regulars and go off-the-grid or get scooped up by some rich guy or get married. Any girl that is as cute, as nice, and that puts out like she does will hook-up in a hurry and retire. I desperately hope I get to see this one again.

Suddenly Tina reappears in my peephole view and walks by quickly in the right direction. I whisper to myself, "Oh yes, she's definitely a newbie."

Chapter 2

The Relief of Knowing

I knock on the door with the relief of knowing that this appointment is with someone I have seen before and that he is someone I like. I'm looking forward to having some completely uninhibited sex today, and then afterward, just walking away. No strings, no drama, no baggage of any kind. This man treats me the way I wish my past boyfriends would have. This guy makes me feel adored and treasured. That's probably because he's such an old guy. Older men always seem to be extra nice to girls my age. I wonder why?

Anyway, I hope he wants to lick my pussy again this time. I feel a bit naughty for wanting it so bad, but it's been a long time since I've had sex and I'm horny. Why should I waste my time sleeping with guys my age that don't appreciate me nearly as much as my clients do? The cute guys my age aren't any good in bed and they don't pay me for it!

I check into a cheap hotel that's close to where I work. I haul my gear up to the room for my second visit with the newbie. Now that she knows me, I don't need to get the room at an expensive hotel just to meet for one hour. I call the hot newbie's mobile number and leave her a voice message with directions to the hotel and the room number.

I did everything possible to maximize the probability of seeing her again. I waited exactly two weeks to call her, as she requested. This shows that I'm interested, but that I follow her directions. I'm lucky that she's still available and will see me. When I hadn't heard back after a week, I thought I'd never see her again. Her next available appointment was a week later. I'm glad I can work around her schedule to get to see her. This girl could easily get top-dollar rates for her looks, personality, and service. I can't afford the rates that a girl this good can get. I'm not going to see any new girls as long as I can book this girl.

I check the time and see that I am a full hour early for our two o'clock appointment. How am I going to kill a whole hour when I'm this excited? I decide to dive into an intricate task from my job to keep my mind busy and off of the incredibly cute call girl that I booked.

The next time I look at the clock, I see it's getting close to our scheduled meeting time. I check my private home-office answering machine and discover a new message from the newbie. She left it just a few minutes ago. I smile as I listen to her excited girlish voice.

"Sorry, I'm running a half-hour late, but I'm on my way now. I'll see you soon."

I pour myself a drink, get high, and thumb through my dirty magazines while I wait for her to show up. I wonder why she didn't call my mobile number to tell me that she'd be late. Why did she call my home-office number and leave a message there instead of calling my mobile number and talking directly to me? She knows that she can leave a private message there, but she also knows that I'm not there when we are going to meet. I return to my work to keep my racing mind occupied while I wait.

The next time I look up, I see that it is now one full hour past our originally scheduled meeting time. There is nothing that I can do but wait for her. I know how hot this girl is. I know what a great time we'll have when she finally shows up... my thoughts are interrupted by a knock at the door. It's her! I leap for the door. My heart pounds in my chest.

John answers the door right away this time and he peeps at me for only a second. John greets me with a warm smile and a quick hug as I enter. He tells me that I 'smell nice' as I walk past him.

I notice that John has a slightly different look than he did before. He looks older and more distinguished somehow. I can't put my finger on it, but something's definitely different. I study his appearance. What has he changed? Oh, that's it; he got his hair cut short. It looks good on him. I should tell him that he looks good this way. I like his look with his hair short like that. He looks older.

Tina looks even hotter than last time. She has been busy in the four weeks since we first met. She is tanned, toned, and she smells great. Tina has a mischievous gleam in her eye and she's smiling devilishly. I wonder why? She must have something fun planned for later. She can't possibly be excited to be on a call. Tina appears relaxed and happy to see me. We chat like two old friends who are playing it cool for the moment, both knowing that we will be rolling like ravenous lovers in a few minutes.

I put my purse down on the table next to an ice

bucket with a bottle of my favorite brand of diet cola in it. Next to the bucket is a white envelope. It's nice that John remembers the brand of diet cola I drink. I appreciate that he has a cold drink ready for me after the long drive across town. John asks me if he can pour me a beverage and asks how much ice I prefer. I'm thinking, "Just pour my stupid drink, I'm thirsty here." He's so formal that it's comic, but it's sweet. John respects me and that helps me to relax. Even though I have seen John before, I still get nervous before every call, especially after that weirdo I encountered last week. I sip my drink and look around the room. I notice that John has been drinking and is obviously high. He offers me some, but I can't. Not today. I have to be able to drive out there on that crazy freeway in an hour. He has some porn magazines open on the bed.

Tina surveys the dirty magazines that I have spread out all over the bed. Tina's pretty eyes open wide as her high-pitched little-girl voice reveals her excitement.

"You have porn. I LOVE porn! Can I see?"

Tina picks up one of the magazines. She sits down on the bed and blurts out her joy.

"Ooooh, they're barely-legal-age girls. Ooooo. I like this model. She's got an innocent girlish look that I like. The back lighting is good on this shot. Look at her pointy butt. The production and the photography are not all that great, but this shot has a good angle, and the teenage girl is provocatively pretty."

I watch Tina carefully evaluate the girls in the magazines. She reminds me of Lisa and the way Lisa always wants to see the porn as soon as she arrives. It makes her hot.

One of the models is exceptionally erotic. I show John. I can tell by his expression that he likes her too.

Tina turns the page and lets out an unusually low,

involuntarily response.

"Oooooh! Look at this girl."

She can't contain her excitement. I notice that my 'little-buddy' can't contain his excitement either.

I am suddenly reminded of how horny I am. I get up, grab my purse and reach for the envelope on the table. I look up at John to ask if it's for me, but he turns away with a shy grin before I can ask, so I don't need to. Still, I want to thank him for it and acknowledge that I have taken it. I hold up the envelope and I tell John, "Thank you for this." I open up my purse and shove the envelope into it. I stand up and inform John, "I am going to use the bathroom. I'll be just a couple of minutes."

After chatting for only a minute about the cute girls in the magazines, Tina seems suddenly impatient. She quickly excuses herself to the bathroom.

Halfway to the bathroom I stop, turn toward John, and order him, "Your assignment, while I am gone, is to find the girl that you like the best from each magazine. You are to show them to me when I return." Before John can respond, I step into the bathroom and close the door. I change into a new lingerie outfit that I have been looking for an excuse to wear.

I grab a condom from my purse, but something makes me pause. I remember that I am seeing John and I grab a second one. I exit the bathroom and when John looks up at me, he makes a weird little noise. I place the condoms on the nightstand making sure that John sees me put them there.

John has obediently laid out all of the magazines on the bed. He has each one open to his favorite girl. The models he's chosen are the same ones that I like. They are all slim, alluring, and youthful. I point to a photo of a girl's crotch and say, "Look at how tight her butt is."

"Her sphincter is as tight as a drum. I bet you she's a

butt-virgin."

I can't help but ask myself, "How can he tell? What does my butt's appearance reveal about me?"

Tina points to one of the models and looks up at me.

"What do you like about this girl?"

"I like her long slender thighs, her narrow hips and her tight tummy."

"Oooo, I think she's hot too. Look at those abs, I bet she's a gymnast or a dancer. She's in great shape. Oh! Look at this girl, she has a pointy little butt."

I tell myself, "This is just like talking to another guy about hot girls." Tina rubs her pussy with one hand while she points out hot girls with the other. Wow, Tina likes girls too! The thought of Tina with another hot girl makes me unbearably horny.

I see a hot lesbian scene in the magazine. Without thinking, I say aloud, "I'd like to have sex with that girl." I silently wonder, "How come I can share my secret lesbian fantasy with this stranger, but I can't imagine revealing it to anyone else?"

John catches me staring at the lesbian scene a little too long. I feel it's safe to tell him about my secret curiosity because he's just a client to me. His opinion of me is not important like a boyfriend's is.

"Do you like girls?"

"I don't know. I've never been with one."

"Do you want to try it?"

"Yes, I do. I have wanted to for a long time, but I don't know how to set it up. Where would I even find a girl that I can ask?"

Tina looks agitated.

"I can't just ask one of my girlfriends, 'Hey do you want to experiment with lesbian sex?'"

Tina stares me in the eye for emphasis.

"You know what I mean?"

Tina laments as she rambles.

"Suppose I do ask a girlfriend to play with me, and she wants to. What if we have great sex? THEN WHAT'S GOING TO HAPPEN?"

Tina's eyes fill with despair.

"What will our relationship be like afterward? Can we still go shopping together? Can we still talk about cute guys together? Will she think we're a couple?"

Tina's eyes widen with terror.

"What if she wants to come out of the closet? Can you imagine that? Or what if she freaks out when I ask her and she thinks I'm a total pervert? What if she ostracizes me and tells all my friends?"

Tina concludes with resignation in her voice.

"I can't risk all that just to experiment with one of my girlfriends, just because I think she's hot. I don't even know if I will like it."

"What if I were to set it up for you?" Tina's countenance goes blank. She stares at me and blinks her pretty eyes a few times.

"Let me think about that." I'm suddenly horny.

Tina gives me a serious look. I don't know whether I should be scared or excited.

"What would you like to do now?" John knows exactly what he wants to do. He instructs me in a tone that a personal trainer might use.

"Get on top of me in a 69 position with your knees tucked up by your elbows so that your pussy and butt are sticking into my face."

John moves me around with his strong hands until he gets me just the way he wants me. He gently moves the crotch of my panties to one side and starts licking my pussy. I recognize his work and know that I am in for a treat. It makes me smile, but I try to fight it because a smile exposes my teeth and that's not helpful when you are trying to start a bj. John's tongue feels so good on my pussy that I stop sucking, lay my head down on his lap, and enjoy myself. There's lots of slurping and tongue flicking. It feels wonderful but wait, that feels a little strange. John is grabbing my ass; he's stretching me and pulling at my buns. What is he doing to me? Oh no! He's sticking his tongue into my butt! I try to pull away but he grips me tightly and forces his tongue deeper into my butthole. He isn't hurting me, so even though it feels a little weird, I just let him keep going. I am somewhat apprehensive, but at the same time, I am curious. It feels strange but I like it, sort of, in some hard to describe way. It feels better, the more I get used to it. I hold still and let him move his tongue in-and-out of my butt. After a little while, it gets easier. It's different from anything I have ever done with a boyfriend, but he's paying for it so...

I ask Tina to 69 with me and she seems pleased with the idea. I want to lick her pussy so that I can knock at her back door while I am down there. Every girl has either tried it, or wants to try it, and I want to see if Tina will go there.

I lick Tina's pussy until I get the desired reaction. She comes readily and maybe more than once. Now that I have set the mood, it is time to see if she'll take my tongue in her tight little butthole. She tries to get away at first, but I hold her tight and keep going at her. Eventually, she relaxes her sphincter and I get all of my tongue into her. I make a mental note to push her a little further at the next opportunity.

John finally finishes licking me 'back there' and I think, "Well, I've never had THAT before. Note to self: John is a total perv and even though I let him 'rim' me, I am not trying anal sex ever again. He better not try to kiss me on the mouth after doing THAT down there."

I undo the 69 and reach for the nightstand where Tina placed the tiny condoms that won't fit me. I open the drawer and grab an XL-sized condom from the box. I make sure that Tina sees me installing it. I roll her into a scissors position and mount her leg so that I can deliver full penetration, but we won't be face to face. I drive Tina's snug little kitty home. Tina makes sure the entire floor of the hotel hears her climax. I roll off of Tina and she pops up off the bed.

"I'm going to wash up."

I lie in bed and ponder my good fortune while I desperately try to catch my breath.

I return from the bathroom and get in bed next to John. He excuses himself to the bathroom, so I grab one of the porn magazines and open it up.

I'm pretty sure that John will want to go a second round and I appreciate having the porn to help keep a sexy mood.

I drag myself into the bathroom after Tina has had her turn. I never close the door when I'm with a professional girl. Standing in the bathroom brushing my teeth, I see Tina's clothes neatly folded in a little bundle on the counter. I can see the lace trim of her panties sticking out from her blue jeans. I go to pull them out and eat them, but I stop. I silently lecture myself, "These are her 'street clothes'. She has to change back into these panties when she's done... working." I further admonish myself, "Don't violate her privacy. This is her personal space." I am ashamed of myself and I leave the bathroom unable to look Tina in the eye.

John returns to bed and watches me as I look through one of the magazines.

"You are much more appealing than the girls in the magazines." Tina flashes me a warm smile.

"These are luscious little ladies and they're displayed in well laid out spreads."

"You sure know a lot about photography. Have you ever modeled before?"

I tell John about my print work and his eyes get big. To keep myself from laughing, I humor him, "Here, I'll write down some website addresses for you that have some of my professional modeling photos." John has that kid-in-a-candy-shop look as he carefully puts the slip of paper away in his wallet. I repeat my mantra silently to myself, "Don't laugh, don't laugh."

Tina turns the page to an article about girls masturbating. The article has a photo of a cute naked girl in bed with a vibrator in her crotch. The title is: "Jilling Off." Tina bursts out laughing, points to the magazine, and chokes out a comment through her laughter.

"Oh, that's funny! Look, 'Jilling Off.'"

I study the article title and the photo, but I do not understand. I look up at Tina with a blank expression and concede, "I don't get it." Tina's pretty eyes widen in disbelief.

"Do you mean that? You don't get it? You're not just fooling with me?"

I reluctantly confess, "No I'm not joking, I don't get it. I'm sorry, but I just don't." Normally I would just pretend to get it and avoid the embarrassment, but I feel safe with Tina.

Tina stops laughing and patiently explains to me:

"It's a GIRL masturbating, so it's not jacking off, it's jilling off, because she's a GIRL."

"I still don't get it. Who the hell is Jill?" I feel

completely stupid and exposed. I don't know what to say. Tina flashes a disarming smile and coaxes me along.

"You know... Jack and Jill, went up the hill? So for a girl, it's not jacking off..."

I blurt, "Oh wow, that's so obvious, but I would never have figured that out on my own." I feel foolish, but Tina acts as if my stupidity is cute. Her gentle kindness reassures me and now I'm glad I exposed myself to her. Following Tina's lead, we return to our magazines.

I turn the page of the magazine I'm looking through and see a photo spread of a guy with two girls. The girls are pubescent and precious. I let out an, "Ooooooh! That looks like fun." I seize the opportunity to ask John something I have wanted to ask him, "Have you ever had two girls before?"

"Oh, yes. Many times. It's great fun to be with two girls, especially if they're into each other. The dynamics are terrific."

I'm intrigued. I stare John in the eye. He realizes my interest and continues.

"I had a six-hour tag-team sex marathon with a seasoned pro named Alley and a budding law school coed named Wilma Sanders. The coed was a hot cheerleader type newbie. I asked her if we could try anal. She looked me in the eye and said, 'I want to become an accomplished analist. I want to be able to take a big dick like yours and just shove it all the way up my ass, with no lube.' As she finished that statement, she guided my erect penis into her anus. Wow, she was a lot of fun, but she stopped working after she passed her bar exam."

"She whored her way through law school?"

"Wilma had a great sense of humor. She made a joke where she imitated a 'wife' blowjob. She grabbed my dick absentmindedly, looked away bored, chattered gibberish, and used a limp hand to stroke with. She gave only an occasional lick at my penis, and no sucking. It was hysterical. Then, just for contrast, she gave me a 'ho' blowjob, she called it a 'ho-job' and I almost passed out."

Tina stares at me wide-eyed as I conclude, "I was having sex with at least one of them from 3 PM to 9 PM. At 9 PM, I told them that I was done with them. I didn't mention that I had another escort booked for 10 PM. They both yelled, 'Yea, the girls won!' I didn't say anything."

Now I'm interested in hearing about John's experience with threesomes and I ask, "Have you ever shared a girl with another guy?" Secretly I wonder, "Do you want to share me with another guy?" I am not sure if the idea of that turns me on, or if it turns me off. John breaks into a dirty grin as he replies.

"My buddy Jacques and I once used a girl named Barbie like a Chinese finger trap."

John pauses and I'm wondering, "What the hell is a Chinese finger trap?" My expression must show my confusion because John explains.

"You know, a finger trap. You stick your index fingers in each end of a little tube and your fingers get stuck. John holds up his hands as though he is pointing them at each other. The harder you pull, the tighter you are held."

I start to wonder if John is some kind of twisted pervert and I ask, "You did that 'finger-trap' thing with a girl?"

"Well, sort of. You see the girl was the trap and... Jacques and I, we didn't use our fingers. If you know what I mean."

I think to myself, "John had better not try to do that

'finger trap' sex-thing with me." John's story excites me unexpectedly. I'm horny now. I'm going to tell John that it is time for us to have sex.

Tina looks into my eyes as if she has something urgent on her mind. It scares me a little. I ask with some trepidation, "Yes?" Tina leans in toward me suggestively.

"Do you want to have sex now?"

I can't breathe at first, so I just nod up and down. When I can speak, I ask Tina, "Would you like to do it doggy-style while you face the magazines so that you can still see them?" Tina jumps into position and arranges the magazines in front of her. I don a condom, get behind her and admire her cute little butthole smiling up at me. I ease myself into her tight kitty and get a good rhythm going. Once she starts making noises I start to massage her cheeks. I slowly work my thumbs closer to her anus. I spit on my right thumb and press it flat against her butthole. Tina instantly pulls away, turns sharply at me over her shoulder and barks at me.

"I don't do anal, don't touch my butt!"

"OK, I'm sorry." I acknowledge promptly and obey immediately. I want her to know that she is completely 'in-charge'. As I return my hands to her hips, I am reminded of the old expression, 'She owns the pussy, so she makes the rules.' Tina quickly calms down and gets back into the rhythm. I make a mental note: "Make sure that you do not touch her anywhere near her butt for the rest of this date." Within a minute, she's making her low "Ooooh" sounds and I finish shortly thereafter.

Tina returns from cleaning up and apologetically explains her outburst to me.

"I'm sorry that I yelled at you earlier, but I don't do anal sex. I've never tried it and I don't want to. It hurts."

31

I understand that Tina needs to say that she's never tried anal, but I also know that she's either tried it and she didn't like it, or she wants to try it, but is scared. Maybe her friends told her that it hurts. Every girl secretly wants to try it, at least once. The problem is that anal sex has to be approached properly in order for the girl to enjoy it. It only works when either the guy, or the girl, knows how to do it the right way.

I am totally relaxed from the sex and without thinking first, I ask John, "Are you married?" Halfway through asking the question I recall that the last time I asked this, John shat his pants. I prepare for the worst, but surprisingly, John is calm as he replies.

"Yes, I am married."

John seems to feel open to the discussion this time. I decide to cautiously ask, "Does she know?"

John looks thoughtfully at me.

"Yes, and no. She has what I call, 'plausible deniability'. That means that I never do anything to embarrass her, or to threaten her status. As a result, she has no reason to have a fit over it. Besides, to her, it's just another chore that she doesn't have to do."

I admire John's maturity and the respect he shows for his wife. He respects her even though he is essentially cheating on her. I tell John, "Wow, you're quite sexually liberated."

I think aloud to John, "I am curious then, why are most of the men that contact me married?" Without stopping, I add, "Why do married men need to see me?"

John seems to realize that my interest is genuine, and he tries to explain. John tells me that my question reminds him of a cartoon that he once saw in an adult magazine...

Tina asks me, with wide-eyed honesty, why married

32

men want to see her. I can't believe that she doesn't know why. She's a smart girl, but then again, maybe she just hasn't been around long enough see the situation unfold. The world is a simpler place at her tender age. I tell Tina about my favorite porn cartoon and I can't help but grin as I finish the punch line:

> The setting is a wedding ceremony with a young bride and groom kneeling at the alter. The thought bubble over his head says, "I'll never have to go without sex again!" And the thought bubble over her head says, "I'll never have to have sex again!"

Tina's eyebrows rise in concern.
"How sad!"
I am stunned by Tina's reaction. Every guy my age who hears this joke laughs knowingly at the punch line. At first, I figure that she just doesn't get it. Upon further reflection, I realize that she does get it, and that her reaction highlights the stark difference between being an old jaded married guy, and being a modern hopeful single girl.

Tina is deep in thought and I wait to see what she's thinking. Tina tilts her pretty little head to one side with keen interest.
"How young a girl would you have sex with... if there were no social taboos... or legal issues?"
I am afraid to answer. I am too inhibited to answer her. She will think I am a complete pervert if I tell her anything except the standard answer. I have to respond to her question. I chicken-out and say, "At least eighteen, or older. You know, legal."
Tina is clearly disappointed at my refusal to answer her question honestly.

"I've always wanted to ask a man that question."

I feel bad. She knows that I am lying, but I don't dare give her an honest answer. I don't know if she was abused as a child, or if she is just curious about men. Maybe she has a daddy-complex. In any case, that is dangerous territory and I won't go there. Tina lingers over the topic a few seconds, but then drops it. I can't help but speculate as to why Tina would want to ask a man that question. I give Tina a long look and she seems to understand that I want to have sex again because she gives me a look back that says 'OK'. "Can I lick your pussy?"

"Sure, how do you want me? How about like this? That way I can watch you lick my pussy. I love to watch."

Tina props up the pillows and lies against the headboard with her legs spread out and smiles at me. I get between her thin, firm thighs and go to work. In no time she starts rocking and then she grabs for my hair to pull me in, but ha-ha! The joke's on her because my hair is too short for her to get a grip. The short haircut works! Tina keeps pawing at my head trying to get a hold. I intentionally back off and lick her as lightly as I possibly can. The teasing is driving her crazy. I am so proud of myself for protecting my remaining hair. Wait! Oh shit, she's got me by the back of my skull and she's squishing my face against her pubic bone with the strength of a woman deep in the throes of orgasm. Her thighs grab my cranium like a walnut in a nutcracker. If she twists her hips sharply sideways then she'll snap my neck like a bread-stick. I can't breathe. Is this how I'm going to die? How will the Coroner report the cause of death, 'vaginal suffocation'?

John gives me great head. I have a screaming orgasm and go limp.

Tina releases me and I gasp for air.

"That felt sooo good. Let's have sex now."

When I catch my breath, I tell Tina, "I want to do it standing up in front of the mirror." She clearly likes the idea and grins at me devilishly. Tina jumps in front of the mirror, strikes a pose and admires her look. I pluck two pillows from the bed and plop them down on the low dresser in front of her. "These are for your elbows." Tina gives me a perplexed expression. I figure that there is no point in trying to explain. I grab a condom and roll it on while Tina watches me. I stand behind her and wrap one arm low around her hips. I place my other hand on her back between her shoulder blades, push and command her, "Bend over."

Seeing Tina in the mirror contributes to an explosive climax that leaves us both panting. We remain in position and rest a few seconds. Tina looks up over her shoulder and beams at me.

"THAT was good."

Tina stands upright sharply and my condom-covered penis flops out of her. Tina twitches and giggles.

"I'm going to be sore down there tonight."

Tina bounces into the bathroom, commenting over her shoulder.

"But it's worth it to have great sex like that."

I am flattered to the point of blushing.

I know from my last appointment with John to expect two rounds in the hour, but he's gotten me three times already and we still have some time left! I hope he doesn't want to go again. I don't think I can. My pussy is rubbed raw from the condom and John's big dick. I decide that I'll put my clothes on after I clean up so that he knows we are done having sex for today.

I always thought older men would be just one pop and then some conversation until the time is up. I can't believe he fucked me three times. I've never had a boyfriend fuck me three times in a row like that. It must just be that he's excited to be with a new girl and this is the one time in his life that he went three times.

I wipe up with a wet washcloth in the bathroom but I still smell like sex. Then I see that same stick of ladies deodorant on the counter from last time. It smells nice when I put it on. I'm glad I used it because John obviously likes the way I smell. Maybe an old girlfriend used that scent and that's why he keeps some around. I better not ask about it. It might be a painful memory.

Tina helps herself to the ladies deodorant that I always bring and emerges from the bathroom with her arms up over her head. Her tank top reveals her lovely underarms. She is smiling and giggles as she approaches me.

"Oooo, smell me, I smell pretty!"

I smile back at Tina, reach my arms out toward her. Tina closes her eyes and with her arms still over her head, leans her head back as I wrap her beautiful torso up in my embrace. She smells great, just like I remember. Tina melts in my arms and deep-French-kisses me like a lover. I am overcome by my affection for this wonderful woman.

After a nice goodbye kiss, I grab my purse and tell John, "It's time for me to go."

"Before you go, I want to ask you something."

"Ask me what?"

"Would you like me to write a review for you?" I can see that Tina doesn't know what I'm talking about. I hand her a sheet of paper containing a review of her written by another client. Tina looks it over carefully.

"Can I keep this? I want to research this website first and then I will tell you what I want to do."

I give Tina a quick hug and another kiss goodbye. I ask hopefully, "When can I see you again?" Tina smiles and states her reply authoritatively over her shoulder while strutting out my door.

"You can call me in two weeks."

From the peephole, I observe Tina quickly look in each direction and then briskly march the wrong way down the hallway. She does not go as far down the hall as she did the last time. Tina quickly returns to view, but for only a moment as she flashes by, headed in the right direction, toward the elevators.

Chapter 3

I Love My Job!

I step briskly and knock quickly on the door of room number 420. I can hear some people coming down the hallway, but they can't see me yet. They are coming my way. They are still around the corner and I want to get inside before I am spotted. John answers the door right away. I escape into his room and shut the door behind me. I laugh out loud, and announce while I hug John, "Hi honey, I'm home."

Something's wrong! Tina's knock is much faster and harder than usual. Something's definitely wrong. I bolt to the door and pull it fully open without peeping first. Tina pours in through the door as it opens and slams it shut behind her. I am trying to figure out what the problem is when she wraps a tight hug around my neck. Her hard body presses firmly against mine. She can't wait to have me. I instantly 'sport wood' in response to her desire for me.

John is always thoughtful and considerate. He has my diet cola and envelope ready for me on the table. It's no wonder that I look forward to our time together with anticipation and excitement.

Tina fixes herself a glass of diet cola from the ice bucket while she entertains me with her story about the unseen people in the corridor that she successfully eluded.

John is fully prepared for our sex party today. He's got the porn magazines spread out, a porno movie playing, booze pouring, and he is getting high. I join him. The high and the porn will help me get into the mood and I don't have a class or anything else that I have to do today.

Tina and I drink and get high together. Tina has only a little, and says she's done. I figure that she doesn't get high and that she's only having some now to be social about it. After a few minutes, Tina is obviously buzzed.

"That was pretty good, can I have some more?"

We both have a lot more. While we do, Tina explains her request.

"I like to try a little bit and see how well I like it, before I have too much. I like this and that's why I want to have more."

Tina's measured approach reveals her maturity. I tell her that and she seems genuinely flattered. Tina sits comfortably on the bed with her back against the headboard, drinking her diet cola and looking through the dirty magazines.

"I told my friends that I have a dentist appointment today and that's why I couldn't go shopping with them."

Tina tilts her pretty head and looks at me with a question in her eyes.

"What do you tell your friends?"

I wait for Tina to swallow her sip of diet cola. I reply rather flatly, "I don't have any friends." Tina involuntarily spit's a raspberry, chokes and coughs.

"It's a good thing that I didn't have a mouthful of

diet cola when you said that, or the maid would have thought we did a 'brown shower' in the bed!"

Tina glares at me with false anger.

"Don't EVER say something THAT funny to me when I have ANYTHING in my mouth. I could choke, or bite your dick, or... wait, what do you mean by, 'you don't have any friends?' I don't believe that."

"Well I consider you my friend, so you're right."

"Aww, that's sweet. Let me see which porn movies you have."

Tina smiles approvingly while she looks through the collection of porn movies. She frowns seriously at one of the boxes.

"I want to watch porn now. Can we watch this movie?"

Without giving me time to reply, she thrusts it into my hand.

"Start this one up and find us a hot scene. I'll be right back." John seems to like it when I order him around. I like feeling that I am in control of the date; it helps me to get comfortable, so that I can enjoy myself.

I look down at my hand and then back up just in time to see the bathroom door close behind Tina. She's become more authoritative in the four weeks since we last met.

In the bathroom, I change into a sexy but elegant nightgown that I bought last week just for work. I go to grab three condoms from my purse, but then I remember that these won't fit, and besides, John packs his own. That's handy because I don't want to have to carry XL-size condoms around with me as well as the regular sized ones, especially if I have to carry enough for John. I would need to get a bigger purse! I am still laughing at my own joke when I exit the bathroom to join John in bed.

Tina emerges from the bathroom in her work clothes.

41

She is giggling. She stops laughing when she sees the porn movie is playing. Tina slips into bed next to me. Her eyes never leave the screen.

"Oooooh! This is a good scene."

Tina is so erotic and sexual that she entrances me.

I like the porn scene John selected. An enthusiastic, wisp of a girl is getting a double-penetration. I get horny watching it. I am ready to go to work and let John know it with a glance.

Tina has one hand on her breast and the other in her crotch. Her eyes are fixed on the porno movie. I suddenly find myself fully aroused. Tina gives me an unmistakable look. I ask, "Can I get a little head?" Tina lights up with a devilish grin while she quickly nods affirmatively and climbs into position so that she can watch the porn while she's on the job.

Tina's pretty little blond head starts bobbing up-and-down on me much faster than usual. I am reminded of why life is worth living. I am close to climax. Tina forcefully snaps my penis out of her vise-like mouth. It makes a loud pop sound like a Champagne cork. Tina looks up at me with bewildered joy.

"I love my job."

She reacquires said penis and resumes the job that she so obviously loves. As I watch her pretty little blond head bobbing up-and-down on me, I have to remind myself to breathe.

I climax. Tina vacuums the last drop and I whimper from the over-stimulation. Tina flies off the bed and is already in the bathroom. I can't catch my breath.

I hurry to the bathroom to spit out the result of the blowjob and I laugh out loud. What I give John can't legitimately be called a blow 'job' because he comes so fast that it's more like a blow 'catch'. I want to get back to the porno movie and get laid. I'm glad I can count on John for that.

Tina returns from spitting and jumps in bed with me. We watch the porn movie together. She seems to be excited about something. There is a particularly hot scene playing. I'm fully erect. Tina notices.

I'm horny today and I can't get enough sex. Well, not until I'm done, of course, and then I'll just leave. I love knowing that I get paid a fortune just to drive across town in the middle of the day and have steamy sex with an appreciative, mature man that puts-out and truly wants to make me happy in bed. I love my job and I'm ready to perform it to the best of my ability.

Tina quickly sheds her lingerie and reaches into the nightstand. She grabs a condom and rips it open with her teeth. She turns toward me and gives me a serious look that frightens me and excites me at the same time.

"I'm horny from watching these cute girls have sex. You have to fuck me now."

I can't speak. I can't breathe. It's a good thing that I'm sitting on the bed so I can't fall over. It's all I can do to nod affirmatively.

"I want to be on top." I push John onto his back and jump on top of him. He's panting. I roll on the condom and ride him cowgirl style. I like being on top where I'm in control and because I can watch the porn movie in that position.

Tina looks me in the eye silently for a long moment. I don't know what to do. Tina's eyes narrow and she leans in on me. In one move, she pushes me down on my back and mounts me. Tina rises up on her knees, reaches between her legs, grabs my erect penis and inserts it. Tina eases down onto me, grinds against me, and starts rocking slowly.

She is literally dripping wet. I've never considered myself sexually submissive; however with Tina, I feel that anything is possible. Mid-rock she pulls her knees up, one at a time, getting into a deep-knee-bend squatting position facing me. She grabs my outstretched hands for balance and starts bouncing her hot little crack on my rigidity. Tina is panting. In one graceful move, she releases my hands and swings around into a reverse cowgirl position. The view is sublime. We ride into the sunset together.

Either John has come, or he's had a heart attack. Either way, he's finished. I jump off of him and step into the bathroom to freshen up.

I don't have my outfit with me in the bathroom and I can't get dressed because I'm pretty sure that he'll want to go for a third time. How does he do it?

I decide I'll just wrap up in a bath towel and tuck it in like a sexy little tube-dress. On my way out of the bathroom I start yelling a question at John that I have wanted to ask him, "What was your first time with an escort like?" Without giving him a chance to speak I add, "How old were you? How did you find her?"

"I was twenty-two. Wow, that was almost twenty years ago. Things have changed since then. It was a little different way back then. There was no internet or cell phones in those days."

Before the internet? Before cell phones? John's story makes me realize just how much older than me he is. I like that though, older men treat me better than the men my age do. Besides, it fits in with my daddy-complex.

I tell Tina, "You're extremely strong down there, like a clenched fist. You must do Kegel exercises regularly."

"What the hell's a Kegel exercise?"

After a brief human-female-anatomy lesson I ask, "How did you develop those astonishing abdominals you have?"

"I do five hundred sit-ups every day as part of my three-hour work out routine when I'm modeling."

I fondle Tina's abs and they are as tight as a drum.

"Can we back up the porn movie to the end of the double-penetration scene with the skinny girl? I missed it because I was busy coming."

We return to watching porn together and we agree on our favorite scene. We both like a scene with a willowy waif getting a deep double-penetration. I excuse myself for a strategically planned trip to the bathroom while Tina is busy looking for our favorite scene.

Once in the bathroom I extract Tina's panties from her neatly folded little bundle of clothes on the counter. They are an exceptionally provocative pair. I hold Tina's underwear up to my nose. I sniff the crotch and it smells like her pussy. I rub them on my face and wonder if I should take them home with me to keep. Somehow, her personal panties are more erotic than her work clothing. I better put them back. If she catches me in here sniffing her underwear, she'll think I'm a complete pervert, and she will never see me again. I get an inspiration and make a mental note. Next time I will ask Tina to let me undress her out of her street clothes. I carefully return the panties to their original location and step out of the bathroom.

I need a distraction to hide from the guilt of playing with her personal clothing. I tell Tina, "I downloaded a bunch of your professional modeling photos from the fashion websites you told me about. You take great bikini shots. I have a whole folder full of your photos; they make great jack material." After I say this, I fear that Tina may freak out over my perverted interest in her. Tina's eyes light up and she responds with an excited squeal.

"Oooooo! I want to see them. Show me!"

I bring up the photos on my computer and Tina sighs.

"These are from last year, but I've been shooting again recently."

"Shooting? Shooting what?" Tina reads my confused look.

"I've been modeling part time around my college classes, so there should be some new photos of me posted soon. Oh, and next week I'm going to Miami to be a hostess at a luxury yacht show and convention. That should be fun and it pays pretty well." John looks confused.

"Oh! Of course, shooting photos. Sorry, I have only met one model before. I don't speak model-talk."

I am flattered by John's interest in my photos, but at the same time, it makes me wonder, "Maybe he is a perv." I tell John jokingly, "I bet you have pictures of all the girls you've ever fucked. I bet you have them all displayed in your jack off shrine and that you look at them one by one and say, 'I've fucked you, and you, and you...'"

John's eyes get big like he's been caught doing something naughty. He mumbles at me in false dismay.

"Have you been watching me?"

"You're funny."

I would love to take photos of Tina, but I'm too afraid to ask her. I do not want to scare her off. I don't want to intrude into her private life. Most girls insist on complete anonymity in this line of work and are paranoid about leaving any evidence that might connect them to their real lives.

John closes my modeling photos and we return to

watching the porno movie.   There is a hot anal scene playing. I ask John, "Do you like anal? Have you ever done it?" John replies with a dirty grin.

"Yes, I do, and yes, I have. However, I've always been on the 'giving' end of the shaft."

I quickly inform John, "I've never tried it. I don't want to try it. It hurts." To my surprise, John agrees with me.

"Yes, when the guy isn't patient, or the girl isn't ready, then it doesn't work right and it hurts for the girl. I have had successful anal sex with many girls. I have even been the first anal success for at least two girls recently."

My curiosity is piqued, but John is ready for another round and so am I. Talking about anal sex is a lot more fun than trying it and now I'm horny again. I tell John that I like the way he licks my pussy and he buries his face in my crotch without saying a word. He stays there for the longest time. I don't know how many times I come.

I give Tina the mustache ride she requested and when I finish, I look up at Tina's beautiful body and her sweet smile. I want her. I ask hopefully, "Can we go again?" Tina glances at the clock.

"Sure, if you can go again, then we still have time."

Tina removes her towel and wipes between her legs. While I put on a condom, she looks curiously at me.

"How many times can you come?"

I give an engineer's reflex response, "That depends." Tina narrows her eyes and bears in on me.   She interrogates me in a slow accusing tone.

"You use a boner-med, don't you?"

I don't answer. Tina's eyes get big and she convicts me.

"You do! You do. I know you do."

I don't answer; I am silent.

"I know that you must be using something."

Tina smiles at her accomplishment, but then notices my discomfort. She tries to console me.

"Many of the guys I know that are my age say they use boner-meds, and they will openly admit to using them. They have no problem with that. However, they won't talk about it in any detail at all."

"Let me tell you about a conversation I had recently with some guys I work with. An older, rather conservative guy says, 'The boner-pills are great for us guys, but what we need now is something that you can give to the girls to get them to want to have sex.'"

"I promptly answer him, 'But there already is something that you can give to a finely formed female to make her want to have hot sex with you.'"

"The old guy says with amazement, 'There is?'"

"I assure him, 'Yes, sure there is. They're called Ben Franklins. You get them at the bank and they work like magic.'" Tina laughs uncontrollably, tries to stop, but looks at me, and then bursts out in another fit of laughter.

While Tina is laughing, I am working on a problem. I want to develop Tina's interest in trying anal sex. I have brought a bunch of anal porn movies with teenybopper girls to help set the mood to ask her to experiment with anal, but I need to do more. How can I encourage Tina to stretch her limits?

When I finally stop laughing at John's amusing story, I see he is staring at his collection of anal sex porno movies. I am reminded of something that I want him to do. I tell John that I love watching porno movies when we're together and I have an idea. I suggest that we get a movie starring an adult film star I've seen on TV. I explain to John, "Her name is Taylor, she does double-penetrations and she makes the cutest noises during sex. Let's get her porno movies to watch while we have sex. She's so hot, she has the kind of body that we both like.

She said she's from Orange County, Huntington Beach I think. How come I've never seen her at any of the clubs around here? I'd definitely notice a girl that hot and remember seeing her. She's cute, I'd like to have sex with her."

I stare open-mouthed at Tina and I mumble to myself, "She's way too hot to be here with me." I can't believe my incredible luck. I do not speak, I just write down the name: Taylor. I make a mental note. "Get some Taylor DP movies right away."

Whenever Tina talks about having sex with another girl my heart races. I decide to ask Tina again about a threesome. I say as casually as I can, "Would you like to have a threesome with a hot bisexual woman and me?" Tina's eyebrows shoot upward.

"Oui, ménage à trois."

"She's an erotic dancer. Would you like to see her photos? Her name is Lisa and she said it was OK for me to show her photos to you." Tina silently nods with a deadly serious expression. While accessing the photos I tell Tina, "Lisa told me that she has a lot of experience being a girl's first girl and that she knows how to handle it. I haven't shown her your photos yet because I would only do that if you approve of it, but I told her you were cute and Lisa said that's good enough for her."

I open up Lisa's photos and enlarge my favorite one. Tina sees the photo and gasps.

"Oh, look at her cute little pointy butt! She's hot. We like the same type of girl, so I can see why you like her so much."

49

Tina's response appears affirmative. I ask, "Can I show your modeling photos to Lisa?"

Tina slowly nods her pretty little head.

"Do you have any more photos of 'little pointy butt'?"

I start up a slide show of my collection of Lisa's photos and suggest to Tina, "I'll tell Lisa that you want to have a threesome. I'll show her your photos, she'll be excited." Tina is so engrossed in Lisa's photos that she doesn't hear me.

"I'd like to have sex with this girl."

Talking about Lisa makes me horny. I want to advance my work on getting into Tina's butt. I recall the back-door score from our last visit. She took the tongue, but she declined the digit. The road to Greece, I conclude, will start at anilingus. I will need a position that provides good access.

I suggest, "Let's do it standing up." Tina hops out of bed and is standing in front of me. I hold her in my arms like a girlfriend and deep-French-kiss her. I turn her about face and order her, "Spread your legs and bend over." Tina complies. I get down on my knees and separate Tina's cheeks. My tongue enters Tina's anus, she pulls away a little, but only at first. She relaxes and lets me work it all the way into her. We have made good progress this time, so I decide not to push it too far for now.

I grab a condom, unroll it, and get in behind Tina. I latch onto her hips and pound her vigorously for a long time. I have her pinned against the bed, as she stands legs spread, bent over the edge of it. Tina's anus smiles up at me. I wipe the drool from my mouth with my thumb and then cautiously massage Tina's sphincter. I slowly move all around her butthole and I am pleased that it yields no adverse reaction. Next, I gently push my thumb flat against her anus without actually entering it. Tina doesn't say anything. I make a mental note that I can move her to the next step when I see her again. That is, IF I ever see her again.

We've been going at it for so long that the condom's lube is wearing off and the latex is getting hot from the friction. It smells like an over-inflated balloon in the sunlight. I am afraid that Tina is getting too much friction and that she will start complaining and insist we stop before I can finish. I try to climax while she's still willing. I pound her harder and faster. The interface gets hotter and Tina's noises become increasingly incoherent. I grab her hips tighter and keep pumping. Tina is bouncing from my thrusts and to keep a hold of her I get rougher than I intended to. We're both making a lot of noise by the time I finally come.

I hope that I haven't hurt Tina. I hope she isn't angry with me. I squeeze out the last squirt and Tina grunts loudly when my penis twitches inside her. I fear the worst, which is that I got too rough with her. Tina turns her head sharply back over her shoulder and declares triumphantly.

"THAT was good!"

I am dumbfounded. Tina straightens up and my still-firm penis pops out of her vagina as she spins around to face me. She gives me a quick kiss on the mouth.

"I will file that one away in my spank bank to use later. I'll be thinking about THAT one when I'm... jilling off!"

I reflexively accuse Tina, "There is NO way that YOU

are going to fantasize about ME when you're masturbating."

"Well, no, I won't. Girls don't think about it that way. What I will remember is the way that it felt. I'll remember the hard, fast pounding up against my butt just when I wanted it. A guy hardly ever lasts long enough to get me to orgasm that hard. THAT was a good fuck."

I stand motionless, with gaping mouth, as Tina heads for the bathroom.

The sex has been pretty good today but I've been here over an hour already. I tell John, "It's time for me to go. Do you mind if I take a shower?"

"You can do anything you want to do."

The hot shower feels great and I like feeling comfortable enough with John that I can take a shower afterward. It is particularly convenient that he provides the deodorant and that I get to put on my client's favorite fragrance. I should ask John about it, since he has a positive connotation with the scent.

Tina springs out of the bathroom, grabs her purse and shoves her envelope into it. She throws her arms around my neck and gives me a hard wet kiss. I wrap her up. I tell her that she smells great and DFK her like a lover. Tina melts in my arms. I have to hold her tightly to keep her knees from buckling underneath her. Tina looks at me with a question in her eyes.

"There was something I was going to ask you, but now I can't remember what it was. Oh well."

Tina shakes off the daze, checks her belongings and heads for the door.

"I'm going to leave now."

I move quickly to meet Tina at the door. I offer for the third time, "Would you like me to write a review for you?" I've been puzzled by Tina's lack of enthusiasm

regarding the review. Most girls are appreciative when I offer to post a flattering review of them because they get lots of good calls as a result. This time Tina has done her homework.

"Oh yes. I do. I knew there was something that I wanted to ask you about. Do you have a copy of all the questions?"

I pull a sheet of paper out of my briefcase and hand it to Tina. She studies the review questionnaire and authoritatively issues her instructions in rapid succession. I write down her responses as fast as I can.

I have discovered that the men that are members of the escort review site are better clients than the ones that just see my escort ad page. I tell John that I want him to write that review that he keeps asking me about. I tell him, "OK, here is what I want you to report: for kissing check the box that says 'Yes on the lips', but also check 'no tongue', then check the 'Yes' for bj, but also check 'covered only', check 'never' for anal, ewe! For multiple pops say 'that depends'. That way if I don't like him, then I only have to do it once."

Tina's last comment makes my stomach turn over. I turn away from her to hide my revulsion at the thought of her having sex with a man she doesn't like. I feel like I'm going to throw up. I try not to think about it.

Looking at the clock, I see that I have been here for over ninety minutes. I head for the door and explain, "I have to go now."

Tina is in a hurry to exit so I quickly ask, "Can we meet for two hours next time?" Tina stops in her tracks, thinks for just a second, then replies in a business-like tone.

"Well, it would be twice as much."

I bobble my head affirmatively, "Of course, that's what I would expect. When can I call you?"

Tina purses her lips.

"I would prefer that you text message me, rather than call me. I feel weird talking on the phone. Let's just text each other from now on."

I fully appreciate that she doesn't want to answer a phone call from a client when she's in her real-life, but I am not text-capable. What do I do? I sheepishly confess, "I don't know how to send a text message." Tina barks at me in dismay.

"What?"

I weakly offer, "I have never done it before."

"What? You're a nerd and you don't know how to text?"

Tina senses my embarrassment, smiles gently at me and offers her support.

"Here I'll show you how."

Tina whips out her phone and presses a few buttons while barely glancing at it.

"Give me your phone. Here, look, I've sent you a text message."

From: Tina
Msg: Hi

Tina looks at my phone briefly. She pushes buttons too quickly for the eye to follow and then she shows me her phone. I had replied back:

From: John
Msg: OK

Tina hands me my phone and I realize that this worldly woman can teach this old fart many new things. Tina gives me a quick kiss on the lips and heads for the door.

"I've got to go now."

I open the door and Tina steps out into the hallway hesitant to pick a direction. I close the door quietly and watch Tina through the peephole; she takes one step in the wrong direction, stops, pirouettes to the right direction, and walks out of sight.

Chapter 4

He IS a Perv

I am about to knock, but I stop at the last second. Is this the right room? I don't want to knock on the wrong door. THAT would be embarrassing! I check the text message from John for the third time to confirm the room number before I knock on the door. Why am I so distracted today?

From: John
Msg: Room 840

While I knock I wonder, if he comes three times in one hour, then how many times will he want to have sex in two hours? The door flies open and there stands John wearing nothing but a smile. He isn't even wearing a hard-on. I burst out laughing and enter. I continue to laugh uncontrollably as I shut the door behind me. I look at John. He is naked and dripping wet. Without taking my eyes off John's shriveled up penis, I set my purse and my drink down on the carpet and kneel down in front of him. John gasps as I take his limp penis into my mouth.

I arrive in the room only fifteen minutes prior to our

two o'clock appointment. I get a text message from Tina.

From: Tina
Msg: On my way
I'm sexcited!

That means she'll be here in an hour. I text Tina the room number and jump into the shower. I have plenty of time to get ready before she gets here.

I turn off the shower and I hear Tina's knock at the door. She's right on time, which means that she's early. I'm not ready for her. I step out of the shower. I don't grab a towel. I don't even peep first; I just pull the door fully open. I realize my stupidity too late. I am grateful that it's Tina and that she is alone.

Tina examines my nude body and enters. I smile hopefully. I expect her to frown, or maybe sneer at my shameless behavior. Tina, however, surprises me. She laughs off the unexpected nudity. She kneels down in front of me and sucks my tiny flaccid penis into her mouth. I lock my knees and we form a tripod. In no time, I am about to come and although Tina will let me come in her mouth, I ask her if I can give her a facial. With my fully erect penis deep in her mouth, she nods in agreement. The movement almost makes me orgasm right there. A moment later I announce, "I'm going to come." I prepare to deliver our first facial. Tina strikes a perfect porn star pose. Her talent amazes me; she looks just like the girls from our movies. Tina patiently waits for me to squirt. Her mouth is wide open, her eyes are tightly shut, and her tongue is sticking completely out. Tina holds the pose while waiting for me to ejaculate. She's too hot to be real. It distracts me and it takes me a little while to come. Tina holds her position the whole time. I finally squirt all over her pretty, giggling face. Tina looks great covered in my semen. I burn the image into my brain. I'm going to bring a camera next time, if there is a next time.

John sprays my face with three big squirts. His grunts are so comical that I can't stop laughing. Some of his semen hits the back of my throat and I almost gag. I swallow hard and as soon as he is done I ask, "Could you excuse me for a second while I go and wash your sperm off my face."

When I see myself in the bathroom mirror, I scream with laughter and close the door. John has pasted one of my eyes shut. My makeup is running down my cheek. I look like a cross between a sad circus clown and an adult film actress at the end of her scene. The spontaneity of the sex, and the sight of John's empty-headed expression, help to make up for the rug-burns on my knees.

After I wash my face, I go to change into my work clothes but for some reason I don't have my purse with me. Then I remember that I set it down in the entryway for the blowjob. I open the bathroom door to get it, but it's not there. John has moved it and my bottle of diet cola over to the little table. I decide to sit down and have a drink before I change. Nothing washes down sperm like diet cola.

"That was... certainly unexpected. You never cease to amaze me with your sexuality and your poise."

"That's a nice thing to say. I think spontaneous sex is more fun. Don't you agree?"

"You've made a believer out of me."

I get up to change and I grab my purse and the envelope. I notice that the envelope feels thicker than usual. I'm about to ask him about it, when I remember that this is a two-hour session. "I'm going to get changed now."

"Instead of changing in the bathroom, can I undress you?" The question catches Tina off guard and she freezes up.

I have never done that with a client before so I think about it before I answer. I prefer to change into my outfit for the session and get ready before the client starts touching me. I guess it is OK to let the client undress me. I decide sure, I will let him do that. Why not? When a boyfriend undresses me, it's sexy.

"Let's have a drink and get high first. Then I want to make out and undress you, like a date."

"Sure, I love to get high before sex, and I don't have to drive for a couple of hours. That sounds like fun." John pours me a drink and we get raucously high sitting together on the little couch in his room. I finally get a chance to ask John about our date with the pointy butt girl. I'm disappointed to hear that she's been out of touch since I last saw John four weeks ago.

Tina doesn't seem ready to start yet. I decide to tell her a story that might help her get into the mood. "Last week I got my annual physical from a fabulous female Physician's Assistant. She gave me the hernia check and inspected the twins, which I was expecting, but as an added bonus, because of my age, she gave me a prostate tickle this time."

"What the hell is a prostate and why did your lady doctor need to tickle it?"

"It is a walnut-sized gland between a guy's butt and penis. The doctor reaches in and feels it to see if it is swollen. The tickle is to screen for prostate cancer."

"What do you mean by 'reaches in'? Does she cut you?"

"No, she shoves two fingers all the way up my asshole

to check it. I couldn't resist telling her, 'Be gentle, it's my first time.' She said, 'I have tiny hands and a ton of lube; you'll be fine. Now bend over and spread your legs.' I'm always telling a girl to do that, but no one has ever told me to do that before."

Tina gets a worried look on her face.

"Do girls have a prostate?"

"It's the gland that makes a guy's semen, so no, you don't have one."

"Good. Did you like it?"

"Well, at my age I have to have it checked anyway, so I figure that I might as well get finger fucked by a delightful damsel with tiny fingers instead of by a grisly old dude doctor who's fingers are as big as mine."

"You are such a pervert. I like that about you."

Tina's mood seems to have improved, so I transition back to the purpose of our meeting. "Speaking of playing doctor... can I undress you now?"

I let John undress me. He clearly has a fetish for my panties; he takes them off me using only his teeth and then plays with them. John is a total perv.

I kiss Tina and grope her through her street clothes. I'm getting turned-on, but I notice that Tina seems to feel somewhat awkward about it. I decide to mix it up a little. I ask her, "Will you stand up for me and turn around so that I can play with your cute butt in your tight jeans." Tina is usually extremely graceful and poised, but she isn't right now. Her movements are stiff and klutzy. I wonder if she is out of sync because she didn't get her time alone in the bathroom at the beginning of the date. She wasn't able to change her clothes along with her character before we got started this time. I unsnap Tina's low-cut jeans. It excites me, but it seems to confuse her. Maybe she needs to change in the bathroom and spend some time with the porn to prepare herself and to 'get into the mood.' Maybe she needs those things more than I realize.

I peel Tina's tight blue jeans halfway down her thin thighs and go to work on her clit with my tongue through her panties. She giggles a little but she doesn't come. I remove her trousers so that she can spread her legs for me. Her panties are soaked by the time they hit the floor.

I remove Tina's top and slide my hand behind her back to her bra strap. It has the kind of fastener that I can unhook with one hand so I unfasten it in one quick move. Tina's eyes get big. I gently guide her to the bed and have her lie on her side. I get on my knees, straddling her straightened lower leg while I push her bent upper knee toward her chest. I install a condom and guide the tip toward heaven. I have to push fairly hard to penetrate her. I compliment Tina, "You're tight." Tina compliments me right back.

"You're big."

I don't last long because I come the moment that Tina climaxes.

After John has stripped and screwed me, I finally get into the bathroom with my purse and the envelope. I brought a bra-panty set with me to wear today. I start to dig them out of my little purse, but I stop. I ask myself, "Why bother to change at this point in the date? That moment is gone. Why get my work outfit dirty now?" I just shove the thick envelope into my clutch with the set and then wrap up in a bath towel.

Tina emerges from the bathroom wrapped in a towel that isn't big enough to cover both her ample breasts and the fur on her hot snatch. It seems much more like a girlfriend scene than a call girl visit. I just stare at her.

"Do you have any porn?"

"Yes! Oh, that's right, I have presents for you. But they're still packed." I didn't expect Tina to arrive on time and as a result, I have not unpacked yet. I pull several large catalog-sized envelopes from my bag and throw them on the bed. I look up and see that Tina's drink is empty.

"Are my presents in those big envelopes?"

"No, those are just our old porn magazines that I always bring."

"Why are the magazines in envelopes?"

"Oh, the envelopes. There is a story behind that." Tina gives me an expectant look. "I'll make us some drinks while I tell it to you. I was at an airport with some ultra-conservative people that I work with and the security guard selected my carry-on bag for additional screening. Thankfully my co-workers continued on through the detectors to the boarding gate while the security guy opened my bag on a table, right in front of me and in full view of all the people in line, and all the people walking through the terminal.

The guy unzipped my bag and opened the top. Then he reached to the bottom and lifted up the entire contents to swab the bare bottom of my bag. Like an idiot, I had packed my pornographic magazine at the very bottom of my suitcase. As a result, the guy was showing the entire airport my jack material. Worse yet, he couldn't see it, so he patiently took his time. So I'm standing there in front of the back cover of the magazine, which is designed to broadcast nude girl's pictures for sale. The effective result was about as subtle as a loud fart in a quiet church." Tina laughs between sips of her drink and then looks like she's just remembered something.

"Oh, that must have been embarrassing for you. Your story reminds me of when I was moving to a new place and all my stuff was packed in boxes. A mover guy picks up one of the sealed boxes in my bedroom and my vibrator starts running inside the box! We could all hear it. I didn't know what to do. I grabbed the box from the guy and ran out of the room with it saying, 'I'll take this box with me in my car.' I heard them mumbling in Spanish about 'la máquina'."

"Your story is much funnier than my story."

"Did you say earlier that you had a present for me?"

"Oh, that's right. Here you are."

John gives me two, still-wrapped, Taylor adult movies! I tell John that while I use the bathroom, I want him to open them up and play one right now.

On her way to the bathroom, Tina bends over to pick her panties up off the floor. I gasp involuntarily at the sight of Tina's tight butt bent over. She hears me. She stands upright, turns around with a flattered grin, and questions me through her laughter.

"I'm sorry, did you say something?"

"The other day there was a cute girl at the grocery store. I walked around the corner and she was bent over trying to reach the bottom shelf. I unconsciously made that same 'audible noise' and she heard me."

"What happened? What did she do?"

"She glared up at me as though I was a total pervert."

"What did you do?"

"I turned around and got out of there in a hurry."

I think to myself, "But you ARE a perv." I've heard stories about dirty old men, but I never thought that I'd actually meet one. I walk into the bathroom and close the door.

Tina appears to be simultaneously attracted, and

offended, by my perverted behaviors. She confuses me sometimes.

When I return from the bathroom, the new Taylor movie is playing. I get instantly horny watching her bent over taking a huge cock in her butt.

Tina arrives and seems excited, like a cat watching a mouse. She has a scary, expectant look in her eyes. What does she want?

"I want to have sex in a position where I can still watch the movie while we're fucking."

I grab an XL sized condom and direct Tina, "Get on top, facing the movie and me." I let her do the work until she is fatigued. When she stops bouncing, I tell her, "Hold on to me by my neck." I then wrap one of my arms around her tiny waist and I put the other behind me for support. I tell Tina, "Hold on." I flip us over in one swift move, so that she's suddenly on the bottom. Tina's eyes widen.

"Wow, you're good."

I push Tina's arms up over her head and pin her down firmly while I ride her. Tina likes it, she gets loud.

"Oh, that feels so good. I'm going to come, I'm going to come, I'm going to ahhhhhhhh, oh yes!"

Tina's obviously been doing her Kegel exercises. Her pelvic floor muscles are so strong that I immediately climax when she does. I roll off of Tina and see the box of condoms on the nightstand. I want to be ready to go again as soon as Tina is ready and not have to fumble around for more condoms, so I check the box and announce, "There are only three left in the box, that won't do."

John gets another box of one dozen horse-sized condoms out of his suitcase of sex paraphernalia. I start to wonder silently, "How many orgasms does he plan to have today?" How does he... oh that's right, he takes boner-pills. That must be how he does it. "Do you always bring your own condoms? Do you buy condoms by the gross?"

"When the girl gets her regular-sized condom out, I like to say that I brought my own and pull out a half-dozen strip of XL sized condoms. If she has not seen my erection yet, she gets a concerned look when she sees the XLs and asks, 'Are you big?' I try to relax her by saying, 'I don't actually need the XL size; I just like buying them at the drug store.'" Tina chortles at me.

"Trust me, you need the XL size. But why do you have so many boxes?"

"I always look to see if there is a schoolgirl-aged cashier on duty at the checkout. If there is, then I will buy a box of condoms even if I don't need any at the time. The girl usually blushes. One time I even got hit on."

Under my breath, I say, "John is definitely a dirty old man. There's no question about it, he IS a perv." Then I realize that I like that about him. I ask, "Have you ever snapped a condom? Is that a myth or can it really happen?"

"Yes, it happened to me once. There was this tight wiry girl that refused to use any lube or spit. She insisted that she was sufficiently wet after some finger-play so we went at it. I don't feel much with a condom on, so I pounded her as hard as she would let me. We went at it for a long time. We were doing it doggy-style. She got dry. She got tight and I kept pounding fast and hard so I could finish. I could literally smell burning-stretching rubber and the condom was pulling on her pubic bone. Suddenly the stroke was easier, and I could feel my bare penis against her vagina. I pumped her hard and she was smooth and wet. After I came and pulled out, only the base of the condom was still there. The top two thirds was gone and only a ragged edge remained."

"Don't break a condom in me. Don't get me pregnant. I'm never getting pregnant. I'm never having kids. Never!"

"You don't have to worry about that with me. I was fixed over a decade ago. There's NO WAY that I can get you pregnant, even without the condom."

"Good. Thank you for telling me. That makes me feel a lot safer. Let's watch some more of my new Taylor porn movie."

Tina makes sexy noises as she watches the porn movie. In the scene, Taylor grabs the guy's balls and sucks them into her mouth. I squeal involuntarily and Tina looks at me alarmed. I explain, "I have glass balls." Tina's pretty eyes widen in disbelief. I extrapolate for her, "You know, like a boxer with a glass jaw. The fact is that not all guys like to have them squeezed. Mine are extremely sensitive. It hurts my balls if a shadow hits them."

"OK duly noted, I won't ever squeeze your glass balls or let a shadow hit them."

"Good. Thank you for telling me. That makes me feel a lot safer." Tina turns back to the porn movie. A new scene is starting.

"Oh my goodness! Now that girl looks under-aged. She's barely eighteen years old, if she's legal at all. Look at her mouth; she has 'little girl teeth'. She's so cute!"

"You're right. She does... and she is."

I decide to seize this opportunity to reiterate an unanswered question that I posed to John previously, "How young a girl would you have sex with, if there were no social taboos or legal issues?"

I don't answer. I am less inhibited this time, but she'll think I'm a pervert if I say anything other than, 'Legal age of consent.' I don't know if this is just a curiosity of hers, or if she has been abused. That's not something that I can ask her either.

I want to explain the conflict that a man can feel, but I don't want to risk upsetting her. I see that Tina's question is genuine, so I decide to say, "The old expression some people use is, 'old enough to bleed, old enough to breed.'" I measure Tina's reaction. She's disappointed. I feel as though I have let her down, so I add, "A man may notice a girl as soon as she is physically mature enough to breed. That is merely nature's law." Tina knows I am holding back. She pleads for an honest answer.

"I've always wanted to ask a man that question."

I can see that Tina's interest is sincere. "Let me share a conversation I had with a mature escort named Kitty, who told me this:

> Do you know how many guys ask for me to wear my 'schoolgirl' outfit? Clients can request it as one of the booking options on my website. I have a photo of me in it. It's just the classic schoolgirl outfit. You know plaid skirt, white long-sleeved high-collar button down shirt, white knee socks and of course, white granny panties. Now it's not because I look young, or because I am young, that they ask me for that outfit. On my website is a recent, untouched photo. They can see how old I am, and they still order it.

That's fine with me that men request the schoolgirl outfit. I'd rather they have an adult outlet for that kind of stuff. It's better for everyone that they fulfill those fantasies with a professional like me. If these guys can hire me to get that out of their system, then all those repressed feelings don't have to stay bottled up. It makes the world a safer place.

I have to agree with her." Tina is silent with thought for a long moment, then she looks me in the eye.

"Do you want me to dress up like a school girl?"

I look straight back at Tina, "I'm not into that. I do however, want you to get in the doggy-style position." Tina smiles at me.

"OK, but I'm getting sore down there, so keep the bottle of lube handy."

I gently massage Tina's tight, pretty little sphincter with my thumb while doing her doggy-style. I can feel her anus relaxing. I start to penetrate her with my thumb, but she flinches and pulls away. Without turning to look at me, she calmly delineates her limit. "Not inside me."

I go back to the circular massage and she goes back to relaxing and enjoying it. I climax but Tina doesn't.

John is in love with my butthole. He is such a pervert.

I go into the bathroom and wash my hands while I tell Tina, "I have posted the escort website review of our session that I said I would write for you. Have you seen it? Would you like to see it?"

"Sure I want to see it."

We go online to her profile and reviews. I nervously pull up my review of her.

"Wow, look, I have an A+ for appearance on all four reviews. I can't believe it. There must be lots of girls with all A+ ratings. Every girl that a guy has just fucked is the cutest girl on earth."

"I have seen hundreds of escort profiles and I have never seen a girl's profile with more than a couple of A+ ratings for appearance. I assure you that I have never seen a profile with all A+ ratings for appearance on all her reviews, yours is the only one. Let's have sex pretty girl."

John rolls on a condom, lubes it up, gets on top of me and inserts before I even realize what he's doing. I can tell after just a few strokes that my pussy is too sore for any more sex. I can also tell that I have to make John come again. I tell him to gently pull out, take the condom off and that I'll finish him with a hand-job. "You can come on my boobs."

I lube up my fist and pump his penis with one hand while I reach for his balls with the other. No, wait he's the one with the glass balls. How am I going to get him to come? I think about his sexual preferences. He likes to play with my butt, and he likes it when his lady doctor fingers his butt. Maybe he will like it if I play with his butt. I reach under his balls and shove my knuckle into his butthole. John yelps and squirts his load all over my chest. I squeeze his cock until he pulls away. I'm covered with sperm. John's a total perv. I need a shower.

I get worked up looking at Tina's reviews. Her pussy is too sore to have any more sex and I'm afraid that I'm going to be left hanging, when she suggests giving me a hand-job. I've never had a hand-job from a girl. Tina is so exciting that I come right away, all over her ripe breasts. Tina

70

admires her work and rubs my semen around on her chest before she excuses herself to the bathroom.

It takes forever to wash John's wad off of my chest. I use the deodorant and then find that the panties I wore here are soaking wet. It's a good thing that I brought a bra and panty set for work today so that I have something clean to change into. I ask myself, "How come I don't know why John always has a stick of this particular ladies deodorant?" I remember now. I was going to ask him for the story about it last time, but he swept me up in his arms and told me that I smell nice, he kissed me all over and then I forgot to ask him.

I double-check to make sure that I have the envelope in my purse. It seems too thick. Oh, that's right, this was a two-hour appointment. It's a blessing that John will pay for a two-hour session. Now I can afford my tuition that's due next week without any more appointments. Maybe I will only see my regulars from now on; after all, I have enough money to pay the rest of my bills this month. With these two-hour sessions, I can afford to see only my regulars and still easily pay all my bills. That sounds good to me. I like my regulars and I'm uneasy with the risks of seeing new clients. I'm not going to see any new clients unless I have to.

I'm happy and excited. When this session is done and I get to my car, I'm going to text my girlfriends to see if they want to go out clubbing tonight. I can afford to buy all the drinks we want. This is so much fun.

Tina emerges from the bathroom singing. From the bed I ask, "When can I see you again?" Tina responds thoughtfully.

"I can see you in two weeks, but we need to change the time. I have a different class schedule now plus I'm busy shooting and I may have some more conventions to hostess at. I had a great time in Miami at the yacht show. Text me and we'll see what works out."

I start to get up out of bed. Tina snaps at me.

"Stay in bed, you look comfortable. I will see myself out."

I hold up her movies, "Do you want to take your presents with you?" Tina glances at the tiny little purse in her hand and then looks back at me with an exaggerated frown. I quickly add, "Or do you want me to keep them for you, and bring them next time?" Tina smiles at me.

"I want you to keep them for me." Tina purses her lips and adds, "Since you haven't heard back from 'pointy butt', your mission is to get us a date with Taylor."

Tina spins around and heads for the door. She has been here for over two and a half hours. The door closes behind her.

I'm appreciative, but I'm also dismayed, at how much effort Tina puts into our time together. Usually, cute girls are bitches. Tina is the cutest girl I have ever seen and she is easily the nicest girl I've ever met. She's even nicer to me than the girlfriends I have had. I snuggle under the covers and replay our date in my mind. Tina is a delightful girl; I hope I get to see her again.

I doze off. My phone wakes me and I see that I have a new text message.

> **From: Tina**
> **Msg: Thanks! That was**
> **Sooooooo much fun**
> **XXXOOO**

Oh, how sweet of her. She's been sitting in her car for the last twenty minutes catching up on her text messaging and she finally counted her money.

Chapter 5

Not a Single Word

I knock on the door afraid that John is going to be unhappy that I am so late and that I can't stay for the two hours he asked for. Besides that, I'm just not looking forward to the next sixty minutes that starts the moment I knock. My body feels weird. Maybe I shouldn't have taken that new brand of diet pill this morning. I've got to lose this extra weight if I'm ever going to get back into modeling. I don't like modeling, but a girl has to pay her bills. That's the only reason I'm here today.

It sounds like John is knocking over the furniture, and he's yelling obscenities. It's taking him forever to open the damn door. It is terribly embarrassing to be left waiting at a hotel room door like this. I have just driven for over an hour on that stupid freeway, and he makes me stand here and wait to use the bathroom. This is almost as bad as modeling. John should be more considerate.

That's not Tina's knock. It's far too slow and it's missing a beat. I stop to tidy up the place a bit before I go to the door. Who could be at the door? I wonder if I called for room service, or housekeeping. I can't recall doing so. I bang my little toe on the table and it hurts like hell. I hobble to the door and look out the viewer. I do a double-take because at first I don't recognize her. She has changed her look substantially in the four months since we last met. Tina hustles quietly into the room as the door opens. She whispers over her shoulder that she is going to use the bathroom and disappears into it.

I don't have an outfit to wear today but I have a lace bra and panties set that will do. Wait. Why should I go to all the trouble to wear something nice that I'm just going to take off in five minutes? We have so little time, there's no point. I'll change into this set when I'm done. That will save me time now. I hurry out. The sooner I get started, the sooner I can get this over with. I can't be late to a job that I've just started.

I check the clock, it is two-fifteen now, and she needs to leave by three o'clock? She arrives more than an hour late on the one day when she has a fixed departure time. Tina scurries out of the bathroom in her bra and panties mumbling.

"It's not my fault that I'm so late, traffic was terrible." Tina mutters discouragingly. "It's such a long drive to this part of town."

I immediately counter, "I'll see what I can do about that for next time." Tina is still frowning at me. I offer, "Maybe we could meet somewhere closer to your place, so that it's more convenient for you." Tina either doesn't care or didn't hear me, I don't know which. She climbs into the bed and complains that she's cold. I pull the blanket up around her and she shivers. I get undressed and get into the bed. Tina grabs my limp penis and lets out an annoyed sigh.

74

"Why aren't the porn movies playing? Have you set up the threesome with the pointy butt girl? Did you get us a date with Taylor?"

I slowly shake my head, no. Tina snidely admonishes me.

"Well you better get a hold of 'pointy butt' since you failed miserably on your mission is to get us a date with Taylor."

I think to myself, "The woman hasn't ever been married and she still uses that tone that a wife uses."

I ask Tina to lie on her back. I lick her pussy. It isn't fresh like it always has been before. Maybe Tina hasn't showered since first-thing this morning. I am not getting any reaction from licking her pussy, so I put my tongue in her butt. Error! It tastes like shit! I know better. I lecture myself; I should have sniffed around the area before I plunged in. My disappointment mounts.

I want to get up and brush my teeth, but that will further deteriorate this already limp date. A more pressing problem is that 'time is of the essence.' I evaluate the position options: mish, no, face to face is no good when I smell like shit. I know what to do; we'll do it doggy-style. I announce, "We're going to 'walk the dog.'" Tina barks back at me impatiently.

"What the fuck are you talking about?"

I ask Tina to get in the doggy-style position. I install a condom, get behind Tina and slap my half-staff against her tailbone. I don't know why it is taking me longer than usual to get hard. I should be hard already, considering how cute a girl Tina is. I don't care if she is 'into it' today or not. The only thing I care about is that she shows up and that she is willing to let me do what I want to her. I don't give a rat's ass if the girl is turned-on or not. Hell, I'm busy screwing; I don't have time to notice shit like that. I get hard, put it in and pump away. I am enjoying it, but I can't help but notice that Tina is disinterested. It surprises me that I seem to care. I should just act as if I haven't noticed anything and change the position.

I must be making some ridiculous face because Tina peeks over her shoulder at me for a second. She looks me in the eye and then gets quiet. She looks embarrassed, like she's been caught faking it. Not a single word is said by either of us about it.

John is practically impotent today. He must have run out of his boner-medication and can't get an erection without it. I wish he would just hurry up and finish so that I can get out of here with my money. I can't be late. I have just started work at that real estate office and I have to be on time. I wouldn't have even set up this appointment if that stupid job would pay me before the end of the month when my bills are due.

I finish and pull out immediately. I look at the clock, it's 2:35 and she has to leave at three. That means that we'll be 'done' and she'll head for the bathroom by 2:45.

Tina looks at the clock and then at me.

"Well, if you want to go again, then we had better get started."

I quickly wash up in the bathroom, return to bed, and ask for head. Her performance is effective even though I can tell that Tina's thoughts are somewhere else the whole time. I ask Tina to get on her back and I grab a condom. I close my eyes for the first time with her. She is distracting me with her distant and disgusted expression. She can't wait for this to be over. Just as I am getting close to orgasm, Tina starts making the worst fake orgasm noises I have ever heard. I try to ignore her sounds. If I can concentrate on the sex then I can finish. Tina gets louder and more obvious.

"Come for me, come on, come in me, I want you to come in me, come on..."

I can't concentrate with all this drama. I finally lift up my head and give Tina a long look in the eye. Tina looks justified, at first, and then admits her guilt with her eyes and looks away. I disengage the female. I roll her one-quarter turn and penetrate in a scissors configuration. In that position, I can admire her above-average butt, while her below-average gibberish is pointed away from me. I start to ejaculate and make the mistake of informing Tina, "I'm coming." Tina jumps up and is in the bathroom while I am still spewing in the condom. I look down at my penis to jack off the rest of my load and see the condom is bloody. I've started Tina's period. Well, that's a relief because it explains her ill-tempered mood today.

I don't plan to take a shower today because I can't be late for work, but when I wipe between my legs, I see that John has started my period! Shit! I'm not due for another three or four days. I don't have any tampons, just some crummy panty liners. I take a quick shower. I look for the deodorant, but it's not there! I can't count on John for anything.

Tina bursts out of the bathroom and barks right into my face.

"I have to leave right now, I've just started working at a real estate office and I am already late."

I don't know what to say. I weakly utter, "OK." Tina's eyebrows narrow. She steps toward me and looks down at me fiercely.

"Don't make me ask for it."

"Ask for what?"

"Are you going to give me some money?"

My hand covers my mouth in embarrassment. I gasp, "Oh shit, I am so sorry. Give me just a second." I scramble to get the empty envelope, which is still in my briefcase. I left it empty and in there because I was not sure whether it should be stuffed with a donation for one hour or for two hours. It depended on when she arrived. I could not prepare it in advance, as I always do. The change in procedure confused me and I was unprepared when it was time for her to depart. I fumble with the Ben Franklins and a bunch of old lottery tickets fall out of my wallet. I feel the need to explain, "I'm playing the lottery so that I can win enough money to afford to see you every day." Half under her breath, Tina smirks.

"That's the only reason that I'm here with the likes of you."

Tina frowns at her watch and then at me. She complains emphatically to me.

"I've just started at this job and I can't be late!"

I hand Tina the envelope, "I'm so sorry."

Tina snarls at me and snatches the envelope without saying a word. She throws open the door and flies off in the wrong direction down the corridor. As the door slams itself shut, I sadly conclude aloud, "I've known her for only seven months and the honeymoon's over already. She'll never reply to my text messages again. That was the last time I will ever see her."

Chapter 6

A Cute Butt

All day long, I haven't been able to think of anything else. I tried to keep busy at work to keep my mind off sex, but my job at that stupid real estate office is so boring that I couldn't stop thinking about getting my pussy licked tonight. I am seriously horny today. I am going to ask John to lick my... Wait, I don't have to ask John to lick my pussy. John always asks me if he can lick my pussy. John is the only guy I've been with who wants to do that more than I do, and he's the only one who stays at it until I'm done. John keeps going even when I pull his hair out! He's more of a gentleman about giving head than any boyfriend I've ever had. I've never had a... Why is the door opening? Did I knock? I don't recall doing so.

Tina's knock is fast and powerful today. She's right on time and it startles me. I'm so excited from just hearing her knock, that my crotch is already tingling. I barely get the door open and Tina slips in and wraps her arms around my neck. I struggle to close the door behind her.

"This is a great place to meet. I live just a few blocks

down the next major street. It only took me five minutes to get here."

Tina gives me a long, sloppy wet kiss that tells me how much she appreciates the convenient location. She eventually let's me up for air. Tina presses her pubic bone against my crotch, looks me in the eye and teases me.

"I would see you everyday if we met here. I love this hotel. I can park near the rear entrance to the lobby and get right to the elevators from the parking structure without anyone seeing me. I like the rear entrance because it's... less crowded... than the lobby. I don't like to valet park, the valet guys always give me funny looks."

Tina releases me from her embrace, struts over to the bar, and pours herself a strong drink.

"Let's get high. I don't have all that far to drive home and I'm not leaving for a couple of hours. I like meeting at night; I work days now. At night I can get buzzed because I don't have to go to work afterward."

We drink and get raucously high. It's been three months since we last met and we both want to forget about the last time. Neither of us says a single word about it. After our last meeting, I thought I would never hear from Tina again. I am relived that this meeting is starting out positively. Tina seems to be in a playful mood and I want to keep it going.

John has a gift for me. He ceremoniously presents me a still-wrapped porn magazine on a pillow. It's the kind I like, full of teenage girl models. John asks me if I want to open it and play with it while he steps away for a moment. I snatch the magazine off the pillow and tear the wrapper off. John's eyes get wide and he scurries into the bathroom.

I give Tina her new magazine and I hit the can. I tell her, "I'll be just a minute. You can pass the time by jilling off."

Even though John is goofy, he is also mature, which I appreciate. He is nothing like the guys my age that I have dated. I especially hate it when my boyfriends try to act like tough guys by being as gross and as graphic as possible in announcing that they are 'going to use the bathroom'. Why do these cavemen think that's a cool thing to do? I prefer older men because they are more fun to be around than young guys. John makes me feel cherished. He adores me the same way my dad does. I love the way he treats me, and I crave the affection I feel from him.

I return from the bathroom to find Tina thoroughly engrossed in her new magazine. She smiles up at me, her eyes sparkle.

"Oh look, I have that same vibrator."

"Is that the one that started spontaneously in your moving box?"

"Yes, it's the kind with a twisting speed control. When they roll they can easily turn themselves on."

"A roll with you always turns me on."

"You're funny. This is hot porn, look at this girl; she's got the type of body we like. Do you like her?"

"Yes I do. She's cute. You have taught me so much. I'm lucky to have met you."

"Aww, how sweet. Wait, what did I teach you?"

"I was always ashamed that I liked porn. That is, until you joyfully squealed that you 'LOVE porn' on our second date. I've thought about that a lot. I am envious of how liberated you are. "

"Why are you ashamed of liking porn?"

"I am afraid that conservative people will judge me negatively for it."

"Screw them. Who gives a rat's ass what they think

anyway. They're just envious of anyone who lives with passion and who is in touch with their sexual feelings, because they repress theirs. They're like all those women that look down on escorts just because they are jealous of them. They feel threatened by escorts because they are too insecure to do it."

Wow, Tina is not only liberated, she is courageous and insightful. She is quite worldly for her tender age. I hear myself talking without thinking. "Time spent with you is like a therapy session for me. Being with you makes me a happier person."

"That's nice to hear. It makes me feel good to know that I help you."

Tina sees me looking at her hand in her crotch, "Without your help, I would NEVER have gotten that joke about jilling off." Tina smiles warmly at me over her magazine.

"We make a good couple; we help each other understand things."

Tina gets a thoughtful look in her eye. I pause to give her time to think. She seems to need some prodding.

John can see that I have something I want to say. He looks at me nervously.

"What...?"

"You won't believe what happened to me the other day at an open house. A man made that peculiar sound of yours that you told me about. I couldn't believe it; I thought you were joking about making noises."

I judge John's reaction to see if I should continue. He seems secure with the topic. "I was doing an open house with a real estate agent. She was at the front door greeting people and I was in the kitchen where I was supposed to talk about all the upgrades. Suddenly a man walks into the kitchen without watching where he was going. He wasn't expecting anyone else to be in the house. He was startled when he looked up and saw me. He gasped aloud and then he looked me over the way men do. The poor guy was terribly embarrassed. I can't imagine the expression I must have had. He got out of there in a hurry."

John's eyes are big like a little kid at Christmas.

"Did he ask if you were included in the price of the house?" We both laugh, but I'm too horny to waste time on comedy.

Talking about the open house has made me horny. There is something about being at an open house that turns me on. I 'm ready to get the action started.

Tina grabs her envelope, stands up, and informs me that she's going to change in the bathroom. I stop her and ask, "Can I undress you?"

John asks me if he can undress me. I know what he's asking, and even though I let him undress me before, I pause to think about it. John can tell that I am stalling.

"You know, instead of changing in the bathroom, can I undress you here?"

I don't say it aloud, but I protest silently to myself, "No, you can't undress me." I like to change in the bathroom. It helps me to prepare. I change more than just my clothes in the bathroom. That's also where I get myself ready to provide the service portion of the appointment. I need some time alone to get into character both emotionally and mentally.

Tina gets quiet on me. She doesn't like the idea of me undressing her, but she doesn't know how to tell me. She's deep in thought. I remember that she didn't like it the last time I did it. Maybe I've crossed a line.

This is not a date. You are not my boyfriend. Then again, John is not like a client to me either. It took me only five minutes to drive over here from my place. I don't need to take a shower, or use the bathroom like I need to when I drive all the way across town to see him.

She's still thinking about it. Maybe I should back off. I don't want to upset her. We're getting along so well this time.

Even though I didn't enjoy it the last time he undressed me, it's not that big of a deal. Besides, he's paying me a fortune, so if it's not too weird of a request, then I should be willing to give him what he wants.

I'm about to apologize for asking, just as Tina shakes herself out of the trance.

"Sure, you can undress me. It's just that last time you got my panties so wet that I had to wear my sexy pair home. They're the kind that are sexy but they aren't comfortable, especially to wear under my jeans. It's a short drive home from here, so it'll be OK this time. I'll bring an extra pair of comfy ones to wear home next time."

I grope Tina's clothed body shamelessly and thoroughly. She is neither into it nor aroused by it, but I am enjoying it completely. I feel the need to explain myself to Tina. "When I see a cute girl in tight pants out on the street, this is what I want to do to her."

"You'd get slapped, or worse, for being a perv."

I bury my face in the crotch of Tina's denims and she giggles at me.

As John is pawing me through my clothes, I can't help but wonder, "Maybe perverts aren't that bad after all. John is certainly a pervert. That should creep me out, but instead it's fun. It's his one redeeming quality. Well, in addition to his tongue. I wonder if he gives good head BECAUSE he is a complete pervert. The great head he gives me is definitely a good thing. So maybe his being a total pervert is not a bad thing and that makes it a good thing. See?"

I undress Tina slowly while kissing and licking her everywhere.   She seems to be preoccupied with deep thought the whole time. What is she thinking right now?

I want to get my pussy licked, but I feel selfish asking John to give me pleasure when he's paying me to give him pleasure. As soon as he has me striped naked, I suggest that we 69, but instead of that, John wants me on my back. I lie down and he gets between my legs. He looks at me like I'm dinner and goes down on me. I put my hand on his head and pull him against me.

I get between Tina's long milky thighs and I go to work on her cute little cat. I put to use what I have learned about her "hot buttons" over our first few dates. Tina responds quickly and I take her to the first orgasm right away.

I let Tina's pussy rest a few moments while I lick her erotic thighs. I slowly work my way back to her crotch and the moment my tongue brushes her clit, she grabs for a handful of my hair. Luckily my hair is still so short that she can't get a grip on it. She tries repeatedly with no luck. I don't want to be suffocated again, so I give her the increased pressure she's looking for and she goes immediately into another climax. It seems like once you get a girl past her first orgasm then she can have one per minute until that big one that makes her too sensitive and then she'll want to take a break.

Now that I have Tina relaxed, I decide it's time to go to work on the back door.   I rearrange us into a 69 position and Tina sucks my erect penis into her soft wet mouth. I gradually move Tina's butt around until I get to where I can put my tongue deep into her butthole. She has figured out what I am doing and she is fully cooperating with me.   She releases my penis from her mouth and adjusts her hips to allow me to fully penetrate her anus with my tongue. She is perfectly clean. She must have taken an enema before she came here.

I spread Tina's cheeks with my hands and thrust my tongue as far as I can into her little butthole. Tina makes a sexy noise and locks her mouth onto my penis. I immediately ejaculate. Tina drains me like a soda through a straw. To my surprise, instead of popping out of the bed to go spit in the bathroom, Tina rolls off, looks up at me, and swallows hard. She smiles fiendishly at me.

"You taste good!"

I reach my arms out for her and she lies down beside me with her head nestled on my shoulder. I put my arms around her and we lie in silence together. After a long time, Tina breaks the silence.

"Let's have some drinks, get high, and watch porn."

It's great to meet at night, near Tina's residence, because we get to party together. She is wonderful to spend time with.

We watch the porn movie on my notebook computer. I notice Tina tilting her head to one side in an effort to get a better angle. I unconsciously do the same thing, but because the image is flat on the screen, you cannot change the perspective. I recognize the move because I catch myself doing it all the time. I confess to Tina, "I do the same move. I try to get a better angle to see the action. It doesn't work for me either." Tina tries for a second to remain composed, but loses it. Tina laughs out loud as she pleads guiltily.

"Look at us, we're such dorks!"

I look Tina up-and-down while smiling at her. She's way too hot and poised to be any kind of a dork. When she laughs I can see her strong, tight abdominal muscles ripple. "You have great abdominal muscles. Are you still working out regularly?"

"Yes I am, but now I only do two hundred sit-ups a day."

I ask Tina with some trepidation, "What do you mean 'only' two hundred a day?"

"Well, when I'm modeling I do five hundred sit-ups every day. It is so hard to look like that every day. You can't eat. If you eat anything, then your belly sticks out. I don't miss modeling for a second."

"It sounds like a demanding profession."

"It gets worse. If you have hair like mine, that curls when it's wet, then you are the first one hosed-down, always with freezing water, so that your hair will curl when it starts to dry. You know how skinny girls are always cold anyway. When you're modeling, you are always cold. The photographers like the way your skin dimples up with goose bumps when you're freezing. Those bastards."

"You don't like photographers do you?"

"All the photographers are jerks. The ones that are gay try to give you an inferiority complex. They're jealous because they want to be a cute girl so bad that they can't stand it. The one's that aren't gay are always trying to get you on the 'casting couch'. I don't miss modeling at all. I try not to even think about it."

Tina seems to be blocking out the memories from some bad experiences during her modeling days. I try to show her some empathy, "I've never realized the burden that an appealing girl like you bears. I always thought that life was easy for a pretty girl. I'm sorry that so many men are assholes. They behave like that because they are insecure. I know because I have been a man my whole life. I understand men and their insecurities towards women. Most men are jealous of what you have. They are jealous of the power that you have, and knowing that they will never have it. I think that is why men try to impose on attractive girls."

John is the only man I have ever met that would say that. I like being with him. I like the way he helps me to understand things.

Tina is giving me a cryptic look. I feel the need to explain myself, "I don't know anything about what it must be like for a woman. I have never been a woman, but I bet it's hard."

"Do you want to fuck me now?"

"Yes, I do. Lie down in the middle of the bed, on your back."

"Like this? Is this how you want me?"

I mount Tina in the missionary position; she puts her arms around my neck and pulls me toward her. Tina playfully issues her commands to me.

"Kiss me. I want kisses, everywhere that I point."

Tina points at her drum-tight belly. I kiss her there. Tina points to her left breast, then shoulder, chin, lips, then her other set of lips. I kiss her there and keep kissing her there. Tina shudders a little and I think she's faking the excitement, until she pulls my head out of her crotch by my ears and barks at me.

"Fuck me right now, and fuck me hard!"

I quickly ready the condom and do as she orders. I get on top of Tina, enter her, and pound her as hard as I can. I continue until we come simultaneously. I lie on top of Tina and doze off. I awake still hard and still inside her. I try to get up but Tina immediately wraps me up in her legs and arms, grabs my cheeks and pushes me back into her.

"Don't pull out just yet."

Tina whispers insistently.

"Hold me. Hold me tight."

I hold her tight. I can't believe how happy Tina makes me. I remind myself to relish every moment of her company as much as I can, but at the same time, I don't want to fall in love with this girl. I may never see her again after tonight. I must enjoy tonight as much as possible. I eventually get soft and fall out. Tina releases her embrace and rolls me onto my side next to her. I lie there lost in her pretty eyes. Tina gets up on one elbow and looks me in the eye a moment. She gives me a quick sloppy kiss.

"That was fun. Let's do that again. Get a good porn scene going for us to watch and I'll suck your cock when I get back."

Tina slowly rises from bed and saunters into the bathroom singing softly. For the first time, Tina leaves the bathroom door open while she pees.

Tina yells to me from the toilet.

"John, I've got 'cotton-mouth' from getting high and I can't give you head with a dry mouth."

"I'll show you a trick that a porn actress showed me." Tina bounces out of the bathroom still wiping up.

"What trick? What porn star? You never told me that you know a porn star. Who is she? Do you have any of her movies? Is she hot?"

John doesn't answer my questions. He gives me a mischievous look as he grabs his bag of tricks. John rummages around and pulls out some sour candy, the kind that little boys would buy. He tells me to put some on my tongue and then he cringes and turns away.

"I can't watch."

"Why not?"

"When the girl makes the sour face, it makes me feel

like I have hurt her. I can't watch that."

Wow, either John is a pussy, or he is overprotective of women. Maybe that's why I trust him so much.

I shake off the bitter taste of the sour cherry candy and my mouth is still dry. I pucker up into a frown. I think, "This isn't going to work." A second later my mouth is watering like crazy and I'm about to drool. I get into position for the bj. I open my mouth and a river of saliva pours out. I can't believe it. I start giving head and my spit flows freely out of my mouth and all over John's fully erect penis.

"Look, I'm drooling like a porn star! Is this how the girls get all that slobber going in the movies? This is great! I'm going to give you a 'porn star' blowjob."

I climax. Tina swallows and looks up at me with a big wet grin.

"That's a great trick the porn star taught you. Did she teach you any other tricks?"

"Well, she also told me that the candy comes in a couple of different flavors and more importantly, in different colors. She cautioned me, 'Be sure to get the red one, which will be either strawberry or cherry flavor, because your tongue will turn the same color as the candy.' I think the idea is that a red tongue isn't as weird as a blue or a green one."

"I need the spit to get your big dick completely into my mouth."

"Am I honesty bigger than average? Would you tell me the truth if I were only average or only a little bigger? The only hard-ons I ever see are in porn movies and they're almost always bigger than me."

"When you watch a porn movie you must think, 'That guy's average.'"

"As a straight guy, I only see regular guy's limp dicks in

locker room showers and they are usually much bigger than mine when it's limp."

"Girls don't give a fuck how big it is when it's limp. There's this expression that goes, 'There are show-ers and there are grow-ers', and trust me, you're a grower."

"That reminds me of a great joke. A grade school kid is in sex education class. The teacher asks, 'How many penises does a man have?' The kid answers, 'Two.' The teacher asks him if he knows what a penis is. The kid says he does and that his Dad has two of them. The teacher asks the kid to explain. The kid says, 'My Dad has a little one that he uses in the bathroom, and a big one that the babysitter uses to brush her teeth.'"

While Tina is still laughing at my joke I grab a condom, put Tina in the doggy-style position and enter her. After a few strokes, I wipe my thumb across my lips to coat it with saliva and press it flat against her anus. She pulls away a little bit at first, but then relaxes and I slowly massage her sphincter with my wet thumb. As Tina starts approaching orgasm, I pull my penis most of the way out of her vagina and I pop my thumb one-knuckle-deep into her butt. Tina's head snaps up and she utters a short gasp. Without turning to look, she calmly instructs me.

"Not too deep."

I hold my thumb in her shithole, push my penis fully into her vagina and give her a few strokes while the tip of my thumb is still in her butt. My thumb and penis can feel each other. I pull my penis completely out and then gently ease my thumb out of her anus in one move.

This is where I would normally try to butt fuck the girl, however I don't want to push this girl too hard. I like her and I'm willing to take the long road to Greece. I insert my penis back into her pussy and pound her. I am silently pleased with the progress we are making. I am optimistic that we may visit Greece together someday. The thought makes me climax.

I collapse onto the bed next to Tina. I am panting heavily. She gives me a concerned look. Between breaths I instruct her, "Tell the mortician; don't even bother to try to wipe the smile off of my face." Tina laughs playfully as she gets up to use the bathroom. Tina leaves the door open again this time and calls out to me while she pees.

"You cured my cotton-mouth, but do you have anything for my cotton-twat? I need a shower. I want to ask you something. Why are you so fond of my butthole? Are you into every girl's butthole, or only mine?"

"Only those rare girls with adorable butts, that are open minded enough to try it. You have such a cute butt that I've always wanted to play with it."

"I'm going to take a quick shower, I'm not leaving, I just want to clean up."

"That's a great idea, then I can lick your pussy to cure your cotton-twat."

Tina returns from her shower, lies on her back on the bed and gives me her bedroom-smile. I go to work licking her freshly cleaned pussy. It doesn't take long until she is in the throes of orgasm and I'm certain the entire hotel hears Tina climax.

"I'm going to come, I'm going to ahhhhhhhh, oooooh yes!"

Tina catches her breath and then rolls over onto her stomach. She starts looking through her new porn magazine. I grab a condom, the bottle of lube and climb on top of Tina's backside. She doesn't even seem to notice me. I settle in with my dick just below the crack of her ass. Tina looks sharply over her shoulder at me and I'm afraid she's going to tell me to get off of her. Instead, she flashes an excited smile at me.

"Look at how hot this girl is! We need to find a hot, skinny girl like this one to join us."

Tina sees what I'm up to.

"Oh, use lots of lube, I'm sore from all the sex." John must have taken a double-dose of boner-pills today. Wait, several of the guys my age that I've been with used boner-meds and most of them didn't even come twice. I'm curious about this. I'm going to do some research on this subject when I get home.

I lube both her pussy and my condom-covered penis before I enter her. Tina grunts. I start slowly. As she gets into it, I penetrate her fully and then pound her hard. Tina's sounds become more urgent, I must be hurting her. I slow down the stroke. Wait, what is she moaning?

"That feels so good. Don't stop. Don't stop."

I can't reach the lube from here and if I pull out she may be so sore that she won't let me re-enter. If I stay in then she'll feel obligated to let me finish if she can take it. I decide that my best strategy is to go at her as hard as I can and try to blow my load before she objects and tells me to stop. We wrestle vigorously until I come. Several pages of Tina's new magazine are accidentally torn in the process. I get off of her and go to the bathroom. Tina stays in bed. When I return I see that she hasn't moved. "Are you alright?"

"I'm covered in lube. I'll probably slip if I try to get in the shower. I better draw a bath."

While Tina is in the tub, I slide her two-hour-stuffed envelope into her new magazine. I want to make sure that I don't forget to give it to her this time and that she doesn't have to ask for it. That was a horribly rude mistake for me to make. I can't believe that I forgot to give her the money last time. It must have been terribly humiliating for her to have to ask me for it like that. I need to be more careful to show her the proper respect. I'm lucky that a terrific girl like Tina will see me.

I'm sure that there is something that I need to ask Tina, but what is it? There was something about the magazines. Tina likes the magazines. Oh, that's it, Tina likes girls.

Tina emerges from the bathroom with one towel wrapped around her body and another wrapped around her hair. She glances around the room.

"Where are my clothes?"

"Never mind your clothes, I've got important news that I forgot to tell you earlier."

"What news?"

"Pointy-butt saw your photos and she wants to set up a threesome!" Tina's pretty eyes get wide with wonder.

"You finally saw Pointy-butt! What did she say?"

"I've seen Lisa three or four times since we last got together. When Lisa saw your photos she said, 'She's got a cute round butt!'"

"Let me see her photos again. Do you have some?"

I bring up Lisa's photos. Tina scrutinizes them.

"Oh, she's so cute. I want to play with her pointy butt. Can you get us a session with her?"

"She's not Taylor, but she's available in two weeks."

"Oh, I want to do this! Go ahead and make the arrangements with her and then let me know when she can meet. Good thing I've just had a ton of sex or I'd be too horny to sleep."

"When I win the lottery, we'll have threesomes every

94

day!"

"You HAVE to win the lottery. Then we can play with cute girls all the time. I'm so excited about Pointy-butt. I'm going home with my new magazine to jill off. I hope I'm not too sore to use my vibrator. Where are my clothes?"

"Can I keep your panties?"

"Well, they're soaked, so I can't wear them. You might as well keep them. I guess I can wear the pair that I brought with me, even if they don't match my bra. I'll bring an extra pair next time so that you can have your souvenir and I can still have matching undergarments."

I help Tina gather her clothing that is strewn about the room. She dresses in front of me and I'm spellbound by the sight. Tina laughs at me for staring at her while she puts her clothes on. Tina gives me stern look as she grabs her purse and magazine.

"You are such a pervert. It's a good thing that I like that about you."

"Do you have everything? Do you have your... magazine?" Tina gives me a big grin as she sees the fat envelope bulging inside the magazine.

"Yes, I've got it all."

"When can I see you again? It's been a long time."

"I'm sorry. It's just that I'm working a lot more hours at the real estate office, it leaves me with less time for sex. The market has gone as soft as a limp penis. I have to go to open houses both days of every weekend. It's better to get together at night during the week like this. Text me in a couple of weeks, or when you confirm with Pointy-butt and we'll work something out."

"It's dark out. Can I walk you to your car?"

"Thanks, but it's OK, I'm parked just outside the lobby."

Tina is giggling as she exits.

"I'm so high, which way are the elevators at this hotel?"

I close the door all but a crack and watch Tina as she saunters off singing softly to herself. This hotel has rooms in a square surrounding a big atrium, so she can go either way out the door and still get to the elevators. I latch the door and think about how lucky I am to know her.

I lie in bed fondly reminiscing over the events of the evening. My phone chimes as a text message arrives. It's been about thirty minutes since Tina left.

From: Tina
Msg: Thanks for the
hot time xxxooo

Chapter 7

I've Always Wanted To

I knock on the door confident that I will get two things out of my time spent here tonight. First I know that I will get all the sex that I want, and second, that I'll get the money I need to pay my overdue rent. The idea of fulfilling both needs with one night's work is both exciting and relieving.

I feel like I'm on a date to see an old friend and fuck my brains out. The trust that I have in John makes me feel secure. I didn't even count the money he gave me the last time; I just spent it.

Tonight's appointment is such a nice break from my real estate office job. That place is so full of drama and bullshit. It's fun and easy to see John for a couple of hours. It certainly pays better. Even though I'm too tired to go out bar hopping with my friends tonight, I'm looking forward to getting drunk, high, laid, and paid. I'd go fucking crazy if I had to live off the paycheck from that stupid office job.

I am terribly horny today. All day I have been thinking about John's mouth in my crotch. I like the way he stays at it until I'm done. He knows how to treat a lady. I've never been with a guy my age who was THAT considerate of my pleasure. The door flies open and there stands John wearing nothing but a hard-on and a smile.

I'm sure that I'm forgetting something, but what? I receive a text message.

From: Tina
Msg: on my way
what room num?

Oh shit! That's what I forgot. I forgot to send Tina the room number. I am such an idiot.

To: Tina
Msg: room 269
C U soon

Tina's knock is right on time again, which means she's forty minutes early, but I'm ready for her this time. I took my boner-medication a full hour ago, I'm fresh out of the shower, and I've got a raging-boner from watching our porn movies. I take a quick peek to make sure that no one else is in the hallway, then throw the door fully open to expose myself to Tina. This should shock her.

I burst out laughing and continue uncontrolled as I enter John's room. I shut the door behind me without taking my eyes off John's penis. I set my purse and shopping bag down on the carpet and kneel down in front of John. He gasps. I grab his erect penis and he grunts. I put it in my mouth and start sucking. John trembles and makes the funniest noises. I start laughing and bite down gently on his hard cock to keep it in my mouth. John squeals and shakes. I bite down harder and John cries out. I reach behind John's glass balls and start to put my index finger up his butt. John comes instantly. Another blow-catch. "I'm going to wash my hands."

Tina attacks me the second I open the door. I love this girl. Tina swallows and goes in to the bathroom. I pick up her purse and fancy shopping bag, take them over to the table, and set them down next to Tina's envelope. I sit down and pour myself a stiff drink. Tina pops out of the bathroom still clothed. She casually issues instructions at me, like a close friend would. I feel loved.

"Let's party! Pour me a strong drink. Put the porn on. Let's get high. I don't have far to drive, and I've got nothing else that I'm doing tonight. I like meeting at night since I work most days and I'm a lot more horny at night. Let's take our time tonight, I'll still stay for the full two hours after we get high."

I love this girl. She is so friendly and affectionate that I can't believe it.

"This is so much fun and I definitely needed a break from my real life. I told my girlfriends that I was going Christmas shopping. They asked to go with me, and THAT wasn't going to work, so I told them, 'If you go with me then I can't get you a present, because then it wouldn't be a surprise.' They believed me."

Since it is near Christmas time, I concluded that I should bring Tina a gift, but I am too cheap and disorganized to get my act together in advance. At the last minute, on my way out the door, I thought about greeting her today. What if she has a present for me and I don't have anything for her? How stupid am I going to look? Tina's so thoughtful that she might have a gift for me. I figure that I must bring her something. I brought her a new porn movie and magazine, but those are just props, not gifts. I decided to go for the novelty gift approach and brought her a little bottle of lube wrapped in holiday paper with a bow. To my surprise, Tina genuinely lights up when she sees that have I brought her a present. I suddenly feel ashamed that I brought her such a cheap present. Tina is so classy that she receives it warmly and gratefully.

"I'm going to need this today; I haven't had sex in a long time." I don't tell John, but the truth is that I've pretty much stopped having sex with anyone other than my favorite clients.

Tina is in a great mood and her infectious joy lifts my spirits.

"I like having two hours and being able to take our time, but I don't know how much sex I can have in one night. Good thing I've got a new bottle of lube!"

I visually explore Tina's hot body and ask her if I can undress her. Tina snaps at me authoritatively, but playfully.

"No, you can't undress me today. I have a new outfit that I brought just to wear for you. You can take it off of me though. That will be your Christmas present."

A giggling, excited girl bounces into the bathroom with a boutique shopping bag and shuts the door.

A few minutes later, Tina slinks into the room moving like a fashion model on the runway. I mumble to her, "Your posture is perfect."

"That's my ballet training. I have an idea, I'll do a runway-model strut for you."

Tina walks the length of the room a few times acting just like a model in a fashion show. Tina steps up to me, looks me in the eye and licks her lips. She is every hot girl that I have ever wanted to have sex with. I grab her and she melts into my arms like a lover. I deep-French-kiss her and grope her tight little butt.

"Like that! Squeeze my butt like that."

I fondle Tina's butthole through her lingerie panties and she giggles nervously. I am contemplating our next romp. I try to remember, "Does she take a finger in the butt?" It's been so long since I've been with this one that I don't remember. Oh yes, I remember now, she said, 'Not too deep.'

"Have you had anal sex with your friend Lisa?"

"I taught Little Lisa how to have anal sex."

"You did? Does she like it?"

"Once she learned how to relax, she started coming hard during anal sex. Now she asks me for it."

"Can you tell if a girl has had anal sex by looking at her butt? I can't see my butt. I don't know if it's cute. Does my butt look like I can do anal? Maybe I should have you take a photo of my butt so that I can see it."

I like the idea of photographing Tina's butt. I would love to have some souvenir photos of this gorgeous girl. I'll definitely bring my camera next time.

I remember that Tina doesn't mind when I use the lubricant on her. I remove her outfit so it doesn't get messy from the lube. I put Tina into the doggy-style position and lube up her pussy and butthole. Tina talks the entire time.

Tina watches as I unwrap an XL sized condom and roll it onto my erection.

"I am so glad that you always bring these, I can't haul around every sized condom. Especially if I have to carry around enough for you."

"I learned to bring my own condoms because I don't want to miss out on having sex just because the girl does not have a condom that fits me."

I slowly rub Tina's sphincter until she relaxes. Then I insert my index finger fully into her anus. She doesn't even seem to notice that I'm three knuckles deep in her shithole. I gently ease my finger out of her butt. I get behind Tina and poke my penis into her pussy. Tina stops talking the moment I penetrate her. I pound her hard and fast.

"Oh yes, like that. Oh, that feels good." John lasts a long time. He grabs me by my hips and pounds me hard, just when I want it.

Tina is making a lot of noise by the time I finish. I pull out and Tina starts talking again.

"Have you talked to your pointy-butt friend Lisa about the threesome? I definitely want to do this. Can you arrange it? Can I look at her photos? Do you have any new ones? Do you take photos of her?"

I explain that Lisa has not replied to any of my messages, however that is completely normal for Lisa. I pull up some photos from Lisa's new escort website. Tina's big blue eyes light up.

"I love this shot of her. It shows off her cute pointy butt! This is a good escort ad. I like the way her text is simple and direct. The layout has nice balance and symmetry."

"Have you thought of changing the photo on your ad?"

"I've pulled all my ads off the escort websites, I only see a few of my favorite regulars now. I'm happy about that. I'm a lot more comfortable this way."

"Come here, I'll show you the review I wrote on Little Lisa."

"Oh, let me see what you wrote about Pointy-butt."

Tina reads the entire review in complete silence, then looks up at me in wonder and asks me in a disbelieving tone.

"Did she actually do all those things?"

"Yes, she did."

"Did she really fuck you four times?"

I can't hide my smile as I look Tina in the eye and playfully respond, "No, she actually fucked me six times, but nobody is going to believe that, so I wrote four times."

"You have to keep trying to make contact with her and set this up. I want to do this. Be sure to arrange for Pointy-butt to see us at night. I'm more horny at night and I'll have more time. I want to be able to take my time with her."

"I'll do my best."

"You fucked Pointy-butt six times! How is that possible? What kind of boner-pills do you take?"

"Oh, those don't increase your libido, nothing can."

Dammit, I forgot to look up the effect of boner-meds on sex drive in men. I don't want to ask John about that. It might be awkward. I'll just look it up.

Why is Tina completely incredulous regarding the number of times we have sex? She's right there. How can she not believe how many times I fuck her when she's the one I'm fucking? She's been around, she must have had a multiorgasmic man before.

"Oh, I hope you don't mind, I've got to check for a text message from my best friend Stacie. I try to never do this when I'm with you, but we need to confirm a shopping date for tomorrow. It will only take a second."

When Tina is done texting, I use the opportunity to ask her something that I've been worried about, "I hope that I am not annoying you by sending you so many text messages?" Tina snaps back her response like a close friend would.

"No, of course not, don't be silly."

I am deeply pleased by Tina's friendliness. I beam at her, "I am just happy to see you again. It's been two months since our last time together."

"Has it been that long? It seems like it has been, at least... forever. I can't remember when I last had sex. I have been so busy at work lately. I have to use a stupid open house checklist that has been implemented by the new real estate office manager. I think she's on speed, I swear. This stupid bitch wants me to check mark every little stupid thing on her checklist. Even the most obvious shit like turn on the lights, and flush the toilets. I've been constantly working open houses, every weekend."

I immediately volunteer, "I would love to visit you at your open house some time. I think that would be great fun."

"Especially if there are other people there. We will pretend that we don't know each other, and act formal, until we're alone there. The market is so bad right now that I'm often alone at the house."

Tina's pretty eyes flash as she admits a secret desire with more than just a hint of suggestion.

"I've always wanted to... 'get busy' at an open house."

Tina looks at me for confirmation and I give it to her with my eyes.

"The next time I'm doing an open house in your area, I will text you the address and hours that I'll be there."

Wow, Tina is a bit of a perv. How exciting! I lament, "I just wish I could see you more often."

"I'd like to see you too, it's just that this stupid job takes up all my fun time. I'm making more money but I'm working so many hours that I don't have much time for appointments. Don't worry, whenever I need some good sex, I'll find the time to see you."

I complain to Tina, "You've spoiled me. I don't want any other girl except you and Lisa. You're so good that you're

104

worth waiting for, no matter how long. I'll wait until you're horny like this. I'll wait until you want sex bad." Tina cracks up and chortles back at me through her laughter.

"Until I want sex bad huh, and then what? You'll give me bad sex? Oh great, where's the vibrator? Is this a new battery? How do you turn this thing on?"

After I stop laughing at Tina's antics, I load and play the new porn movie. There is a schoolteacher scene.

"Does the school teacher thing turn you on?"

"No, but I met a school teacher escort once."

"I want to hear about this. You must tell me. How did you meet her?"

"I know this girl named Schelley and one time when I went to see her she said that she could do a double with her cute girlfriend. When I got there, I met the hottest grade school teacher ever. She's an attractive mid-twenties woman who stays strictly off-the-grid and only does doubles with her friend Schelley. She is what I'd refer to as an off-the-grid call girl."

"What was she like?"

"The school teacher was exceptionally entertaining. I had sex with her first and she came hard. Then when she got up, she was wobbly and giggling uncontrollably. I asked if she was all right and she explained, 'I get silly from sex, I get cum-drunk.' I asked her, 'Can I see you again sometime?' She shook her head, 'No, I'm sorry but I can't. I seldom do this and I never see clients alone.'"

"I must have had a puzzled look because she explained her situation to me in detail:

I teach elementary school full time. On rare occasion, when Schelley has a nice client that wants two girls, sometimes I join her. I'm actually a rather conservative person. It's just that once in a while I like to have uninhibited sex, and doubling with Schelley provides me with my sex fix and augments my income. I don't make much money as a teacher, but I love helping the kids. I tell Schelley, 'My horns hold up my halo.'

I saw Schelley again after that, but I never saw the schoolteacher again. Speaking of horns, here are some new pictures of Little Lisa for you to look at while I go and freshen up."

"You have new photos of Pointy-butt! Show me!"

I make sure that Tina is fully engrossed in the photos of Little Lisa before I enter the bathroom. I can't close the door or she'll get suspicious. Tina's street-clothes are in their usual neat little bundle on the counter, in the corner. I find her panties inside her neatly folded blue jeans and carefully remove them. I can't leave any evidence that I violated her personal space. I hold the precious panties to my face and inhale her feminine scent. My penis starts to swell in reaction to the stimulation. I hear Tina talking to me from the other room.

"These are great photos of Pointy-butt, did you take them?"

Oh shit! If Tina catches me sniffing her personal panties she'll think I'm a total pervert and she'll never see me again. "Yes, I took those photos the last time I saw her."

"You can take photos of me if you want to."

"Great idea, I'll bring a camera next time." I quickly stuff Tina's street-panties back into her blue jeans and turn on the sink faucet to make some noise. I hurriedly wash my hands and step out of the bathroom without looking where I'm going. I practically run into Tina standing just outside the door. Did she see what I was doing?

"About my underwear..."

Oh shit! I'm busted.

John is suddenly flustered for no reason. He doesn't want to discuss whatever it is, so I continue, "This time I brought an extra pair to wear home, due to what happened last time. The sexy ones are not comfortable to wear under my jeans. The only kind that are comfortable are granny pants and they aren't sexy.

"Oh, OK. That's a great idea. Good thinking."

"You seem to be infatuated with my underwear, so I am trying to accommodate your fetish."

I don't know if she caught me and doesn't mind, or if I got away with it. In either case, I am completely turned on by the panty sniffing and now I want to lick Tina's pussy.

I grab her hand and lead her back to the table. I pull a condom from the box, toss it on the table and instruct, "Stand right here." I bend the gorgeous girl over the table and get down on my knees behind her. I spread her beautiful buns and stick my tongue into her pussy as far as possible. Tina grabs onto the table for stability. She stands upright and the angle isn't good. I push her legs apart and she spreads them wide for me. I turn around and lean back with my head between her legs and my face looking up at her hot pink crotch. I work on Tina's clit with my tongue until she's wet and making her noises. She is

107

clearly turned-on and is grabbing at my hair to pull me in. I forgot to get a haircut and she can almost grip it. I make a mental note to get a hair cut before our next meeting.

Tina is shaking from orgasm. I am fully erect. I stand up, bend her over the table, roll on the condom, spit on my dick and shove it into her pussy.

"Oh, my pussy is getting sore, use some of the lube."

I pull partway out and squirt some of the glycerin-based lube on to where my penis is entering her pussy. I shove my penis in and Tina flinches. I hear some clinking noises on the table.

"Stop!"

I look up to see Tina's arm quickly sweep all of the items off of the table. Everything flies; our drinks, the ice bucket, her purse, the envelope.

"Ouch! Oh, that burns."

Tina bolts upright and my penis pops out of her vagina.

"I'm sorry but I'm just too sore to have sex. I know what to do; I'll finish you by hand. Take off the condom.

"I'll bring olive oil next time, extra-virgin. It doesn't sting and it's great for anal."

"You'll bring what?"

"I'll bring extra-virgin olive oil."

"Why?"

"Because extra-virgin olive oil doesn't sting like the glycerin-based lube can."

"Why extra-virgin? Does it work better?"

"No, it doesn't work any better but the joke is funnier." Tina grabs my penis and works it fast and hard. She presses her body against me and I ejaculate onto her rock hard belly.

"I'm going to go wash your sperm off my stomach. I'll be right back."

I pick up the spilled drinks and ice bucket that were casualties of our sex on the table. Tina returns from the bathroom and climbs into bed with a question in her eye.

"I want to talk you about something."

I get worried, but I try not to show it.

"I have a number of questions that I want to ask you. I feel like you are the only person that I can ask these questions. Do you mind?"

"No, I don't mind. Go ahead."

"Do you think that escorts are more health-conscious than most girls? Do you think that they get tested more regularly for STDs, and that they are more careful, for example, as in using condoms?"

"I definitely think that they are."

"Why do you think that?"

"The girls that I see all tell me that they get tested anywhere from every month to every three months. They always use condoms, that is, unless they trust the guy and they know that he gets tested regularly. All these girls know how to do a dick check and they screen their clients before meeting them. Therefore, I would say that the escorts that I have met are all much more health conscious than amateurs are."

"Do you get tested regularly?"

"I've told my MD that I see girls and he orders tests for me every three months, or at least twice a year at a minimum."

"I would like to dispel some of the myths about escorts."

"I think that there are many misconceptions and wide-spread ignorance when it comes to the general population's ideas about escorts and their clients."

"It helps me to talk to you about these things but now

109

I want to play. Let's watch porn."

I start up the porn movie. There's a scene of a teenage girl with an old man. I carefully ask Tina, "Does it ruin the scene when the guy is old like that?" To my surprise, Tina snaps her response back at me.

"No, I like older men. Older men know how to treat a lady, and they appreciate me a lot more than guys my age do. Besides, it goes with my daddy-complex."

I give Tina a look and she immediately answers me.

"My pussy is too sore to have any more sex, how about a blowjob? Where's the porn-star-blowjob candy?"

Tina finishes me and giggles as she turns toward the bathroom.

"I'm going to take a shower and use the mouthwash before I go." I get into the bathroom and there is that same stick of ladies deodorant. I keep forgetting to ask John about the story behind the ladies deodorant. I know what a pervert he is. I bet there's a story there. I'm going to see if I can get the juicy details out of him.

Where is Tina's envelope? Did she take it to the bathroom with her? No, her little purse is still out here on her chair. The envelope was on the table earlier, when we were talking. Where could it be?

I look around and find the envelope under the table. It must have been knocked off the table during sex. I'll just tuck it into Tina's new magazine and put it on the table under her purse so she doesn't forget it.

Tina emerges from the bathroom ready to leave.

"I'll take my magazine with me, so I can jill off at home, but I want you to keep my Taylor porn movies for me. Be sure to bring them next time."

"I hope there is a next time and that it is soon."

"Why wouldn't there be a next time?"

110

"I'm always afraid that you're going to meet some handsome virile doctor, get married, and that this is the last time I will ever see you."

"I would tell you if it was the last time."

"Don't ever tell me that it will be the last time. I won't show up."

"Why not?"

I don't answer. Tina looks at me knowingly.

"You wouldn't come because it would be too sad for you to bear?"

I silently look into Tina's pretty eyes.

"Don't worry. I'm going to go now, but I simply must see you again."

"Why is that?"

"Because you have my Taylor porn movies."

"Do you have everything? Do you have your... magazine?" Tina smiles while looking at the envelope, then pats it.

"Yes, I've got everything."

Tina steps out the door. I shut it quietly behind her. I look out through the peephole to see Tina stop, think for only a second, and then strut off in the right direction down the hallway toward the elevators.

I go to use the bathroom and Eureka! Tina's dirty underwear are lying on the bathroom floor! I grab them and sniff them. They smell like her pussy. I place them in a clean plastic storage bag, seal it shut, and place it in my bag. I'm thrilled with the wonderful present she's given me.

Chapter 8

Am I a Perv?

I knock on the door afraid that I'm about to throw up. I can't believe that I'm here tonight to meet a girl for sex. I am so nervous that I can barely breathe. Playing with another girl is all I have been able to think about since John texted me two days ago that he finally got us a date with the pointy-butt girl. I couldn't sleep last night even after using my vibrator twice. I'm consumed by questions. Am I going to like being with a girl? Am I going to like this girl? Is this girl going to like me? What if she doesn't like me? Can I handle that kind of rejection? Should I go through with this, or should I just leave right now, while I still can?

"No!" I hear myself talking out loud and it helps to bring me back to reality. I have wanted to do this for the longest time. This is the best opportunity I'm going to get. I desperately want to fuck a girl. I'm going to go through with this no matter what. Good, that's decided. I suddenly feel calmer, maybe because I have made my decision. In my relaxed state, I become analytical. I stop and ask myself, "Am I a perv?"

Tina's knock is somehow different today. I answer it worrying, "How disappointed is she going to be?"

Tina shoves past me and quickly scans the room for the other girl. When she doesn't see anyone else there, she turns and narrows her eyes at me. I'm scared. Tina corners me, takes a deep breath, and fires-off questions like a machine gun.

"Is she here yet? Is she on her way? Have you heard from her? Is she coming?"

Oh shit! This girl is ferociously worked up. I need to be careful. How do I break the news to her? I hope the disappointment doesn't ruin the evening for her.

"Let's sit down, have a drink, and I'll tell you what I know." I pour Tina a strong drink and serve it to her with a gentle smile. Tina snatches the drink from me, drains most of it, slams the glass down on the table and stares at me expectantly.

"Well?"

"My plan was that Little Lisa would be your present for our one year anniversary tonight. However, a few minutes ago she sent me a message with her apologies for her last minute cancellation."

"Do you think she canceled at the last minute because she doesn't want to do this with me?"

"No, not at all. I am certain that Little Lisa wants to see you. What you should know is that when Little Lisa says, 'Sorry, but something has come up,' that usually means it has something to do with her daughter." Tina quickly composes herself.

"OK. Well, then I can be flexible. I can meet on short notice anywhere anytime. Just let me know when she's available. Pour me another drink and let's get high."

Tina sets her purse down on the table and looks up at

me with a question in her eye.

"Wait, you said that Lisa has a daughter?"

"Yes, that's what she's told me."

"And she's still tight?"

"Oh yes. Lisa is incredibly tight. She's almost as tight as you are. That's why I call her 'little' Lisa. She had her daughter when she was still a teenager and I think that she snapped right back from it as a result of her youth."

"I'm never going to have a baby. My pussy's the size of a grape and it's going to stay that size. I'm not getting pregnant and having my pussy stretched out to the size of a... of a grapefruit!"

"I'm sorry about Little Lisa not making it."

"That's OK. Maybe it's better because I've been a nervous wreck over seeing a girl. I'm worn out. I'm also horny from thinking about it, so you'd better fuck my ears off tonight. I need another drink. Let's get loaded."

I pour us some strong drinks and we get buzzed.

"Are you going to play with my butt tonight? I showered myself extra clean to see the girl tonight so you can do anything you want to me. I know how oral you get."

I reach between Tina's legs and stroke her thigh sexually. Tina doesn't even notice my advance; she's too busy talking at me.

"Is my butt cute? Will you look at it and tell me. I can't see it, and I can't ask anyone else that question. There are so many questions that I can ask only to you. I can't ask a boyfriend or my mother or... anyone else."

I rub Tina's crotch through her clothes and she finally notices that I'm groping her.

"Oh, are we going to fuck? How do you want me? Should I get undressed? Sometimes you like to fuck me with my clothes on."

"Come here, strip, and give me a blowjob."

"I've got cotton-mouth, where's the porn-star-blowjob candy?"

Tina sheds her clothes onto the floor while I dig into my bag. I give the candy to Tina and I turn away.

"Ooooh, that's sour. I need to suck the sperm out of you to get the sour taste of this shit out of my mouth."

I climax quickly; Tina swallows and looks up at me casually.

"Is Lisa married to the baby-daddy, or is she divorced, or was she never married?"

"I don't know. We've never discussed it."

"My mom's married friends sit around her house and talk about their husbands. They say that they only have sex with their husbands twice a year, on New Year's Eve and on their husband's birthday. Is that true? How come? I have so many questions about marriage that I want to ask a man. Do you mind? Why do married men need to see escorts?"

"I've always said that putting a wedding ring on a girl's finger is like pulling the ripcord on a self-inflating raft."

"No wonder married men want to see escorts. I'm never going to be one of those fat-assed wives that their husbands cheat on. Why do women get married if they hate their husbands so much?"

"For many women, a husband is merely a social status and a paycheck."

"That reminds me of something I want to ask you. I have been trying to remember what kind of work you do, and I just can't. You keep saying that you're a nerd, but that's impossible. You can't do anything that nerds can do and besides that, you're too good in bed to be a nerd. So just tell me what you do for work again." John delivers his answer while keeping a straight face.

"I am a payload delivery optimization engineer at the

116

Rocket Thrust Institute."

I'm thinking, "What the fuck did he just say?" I ask John half joking, "Are you some kind of a 'rocket scientist' or something?" John pretends to be offended as he quickly retorts back at me.

"Oh, hell no! I'm not one of 'them.' The only thing the rocket scientists can do is... spew hot gasses."

John cringes and then shakes off my inadvertent insult the way my dog shakes off water. John composes himself, grabs a condom for some reason, and continues in a rare tone of voice. He sounds like he is giving me a lecture.

"Now, in payload delivery engineering, we make sure that the precious load gets delivered to exactly the right place, at just the right time, in perfect condition, while optimizing delivery efficiency."

John puts on the condom and surveys my entire body. He smiles devilishly at me, the way he does when we're about to start another round of sex. I ask John as seriously as I can, "Are you done spewing hot gas and ready to deliver...?"

Suddenly I am on my back. John has lifted my legs up in the air and has penetrated my pussy before I can finish the sentence. I close my eyes and let go. I go to places that I have never been to before. When John finally finishes, I have to rest a few minutes before I can get up to take a shower. When I get back to bed, I am curious to know more about John's job. I ask him about it and John swells with pride as he describes his work to me.

"I work in the 'S&M' department. I am honored to have my name on the official department document titled: S&M Contacts List."

"What the hell does that mean?"

"Everyone knows that S&M is a joke making reference

to Sadism & Masochism, but no one ever says anything about it."

"So what does it mean literally?"

"Oh, it's just an abbreviation for science and mathematics, but you never see that spelled out anywhere, you only see and hear S&M."

"That's a hilarious joke for a bunch of nerds."

"We have our moments."

John is giving me that look again, so I ask suggestively, "What do you want?"

"I want to lick your pussy. Get on your back in the middle of the bed." Tina props her head up on the pillow and looks on with anticipation. "I just got a hair cut, so feel free to come as hard as you want to, because my remaining hair is so short that it will be safe."

"You look good with your hair short. You should keep it that way."

"I tell people I keep it short for the convenience. Or I joke that I keep my hair short because then I can't get a grip on it when my job makes me want to pull my hair out. But that's only to hide the real reason."

"What's the real reason?"

"To keep a girl from pulling it out during oralgasm."

"Sorry about that."

"Don't be sorry, I'm flattered." I lick Tina's pussy until she has her first orgasm and then I roll her legs back and stick my tongue as far up her butthole as I can. My nose rubs Tina's clit and she orgasms a second time while my tongue is up her ass. I go back to licking her pussy and slowly work my index finger fully into her anus. I start finger-stoking her in the butt while sucking on her clit. Tina climaxes hard. She rests a second and then seems to notice my finger in her butt. She reaches behind her back

118

and utters a short gasp as she pulls my finger out from her butt.

"That felt good. Even having your finger in my butt turned me on this time."

I quickly put on a condom, roll Tina into the scissors position and start to penetrate her.

"We need lube."

"I can't reach the lube."

"Spit on my pussy and your cock. Spit works better anyway and it doesn't sting like the lube does when I'm sore."

I pound Tina's pussy vigorously while my finger is all the way up her ass. We both climax. I silently note that we've made good progress down the road towards Greece today.

After we rest a few minutes, I tell Tina, "I taught Lisa how to do anal sex and now she likes it." Tina frowns at me and shakes her head from side to side.

"I don't want to try it. I won't like it."

"Maybe you won't like it. Some girls don't ever like it."

"Tell me how old you were when you first had sex..."

Tina pauses thoughtfully, as though she has more to say. I wait for her to formulate her thoughts, and she continues.

"Or, at least, when you first tried to have sex... you know?" John nostalgically narrates for me.

"When I was three and a half years old, I had my first girlfriend. Her name was Margie, probably short for Margaret, and we played 'doctor' in the basement of my house where we could be alone."

"You had sex at three years old!"

"No, I just looked and barely touched her. I liked looking at her, even though I didn't know why."

John takes a deep breath before he continues the historical account of his childhood sexual development. "Keep going! You know I love juicy gossip. Give me the details."

"When I was five years old, I had the two cutest girls my age, that lived in my apartment building, showing me what was under their bikinis while I counted to five as slowly as I could."

"That's a fun age for a girl to show off her stuff to the boys. I did some of that."

"At seven years old, I tried to have sex with the neighbor girl who was my age. The instinct was strong and so even though I didn't know why, I put my finger in her pussy and then tried to put my limp penis into her. I had never had a hard-on before and I was not going to get my first one while playing with her either."

"I can't believe you tried to have sex when you were only seven years old!"

"Well, I didn't succeed, and it was not until age 15 that I even got close again. My mom had a drunken adults party and a thirty-something woman friend of my mother's tried to seduce me in front of her drunken husband. When I was eighteen I got my first bj. I finally got laid for the first time two months later at college."

John is panting and out of breath. I want to ask him a bunch more questions, but I decide not to. He looks like he's ready to have sex again.

Tina has asked about my introduction to sex, and talking about it has made me curious about her history. I don't dare ask her anything about it though. That subject matter is strictly 'out of bounds' in the escort-client relationship. If she wants to talk about it, then she will bring it up. Besides, the questions that she asks me reveal more about her history than she would ever admit to me outright. She keeps asking about how young a girl I want to have sex with. I wonder what happened to Tina and how old she was at the time. I grab a condom and jump her. I climax quickly and roll off. Tina is unfazed by the completed copulation.

"I can't believe how many times you can fuck. I know it's not the boner-meds because I looked it up and found out that nothing can increase a man's sex drive. How do you do it?"

"It only happens when I'm completely turned-on by the girl."

"Can any girl keep up with you? It's always the guy who can't give the girl enough sex."

"Little Lisa gave me the best compliment about that. One time, right after we fucked six times in two hours, she looked at me seriously and said:

You're a catch. I have never been satisfied by just one man before. It usually takes at least two, or three, men and my vibrator for me to get enough sex so that I can go do other things. This is great, it's still early in the day and I've had my sex. I can go get something useful done. Thanks.

Then she stepped into the bathroom to clean up."

"How many times can you come?"

"That depends on a few things like how much time we have, how hot the girl is, things like that. As long as the girl is cute and willing, then I usually come two or three times in one hour, four or five times in two hours, and six or more times if I have all night."

"You DO realize how aberrant that is. Don't you?"

"A few years ago, a girlfriend broke up with me because of my appetite for sex. I met another girl who told me that she broke up with a guy for the same reason. A different girl admitted that she broke up with a guy once because he had a tiny dick."

"Oh, no kidding? Tell me the tiny dick story."

"This girl met a guy that she described as 'a hunk' and she liked him enough, but he kept stalling on getting in bed with her. Finally, she tried to rape him and he stopped her. She demanded that he give her an explanation or she was going to dump him right then. He reluctantly told her that he has a small penis and he's afraid that she'll break up with him because of it. He told her that he likes her and doesn't want the relationship to end because of his small penis. She scoffed and said, 'It can't be that small.' However, when she finally saw it, she freaked out because it was ridiculously tiny, not even the size of her thumb. She was terribly disappointed because she couldn't even feel it inside of her when they tried to have sex. She said it was so small that she couldn't even give him head because it wasn't big enough to get it into her mouth. Then she sadly concluded, 'I did break up with him, right after that first time we tried to have sex.' She said she felt bad about breaking up because of it, but also that she didn't regret it."

"I've seen some pretty small dicks, but she literally said that it was smaller than her thumb?"

"She held up her thumb when she said that, and her hands were smaller than yours."

"I'm so glad that you have a big dick. I want to fuck again but my pussy is rubbed raw from the condoms. The lube will sting."

"Don't worry. It's going to be OK this time. I brought some extra-Virgin olive oil."

"Why?"

"Because I'm Italian and we put olive oil on everything, even our lovers."

"Well at least the Italian part explains your big cock and your stamina."

I grab a condom, oil up the bikini model, and ravage her. Tina reminds me why life is worth living while she informs the entire hotel complex that she has climaxed. Tina returns from the bathroom with her hand under her chin and her index finger on her lips in a shushing pose. She seems to be thinking about something. I wait with delight and wonder.

"I am sure that there was something... Oh, I almost forgot. I told you about the new office manager where I work. You know the psycho-bitch that's on speed and how she has me filling out her stupid open house checklists. I want to show you this one that I modified."

Tina digs trough her purse, pulls out an office form and hands it to me with an expectant glimmer in her eye.

John reads the checklist slowly and deliberately, as though he knows something's up. When he gets to the good part, his mouth falls open as he looks up at me with wide eyes.

I start to read the document aloud to Tina. I stop abruptly at the fourth item.

OPEN HOUSE PREPARATION CHECKLIST
[ ] Turn Lights On
[ ] Flush Toilets
[ ] Open Drapes

[ ] Fuck John Smith

"Do you like it?"

"Can you put a copy in the open house folder of every cute female agent and then send me a list of the addresses?"

"I hope I remembered to erase the copy of the file I modified. Otherwise those stupid robots will be running around looking for a John Smith to fuck, I swear."

"I'm trying as hard as I can to keep from falling completely in love with you."

"Do you want to fuck me again? Can you? Should I suck your cock?"

"Yes I do, and yes I hope I can, and yes you should, and to hell with it, I do completely love you." Tina grabs my limp penis and sucks it into her pretty little mouth while I reach over to the nightstand. I grab an XL and rip it open with my teeth.

"Do you have a vibrator that I can use while you fuck me?"

"Yes, I do. I'll tell you a vibrator story while I put a new battery in it for you." Tina's pretty eyes get big,

"You have vibrator story too?"

"In Vegas I met a famous escort named Ava Nicholson. She was the most sophisticated and experienced escort I have ever met. She carried a big bag of toys and props with her on calls. She opened her bag and pulled out a condom and a little lipstick-sized vibrator. I just watched. She unrolled the condom, turned on the vibrator to full-speed and dropped it into the condom. Then she shoved it up her ass with the end of the condom hanging out like a tail. She then laid down in bed on her back. She said, 'Fuck my pussy and you'll feel the vibrator in my ass.' It was one of the hottest fucks of my life."

"Your assignment is to get the smallest vibrator that you can buy and bring it next time. I want to try that."

"OK."

"Did she do anything else amazing?"

"She was wonderful. She sat down to pee with the bathroom door open, and the toilet was right across from the bed. While she was peeing, she looked over at me. I casually asked if she gives golden showers. She gave me a perturbed look and said, 'You should have asked me for it before I started peeing!' I said, 'Oh no, I don't want one, I just wanted to know if you did them.'"

"We had hot anal sex, and then she took a shower with me. By then it was pretty late, even for an escort in Vegas. It was about 3am. We did a 69 with her on top and we both came. She spun around so that we were face to face and we DFK'd a while. Then she got in a comfortable position on top of me and fell asleep."

"She fell asleep on top of you?"

"I was amazed and thrilled. She's a tiny girl maybe five-foot-five and barely one hundred pounds, so she felt great on top of me. My penis was pinned between our bellies. We were positioned such that I could reach both her butthole and the bottle of lube. I squirted some lube on her anus and put my index finger into her. I was sure that this would wake her up, but it didn't. I kept finger-stoking her butthole and after a little while I got hard. She was still asleep and I didn't want to wake her because she would leave and it felt great to have her gently sleeping on top of me while I finger fucked her butt."

"She slept while you fingered her butt?"

"She was a pretty sound sleeper because I could rub

my erection against her tummy and she kept sleeping. Finally, I decided to try to move my boner to between her legs. I used my hands to push lube in between our bellies until I could slide my hard dick to her crotch. I got so excited that when I rubbed past her little patch of pubic hair I ejaculated. Again, I was sure that this would wake her up, but she stayed asleep. With my dick between her thighs, I could reach her butthole and the tip of my dick. I proceeded to play with them both until about 4am when I got hard again. I couldn't quite reach far enough to guide the tip of my boner into her pussy and the angle was not going to allow anal entry. I maneuvered carefully so that I wouldn't wake her up until I got my uncovered penis into her hot wet vagina."

"She slept while you fucked her?"

"Yes, I penetrated her fully and she was still asleep. I was panting with excitement. I slowly moved in and out of her for as long as I could control myself. I approached orgasm and I knew that we would soon be done sleeping together. I put one arm around her waist to hold her on top of me and with the other I put my index finger fully into her asshole. I fucked her as gently as I could under the circumstances. I soon came and then quickly pulled my penis out of her vagina and eased my finger from her anus. Ava slowly woke up. I was afraid that she was going to be mad. She was sleepy and groggy. It took her a few minutes to fully wake up. She was totally sweet to me like we were lovers. She kissed me and said she was going to take a shower. She tried to get up off of me and said, 'I'm covered in semen and lube!' I tried to look innocent. She never asked me if I fucked her while she slept."

"She fell asleep on top of you, on your first date?"

"She's a terrific girl."

"I can't believe that she fell asleep. I thought that only guys did that."

"It was exceptionally romantic. Here's your vibrator, are you ready to suck my cock." Tina grabs the vibrator with one hand and my dick with the other.

"You're getting hard again. That's amazing. I've never had a boyfriend that could perform the way you do. Fuck me hard from behind. I'm rubbed raw from the condoms and it will hurt, so just fuck me fast and hard until I come. Don't stop this time just because I say it hurts. It's supposed to hurt and don't worry, if I REALLY want you to stop, then you will know it."

I roll on the condom and proceed to test its durability. We both get loud by the time I finish. Tina nymph-limps slowly to the bathroom.

"I'm going to be sore down there tonight. How does a man your age fuck more times than a guy my age? You must be younger than you look."

"Do you think I should I get rid of the gray in my hair?"

"No! Don't change it. Leave it the way it is."

"OK, I will. But why?"

"It looks good on you, and besides, it goes with my daddy-complex."

"Oh, I see. Now I understand. I won't change anything."

"I'm going to get a shower and get dressed now."

I hear Tina singing as she comes out of the shower, so I get her envelope out of my briefcase and place it under her purse on the table. I had kept it in my briefcase during the session so we wouldn't lose it while having wild sex on the table again.

"Thank you for this. My friends keep asking me why I

have so much money when I'm never working."

"What do you tell them?"

"I never tell them anything about my escorting. I absolutely must keep this a complete secret from my friends. It's hard for me to come up with excuses all the time, especially because girlfriends are always nosy about each other's business."

Tina gives me a long, suspicious look.

"Did I leave a pair of panties here last time?"

I don't know what to say to her.

John is just looking at me. Why doesn't he answer me? Maybe he didn't hear me. "Did I leave a pair of panties here last time?" John is blushing. He is such a pervert. I answer for him, "You DO have them. I KNOW you do. Just admit it to me." I pressure him and he quickly breaks down. He pleads with me to allow him to keep them.

"I can't tell you how much they mean to me."

"I'm not sure which of us is the bigger pervert, you for snatching my panties, or me for leaving without them!"

I was worried at the beginning of the evening that tonight would go poorly with Tina. After getting Lisa's message, I feared that Tina would be disappointed because I failed to get her a date with Lisa. But to the contrary, the anticipation of the threesome resulted in three hours of great sex, it's hard to call tonight a failure by any definition.

"I'm going to go now."

Tina struts out the door without any hesitation, and instinctively goes the right way down the corridor toward the elevators. She's not a newbie anymore.

Chapter 9

Oh, That's Right

I hurry up to John's room at the luxury resort hotel. I locate room #1958 and start knocking at the door. I'm shaking with nervous energy. A stream of questions flood into my mind. Am I going to like being with a girl? Am I going to like this girl? What if she doesn't like me? Why did she no-show last time? Maybe I should just bolt out of here right now. I want to do this so why am I so nervous? I hope she shows up this time. Why is John taking so long to answer the damn door? Oh shit, I think I'm going to throw up.

There's a fast and urgent knock at the door. That must be Tina, but she's thirty minutes early. I barely get the door open and Tina rushes in like the wind. Her eyes scan the room with wild excitement.

"Is she here yet?"

"Not yet, but it's early."

"Did she call?"

"Yes, she did."

"Did you talk to her?"

"Yes, I did."

"How long ago did you talk to her?"

"About fifteen minutes ago."

"Is she coming?"

"She was just leaving her place and that's about a forty-five minute drive from here."

"OK, good. She's on her way. That's good. Can we order some room service? All day long I have been too excited to eat and now I'm starved. What do you have to drink?"

Tina selects some appetizers from the room service menu while I pour her a strong drink. Tina gulps her drink while I call in the order. Tina seems anxious. She steps out onto the balcony to use her phone. I set out the toys, lubes, and porn so they will be handy when we need them.

There's a knock at the door, but it's not Lisa's knock. It must be room service with the food we ordered. I sign the tab and our juvenile waitress can't keep from smiling as she looks around the room. I get rid of her as quickly as I can. Tina comes in from the balcony and sits down to examine the delivery. Lisa knocks at the door. Tina's eyes meet mine. She has become a 'deer in the headlights.' I give Tina a playful smile. Tina stares blankly back at me.

I open the door. Little Lisa bounces in and her eyes lock onto Tina. Lisa gives me a quick hug without taking her eyes off of Tina. Tina stands up sharply without taking her eyes off of Lisa. They are both statues.

I introduce Tina to the runway-model-thin, five-foot six-inch, dirty-blond haired, dark-blue eyed erotic dancer.

I introduce Lisa to the magazine-cover-cute, five-foot ten-inch, platinum-blond haired, bright-blue eyed bikini model.

The two girls pause and eye each other up-and-down carefully. It strikes me that they both behave just like a guy does when he checks out a hot girl.

I decide to break the ice and help them to get started. I suggest, "How about if we all sit down and have a snack. The food just got here. I'll fix us some drinks, while you two get to know each other." The two girls sit down side by side on the couch, but not very close together. They still haven't taken their eyes off of each other. I try not to laugh as I pretend to be busy making drinks. Lisa smiles invitingly at Tina and let's her start. Tina's eyes sparkle. Tina composes herself and carefully asks Lisa her first question.

"How old are you?"

Lisa looks Tina in the eye as she replies slowly and deliberately.

"I'm twenty-five. How old are you?"

"I'm twenty-two. How long have you been escorting?"

"About five years now. How about you?"

"Just over a year. How did you get started?"

"I needed some money in a hurry and I was talking to a career escort that knew John. She said he is the nicest client she's got and that he keeps asking her if she knows of any new, teenage girls. She introduced me to him and we did doubles until I felt comfortable enough to see him alone. How long have you known John?"

"He was just my second date, so that was a year ago. Have you always liked girls?"

"Yes, even when I was a little girl I wanted to touch the other girls. I like boys too; I go both ways.

Have you ever been with a girl?"

"I have wanted to try it for a long time, but I didn't know how to set it up. I can't just ask one of my girlfriends if she wants to have sex with me. She might freak out and call me a perv. I wouldn't want to lose a friend that way, or have her tell my other friends. And besides that, even if she wants to do it, and we do, then what? Can we still go shopping? Can we still talk about guys? It's been terribly frustrating for me. I have never told anyone about it before I told John. I trust him."

"I trust him too."

"What other kinds of jobs have you had?"

"I used to be an erotic dancer at a topless club."

"Can you dance on a pole, like the girls do?"

"Oh, sure. I teach a class in pole-dancing to the girls at the studio."

"You 'teach a class' in pole-dancing?"

"I work at a sex club and porn movie studio. It's in a renovated building in the old part of Downtown. It has film studios, a bar area, a bunch of offices, and some little apartments. I work there as the computer admin. Sometimes I stay there a night or two, if there's a party or something fun happening. I just roll around the sex club wearing nothing but my roller skates. That way I can skate in, have my sex, and then just skate away."

"You're the most sexually liberated person I have ever met."

Both girls seem to be out of questions. They pause and look at each other as though they are done getting to know

each other socially, and now they are ready to move on. They each politely excuse themselves to the bathroom and then the three of us meet in the bedroom. We are all standing together waiting to see what happens next. Lisa undresses. Tina and I quickly shed our clothes. We stand naked facing each other. Lisa suggests a three-way kiss. Tina and I both nod. We all move in together. Our three tongues meet simultaneously. Our arms encircle our bodies and our hands roam our hips and buttocks. The girls are breathing heavily. I say, "Let's get on the bed." I sit in the middle with my back against the headboard. The girls lie down, one on each side of me. I ask them if they would take turns sucking and kissing me. Lisa grabs my penis and with her eyes, motions for Tina to kiss me. Soon Lisa strokes Tina's leg and they trade roles. They trade again, and again. I experience complete sensory overload.

Lisa must have swallowed my blast while I was kissing Tina. Not realizing that I have already come, Tina trades off and takes her turn sucking. I am so excited that I stay stiff for several more turns.

When it is obvious that I am done for round one, Lisa studies Tina's body with her eyes.

"Would you like for me to lick your pussy now?"

Tina's jaw goes slack. She silently nods in the affirmative. I tell Tina to sit between my outstretched legs and I have her lean her back against my chest. I hold her in my arms. Lisa smiles devilishly at each of us as she gets into position between Tina's thighs.

Tina shivers with excitement, her eyes follow Lisa's mouth into her crotch. Lisa starts to gently lick her pussy and Tina's jaw trembles. I have never seen Tina so turned on. Her nipples are fully erect. I can tell that this is virgin territory for her. I am happy for her, and I feel proud of myself for bringing her this much pleasure. Lisa looks up at Tina to gauge her reaction and then gets more aggressive with her tongue. Tina mutters at Lisa in a complimentary tone.

"Oh, that feels good."

A minute later, Tina announces her assessment in a much more serious tone.

"Oh, yes like that. I like that. That feels good."

After a few more seconds, Tina emphatically declares her opinion.

"Oh, yes! Yes, just like that! Oh, yes! That feels sooooo good. I'm going to come. I'm going to... ooooooooooh!"

Tina is panting so hard that she's bouncing off my chest with each breath. It's a good thing that she does aerobic training, because an orgasm like that would kill a couch potato.

Tina slowly catches her breath. Her lithe, lean body still shaking from her first lesbian orgasm, she looks down between her legs at the erotic dancer, and mumbles to her through a sly grin.

"That was great. That felt so good."

Lisa sits up, wipes the pussy juice from her mouth with the sheet and looks Tina in the eye.

"Do you want to try giving me head? Are you comfortable enough with that?"

Tina's eyebrows rise with excitement. The two girls quickly switch positions. Tina stares at Lisa's crotch, smiles, and puts her hair behind her ears, the way girls do when they start a blowjob. As Tina goes down to taste pussy for the first time, she flashes Lisa a playful look.

134

"I hope I can remember all of the things that you just did to me."

I hold Lisa in my arms. Tina starts licking away at her pussy. Lisa leans her head back to kiss me in gratitude. Life is so good. After a minute of girl-on-girl licking, Lisa's hips start to 'shake and grind.' She starts moaning and then she shrieks out the approach of her imminent orgasm.

"I'm going to come! I'm going to come!"

From reflex, Tina snaps her head back from Little Lisa's crotch, closes her eyes tightly, opens her mouth and poses in preparation for a facial. Lisa snaps at her emphatically.

"Don't stop! Don't stop!"

Tina thinks for a split second, and then her eyes get wide as she realizes the situation.

"Oh, that's right, you're not a guy!"

Tina quickly plunges her head back down into Lisa's crotch to finish her first carpet-cleaning job. A few seconds later Lisa has a toe-curling, back-arching, noisy orgasm that I'm sure the people in the next room heard. Tina's words keep resonating in my mind, 'Oh, that's right, you're not a guy!'

Tina lifts her head up and Lisa compliments her.

"You're good at it, especially for your first time. That felt so good that now I have to go pee."

Lisa hops out of bed leaving Tina looking at me with wide-eyed wonder. I reach out for her and plead, "Kiss me, pussy-face."

When both girls have had their turn in the bathroom, we meet in the seating area. The two naked girls sit down side by side together on the couch. This time they are right next to each other, touching.

I get the blanket that was pushed off the bed and wrap it around the two of them. I fix us some drinks and we get high. Tina glances at Lisa's crotch.

"Do you always shave your pussy?"

"Yes, I like being shaved."

"Why?"

"Well, for one thing, when you are fully shaved, you don't have to wear panties."

"It looks like you shave everywhere, even down there beside the lips."

Lisa cautiously replies.

"Sure, why?"

Tina looks apprehensively at Lisa's crotch as though she's nervous about the thought of shaving the part down by the lips. Tina pauses and musters the courage to explain.

"I was shaving my pussy for the first time and I was doing it with an electric razor. I was just a teenager and I didn't know how to use the thing. It slipped and it cut my lip right here. If you look you can still see the scar where it cut the edge."

"Oh, no! You poor girl. Did it hurt? Did it bleed a lot?"

"No, it didn't bleed or hurt that much, but I've never tried to shave down there since. I don't have much hair down there so I just trim the top into a landing strip when I do my bikini shave."

Tina probes Lisa.

"Speaking of bleeding. Has John ever started your period when you weren't due?"

"Oh, sure, lots of times, and once he even gave me

a bloody nose during sex."

"Are you kidding, a bloody nose!"

Tina gives me a sharp stare.

"You gave her a bloody nose?"

"I didn't hit her, I didn't even bump, or touch, her nose. We were just screwing, and it was no harder than usual, when she spontaneously started hemorrhaging from her right nostril."

Tina glares at me in disbelief and then turns to Lisa for confirmation. Lisa laughs as she explains.

"John makes me come pretty hard."

Her eyes still wide, Tina interrogates me with more than just a hint of jealousy.

"How come you've never given ME a bloody nose?"

Tina gives me a brief annoyed look, then turns to Lisa smiling and inquires curiously.

"Do you have anal sex?"

"Sometimes, but only with certain men."

"Did John teach you anal sex?"

Lisa smirks as she replies suggestively.

"No, but he taught me how to enjoy it."

"What do you like about anal sex?"

"I don't know... maybe it hits my G-spot. John, do you remember that one time when I asked you to fuck me in the butt?"

"I'll never forget it. I was thinking, 'The mortician will never get the smile off my face.'"

"It makes me cum hard, a lot harder than getting fucked in my pussy does."

"How many times does John come when you see

him?"

"I don't know, a bunch of times. Why?"

"Have you ever met a man that can come as many times as John?"

"No man fucks as much as John does, he's a catch."

Lisa gets a mischievous look in her eye.

"It's your turn John, what do you want?"

"Lisa, I want you on the edge of the bed, doggy-style. Tina, I want you standing beside me where I can kiss you while you spread Lisa's cheeks for me."

"Tina, when I pull out of Lisa's pussy I want you to suck my cock. You know, pussy-to-mouth. Is that OK?"

"OK."

Tina watches intently. I put my thumb in Lisa's butthole and I insert my uncovered penis into her pussy. "Oh baby, baby, baby." I reach around and put my finger in Tina's butt while I French-kiss her.

"Tina, get down on your knees so I can put my dick in your mouth."

"OK."

My knees are shaking as I shove my penis into Tina's pretty little mouth. Tina sucks me hard and I'm afraid I'll come in her mouth and miss my chance to get Lisa for a trifecta. I pull out of Tina's mouth and re-insert into Lisa's pussy just before I ejaculate.

The three of us get into the shower together. Soap, suds, and fingers go everywhere. The girls both giggle the whole time.

I pour us another round of drinks and we get high again. When the girls are ready, I inform them, "We're going to make a Bermuda Triangle." Lisa smiles at me with quiet curiosity. Tina frowns at me and demands an explanation.

"What the fuck's a Bermuda Triangle?"

"It's easy, our bodies are the sides of the triangle, and the vertices are our mouths and crotches. Each person gives head, and gets head, simultaneously." The girls are agreeable. It takes a while to get it set up, but then they like it. After a while we change the direction and we each get to give to the person we were getting from. Licking Tina's pussy makes me want to penetrate her. I grab a condom and announce that we're changing the position.

"Tina, I want you to stand up at the edge of the bed so I can get you from behind. Lisa, I want you to stand beside me and kiss me while you play with Tina's clit."

My plan doesn't quite work. Lisa isn't tall enough to kiss me and still reach Tina's pussy. Lisa gets down on her knees behind me and licks my ass while I'm pumping Tina. From there she can reach Tina's pussy to rub it. I have never had a rim job before and getting it while driving Tina's tight pussy blasts me over the edge. Tina joins me and the entire resort hears Tina's climax.

We all agree to take a short commercial break from the festivities. Tina wraps up in the blanket and goes out on the balcony with her cell phone. Lisa turns and looks me in the eye seriously.

"I like her, she's nice."

I reply to Lisa, "She's every bit as nice as she is beautiful. I wanted you to meet her. I'm so happy that I have gotten to know her."

Tina comes in from the balcony and looks innocently at Lisa and me.

139

"What are we going to do now?"

Lisa looks me directly in the eye.

"Do you want to put it in my butt?"

Tina watches closely and applies lube as I push my uncovered penis into Lisa's anus. Tina looks up sharply at me. I smile at Tina.

"No! I know what you're thinking, and the answer is NO, I won't do ass-to-mouth! Don't even think about it. I'm not doing it."

"Fuck me in my butt Daddy."

"Take Daddy's fuck little girl."

"Fuck her tight little butt."

Tina fondles Lisa's buns as she watches intently. I don't last long uncovered in Lisa's tight butt. I pull out and Lisa heads straight for the shower. I go to the sink and wash my penis and my hands. I return to bed. Tina cuddles up with me under the covers. We embrace tightly, but we don't speak.

Lisa returns from washing up and is fully clothed.

"I've gotten my sex, I'm leaving now. It's been nice to meet you Tina, I enjoyed the evening."

"I'll walk you to the door."

"No, you're both comfortable, stay in bed together, I'll see myself out."

I get out of bed anyway just in time to see Lisa fly out the door and strut down the hall the right direction. I return to the bed and Tina has a concerned look.

"Did we do something to upset her?"

"No, that's just how Lisa always is. Once she's had enough sex, there are no good byes, she just 'skates away.'"

"Just like she said she does."

"Isn't she great? I got her for a trifecta tonight."

"What the hell's a trifecta?"

"It's a term I borrow from horse racing. A trifecta bet is where you pick the horses that finish in the top three spots in the exact order in which they finish in a race. In sex, it means shooting a load into each of a girl's three orifices."

"You are so bad. You're a prodigal profligate."

"You call me the sweetest things. If you did anal too, then I could have gotten a prestigious six-pack!"

"Maybe some day. Right now I want to stay here with you for a while. Can we have a drink and get high?"

"Sure, I'd love to."

"Good, I'm too excited to drive home just yet."

We cuddle in bed quietly together. Several hours pass. We have sex and doze off. Dawn breaks and it starts to get light outside. Tina showers and dresses. I give Tina her envelope, she looks at it puzzled.

"Did Lisa get an envelope?"

"No, I've been seeing Lisa for so long that I have a direct deposit relationship with her. I'll send the money to her account some time later today or tomorrow."

"This was fun. I'm worn out. I'm going now."

I walk Tina to the door. She gives me a tight squeeze and a long hard kiss on the mouth. She releases me and looks me in the eye for a long moment, then turns, steps out the door, and absentmindedly strolls the wrong way down the hallway.

Chapter 10

I've Gone Bald

I knock on the door thinking about how nervous I was the last time. I can't believe that I almost puked on my way to see John and Little Lisa. I don't know why I was so neurotic about seeing a girl for the first time, it ended up being so much fun. Today I'm going to show John how much I appreciate him for setting that up for me.

It's so nice to be able to see John whenever I want to. Especially since today's money is going straight to my rent. John has been a blessing to me.

Our last date was so delightful. I hope that Tina feels the same way about it. I can't believe that I've literally been dreaming of seeing Tina again. My phone is making noise. I've got a message.

> **From: Tina**
> **Msg: On my way.**
> **I can't wait. I'm**
> **sexcited!!!**

Oh shit! I haven't sent her the room number yet.

**To: Tina
Msg: Great. Rm
469 facing the
pool. C U soon**

Since Tina lives only five minutes away from this hotel, she'll probably be at my door in fifteen actual minutes, not fifteen escort minutes, which is equivalent to forty actual minutes. I don't have much time to prepare for her arrival.

I'm so glad I remembered to bring my camera today. I should leave it out so that Tina will see it. No. Wait, what if she didn't mean it when she asked me to take a photo of her butt? What if that's one of those things that a girl says, but she doesn't really mean? A mistake like that could scare her off. I can't risk that. A cute girl like her has lots of clients that are better than me. She isn't going to put up with any client that threatens her anonymity. I'll keep the camera hidden in my bag until I see how it goes today.

Tina's knocking at my door! My heart pounds as my feet fly across the room. I try to calm myself down so that I don't rip the door off its hinges.

Our eyes meet. We both smile devilishly and start giggling. Tina strolls in and our eyes never leave each other. Tina wraps me up in her arms and gives me a big wet kiss on the lips.

I don't have the words to tell John how much fun I had last time so I give him a kiss to show him. We don't need to say anything; we both know that we feel the same way.

"Make yourself comfortable. I'll pour you a drink."

"I normally wouldn't get high in the middle of the

afternoon, but I'm not working, I'm not taking any classes, and I'm too broke to shop or go clubbing, so let's get loaded today." Besides, John is fun to hang out with.

Tina and I drink and get high together. The conversation is light and playful. It feels like we're best friends.

We're having an exquisite time when my phone utters a ring-tone indicating a call from work that I must take. "I'm terribly sorry, I need to answer this. It should only take me a minute to get rid of them."

"That's OK, I'll jump in the tub." It must be an important call because neither of us ever answers our phones when we're together. It's probably his wife, that's why he's so apologetic. I want to eavesdrop, but I decide to close the bathroom door tight so that my noises will not disturb him. I hope this call from his wife won't ruin our time together today. I put my ear to the door and I can hear John talking.

"Payload Engineering, this is John Smith speaking. What can I do for you?"

I'm glad it's not his wife. I get into the tub and run the water until it is warm. It feels good as I splash it onto my pussy. I wash my butt thoroughly because I know that John will go down on me back there.

Tina will be busy in the bathroom for a few minutes. I should be able to dispose of this interruption by the time she returns.

I turn off the faucet and hear a strange man's voice in the bedroom! Why would John let a man into our room? My heart stops. Oh shit, could it be cops? Are we busted? The thought that this is technically illegal is never far from my mind, whenever I'm with a client. I grab a towel and open the door just a crack to listen in. Who's talking? What is he saying?

"No, I'm not coming over to the stadium right now. I don't care how good your seats are. Just calm down and tell me what the problem is, and we'll come up with a solution right now, over the phone."

Wait. That's John's voice. Why does he sound so authoritative and businesslike?

"I understand. Where are you sitting? How close to home plate are you? I've got it. He's got a luxury suite up in the second deck, right? OK, this is an easy one."

John sounds confident. Whom could he possibly be speaking to?

"You're going to be a big hero in a few minutes. Just tell him to relocate to the seats in his suite and everything will be fine."

I've never heard John talk like this. What is he even talking about?

"What? He wants to know why that will work? Tell him it's basic physics. What? He says that moving upstairs won't fix the delay in the television sound. Did he say he doesn't believe me? He said I put the satellite in the wrong place! Who is this guy? He's a what? Oh, I see. That explains the arrogance and ignorance. Put him on the phone, I'll set him straight."

Wow, John is a tiger when he's on the job. I've never seen this side of him. He's forceful and demanding when he's working. He's acting completely different from how he treats me.

"OK buddy, listen carefully, I'm only going to say this once, so follow along. You are sitting about ten meters from home plate right? So the sound from the crack of the bat reaches your ears about the same time as it reaches the microphones for the live TV broadcast. Now you have to understand that the sound from the crack of the bat is digitized and sent to a satellite that is almost 36,000 kilometers above the surface of the equator. What? Because that is the distance required for a geosynchronous orbit, that's why. Now by the time the signal is sent back to your dish antenna, it has traveled about 72,000 kilometers. Actually, a little farther due to our latitude. Now the speed of light is only 300,000 kilometers per second, so it takes about a quarter of a second to make the round trip. Got it?"

Holy fucking shit! What language is John speaking? Is that nerd-talk? I can't believe that he's rattling this gibberish off the top of his head. Any normal person would have to research this first.

"OK good. Now a human ear can distinguish two separate sounds if they are more than one-tenth of a second apart, so that's why you hear the crack of the bat twice. What? No pal, even you can't change the speed of light, although you can easily fix this by merely moving to your seats in front of your suite up in the second deck."

Oh my God! John is terribly condescending to the person on the phone. He must be talking to some low-level subordinate that works for him. John would never speak this way to a peer or a supervisor.

"The reason that the sounds will match up when you are in the upper deck is simple. Sound travels through air at only 343 meters per second, so by the time the sound from the crack of the bat reaches the second deck, which is on the order of 86 meters away, it will be delayed by about the same one-quarter of a second as the sound emanating from the television audio. As a result, they will both reach your ears at roughly the same time. Problem solved, now go along and enjoy your game."

Jesus fucking Christ! I knew that John was smart, but

what the fuck was that? I never had any idea what engineers actually did. I've never met one before. I thought they drove trains. I should keep him around to help me solve my more difficult problems. Let me think, which of my problems can I have John help me with? Oh, he's finishing the call.

"Thank you for calling the Rocket Thrust Institute. There's no charge for today's lesson; however, I'm busy with important matters for the next few hours and cannot be disturbed. Good bye."

John sounds like a fucking genius when he's working. The expression on his face and his tone of voice are so serious that I don't recognize him. It scares me a little.

I set my phone down laughing and look up to see Tina wrapped up in a towel. She is staring at me with an open mouth and a blank expression. I wonder what she is thinking.

John must think that I'm pathetically stupid compared to him. He probably notices every mistake that I make, but he's just too polite to point them out to me. I suddenly feel insecure and outmatched. John looks up at me with a big warm smile. Well, at least he likes me anyway. I move over to him and he hugs me. He returns to his normal voice.

"I'm sorry for taking that call. I feel like I've been rude, talking business on the phone like that."

"Oh, don't be. I thought it was interesting, not rude at all. I've never heard a conversation like that before.

"Thanks for being nice about it, you are such a kind person."

"It sounded like someone that works for you screwed up."

"No, that was just my brown-nosing boss."

"Your boss! You talk to your boss that way? You're

148

kidding, right?"

"Well, you're right. My boss gave the phone to some clown that was complaining that the sound from his portable television did not match the live sound at the stadium."

"What clown? Who is he?"

"He's one of the team's owners. My boss only called me because he was trying to impress him. That's why I lectured them both like disobedient children."

"I can't fucking believe that you talked to a team owner like that."

"I don't give a rat's ass what he owns, he's an idiot, a rich idiot, but just an idiot all the same. I don't put up with any bullshit from idiots just because they're rich. In fact I'll go out of my way to expose their ignorance, just to have a laugh at their expense."

"You are the most impressive person I've ever met."

"I feel the same way about you."

"I like you."

"I like you too." We gaze into each other's eyes. Tina smiles fiendishly at me.

"I'm so high and horny that I forgot what I wanted to tell you... Oh, that's right. Wait here. After I hang up my towel in the bathroom, I have something new to show you."

Tina emerges from the bathroom wearing nothing but a sly smirk. She acts like she's giving me a chance to notice something about her appearance.

I scrutinize every inch of Tina's body. There is definitely something different about Tina's look today. What is it? I stare at her naked body as she proudly presents it to me with a glimmer in her eyes. Tina can tell that I've noticed something different about her, but that

I can't figure out what it is. She smiles mischievously.

"I got inspired by our little pole-dance instructor. I've gone bald!"

"You look great."

"Do you want to kiss my bald pussy?"

"I'll do anything you want."

"Great. Move the computer to the bed and put on the porn movie with the girlish-looking actress that we like. You know the one that has 'little girl teeth' and takes it up her butt."

I do exactly as instructed. I find the requested scene. Tina crawls onto the bed and moves close to the screen.

"Turn up the volume! I want to see if she has a little girl voice to match her teeth."

I increase the audio while the actress is still being interviewed. She sounds like she's twelve years old as she speaks through her adolescent buck-teeth.

"Oh, yes! Start this scene from the beginning so that I can watch it while you lick my pussy. Begin slowly at first and do that thing you do to me. You know, the way I like it, and don't stop until I push you away."

I give Tina everything she wants and use the opportunity to penetrate her butthole a few times with my tongue. She readily accepts the rim job. I keep thinking that I should get my camera out and shoot Tina's shaved pussy. The photos would make for the most priceless jack material. I want to, but I'm afraid to ask Tina to pose for me. I'll give her a big orgasm and she'll be so cum-drunk that she won't even notice me snapping away.

I lick Tina and she makes so much noise that I'm betting that I get one of those phone calls from the front desk telling us to quiet down.

I love the way John gives head. I wish he would give lessons to my boyfriends. "You made me come twice. I

150

can't make myself come twice, even with my favorite vibrator. I'm going to use the bathroom and then I'm going to do that to you."

"OK." My heart pounds while Tina is in the bathroom peeing and singing with the door open.

I give John a blowjob and he lasts a lot longer than he usually does. That's nice because it gives me enough time to do a good job.

Tina blows me like a porn star and I surprise myself with how much noise I make when I come. Tina swallows and looks up at me with a big smile. She giggles at me as my semen runs down her chin.

"I love to suck cock."

"Girl, you could make me believe in God."

"Do you love to eat my pussy and my butthole?"

"Yes, in that respect I am different from the Big Bad Wolf."

I can tell that John is setting me up for a story so I play along. "Which Big Bad Wolf is that?"

"Why the Big Bad Wolf from the story of Little Red Riding Hood of course."

"So how are you different?"

"Oh, you see when the Wolf jumps out at Little Red, he says, 'I'm going to eat you in one bite!' and Red cries, 'Are you going to swallow me whole?' and the Wolf notes, 'No, I'll spit that out.'"

"You are so perverted that you can even corrupt a children's story."

"There's nothing wrong with being a pervert. Lots of people are perverts. Speaking of which, I have something for you." I give Tina a lipstick-sized vibrator. Tina gives me a blank look back. "You said that you wanted to try this."

"Try what?"

"Don't you remember? I told you last time about the Vegas call girl I saw who put one of these up her ass and then I fucked her pussy? You told me to get one so that you could try it. Remember?"

"Was I cum-drunk when I said that?"

"Probably. Does that matter?"

"Are you going to take advantage of a cum-drunk girl?"

"Maybe I should just shove it up MY ass before we screw?"

"Oooo, that sounds like fun. A vibrating flesh-and-blood cock. I've never had that before."

"Oh shit. You're serious. Can we just fuck like normal people?"

"That's the first time you've ever asked for THAT."

I get on top of Tina. She flinches as my bare penis brushes against her shaved pussy. We look each other in the eye.

"You and Lisa don't use condoms do you?"

Tina thinks for a long time. I wait silently.

"Don't you worry about getting a girl pregnant? I worry about getting pregnant. Shit, I'm on the patch and I've got an IUD. I'll do anything to make sure that I don't ever get pregnant. That's one thing a girl can control. I don't even care that the IUD is uncomfortable and the hormones make me feel bloated. It's worth it; pregnancy and children are so gross. I'm never going to have any kids."

"I know how you feel, but it was too late when I did something about it. I got fixed a long time ago. As soon as I figured out what was causing me to have kids, I fixed it. I haven't been fertile in fifteen years. I'm never having any more kids either."

"I remember you telling me that, but I still want to be safe from any STDs. I want to use condoms this time."

I get a condom out of the nightstand and put it on. I mount Tina and penetrate her. "Oh, baby. Yes, baby. That's my baby girl."

I can't tell if Tina has climaxed or not, but she's panting and I know that I did. Maybe I should let her rest for a while.

"That was great... for normal-people sex."

"Do you want to watch one of our other porn movies?"

"Do you have the one with the double-anal? That is such a hot scene."

I insert the disc and find the requested scene. A svelte seductive schoolgirl is doing a double-anal.

"She looks like she's enjoying anal sex."

"I used to think that the girls in porn movies didn't like to have anal sex. I thought they only did it because the producers know that it's what guys want to see and so the girls do it because it sells. I thought the girls only pretended to like it so that they could get paid top dollar. Then I met Lisa. Once she got used to anal, she loved it. We did anal at least once during every session. After a few times, she started asking me for it and now we do it two or three times during any given session."

"I wonder how a tiny girl like Little Lisa can take your big cock in her little butt?"

"Since then, I have met several other skinny girls that love anal sex."

"Which girls? Have you told me about them before? What are their names?"

"Well, there's Gina and Bella; they both like to have anal sex every time. Then I met a girl named Fiona. When I asked her if I could fuck her butt, she said, 'Sure! That will make me come super hard,' and it did."

"Do you have any photos of them? Are they from around here?"

"Those three girls are from out of town."

"Do they ever visit Orange County?"

"Yes, they do. They visit here on vacation to go to the theme parks and do other touristy shit around here."

"Have you ever seen a girl when she's visiting?"

"Oh yes, many times. I've even flown them in, or to meet me traveling. It's fun. I'll dig out their photos to show you next time we get together and if you like any of them then I'll set it up to introduce you when they visit. Most of them like girls. I always ask the cute ones if they like girls, and most of them say that they do."

"Where's that little vibrator you want me to shove up my asshole?"

"Here, let's put it in a condom so it will be easy to pull out."

"And so it doesn't get covered in shit?"

"That too."

"Oh, that's not going to fit. It's too big."

"That's the smallest one that they had."

"Then tell them to shove that big thing up their ass."

"Let's just do it doggy-style." I roll on a condom and pound Tina's pussy for a long time. She starts making noise like she's in pain.

"Are you almost finished? I'm getting sore."

I finish as quickly as I can. Tina squeals when I pull out. We may be done with sex for the day. I pour Tina a strong drink. She gulps it down.

"I need to rest. Let's talk. Have you seen Little Lisa?"

"Yes, and she had a new story for us. A Beverly Hills female police officer recently pulled Little Lisa over while she was driving. Here's exactly how Lisa told it to me:

> So I get pulled over in Beverly Hills by a woman cop. She gets out of her car and she's walking up from behind my car and I hear her talking into her radio. She says real loud into her radio, 'Dispatch, I've got a juvenile female, code number... whatever the fuck they say... and she's in an old beat-up VW bug, and get this, she's got a decal on her rear window with a picture of a pissed-off black cat. You know with its back all arched and its tail fluffed up. Underneath that it says, 'I've got a killer pussy'. What am I supposed to do with this little tramp?' I remember thinking, 'She's a fucked-up jealous bitch.' She just checked my license and registration while she kept looking down my shirt. I think she was a dyke.

Doesn't that sound just like her?"

"Oh, God. Little Lisa is the greatest! She's outrageous. She's our preposterous little prostitute. She is my sex hero."

Tina slowly shakes her head with obvious admiration.

"Don't you feel lucky just to know her?"

"Oh, yes, I feel incredibly lucky to know her. I'm glad you got to meet her too. It's hard to fully appreciate her stories if you haven't met her in person." Tina corrects me.

"I wouldn't believe any of her stories if I hadn't met her, and fucked her."

"She's fun to have a threesome with isn't she?"

"That was... so much fun. We definitely have to do that again."

"I'll mention that to Little Lisa the next time I talk to her."

"You look like you're ready to go again."

Tina sees that talking about Little Lisa has given me a boner. I put on a condom and lube it up. I try to enter Tina and she seems open to the idea. My condom-covered penis starts to enter her pussy and she pushes me away screaming in pain.

"Stop! Ouch that hurts! I'm sorry but I'm rubbed raw from the condoms. I know what to do. Take off the condom and I'll give you a hand-job. You can pretend that I'm a hand-jobber."

"What's that?"

"That's a girl that doesn't provide full service, she only does hand-jobs."

The hand-job is surprisingly exciting. Tina works me hard while talking dirty. I come quickly and Tina is proud of herself.

"That was fun. Do you ever ask for hand-jobs from girls?"

"No, I have never asked for one, but I have settled for one on a few occasions."

"I can understand why. You can fuck more times than a girl can, so I expect that a hand-job is often offered as a last resort. Has Little Lisa ever given you a hand-job?"

"No, Little Lisa is the only girl that can fuck as much as

I can every time. She is the most sexually active girl I have ever met."

"I wonder if she's always been like that."

"I've wondered the same thing about her. I remember the time when I asked her if she has always been erotically intense. I specifically asked her if she was sexually aware even when she was a little girl."

"What did she say?"

"She told me this story:

> I remember back when I was just a little girl and I was playing dress-up in my Mom's clothes. I had put on her most sheer negligee, her fishnet stockings and her stiletto high-heels. My Mom looked at me and smiled. Then she asked me, 'What do you want to be when you grow up?' I struck a pose and answered her right back. I told her, 'I want to be SEXY!

Can you believe that?" Tina's eyebrows narrow in deep thought. I wait patiently for her as she forms her question.

"Last time, when you were fucking Little Lisa in the ass, she was calling you Daddy. Does she have a daddy-complex?"

"A couple of years ago, while Little Lisa and I were fucking, she said to me, 'I want to call you Daddy.' Without thinking, I said right back to her, 'I want to call you my little girl.' She gasped at me 'Yes, call me your little girl.' As soon as I called her that, she came. We fucked hard for a long time while she kept whispering, 'Fuck me Daddy.' She's so much fun. I was never into that kind of thing before, but Little Lisa has helped me to grow sexually."

"I can't believe that our Little Lisa works at a real live sex club!"

"Have you ever been to a sex club?"

"I don't have the balls to go to a sex club, even if I knew of a good one to go to. Besides, whom would I go with?"

"I'd go with you to a classy sex club, like the one Lisa works at. You could do your hair and makeup so that nobody would recognize you. Would you want to go then?"

"Let me think about that."

I can sense that Tina is getting tired. I pause the conversation to see if she wants to end the session.

"I'm going to take a shower and get dressed."

Suddenly, Tina's tone changes from notifying me to interrogating me.

"Did you bring me my underwear that I left behind by mistake?"

"Are those the ones from Victoria's Secret with white lace trim and little pink flowers?"

"Yes, that pair. I want those back."

"I can't tell you how much they mean to me."

"I'm not going to get those back am I?"

I don't answer. Tina's brow narrows as she zooms in on my frightened eyes, she grimaces, looks away and swears half under her breath.

"Dammit!"

She continues angrily.

"They're part of an expensive set! RATS! I should give you the damn bra that matches them."

Tina snarls at me a few seconds, then shakes it off and

sits down on the bed beside me.

"You are such a twisted deviant. From now on, I'm only giving you my old worn-out underwear that I'm ready to toss out anyway. I can't afford to give away my good underwear. Shit, I can't afford my rent!"

Tina laments the state of her current employment in a melancholy tone.

"The real estate business totally stinks lately. I'm not working enough hours to pay my bills. They aren't paying me to do open houses anymore. I'm going to put up an escort ad for in-call down in San Diego. I don't want to see any new clients in OC any more. Shit, what if it was someone I know. Fuck that. Don't shit where you eat. Right? I'd rather make the drive to San Diego, stay there overnight in a luxury hotel, and do high-end in-calls. I'm asking you and my other two regular OC clients that I still see, to write reviews for me. Say that you saw Sunny Knight in San Diego and paid her posted rate."

"How much should I say I paid?"

"My new one-hour rate is double what you give me."

"But I give you a two-hour donation."

"Yes, my new one-hour rate is twice what you give me for two hours."

"Wow! I know you can get that much, but that's a fortune. Are you going to grandfather me in?"

"What the fuck does that mean? Is that some kind of perverted sex act?"

"Do I get to keep the old rate?"

"Of course you do, silly. Besides, the truth is that the sex with you is so good, that if I didn't need the money, I'd probably see you anyway, just for the sex and the laughs."

My heart pounds and I can feel myself blushing.

"I am going to post my web ad tomorrow, so please

159

write the review for me as soon as you can. I will easily be able to book a full schedule of appointments, even at that ridiculously high hourly rate, if I have three great reviews from established hobbyists like you three. I will get a lot of good inquires by phone and email from members that see your reviews. I am only going to see clients that I can screen to my satisfaction. That way I'll get nice, generous, older, married gentlemen who usually don't want that much sex, so it will be easy to see several of them on one overnight trip down there."

I wish I was in a financial position to solve all of Tina's money problems, but I simply can't do that under the circumstances. I feel terrible, but try to be as helpful as I can.

"I need to make some money fast, and this will do it."

"OK, send me the link to your web ad and I'll post your review by tomorrow night."

"How can I thank you?"

"You're a smart girl. Use your head... you'll think of something."

"I have to use my head. You've fucked my pussy raw. I can't have that much sex using condoms. Get on your back. Put your knees up so I can finger-fuck your asshole while I suck your cock. That will make you come. You like that, you warped freak."

Tina gets in position and goes to work. I've had a lot of sex today and I'm slow to respond but she stays at it until I'm big and hard.

I give John a bj but he takes forever and my mouth is getting tired. I give it one last shot. I suck hard, cover my finger with the saliva that's everywhere and shove one finger into his butt. John yelps and comes at the same time. "I'm going to take a shower and get dressed now."

Tina saunters into the bathroom. As the shower starts

160

up I hear her singing though the open door. I get the envelope that I prepared for her and put it under her purse. I'm glad that I have the grandfather rate or I couldn't afford to see her. She has been here for over three hours. I am so spoiled by Tina and Lisa that I don't want to see any other girls. Tina emerges from the bathroom wrapped in a towel, holding up the stick of ladies deodorant in her hand.

"Does Little Lisa use this brand of deodorant? Did you get it from her?"

"I didn't get it from her, but she uses it sometimes when she visits me."

"I like it. I'm going to use some before I get dressed."

A few minutes later, Tina strolls out of the bathroom dressed and ready to leave. She pulls the envelope from beneath her purse, folds it in half and shoves it into her purse without looking inside.

"Thanks for this. It helps me a lot right now."

"Thanks for seeing me and for being so nice to me. You help me a lot. I just wish that I could give you enough money to solve all your problems. I'm afraid you're going to marry some prosperous doctor who's half my age and then I'll never see you again."

"Oh, don't worry. I'll still see you after I'm married."

I must have a perplexed expression because Tina smiles at me and explains herself.

"Well, I won't see you for the first six months or so, but after that, you know once the honeymoon has worn off, then I definitely will want to see you again."

"Do you truly mean that? Are you just joking with me?"

"No, I'm not joking. The fact is that everybody knows that wives don't have sex with their husbands. I'm sure

161

that I will want to see you again. My mother's friends are all a bunch of old married ladies and they all say that they only have sex with their husbands twice a year: on New Year's Eve and on their husband's birthday. I'll need more sex than that."

"You are so wonderful. When can I see you again?"

"I can see you next week. It's not like I'm busy with a job, or going shopping, or anything like that. Just text me."

"I think I can get another envelope together in a week. It's starting to get dark outside. Can I walk you to your car?"

"That would be nice. The hotel is busy today and so I'm parked at the far end of the parking structure."

We have never been out in public together before. Neither of us is too sure how to act towards each other in this environment. What do we do if we run into someone we know?

It is considerate of John to walk me to my car. He is always a perfect gentleman to me. I like the way he treats me. He seems to be a little nervous. I wonder why?

We exit the door together for the first time. I show Tina the right way to go toward the elevators.

Chapter 11

Have You Been Tested Recently?

I knock on the door wondering if I did this just last week, or if it was two weeks ago. I feel like I was here only yesterday, but I need the money. It helps that I like seeing John. I feel like my time spent here tonight will be... Oh, the door is opening. John is surprised to see me. I wonder why?

That's Tina's knock, but she's early. Why is she early? I'm not ready yet. I'm standing at the door so I pull it open. Tina scoots in and gives me a quick hug.

"Were you waiting at the door for me to arrive? How sweet!"

Tina struts over to the little table where she sees a bulging envelope full of bills.

I go to put my purse down on the table and there's an overstuffed envelope full of cash. The scene looks like a drug deal is going down.

It has only been two weeks since our last visit. I haven't had a chance to get C-notes, therefore I have twenty-dollar bills instead of hundreds this time. Upon seeing an envelope, which is five times thicker than usual, Tina bursts into uncontrolled giggles. She points at the envelope, raises her eyebrows in false shock, and fakes a scream.

"Aaaaaaa! Oh shit! Look at all this money. What kind of kinky shit are you going to want today? Are you expecting a midget orgy and a brown shower?"

"I'll pour you a drink and we'll get high before we navigate the evening's festivities. Give me a second to get set up, I'm still unpacking."

"Thanks, I need a drink. The real estate business is bust. I've essentially been out of work for two months now and my bills are piling up."

"Have you had any appointments in San Diego yet? I posted a review for you. Have you seen it yet?"

"No I haven't seen it. Can you show it to me?"

I set up my notebook computer and log into my escort review account. "I'm going to jump in the shower while you look over your reviews. I'll just be a minute."

I'm terribly nervous about how Tina will react to the review I wrote on Sunny. I had to make it sound realistic and discriminating or it wouldn't have been posted by the escort review website administrators.

I'm a little nervous reading my reviews by John and my other two OC regulars. I read John's review first.

> I saw Sunny's ad and decided to email her. I sent her the extensive screening information she requires. A few days later she emailed me and said that she needed to talk with me on the phone to set the appointment. While on the phone I confirmed her menu before committing to her upscale rate. Arrived at her swanky in-call hotel and called from the parking structure. Got the room number and headed up.
>
> When the door opened I was stunned by how gorgeous

she was. Sunny looked much better in person than in her web ad photos. Her look is a little different than the photos on her website, but they are representative of how good she looks. It may just be that she's changed her hairstyle and makeup since those pictures were taken.

We took care of the donation and had some engaging conversation before she changed into a sexy outfit and the fun began. A fairly broad menu with safe full service, delivered with skill. She provides true GFE. A rare treat to find, in such a pretty and accommodating provider.

Highly recommended if you can afford the price of admission. I plan to repeat as soon as she is available.

John returns from the bathroom wearing a white terrycloth robe. "You noticed that they're not my photos. I chose them because they show a pretty girl's face and guys like that. There's no way I'm putting my real photos on an escort ad. It's bad enough that my modeling photos show up all over the place. The men I've seen in San Diego have been nice. Well... most of them were nice."

I am sickened by the thought of Tina with other men. I turn away to hide my revulsion. I begrudgingly accept it as an inherent part of the escort-client relationship. I compose myself, look up, and address Tina, "Girls have told me that they get a lot of good calls right after flattering reviews like those are posted."

"I hope so. I've increased my screening and I've become more selective. As a result, I am making so few appointments lately that I need the money and I'm starting to look forward to the sex. Are you ready?"

"Let's start with a blowjob. Is that OK?"

"I like the taste of your dick in my mouth."

Tina attacks me like a lover and blows me like a porn star.

John comes quickly and not very much so I just swallow it and chase it with my drink. Swallowing isn't all that enjoyable and semen doesn't taste all that great, but John is so happy when I do it, that I don't know why so many girls are opposed to it. John loves to come in my mouth and then French-kiss my spermy mouth.

"Is this a good hotel for you to meet at? Do you mind meeting me at night?"

"I like meeting at night, especially when it's near my apartment like this."

"What do you want to do next?"

"Do you have our porn magazines?"

"Of course I do. Are you kidding? I ALWAYS bring the dirty magazines every time now."

"Why do you say it like that? What happened?"

"There was this one time I saw Little Lisa and the first thing she asked me was, 'Where are the adult magazines?' I sheepishly muttered, 'I forgot them.' She scolded me, 'What! You forgot the magazines!' Ever since that time, I bring magazines to every meeting."

"I bet Little Lisa has all her lovers trained. Oh, look at this girl. Look at her butt. Oh, and here she's got her finger in her butt. I want a photo of my finger in my butt. Does my butt look that good? It's not like I can see it."

I reassure Tina, "Your posterior is particularly pretty. I consider your beautiful backside much more appealing than any of the rumps in these magazines." Tina thinks a second.

"You could take a photo of my butt for me. Then I could see it for myself. I can't get a good angle when I look at it in the mirror. I want to see how I look bent over, the way a guy sees me during sex."

I can't speak. The thought of taking pictures of Tina's tush for my collection makes my heart pound. I have my

166

camera, but I'm afraid that Tina will get spooked if I ask to take photos of her. I'm not sure that she genuinely means it. I'll wait and see how this evening goes. Maybe I can ask her later in the date.

He's not saying anything, but he's got those kid-in-a-candy-shop eyes again. He wants to shoot my butt. I know he does, but he's too shy to tell me. That's cute.

"Can I undress you?"

"Yes, but let me change into a cheap pair of panties that I brought specifically for you to keep. That way you won't abscond with my expensive ones again."

Tina grabs her purse and bounces off to the bathroom. I smile at the fat envelope still sitting on the table.

I wanted to wear something nice for John tonight, but I didn't have the cash to buy something new. I was quite pleased to find a lace-up bustier in my old modeling clothes. I like this corset because it has push-up under-wire cups and boning that gives my boobs lift and emphasizes my curves. The best part is that I have several pairs of panties that match this top and the pair I brought are too worn out to wear for a boyfriend. They're perfect for John.

Tina slinks out of the bathroom wearing a sexy outfit that pushes her perfect-sized boobs up into a tight cleavage and then flatters her slim waist and tight belly. She looks so hot that I spill my drink trying to set it on the table without letting my eyes leave her gorgeous body.

"How do I look?"

I stand up and Tina walks into my arms. We kiss deep and long. I drop to my knees because they're getting weak and so that I can nuzzle her pussy through her panties that will soon become my trophy. I rub them against her lips to make them smell like her pussy. I take them off of her using only my teeth.

John is such a pervert, but he knows how to make a girl feel noticed and appreciated. I like that about him.

Tina's panties hit the floor. I pick them up reverently, sniff them and carefully place them in my bag. "Those will make a nice addition to my collection."

"You have a collection?"

"Lately, I've started to keep the girl's panties. I hoard them all together in an air-tight plastic bag. The dirty ones keep their scent for a week or two. I sniff them while I jack off."

"You are a complete pervert. That is so depraved. Then again... Do you think I could get a pair of Little Lisa's panties for me to sniff when I'm jilling off?"

"Uh, I'm sorry but Little Lisa doesn't wear panties, remember?"

"You're right. Fuck!"

"Good idea. Lie down on the bed."

"Do you want me on my back like this?"

I lick Tina's pussy and she has a big orgasm. It's a good thing that I got my hair cut recently.

"Oh, that feels so good. Like that! Yes, like that! Oooooooooooo!"

I get up on my knees between her legs and admire her pretty cat. I go to mount her, but I pause. We both look at my raging uncovered boner hovering just over her dripping pussy. We look deeply into each other's eyes for a long moment.

"Have you been tested recently?"

I look Tina directly in the eye and answer quickly, "Yes." Tina looks me in the eye and immediately responds.

"So have I."

I slow down to savor this rare and precious moment. I carefully maneuver into position and reverently penetrate

168

her for the first time uncovered. She is saturated, and in spite of how tight she is, I slide right into her. The sensation is mind-blowing. Tina's beaver squeezes my cock when she climaxes. "You're tighter than a clenched fist."

"Can I get on top?"

"Sure! You can do anything you want, pretty girl."

"I'm horny; I haven't had sex in a long time." I grind my crotch onto John's big cock and close my eyes.

"Yes, baby. That's my baby. Oh, baby."

This is why I haven't had sex in so long. The guys my age don't fuck half as good as my favorite clients do. They aren't as nice to me. They waste my time. I have to worry about getting pregnant because none of the guys my age have had a vasectomy, and most of all, they don't give me a big wad of money every time we fuck. No wonder I'm only having sex with my favorite clients.

We come simultaneously. Tina collapses on top of me in a sweaty heap. She is panting and cooing. Between breaths Tina utters the nicest compliment to me.

"I have never done that with a boyfriend. It felt so good to feel your hot semen squirting inside me while I was coming."

Tina pauses and looks at me with a perplexed expression.

"How come sex with you is better than sex with any boyfriend I've ever had?"

I can't answer Tina. I don't know how to answer her. We lie together, breathing hard, without speaking, for the longest time. I feel like I'm with a girlfriend, but it's even better somehow. Eventually, Tina rolls off of me, props her pretty head up on her elbow and looks at me inquisitively.

"Have you seen our little killer-pussy lately?"

"No, I haven't seen Little Lisa since you and I last got together, but I remember something she said about jilling off that I want to tell you."

"I bet she has an industrial strength vibrator."

"These are the exact words she said to me:

I love to masturbate. I enjoy it when I can take my time and masturbate as much as I want. I have gotten pretty good at getting off. I can come more times by myself than I can with a partner and it's a lot faster. Plus, it's much more convenient, I don't have to involve another person. I don't have to deal with them and their needs. I can have as many orgasms as I want, then just stop, and go to sleep when I want to. Masturbating can be every bit as satisfying as sex. Sometimes it's better.

Little Lisa helps me understand things."

"That sounds like our little... carnal courtesan."

Tina reaches for her drink on the nightstand and presents her bare butt to my admiring eyes. I study Tina's adorable ass and I suddenly wonder if an attempt at anal sex would also be uncovered. I start to get an erection just from the mere thought of finding out.

John is looking at me with a question on the tip of his tongue. I prod him into asking it, "What?"

"Can I lick your pussy?"

"Sure! Let me prop up my head on the pillows so

170

that I can watch."

I take Tina to a big orgasm. While she's catching her breath I tell her, "Your pussy tastes like my semen."

"Kiss me sperm-face!"

I kiss Tina on the mouth and attack her pussy with my uncovered penis. I get close to orgasm and wonder if I should try to pull it out of her pussy, and see if she'll let me stick it in her mouth. Then I could come in her mouth. I love fucking her uncovered like this!

"Oh, baby, baby, baby." There's no way I can keep myself from falling in love with this girl. I should just accept it. I come hard in Tina's pussy and collapse on top of her. She rolls me off and prances into the bathroom while asking me a question.

"When we have sex, why do you call me 'baby'? You called Little Lisa that too. How come?"

"There's a good reason why I call you both by the exact same term of endearment and I'll tell you why. There was this one time, in bed, I called my girlfriend by my wife's nickname, and holy shit, she got pissed-off at me. I didn't get any for a long time after that."

"You're lucky she didn't kill you for that."

"A few years back I was talking with a buddy of mine over drinks at a bar. I told him about my error. My buddy laughed knowingly and lectured me:

> That's a rookie mistake. However, there's an easy solution to preventing that error from occurring ever again. I've never called a girl the wrong name in bed. It's simple. There are two steps for staying out of trouble; the first step is to pick some common term of endearment that the wife likes and then you use it like a nickname. It doesn't matter what the nickname is. It can be: snuggles, honey, sweetie, darling, etcetera. The

171

second step is that you simply always call her by this nickname and you never call her anything else. You call her this in bed. You call her this at breakfast. You call her this on the phone. The drill is: you use this nickname and you only use this nickname, both in, and out of, the heat of passion. The trick is that you also use this nickname for every other girl you are ever with, especially when you are in bed. The nickname will become a reflex. Eventually, you will call out only this nickname from habit, no matter how excited you are. That way you never call out the wrong name.

The other thing you learn to do is: you never, never, never talk while you're fucking. The problem is that a guy can't think while he's fucking, that's a proven medical fact. That's because all of his blood is down in his pecker. Shit one time, as a compliment, I told my girlfriend, while we're fucking, 'You are so much better a fuck than all those other girls.' Oh shit, what a mistake that was. She bitched about that until she broke up with me shortly thereafter. That's why the rule is: You never talk while you're fucking, unless to grunt or bark instructions.

I told him, 'That's damn good advice.'"

"That sounds like guys at a bar. That's hysterical. Does it work?"

"I have been following those instructions as accurately as I possibly can ever since. When I tell my buddies this story, they all say, 'Hey that's good shit, I'm going to use that!'"

"I would kill a boyfriend if he called me the wrong name in bed. Besides, a guy should be smarter when he's inside a girl."

"Why's that?"

"Because, he's plugged into a fucking genius!"

"You're funny, I like you." I'm not going to mention to Tina that when a guy tells that joke, it ends with the line,

'Because he's plugged into a know-it-all.' I like Tina's girl-version of that joke better.

"Do you want to have sex now?"

I don't answer; I just pull a small lipstick-sized vibrator out of my bag, hold it up, and give Tina a suggestive look. I hope that she'll figure out that I want her to shove it up her asshole.

"Oh, I remember that trick. You want me to try it, don't you? I can tell that you do. Get me a condom for it. Thanks for getting a smaller vibrator."

I quickly open up a condom, turn on the vibrator, drop it in, and hand it to Tina. She takes it from me cautiously and looks at it with a perplexed expression.

"Do you have any olive oil? I'm going to need some lube to get this big thing in my butt."

I grab the little bottle of extra-virgin olive oil from my bag and hand it to Tina.

"Good job. I like this stuff; it doesn't sting like the glycerin-based lube does. OK little butthole, get ready."

Tina coats the vibrator and takes a deep breath as she reaches behind her and tries to insert it. She tries several times and grimaces before giving up.

"It's too big for my butt, I can't do it. I'll have to practice with my vibrator at home to get my butt used to it. I've never put anything in my butt before so I'm not surprised that I can't do it. We can try again next time."

I get on top of Tina and push her long legs up by her ears. I grab her butt cheeks and lift her up while I penetrate her. I reach under and finger-fuck her butt. I can feel my penis from her anus. I climax and release her. She rolls out of bed and heads for the bathroom.

"I need to rinse off. I'm not leaving; I just need to take a quick shower. If I rinse off with warm water after sex then I don't get as sore. That's the only way I can have sex almost as many times as you can."

Tina leaves the door open and talks to me while she pees.

"Your semen is dripping from my pussy. It's sexy."

That does it. I am completely in love with this girl. Tina returns a few minutes later wrapped in a towel.

"Do any of your friends see escorts? Can you talk about it with your friends? Do you have any friends that you see girls with?"

"I have only a couple of old buddies that I can share references with. It's a bit tricky, because you don't know how a guy feels about seeing professional girls. He may freak out on you. Most guys don't like to talk about it at all and precious few will discuss the hobby honestly."

"I can't tell any of my girlfriends. It's like being a member of a secret organization and you can't ever say anything to anyone who's not a member of the secret society. There are code words and everything. If you don't know the code words, then you're not in the club."

"Would you like to meet a buddy of mine?" Tina pauses and thinks carefully before answering. I get worried. Have I crossed a line?

Why does John want me to meet his friend? If I see his friend then will he view me differently? I could use the money, but what if the guy doesn't like me? What if I don't like him? Shit, John doesn't know what this guy is like in bed. If it goes bad, will that affect how John feels about me? Is it worth the risk? The most important thing is that I trust John. "Sure, if you say he's nice, then I will."

"You'll like him. He's even nicer than I am."

"Bullshit."

"No, in truth he is. All the girls I have introduced him to have told me that. I was telling my buddy Marty about you last week at a titty-bar over a business lunch and he's

174

interested in knowing more. Can I show him your modeling photos?"

"Sure. But wait a second. You guys were at a topless bar? During work?"

"Well, it's a high-end titty-bar. You know where businessmen have lunch and the daytime girls are pretty."

"You go to strip clubs for business lunches!"

"Part of my new job is to sell payload delivery services, and entertaining potential customers is inherent in my work."

"Oh my God. You're a professional pervert. You get paid to lust after naked women."

"I have a story to tell you about something that happened to us at the gentleman's club. First you have to know that Marty and I look nothing alike. We were seated and the waitress comes over to take our order. Marty ordered the Club Sandwich and an Iced Tea. Then the waitress looks at me and I say, 'I'll have exactly the same as my identical twin brother'. The waitress looks at Marty, then back at me and says sarcastically, 'Identical huh.' So I say, 'OK, we're not identical. He got all the brains, all the good looks, and all the money.' The waitress looks Marty up-and-down carefully. Then she turns to me with a questioning look and asks, 'So what did you get?' and I say, 'Oh, I can't show it in public.' The waitress looks me over for a second, smiles at us both, and then walks away."

"That's priceless. A good sense of humor can turn a girl on. Did she hit on you?"

"There is no way any girl at a titty-bar is ever going to hit on me."

"You might be surprised."

"I would definitely be surprised if that happened."

"If you have money, then there are a lot of cute girls

that will hit on you."

"You're the only cute girl I want. Can I lick your pussy?"

"OK, I'm always ready for your tongue."

I move down between Tina's legs and she spreads them for me as she arranges her pillows. I begin cunnilingus and she sighs.

"I wish I had you in my bed at night instead of just my damn vibrator."

I roll Tina onto her belly and shove my tongue deeply into her butt. It goes in easily so I work it around in there before pulling out. I squirt some extra-virgin olive oil on her asshole and then try inserting one finger. She takes it easily. I slowly pull the one finger out, and then try to insert two fingers.

"Ouch!"

"Sorry. One finger seems to work, but two fingers are too much."

"I'll never fit your big cock in my butt. Maybe if you had a little one it would work."

"Some girls that routinely do anal see mine and tell me that they have anal with small dicks but they refuse to even try anal with me."

"Oh that's just great! I have to break in my virgin butthole with a guy that has a huge cock. I guess that I'll just have to practice at home until I'm stretched out enough to fit your big boner into my poor little butt."

We're obviously done playing finger-in-her-butt for today, so I climb on top of Tina's backside and shove my uncovered penis between her oiled cheeks and into her pussy. I reach around under her pelvis and Tina lifts her hips up so that I can put my hand under her taunt tummy and rub her clit. Tina has a couple of strong orgasms

176

before I finish.

"That's the first time we've done it that way."

"Did you like it? You seemed to."

"I came hard several times. I like being rubbed on my clit during sex. I need to rest. Do you have any new porn or photos?"

"Yes, I collected the photos of those girls I told you about."

"Which girls?"

"The girls from out of town that like anal sex, that like girls, and that sometimes visit OC."

"Show them to me."

I pull up the photos and Tina watches intently.

"Oh, now this girl is cute. Wow, what a hot body she has. Is she nice? What's her name? Does she visit OC?"

"Her name is Gina, she likes girls, and she's nice. I've seen her a few times in San Francisco. I will send her a message and ask if she plans to visit OC any time soon."

I get horny imagining having sex with a hot girl. John is a fabulous sex partner. No other man I know would set up a threesome for me and then pay me to fuck a cute girl. I love this dirty old man.

Talking about getting these other girls together with Tina has given me a boner. Tina is fondling her breasts with both hands.

"I want to do this. See if you can set it up with her."

I'm totally turned on by screwing Tina without a condom tonight and even though I want to go again, I feel obligated to give Tina an opportunity to get out of it, if she wants to. "Are you too sore, or can we go again?"

"You can fuck me again."

Tina shot back her response like she was worried that I WOULDN'T fuck her again. I love this girl. "I want you

177

on your back."

"OK. Let me get a hair band and put my hair up in a pony tail or else it will get a little too much volume."

I get on top of Tina. Without saying another word, I slide fully into her and start pounding. After so much sex I don't know if I can come again or not. I start to go soft and Tina can feel it. She reaches down and grabs the base of my penis like a cock ring. I get hard and she jacks herself off with my dick like it's a dildo. We both come quickly.

"I love sex without condoms. I don't get as sore and I can feel you squirt your cum into my pussy. That's so sexy."

"Thanks for the hand-job cock ring. That was great."

"I had to do something. I wasn't finished with you and you were losing your mojo."

"Did you know that these hair bands that you use to make your ponytail with can also be used for a makeshift cock ring? I borrowed one from a girl named Barbie one time, and she said to me, 'I've learned not to put those in my hair after they have been around guys.'"

"I've never seen you use a cock ring?"

"I've never fucked you six times before."

"Oh my God, did we fuck six times today? Shit, that's a lot of sex. I know I've never been fucked that many times before. Are you sure? Have you been counting?"

"Don't you count your orgasms?"

"Are you kidding? I can't count that high!"

"I can't move but I need to wipe up."

"Do you want me to bring you a hot towel?"

"Thanks. You're so sweet. I will show you Beth's cock sauna. She always does it after sex or a bj, and it's pretty nice."

"How does it work?"

"You make a hot, tightly wrung-out wash cloth and after wiping off the penis and groin area, you wrap up the package with the wash cloth and tuck in the end. It feels great. I always like it. I leave it there while she has her turn first in the bathroom."

I bring John a hot washcloth and he wraps his cock up in it.

"Thanks, I'm just going to enjoy my cock sauna while you take your turn in the bathroom."

"Sometimes the weird shit that other girls will do just amazes me. I'm going to take a shower and get dressed. Oh, that reminds me of something I've been meaning to ask you."

"What's that?"

"Why do you always have a stick of ladies deodorant? Do you mind me asking?"

"Oh, that's from a cruise I took with the wife a few years ago."

"You kept the deodorant from a cruise?"

"Let me explain. When we first got to our cabin there was a little basket of soaps, shampoos and shit like that."

"Like a hotel room has?"

"Yes, just like that, but more shit and name brand products. I think it's some kind of promotional thing. The first thing I did was rifle through the basket. When I smelled the ladies deodorant, I liked the scent. I knew that the bikini-clad chicks on the cruise would be wearing it and I got an idea. I hid the deodorant in my luggage before my wife saw it, so she wouldn't know it was ever there. All during the cruise there were hot new brides and teenage girls in string bikinis wearing this scent. I made a strong connotation in my mind matching the scent to the hot girls."

"What good is that?"

"When I got home, I would get the deodorant out when I jacked off, and the turn-on was great. The effect lasted for almost a year. Now I use this particular scent only with escorts and for jacking off. The scent helps me to connect the two."

"You are such a devious degenerate. That's why every time I use this deodorant it turns you on. I'm going to shower now and then put on your jack off scent."

Tina will get dressed and leave after she showers, but I'm still too nervous to ask her to let me take naked photos of her. I'm afraid that she didn't mean it when she said I could. She's getting ready to leave; it's now or never. I muster the courage and blurt out my request at Tina, "Can we take some photos?"

"Sure, that would be fun. Did you bring your camera? I'll get undressed."

Wow! I love this girl. I totally love this girl.

"I'll strike the same pose as the girl in the magazine. Shoot me at the same angle and frame it the same. Be sure to get the magazine in the shot."

"Oh yes, like that."

"Are my pussy lips all scrunched up? That's not good, I'll spread them out all pretty for you."

"Perfect."

"Now shoot my butt. Get a close up so I can see if my asshole is as cute as you promise me it is. Should I pull my cheeks apart? Is that better?"

"Oh, that's fabulous."

"I want one in this pose. Stand on the bed above me and shoot down on me."

"Oh my God!"

"Is the lighting bright enough? Turn on the other

lamp and shoot from over there to catch the back-lighting. Move to your left until you like the crescent of the back-lighting against my breasts."

All this photography of Tina in the nude has gotten me excited. I want to fuck her again, but she has been here over four hours already. She has graciously stayed with me way past when she was dressed and ready to leave the first time. She's getting dressed. Should I ask for another fuck? That seems rude after fucking her six times already. I better not ask. She wants to leave now. She won't fuck me again today anyway and it will just piss her off if I ask for it. I must just let her go, tell her how great it was, thank her for the photos and beg her to see me again.

"That was fun. I'm going now."

"I had a wonderful time too. When can I see you again?"

"Well, it's not like I'm working a regular job right now."

"Can I see you next week?"

"I don't know if I can. I might be sore for a whole week!"

"I'll text you and we'll see what happens." Tina picks up her tiny purse and the bulging envelope.

"Oh shit! How am I going to fit all this cash into my little clutch? I look like I've been giving twenty-dollar hand-jobs all night!"

"Can I walk you to your car?"

"Yes, I'd like that, if you don't mind. But let me give you a proper hug goodbye here instead of in the parking lot." I hope we don't see anyone that he knows. They'll know that I'm his escort. I hope I don't get seen by anyone I know. Shit! They'll know that he's my client.

I return to the room after Tina drives away. I upload the camera files to my computer and look through my new

181

photos of Tina. I set up a slide show loop of them on the computer screen. I grab the bottle of lube and jack off. Tina is wonderful. I'm completely in love with her. I am an exceptionally lucky guy.

Chapter 12

I Think She Was a Hand-Jobber

I knock on the door feeling like I'm on a date with an established boyfriend, instead of seeing a client. I haven't even shaved yet. I'm feeling kind of embarrassed about it. A call girl would NEVER show up unshaven at an appointment. Well, that is she wouldn't unless the client specifically asked her for it, and if he paid her for it! But that isn't the case here, so I feel like I'm a fuck-up for not preparing properly and thus arriving with a bushy beaver. I hope John isn't disgusted with my furry kitty. He brings so much shit in his ho-bag that I'm sure he's got a razor I can use.

The door opens to reveal John's beaming smile, open arms, and wide eyes. I smile back at him and step into his warm embrace.

Why am I uncharacteristically calm waiting for Tina to arrive? Normally I'm neurotic as hell, but tonight for some reason, even though I'm excited, I'm relaxed at the same time. Our last date two weeks ago was incredibly romantic. Tina was as affectionate as any girlfriend I've ever had. Things are great between us right now. I'm looking forward to her charming company tonight as much as I'm anticipating the hot sex.

My phone chimes. There's a message from Tina!

> **From: Tina**
> **Msg: On my way will be**
> **there by eight or so I'm**
> **sexcited!**

It's exceptionally accommodating of Tina to drive all the way over here just to meet me in my part of town. I want to show her how much I appreciate it by making sure she has a good time. I jump into the shower to make sure I'm as fresh as possible for her, and then I put on my robe. I don't want to have to waste time getting undressed once she gets here. I want to be ready to penetrate her upon arrival.

It's almost eight o'clock; she'll be here soon. Let's see, I am all set up with her favorite drinks, snacks, porn, and lube. What else can I...? That's Tina's knock at the door, but it is less urgent than usual. Somehow it's more casual than normal.

I can tell the moment I open the door, that Tina doesn't have her typical charming smile. Tina is in a pensive mood, even though she seems genuinely happy to see me. She walks straight into my arms and hugs me playfully.

Tina is an absolutely wonderful human being. She is one of those incredibly rare people, who genuinely wants to make others happy. I have never met anyone as nice as she is. I am fortunate to know this delightful young lady.

We sit down on the couch so close together that our thighs are touching. Tina looks like she has something on her mind. I smile and look at her inquisitively.

"Do you have a razor?" John's eyes widen in fear before I can add though my laughter, "So that I can shave my legs."

"Oh, a razor to shave your legs. Sure, in that case, then yes, I have one you can use."

"Do you mind if I shave and shower here?"

"No, of course not. I don't mind at all."

"Are you sure? You really don't mind? How is that possible?"

"Quite the contrary, that's a big turn-on. It feels like you're here as my girlfriend."

"Why on earth would you want me to act like I'm your girlfriend?"

"Huh, why not?"

"If I was your girlfriend then I'd be bitching at you to get my oil changed and then I'd tell you that I have a headache tonight! You don't want a girlfriend, you want a call girl."

"You've had a long drive. Can I pour you a drink before you start getting ready?"

"That would be nice. I don't have anything going on later, and it's not like I have to go to work tomorrow, so we can get blitzed and take all the time you want tonight."

"Let's have a drink and get high." Tina seems relieved about the furry legs thing and returns to her usual good mood.

"OK, but I can't get too buzzed before I shave, or your bathroom will look like a scene from the movie 'Psycho'."

"Can I feel your legs?"

"No! They're all hairy!"

"What if I like the hair on your legs?"

185

"You couldn't like it."

"What if I love you so much that I love the fur on your lovely legs too?"

"You don't love me that much. Trust me."

"Is your pubic hair long too?"

"You incorrigible dirty old man. I suppose you think that's sexy too?"

"I would love to play with your long-haired kitten. I've never been with you when you weren't all prepared for our date. I think the change is exciting."

I am relived that John isn't grossed-out by my shaggy legs. I was worried sick that he would be disappointed in me. Instead he's turned-on and thinks this is a girlfriend experience. Has John ever had a girlfriend? Does he realize how much maintenance a girlfriend requires?

Tina is distracted by something. I try to get the conversation back on track. "Let me give you your envelope now, so that we don't forget it later, when we're both cum-drunk." I place an envelope full of C-notes on the table and go to the bar to fix our drinks. Tina picks up the envelope, and without looking inside, shoves it into her purse. She thanks me for it and comments with exaggerated relief.

"I'm glad to see that it's a normal sized envelope this time. Thank God there won't be any midget orgy or brown shower tonight."

I laugh so hard that I spill our drinks and have to start over.

"This session tonight is just what I needed. Being out of work is depressing and filling out job applications for asshole managers is totally humiliating. I've been looking forward to this date all day."

"The job hunt is not going well?"

"I'm signed up with a new modeling agency and they might get me a hostessing job at a motorcycle convention in Vegas next month. I did an overnight trip to San Diego and did some high-priced, one-pop, one-hour-long in-calls. I'm starting to get more phone calls from new clients in San Diego. Thanks for writing that review for me."

"Sunny Knight has two new reviews. Have you seen them?"

"No, I haven't seen them? Can you show me?"

I pull up Tina's reviews under her alias for San Diego. There are five total, including mine.

"Look, I have all A+ ratings for my appearance!"

"I'm not at all surprised."

"I bet there are lots of girls with all A+ ratings for their appearance."

"No, there are not."

"Why not? I was sure that there would be, cuz every girl that a guy has just screwed is always the cutest girl in the world."

"Yes, you're right about that; however, as I told you before, I have read hundreds of reviews and I've never seen any girl that has all A+ ratings for appearance. I think that the guys are no longer cum-drunk when they write the reviews."

"That might explain why I'm getting so many calls, even at my astronomically high rate. I'm being super selective about choosing which new clients I see in San Diego."

"I hope it works out for you." I turn away. I'm nauseous at the thought of Tina seeing other men, but since that is an inherent part of this relationship, I must accept it and just deal with it the best I can.

I can see that John is repulsed by the discussion of my activities down south. He is such a typical guy. I'll explain and then quickly change the subject. "I

187

desperately need the money right now. I applied for a job at a call center yesterday, but I don't know if I'll get it yet. It doesn't pay much, but the hours are flexible, and the only requirement is that you can talk on the phone. It's easy work and I get to keep my clothes on."

"I'll see you as often as you want to. I'm thrilled that we could get together again so soon."

"Well, I'm not working, so I might as well enjoy being unemployed as much as I can."

"I'm just happy to see you, and thanks for driving all the way over here to my part of town."

"Oh sure, it's not that far."

"You are so nice to me. I'm lucky to know you."

John always appreciates my efforts and he absolutely adores me. I like the way he respects me and he provides for me at the same time. It's like getting paid a fortune to get therapy and have hot sex. I love seeing John. I would never see any other client this often. I love this job. I'm horny. That reminds me, I need to get shaved and get to work.

The thought of playing with Tina in her natural state is too much to resist. I'm going to ask her to let me play with her unshaven, even if I risk pushing her boundaries.

"I'm going to get ready now before I get too loaded."

"Can I have you right now, just the way you are?"

"But I'm dirty."

"Yes, I know."

"But I'm hairy, and I smell."

"But I want to have you this way, please."

"You complete pervert! You are such a deviant. You are so depraved. You smutty tomcat. How do you want me?"

"Stand up." I undo Tina's pants and peel them down to

her knees. "You're not wearing any panties!"

"Now that I've gone bald, I don't have to wear them. That's why I need to shave. I had to wear denim pants and a long top today or everyone would have seen that I'm packing a bush. Look at this old-growth forest. I've got a jungle down there. That's how you know for certain that a girl isn't getting any ass."

"Oh, your pussy is furry!" I bury my face in Tina's silky blond bush and lick at her labia. Her scent is strong and the strangeness of the fur on her cat excites me beyond my control."

"Yessssss, like that!"

"Bend over." I spit on my dick and work the tip into Tina's pussy but she pulls away.

"Just a second."

Tina spits on her hand and wipes it on her pussy.

"OK, put it in now."

I enter Tina and pound away. Tina gets loud by the time we finish. Good thing it's still early in the evening or we'd get complaints about the noise.

"That felt good. I like the spontaneity, I think that makes sex better." John is so dirty in bed. I've never had a lover that was such an animal. Yet, John is also a gentleman in bed. How does he do that?

"Screwing you makes life worth living."

"What do you mean?"

"Every once in a while, if you're lucky, you get a 'charge' out of life that makes it worth going through all the trouble just to stay alive. Having sex with you is the charge that makes my life worth living."

"That's a sweet thing to say. It makes me feel good to know that I make you happy. I'm going to get cleaned up now. I'll leave the door open in case you want to talk to me while I shave."

I wait until after Tina pees to step into the bathroom. She climbs into the tub and draws a short bath. I stand at the sink and wash my penis. "That was a sexy surprise to pull down your pants and find you panty-less."

"Do you like me that way?"

"Yes, but I still want a pair from our date to keep."

"I know you do, that's why I have three old pair in my purse. You can pick out a pair to keep for your collection if you want to."

"Will you wear them while we have sex and keep them on afterward, so they'll smell like your pussy?"

"You pervert. Of course I will. I'm done shaving and I'm going to run the shower now."

"I'll fix us some drinks for when you get out."

"Put on a porn movie too."

Tina glides out of the bathroom wrapped in a towel. I'm pleased that she is keeping with the girlfriend ambiance. "You look great!"

"It's only a towel."

"Not when it's on you." Tina gives me a look like she is flattered. She walks up to where I am seated and kneels in front of me with an expectant look in her eye. "What do you want?"

"I want to taste your dick in my mouth."

Tina moves my robe aside and shoves her mouth in my crotch. I push my dick toward her and she sucks it into her pretty little mouth. I come quickly. Tina swallows, wipes her mouth on my robe, sits down on the couch next to me and drains her drink.

"Can you pour me another? This is a good porn scene."

Tina watches an orgy porn scene while I mix our drinks.

"Have you ever been to an orgy?"

190

"That depends. Does two-plus-two count as an orgy?"

"What the hell does two-plus-two mean?"

"Schelley and one of her girlfriends, not the school teacher, but a different one, got together with Jacques and me at Schelley's beachfront apartment. We made a 'magic square' with our four bodies. Jacques asked Schelley's friend in his French accent, 'Do you like it when he licks your pussy?' She responded, 'Well actually his tongue was in my butt.' Jacques' mouth dropped open in gaping disbelief and his eyes got round with raw wonder. I think he was so surprised because he doesn't even eat pussy, not ever."

"Isn't this Jacques guy your French buddy?"

"Yes, why?"

"He's French, and he won't lick pussy, how weird is that? How come some men won't eat pussy?"

"I can't imagine why a heterosexual guy wouldn't like to eat pussy. To me it's as natural as kissing a girl on the mouth. I can only guess that his first experiences may have been with French girls, and if they have the same hygiene habits as French men seem to have, then maybe I can understand his reluctance."

"I see, that would explain it. I'm glad that you are into hygiene, I find it sexy."

"That's part of the reason that I'm obsessive about cleanliness, because most girls like that."

"What do you mean by 'most girls'? Don't you mean to say that 'all girls' like cleanliness?"

"Well, that's what I would have thought, but some girls have told me that they like the smell of men, you know the primal, sweaty, dirty smell of men."

"Who told you that?"

"It was part of a story that Little Lisa told me. Do you

191

want to hear it?"

"Well of course I do. I love juicy gossip."

"This is what she told me:

I was drunk and horny one night last week and just as it was starting to get dark outside I decided to break into the local high school boy's locker room so I could masturbate to the smell of sweaty guys. I got to a chain link fence, and because I was drunk, I decided I could just climb over it. Well, I got stuck at the top and got my pants caught. I had to undo my pants and wiggle out of them upside down in the dark, out in the open. I finally got myself down on the other side of the fence. Of course I never wear panties, so I'm out there bottomless. I tear my pants getting them off the fence and wiggle them on me. That's when I see that there is a gate just a little ways down from where I climbed over. I was so pissed-off that I just went back through the gate and went home.

That's our little super hero."

"She's completely ludicrous. Only our Little Lisa would do that. She's the queen of capricious behavior. I can't believe the things she does. That's just crazy, even for her."

"Do you want to get together with her again?"

"Yes I do. The last time was... it was so much fun! We absolutely MUST do that again. Does she want to see me again?"

"Yes, she does."

"Are you sure?"

"I'm positive."

"How can you be so certain? What did she say about it?"

"She leaned in on me with a wild look in her eyes and her exact words were, 'Set it up and we can get FREAKY!' She's so cool."

"Good. I'm glad she feels the same way that I do."

"She calls you the nice girl with the cute round butt. She told me she likes you and wants to see you again. The problem has been that it's so hard to schedule her, she's always busy."

"I can't believe how business-like you two are about it. Do you still have a direct deposit setup with her?"

"No, not anymore."

"What do you do instead? Do you give her an envelope like me?"

"No. I wait until she's getting ready to leave. I approach her while she stands naked at the mirror fixing her makeup. I move in behind her with a fist-full of cash. I reach around with one hand and I rub her pussy while I stuff the wad of hundred-dollar bills into her purse with the other. I say to her, 'Daddy loves his little girl. You're the best daughter any daddy ever had.' She turns her head around and kisses me. Most of the time she sticks her butt out and we fuck again, right there, standing at the counter.

"Oh, that is so hot! Will you do that to me?"

"I'll do anything you want."

"I'm horny."

"What can I do for you? Let's do whatever you want to do this time."

"OK! Let's get high and then I want you to lick my pussy and then kiss me with your pussy-face. Talking about our sleazy little slut has put me in the mood to taste pussy."

We get high and giggle like teenagers, until Tina's expression gets serious. I pause to determine what to do next. Tina spreads her legs wide and uses her big blue eyes to tell me it's time for me to go to work. I crawl in between Tina's milky thighs as she arranges her pillows. "Oh, you're clean shaven now. What a great contrast!"

"I bet it's like having two different girls in the same hour."

"I love your pussy."

"I love the way you make it feel."

I lick Tina's kitty to completion and then kiss her on the mouth as I mount her in the missionary position. I inspect her molars with my tongue. I get an idea as I pump my boner deep inside her.

John stops screwing me and pulls out before he has come. I wonder why? He gets up from the missionary position and says he wants to come in my mouth. I agree to it and he comes in a few strokes. He pulls his dick from my mouth and then re-enters me while he's still hard. He resumes fucking me while he French-kisses my spermy mouth.

Tina readily accepts my proposal for pussy-to-mouth and sucks my load out of me. I'm so turned on that I stay hard. I stick it back in her pussy and keep going while I taste my semen in her pretty mouth. I'm falling in love with this girl, I can tell.

"I need to rest a while. I'm going to rinse off and then we can drink and get high while I recover."

"Do you want to see the photos we took last time?"

"Yes I do. Show them to me when I'm done in the bathroom. But you must NEVER let these get out. I'm going to be... President some day and I can't have these floating around. OK?"

I reassure Tina, "I understand that these are just for us." Tina gives me a long look and then turns toward the bathroom. I stop the porn movie and bring up the photos. Tina returns just as I get the photos up on the screen.

"Wow! They came out great. Ooooo, look at this one. I got the expression just right, it matches the girl in the magazine and you framed it perfectly."

"Should I order some photo-quality prints over the internet for us?"

"Oh shit, the internet! That just reeks of security. Why don't you just post them on some fucking social networking website?"

Tina shits her pants and I get scared. Then she immediately snaps out of what must have been a sarcastic rant and returns to being a model.

"I like shooting nude. I like the way I look naked. But I like semi-nude also. I should bring some sexy lingerie to wear the next time we shoot."

"I once met an escort that was working as a Victoria's Secret model at the time. I only saw her a couple of times. The thing I remember most is that her place was on Meats Avenue. I always thought that was an amusing coincidence. She photographed great and I recognized her from the ads, but she wasn't all that hot in person. She wasn't any good in bed either. I was disappointed. There's a big difference between how a girl looks in person and how she shoots."

"I've noticed that about models too. Do you like the way my butt looks. Do I have any cellulite?" Oh shit, did I say that out loud? I shouldn't have said anything. Now he'll be scrutinizing my butt for cellulite. What have I done? I need to change the subject fast.

Tina gets quiet and then rambles uncharacteristically. I wonder why she's so nervous. Maybe I shouldn't talk about models in front of her.

"You say that a girl is a butt-virgin if her butthole is tight. Can you tell that your tongue has been in my butt?"

I don't answer. I look down at my boner. Tina can see from my erection how excited I am from looking at her photos.

"I want to have sex while the slide show of my photos plays. Get behind me doggy-style, so I can watch it."

I last a long time. I pound Tina's pussy hard and deep. She comes more than once before I finally do. I pull out and it's bloody. "Ooops."

"What?"

"Are you due to start your period soon?"

"Oh fuck! Did you start my period again? I'm not due for another three or four days. How is it that you bust my period out of me?"

"I'm sorry, was the sex good at least?"

"Thanks for reminding me. I want to ask you something. Why are you so good in bed? Come with me to the bathroom. I want to ask you about it while I wash up."

I follow Tina obediently. She looks serious. I get worried.

"Why is the sex with you always so much fun?"

"Wow, thanks for the flattery."

"Can you teach the immature guys my age to fuck like that?"

"What?"

"Inexperienced guys don't fuck for shit. They can be cute, and masculine, and sometimes they can even be fun; but they're selfish in bed. They treat a woman like she's just something to jack off into and then they go back to their football and beer. Why are you so different?"

"How would I know? I'm nothing special."

"No, you don't understand. You are the best lover I've ever had... and you know... I've had more than a few, so I would know. So, tell me why?"

"Well, I've never tried to put it into words before. It's like riding a bicycle, you know how to do it but you don't know how to explain it."

I finish washing up and take John over to the couch to interrogate him.

Tina is serious about this line of questioning. She must have had a series of lousy lovers.

"Just tell me. I want to know. You can do it."

"OK, first I think it's because I totally love women."

"Yes I know. I could tell when we first met."

"Since I love girls, I respect them. I adore them. I try to always be appreciative of the wonderful things a girl gives me, even if it's just a smile in public."

"Sure, you make me feel that way. Get to the point already."

"Oh, the sex part?"

"Yes dammit! Give me the details."

"I like to start out with gentle girl-sex and then finish with hard, dirty-old-man, daddy-complex-sex."

"What's girl-sex?"

"That's when I shyly ask you if I can lick your pussy.

197

Then I start slowly, teasing you until you want more."

"That always frustrates the shit out of me."

"But it turns you on doesn't it?"

"Yes it does. But then I want rough sex."

"That's why once I get you turned on, then I get rough with you, and you like it."

"Yes, I do like it."

"But I never start out rough."

"Why not?"

"Because you wouldn't like it. It would turn you off like the infantile guys your age do."

"You're right they do. How do you know all this?"

"I was once that age. I had to learn."

"What else do you do? You are a good lover even when we aren't having sex. What are you doing then?"

"I always try to be respectful, generous, and kind. I try to be supportive and caring. It's easy to do that because I love girls and I want to show them my appreciation for their great performances in bed. That's what I do to keep a girl that I like."

"Does it work?"

"Why else is a drop-dead-gorgeous girl like you hanging out here with the likes of me?"

"Is there any advice you give to other guys?"

"Well, there is one discussion that I've had with my buddies that we all agree on."

"What's that? Tell me."

"We agree that it's more fun to fuck a girl that is climaxing than to come in a girl that's still waiting for her first orgasm. The rule that we use is: Don't even put it into her until she has had at least one orgasm."

"You follow that rule with me, don't you?"

"Yes, most of the time. Unless you get me so turned on

that I have to ravage you before I get you warmed up."

"That's fun too. I like the spontaneity and it mixes it up so we don't get into a routine."

"Whenever I come first like that, I always try to make it up to you by licking your pussy to start the next round."

"We make a good couple. We help each other understand things."

"I'm completely kitten smitten by you."

"Speaking of my pussy, I can't believe that you started my period. I thought for sure that this would be long enough before I'm due. I still want to have more sex. What am I supposed to do with you?"

"We could play the virgin game?"

"What the fuck is that? Where are we going to find a virgin?"

"That's when the girl is on the rag and we fuck in the shower."

"Wow, you are deeply into this girlfriend experience thing. I'll get in the shower. Give me a couple of minutes head start, then come in."

I poke my head onto the bathroom and ask, "Are you ready for me yet?"

"Yes, come on in and fuck the fake virgin!"

I finish quickly and there isn't any blood until I pull out. I wash off first and leave Tina in the shower.

"I need a drink. Make me one while I wash up."

Tina returns from the bathroom shaking her wet hair. She plops down in the chair and drains half of her drink. Tina gives me a suspicious look.

"I can't believe how many times you can fuck. Do you realize how crazy you are?"

"Why is it crazy? Women can fuck a bunch of times. I don't know how many times a man can fuck. I've never fucked a man."

"I'm glad to hear that. Let's drink and get high while we rest and then I want to see if you can fuck again. I'm horny tonight and I'm not getting sore. I think it's because of the olive oil, rinsing off each time, and no condoms. It's great that older men have had vasectomies. None of the contraceptives for women are worth a shit."

"What about the pill or the patch?"

"The hormones make you feel like you're pregnant. It's awful. You gain weight and feel bloated. You don't even want to have sex when you're on those things. Everybody hates to use them."

"What about using an IUD?"

"An IUD is so invasive. They can be seriously uncomfortable and they're expensive. Girls get cramps from them. Nobody uses an IUD."

"Are any of the contraceptives worth using?"

"They all have terrible side effects. I won't use them."

"What do you do?"

"I make all guys I'm with wear condoms. Even my long-term boyfriends always have to wear condoms, no matter what time of the month it is. I'm not getting pregnant, not ever."

"I like having sex without condoms. You were able to fuck me until I'm done without getting too sore. This is great. When I can have enough sex then I don't need to masturbate afterward."

"I am totally satisfied sexually. I won't need to use my vibrator for a week!"

"That reminds me. I was talking with Little Lisa about how much I appreciated her perspective on masturbating when she got a strange look on her face and told me this story:

I have to tell you about what happened to me with my vibrator recently. Late one night I got out my vibrator. I have the one with those big batteries in a big flashlight sized thing and then it has a wire going to a little 'egg' that you can put inside. Well, I was tired but not sleepy, so I wanted to come a couple of times to help me relax and go to sleep for the night. I put the egg inside me and it was buzzing fast and hard because the thing has no speed control and the new batteries made it hum. So I came and then I came again and then I think I fell asleep. The next thing I can remember is waking up the next morning during an orgasm. I was shaking and coming at the same time. I pulled out the vibrator egg and it was still buzzing, but just barely. I felt weird. I tried to get up, but I couldn't stand. My legs and stomach were sore, and I was still shaking. I had to lie back down and I just rested for a long time. I felt better a couple of hours later and I was able to get up and take a hot bath. I think that I was coming all night long. I was sore all *over for the next couple of days and I didn't*

touch my vibrator again for a whole week!

Doesn't that sound just like her?"

"Our little super hero never disappoints in the erotic. She needs to be more careful though. A pussy can only take so much electronic stimulation, she could have hurt herself."

"I'll pour you another drink, let's get high."

"I need to lie down on the bed. Here, take my towel."

I hang up Tina's towel in the bathroom and return. Is Tina asleep? She is beautiful sleeping. Wow, that turns me on. I carefully climb in bed, spoon in behind her, and cuddle up to her warmth. She's still sleeping. I get an erection. I lube it up. I put my penis against her vagina. She's still asleep. I insert the tip into her and start stroking. Tina wakes up laughing.

"Oh, you're fucking me! I thought it was a dream. That feels good."

I pound Tina. She comes hard and that makes me come.

"I've never woken up with a dick in me before. That was fun, but I'm not going to marry you just because of it."

"You're adorable. I like you."

"What time is it?"

"Oh, it's gotten late on us, it's eleven twenty already."

"Do you need me to leave now?"

"No, of course not. Why? Can you stay? I would love that!"

"I'm still drunk and high and I'd like to come down before I make the long drive home. If you don't mind,

I'd like to stay a while, if you don't need me to leave."

"I'm spending the night here, so you can stay all night if you want to. I could buy you breakfast in the morning, just like a girlfriend on a real date."

"I'd like to hang out a little bit and then see if I feel good enough to drive home."

Tina's expression changes as she looks around the room thoughtfully.

"Can we snuggle in bed together under the blankets and watch my favorite late night TV show?"

"I'd love to. You get in bed and I'll put the show on."

"This is great, I love this show. This guy cracks me up. Do you like his sense of humor?"

We watch the TV show together like a couple of old friends. I am overcome by my affection for this wonderful girl. The hour passes in no time.

"That was fun. I'm going to get dressed now. I feel good enough to drive home."

Tina's little purse is too small for the envelope to fit. I see her start to open the envelope. I turn away and pretend to fix a drink to give her some privacy.

I open the envelope to put the money in my purse and see that John has included an extra hundred-dollar bill inside. "Oh..."

Tina is surprised when she notices the extra C-note. I keep my back to her and I don't say anything.

That's nice of him. He didn't have to do that. I feel like I should say something, but I decide not to. I feel that this is something that is best left in the unsaid portion of our relationship.

She's hesitating as though she's considering saying something, but after a moment's reflection, she decides not to. I keep my back to her and she just goes about her business of getting ready to leave.

I like John. I'm going to keep seeing him even if I get that job I applied for. "I'm going to leave now."

"Can I walk you to your car?"

"Thanks, but there's no need to, I'm parked right in front."

"Thanks for seeing me."

"Thanks for everything, I had fun tonight."

"I hope we can get together again soon."

"Text me and we'll see what works out."

Even though it's her first time at this hotel, Tina instinctively goes the right way out the door; she's definitely not a newbie anymore.

It was wonderful of Tina to stay and watch TV with me tonight, even though we were done with the sex and she was on her own time. It felt like we were lovers. She was friendly to me. She openly shared her feelings and questions with me. It was as good as it ever was with any girlfriend I have ever had. She made me feel loved. I will never forget it. I can tell that this will be one of the fondest memories of my life. I will always love her for giving this night to me. Life just doesn't get any better than this.

Is that my phone? Oh, it's a new text message.

> **From: Tina**
> **Sub: U won't believe**
> **Msg: Soooooo funny.**
> **There was an Asian girl**
> **in the elevator with her**
> **body guard counting**
> **her money – how**
> **indiscreet...**

I reply.

To: Tina
Sub: I do believe U
Msg: UR2 funny.
wish I was there 2 C it.

I barely set my phone down and it chimes again.

From: Tina
Sub: Amateur
Msg: There were 5s
& tens I think she
was a hand-jobber.
Scoff.

Oh, that's unbearably rich, Tina engaging in call girl trash talk. I love her. She's wonderful. I'm an incredibly lucky guy.

Chapter 13

I'm Positive

I pause at the door wondering if John is going to be angry with me that I didn't tell him. Is he going to be mad that I exposed him? Is he the one who infected me? Should I ask him if he's been tested recently? Is he going to be pissed-off that I said that I only have one hour today? Is he going to be mad when I tell him to wear a condom? Maybe I'll still give him bareback... The door flies open and John stares at me bewildered.

Did I knock? I'm caught by surprise, but I turn on the charm as quickly as I can.

That's not Tina's knock. Who could it be? Did I order room service? Did I call housekeeping for extra towels? I better hide the porn before I open the door. This is a new hotel for us, so I don't know what to expect. I agreed to meet her in this part of town since it's close to where she is working now and it's not too far from my work.

I smile at John, but I can't look him in the eye. I feel terrible about contracting an STD and having to tell him about it.

Tina avoids my eyes and gives me a quick business-like

hug as she enters. Things have certainly changed since the last time I saw her two months ago.

"I'm sorry that I only have one hour today. I have to go to work early this afternoon. Thanks for meeting me in this part of town. This is much more convenient because my new job is near here. We have the full hour, but just so you know, I must leave right at four o'clock sharp."

"That's fine. I understand. It's nice to see you again. Thanks for arranging this. You look great. Have you been doing your modeling workouts?"

John is talking at me but I'm busy thinking about how I'm going to break this news to him. The reason that I told him that we could meet for only one hour this time is actually because I can only take being fucked three times today. Using a condom will rub me raw. Plus, this way he doesn't have to give me as much money and he won't be as upset that I didn't say anything before we met. Besides, I only have one hour's worth of bills to pay right now. What is he babbling about?

"Did you have any trouble finding the hotel?"

"What?"

"The hotel."

"What hotel?"

"This hotel."

"Oh, I'm not sure."

Tina is unusually preoccupied today. I wonder if she's feeling under the weather or if something's wrong.

"Before we get started, I have something that I need to tell you. Sit down."

Oh shit! Tina has never used this tone of voice before. I start to worry, but I try not to show it. Tina composes herself and speaks slowly and deliberately to me.

"I tested positive for, and I was treated for, chlamydia. I don't know from whom I contracted it, so

I'm just going to always be safe from now on."

"Thank you for telling me."

"I wanted to tell you face to face, not over the phone or through a text. I hope you understand."

"Yes, I do understand."

"Do you still want to see me?"

I get up and grab a condom from my bag. I set it on the nightstand and Tina smiles at me.

I can tell that John is a totally freaked out by the STD news. I would like to keep my favorite regulars if they don't mind using condoms for full service from now on.

It is only by accident that I just happen to have condoms with me today. I've been shopping around for a new girl lately because both Tina and Lisa have been unavailable for so long. I haven't found a new girl, but I've been packing condoms lately just in case I score. I'm not going to tell Tina that.

John is obviously disturbed and uncomfortable with the situation. I'm glad I booked this session for only one hour.

I was expecting uncovered, but it's been two full months since I have seen her, and I considered the possibility that things may have changed. I prepared myself for the idea that she might insist on a cover this time, so I left the condoms in my bag. I'm glad I did. I wonder if she'll still speak directly into the microphone.

I get undressed. John watches me and then he does too. I walk over to him, give him a hug, and press myself against him. Usually this gives him an instant erection, but not today.

"How about a blowjob?"

I get down on my knees and grab John's bare, limp penis. I suck on him like I usually do, but he barely gets hard. I grab the condom and put it on him. I wet my pussy with spit and bend over in front of John. He penetrates me and grabs my hips. He gets hard as he starts pounding me. He doesn't make any of his usual noises. I try to come, but I can't. John seems to because he stops and pulls out. I ask him if he wants to go first in the bathroom, to take care of the condom. He seems confused at first.

"Oh, the condom, yes certainly."

John returns from the bathroom and then I take my turn. When I get back I see that John is not his usual happy self. I try to chat to improve the atmosphere. I look for a suitable subject. "I started a new job."

"Oh, good for you. What are you doing?"

"I'm working at an illegal phone-scam place. We only take incoming calls, we don't make any outgoing calls, and so it's not too bad. There are lots of cute college aged girls working there. After two weeks on the job, I was promoted to first-level supervisor. I completed some easy training and now I'm managing a group of girls in the phone pool."

"Have you given up on modeling? I know that you don't like it."

"The hostess job at the motorcycle show in Vegas didn't go so good. It was booked though a new agency that I haven't worked with before. They aren't as professional as other agencies I've worked for. The clients got the wrong idea about what hostesses are there for. I'm never doing that again."

"How is Sunny Knight doing, is she OK?"

"I don't like making the long drive to San Diego to do in-calls. It's creepy to host new clients and the scheduling is difficult to work out. I won't be doing that any more. I pulled my website ad down. I'm applying for a better job at this same place. The phone pool supervisor position pays a lot more. I think I can get the job after I complete some additional training. I should be able to earn enough to pay my bills. I'm going to stop escorting."

John's eyebrows rise up in shock, so I quickly add, "Except for you. I'll still see you."

Tina is clearly feeling bad today. I'll try to make her feel better. What can I do to make Tina feel better? I get an idea. "Can I lick your pussy?"

"Yes, I'd love that."

I lick Tina's pussy, but I don't get the usual reaction.

John puts his mouth on my pussy and I eventually have an orgasm. I'm ready to have sex, but John hasn't gotten hard yet. I suggest to him that we move into a 69 position. I suck John's cock until I get him hard. I quickly put a condom on him, get on top, and ride him cowgirl style. I know that he likes it that way.

Tina bounces her pussy on my condom-covered penis and although she looks great, I can't feel anything through a condom. She doesn't come, but she pretends to. I shouldn't be too surprised. She can tell that I'm getting limp.

"Did you come?"

"No, not yet." Tina climbs off of me and she removes the condom.

"That won't do. I know, I'll blow you. I'm too sore to fuck any more with my pussy. The condoms rub me raw."

Tina does her best to provide good service, but the mood is ruined and I'm barely able to come.

"I'm going to go wash up now."

I prepare Tina's envelope with our established one-hour rate plus one more Ben Franklin. I had added a C-note last time and now I feel obligated to continue. I want to do whatever I can to keep our relationship intact, if that's even possible at this point. I put the envelope under

211

her purse while she is still in the bathroom.

It's not her fault that this has happened. For that matter, I might be the one who gave her chlamydia. I don't know. She is handling the situation well, in her usual poised and classy style.

When I come out of the bathroom, I see that John is deep in thought. I can tell by his body language that he's never going to call me again. I can't blame him; I just told him I have an STD. I can't help but wonder silently to myself, "Is this the price of being a perv?"

I pick up my purse and the envelope. "Thanks for this." John is completely preoccupied.

"I am going straight to my MD from here to get tested, and if indicated I'll get treated immediately."

"That's probably a good idea."

"I'll text you the test result as soon as I have it."

"OK, thanks."

Tina looks uncomfortable and wants to leave. I can tell that she's never going to reply to my messages again. I try to lighten the mood. "Can I walk you to your car?"

"No need to. It's daytime and I'm just out front. Thanks though."

"I don't want to miss out on any more interesting people you meet in the elevator."

"The hand-jobber chick was totally preposterous. I wish you had walked me to my car last time, because sometimes you do. We would have screamed laughing at her."

"We probably would have pissed-off her bodyguard."

"He probably would have laughed at her too. Well, I've got to go to work now, thanks for seeing me."

Tina shoves her envelope into her purse and is out the door, going the wrong direction down the hallway, before she finishes her sentence. Even at a new hotel, an

212

experienced escort instinctively knows which way to exit the room. Tina is clearly frazzled today.

I mumble to myself, "I wonder if our relationship will survive this?"

Chapter 14

I'm Negative

I knock on the door talking to myself under my breath, "Be professional. Be on time. Just go in and do your job. Stay focused. Get laid, get paid, and get out of here. You need the money."

I appreciate that John tested negative, but I have to wonder how much damage this STD scare has done to our relationship. I could tell that he was not at all engaged in our last session. It's understandable though. I would freak out if he told me he had an STD. I'm surprised that he wants to see me again. I lecture myself, "Get back to the task at hand."

I hear myself say out loud, "It's three o'clock now and we have the full hour, but I have to leave right at four o'clock."

I continue thinking to myself, but don't say it out loud, "I can't be late. I have to get my car from the shop and still be on time to pick up my last paycheck." I don't want to say anything like that to a client. He's paying for someone that doesn't have any baggage. The rules to good call girl etiquette are simple: turn off your cell phone and don't have any problems. If he wants to put up with a girl's baggage, then he'll just screw a regular girlfriend and save his money to spend on her. I have to be a lot more alluring than a regular girlfriend if I expect him to pay this much for my time.

I'll just watch the clock and make sure I'm out of here by four o'clock sharp.

That's not Tina's knock. Who is that? Oh, wait, that's Tina's new knock. I recognize it now. I pull the door open.

I enter the room and immediately check to see if the time is correct on the cheap little clock radio. It isn't. The piece of shit is ten minutes fast. I'll just adjust for it, which means I need to head to the bathroom when it's four o'clock on this little timepiece of shit.

Tina enters nervously and gives me a quickie hug. I guess that must be Tina's new hug. I miss the way it used to be.

"Thanks for meeting me here again. I know it's a long way for you, but I've been working in this part of town. It's more convenient for me to meet over here during the daytime."

"It's not that far. How's the job working out? Do they realize what a star employee you are?"

"I'm seriously looking for new work right now. The phone-scam place got busted last week. The owners moved into another building and got all set up the very next day. The new place is just down the street from here. They sent everybody a text message and we showed up at the new place, so at least I'll get paid for the time I put in. I don't want to work there anymore. The hours and the pay are terrible."

Tina pauses and looks at me as though she has something she wants to confide in me. I smile encouragingly at her to coax her along.

"While I was training to be a supervisor, I learned more about the place. I think the owners are some kind

216

of white-collar criminals, or at the least, they operate on the edge of the law. I don't like it, none of the girls there do. I'm going to quit today; I'm not even going to wait until after my shift. I'm just going to quit and get my check, so that I can look for a new job full time. I'll miss being around all those cute girls though. Maybe I'll give a couple of the hotties my phone number."

"I'm sure that you can find a better job. You're too good for that place. It's nice to see you again, it's been four weeks."

"I got the text message you sent me three weeks ago that you tested negative for chlamydia. I'm glad you weren't infected."

"I went straight to my doctor's office right after our last meeting. They took a urine sample for the test and then suggested that I get the prescription for the antibiotic filled and take the whole dose right away. So that's what I did. They called me a few days later with the negative result from the lab. I was relieved."

"I guess that just goes to show that you don't contract everything that you're exposed to."

I look at Tina not knowing what to say next.

"Even though I'm cured and you were negative, I'm just always going to be safe and use condoms, every time, from now on."

Tina seems to feel the need to explain something. I wait patiently for her to compose her thoughts.

"I don't know who I got it from, but I'm not seeing any new clients ever again. I'm only seeing established clients that get tested regularly. Oh my God, what if I had contracted something much worse than chlamydia?"

I think to myself, "What if I had given it to my wife? How the hell would I explain that?"

"I'm going to always be safe from now on. I'm going to use the bathroom. I'll be back in a minute."

I get naked, grab a condom from my bag and place it on the nightstand. I crawl into bed and wonder what exactly does she mean by 'always be safe from now on'? Can I lick her pussy? Will she give me a blowjob? Will it be covered? The conversation about STDs has put a damper on my sex drive and I'm as limp as an over-cooked noodle. Tina returns naked and gets in bed next to me. She can sense the uneasy atmosphere. She grabs my penis in her hand and tries to get a reaction. Nothing happens.

"Lie back on the bed."

Tina looks at the condom and looks me in the eye. She methodically puts her hair behind her ears and goes down on my bare penis. As soon as I am hard she gets the condom, puts it on, and mounts me. Tina bounces a few times and I come. She can't tell that I came and keeps bouncing on me until I'm so soft that I fall out of her.

"Oh, did you come already?"

"Yes, you're so tight that even in a condom, I don't last long inside you."

"A girl can't feel anything down there when a guy's wearing a condom so I can't tell when you come."

"A guy can't feel anything down there either when he's wearing a condom, so I don't know if you came."

"You should scream 'I'm coming' like I do. Then I would know. You can use the bathroom first, so that you can take care of the condom."

I return from flushing the condom and wonder if it is going to clog the toilet. I wait nervously as Tina takes her turn. She returns from the bathroom without incident so I try to keep things moving along. I can tell by the way that Tina is watching the clock that we are under a time constraint today. I respect her schedule limitations, but at the same time, I want to get my money's worth. "Can I lick your pussy?"

"Sure, I want the pillows for my head, so I can watch. I love to watch, it's like a porn movie, but more fun because I get to participate."

Tina climaxes and I get up to mount her like I usually do. Tina's face instantly takes on a worried expression.

"Get a condom."

We start our usual sex, but using a condom, like we did back in the beginning of our relationship. It's still enjoyable, but it's not the same. I didn't even bother to try to play with Tina's butt today. There's no point in pursuing anal sex if you have to wear a condom. I guess this is just how it's going to be from now on.

I can tell that John is going to have trouble coming while wearing a condom. My pussy is getting too sore to take much more. If he doesn't come soon then I'll have to... Oh, good, I can tell by his grunts that he's finally coming.

If Tina is going to require condoms from now on, then I think that I'd rather see Lisa uncovered instead. I can tell that Tina is not enjoying the sex. I know she doesn't like using condoms. I think about the uncovered sex we've had together in the past and I finally shoot my load.

I don't want to rush John but I don't have the time to let him lie on top of me the way he likes to.

With her eyes on the clock, Tina throws me off of her, pops out of bed, and dashes into the bathroom. I get the envelope out of my briefcase and place it under her purse on the table. I turn around to see Tina emerging from the bathroom fully dressed. She is reaching for her purse as she announces her goodbye.

"OK, it's almost 4 o'clock, I'm going to leave now. Thanks for the envelope."

"OK, thanks for seeing me." This is where I usually ask when I can see her again, but there probably won't be a next time, so I don't ask. I feel like I should be saying my final good bye to her. I look up to see Tina dash out the door in the wrong direction.

Chapter 15

We Exchange Looks

I knock on the door feeling grateful that I will be able to pay my rent and get great sex tonight. I like having John as a regular that I can count on to book a two-hour appointment whenever I need the money. I'm going to give him what he wants today to make sure that I keep him. I'm lucky to have a regular like John.

I unpack my bag of supplies like I usually do, but I stop when I get to the box of condoms. I want to keep the condoms handy, but I think I'll hide them in the nightstand drawer. I won't bring them out unless she asks to use them. I don't like using condoms, but since Lisa has been unavailable for several months now, I don't have any alternative. The simple fact is that covered sex with Tina is the best sex I can get right now. I'll try to have as much fun as I can under whatever rules she imposes tonight. I'm lucky to have a hot escort like Tina.

I am more horny than usual tonight. It seems like it's been a long time since I've had sex. It's not like I have a lot of extra time to waste on finding and seeing a regular boyfriend. I hope I still remember how to fuck!

That's Tina's knock. It's her old knock from before. I throw open the door and beam a big smile in hopes that our relationship will return to its former glory.

I jump toward John when he opens the door. He catches me in his strong arms and I give him a hard kiss on the lips.

Tina sets the mood the moment I lay my eyes on her.

"I've missed you John."

"I've missed you too Tina."

"I'm horny today. I don't know how long it's been since I've had sex. No. Really. How long has it been? Oh shit. I haven't had sex since I saw you two full weeks ago. No wonder I'm so horny."

"I'd be happy to help you with that."

"Remember you told me that you like to start out with girl-sex, and then get dirty?"

"Yes, why?"

"I want you to start the girl-sex part on me right now. Then as soon as I'm ready for it, I want you to get dirty with me."

I undress Tina and I'm pleased to find her wearing panties. I take them off of her with my teeth, sniff them, and set them aside for later.

"Are you going to keep those to add to your collection?"

"Yes, they smell like your pussy."

"Let me smell them!"

I hand them to Tina and she practically snorts the crotch up her nose.

"Oooooo, they do smell great. Where do you keep your collection? What are you going to say if your wife finds them?"

"I will tell her that they're mine."

"What if she thinks that means that you wear them?"

"Then I'll start wearing girl's panties."

"Oh, you are decadent, lewd, and lascivious."

"Personally, I prefer to think that they'll make me feel sexy. Or maybe they'll just make me feel queer. Lie down on your back."

"OK."

I take my time and lick Tina's pussy until she has at least one big orgasm, then I get up to mount her. We both look at my uncovered cock for a second and then our eyes meet for a moment of truth. Neither of us says anything. We exchange looks. Tina spreads her legs, grabs my bare penis, and guides it into her vagina. I stroke her slowly and gently until she indicates she wants more.

"Fuck me hard!"

I do exactly as Tina commands. I pound her pussy with my cock while I reach under her backside and shove my middle finger, two knuckles deep, into her butthole. By the time we finish, the mattress has slid halfway off of the box spring. Tina gets up and staggers to the bathroom cum-drunk. I don't think she realizes that she's talking out loud.

"How can such an old man be such a good fuck?"

I shove the mattress back onto the bed, stagger over to the sink, and wash my hands. I put on my robe and fix two drinks while questions fill my mind. What is a gorgeous young girl like Tina doing with an ugly old fart like me? How can I be so lucky? What can I do to maximize the probability of continued contact? My pondering is interrupted. Tina arrives wrapped in a towel; she is smiling. She gracefully sits down at the table and sips her drink. We get high together like college roommates.

"I needed a good hard fuck, that was great. Thanks

223

for seeing me on short notice like this; my rent is due tomorrow. I only see my regulars now. I don't have many regulars left. I'm not going to see any new clients ever again, that is unless I absolutely have to. I'm still looking for a regular job. I have an interview next week at a legitimate call center. I'm applying for the phone pool supervisor job because I have experience now. The pay is great and there will be hot young women there. It's a full-time job that includes employee benefits like health insurance."

"Have you had any modeling work?"

"I won't go back to modeling. I don't miss modeling at all. All of the photographers are either gay or they're lechers. The gay guys are constantly trying to give you an inferiority complex because they're jealous of every cute girl. They'll tell you, 'You can't be a model, your nose has a big bump'. It does not. There's only one angle where the little flat spot on the bridge of my nose causes a slight imperfection in the profile. It's a result of my deviated septum."

"I'm sorry, what did you say? Your deviant what?"

"No, you perv. I said my deviated septum."

I don't know what Tina's talking about, but I think I'd better just drop it and go back on topic. "Are most of the men in modeling gay?"

"It's no better if they aren't. If they're one of the few that are straight, then they're always trying to get you on the casting couch. Either way they're all pathetic assholes."

"It doesn't sound all that glamorous."

"I don't miss modeling. It's especially bad when they identify you as a model whose hair will wave when it's been wet, because then you are the first one hosed down at the shoot, always with freezing water. You're out there in the freezing cold, they get your hair wet, then you have to wait for it to dry. It's cold outside, you're in a fucking bikini for crying out loud and the Pacific Ocean wind is blowing on you at gale force. I don't miss modeling at all."

"I looked up your professional photos on the websites you gave me. In the shots where you've got wavy hair at the beach, you look cold and pissed off."

"Those sadistic fuckers. Even if my skin condition clears up, I still won't go back to modeling. I'm done working with the sick bastards in that crazy industry. I've had so many bad experiences modeling. I have had to block them out of my memory just to keep from being traumatized by them. I don't even like to talk about it."

Wow, Tina never complains or rants about anything and this is the second time I've heard this tirade on the evils of modeling. She is definitely hiding something traumatic from her past. Modeling is clearly a sore subject that I need to avoid around her. I quickly steer the conversation to a topic I know Tina likes.

"I have another story from Little Lisa. Do you want to hear it?"

"You KNOW that I love her stories. Don't make me beg. What's our little sex fiend doing now?"

"This is exactly what she said to me:

When I'm out driving on the freeway, I like to flash the truck drivers. I do that whenever I have the top down on my convertible. My dad was a truck driver, so I know how much they appreciate it. They are way up high in their rigs and so I can flash them without anyone in a car seeing that I have my skirt up. I never wear panties anyway and so I can flash my pussy at truck drivers. I have a vibrator that plugs into my car's cigarette lighter. I saw it online and ordered it right away. That's a must-have car accessory. It's great for a long drive. What else are you going to do while you're driving? I play with my vibrator in my pussy and then I show it to the truck drivers. I always make eye contact with them. That's important, to look them in the eye and smile at them. You should see the big grin they get and sometimes they'll blow their big horns and scare the shit out of the cars in front of them. That's my favorite place to flash guys.

I love her stories." Tina looks me in the eye and slowly shakes her head from side to side.

"Don't you feel lucky just to know her?"

Tina has made another one of her deeply insightful and thought provoking comments. It deserves notice.

John seems confused by my comment. Maybe he is just thinking. John takes a deep breath and replies thoughtfully.

"She's a gift of adult liberation, I just adore her. That's why I wanted you to meet her. I remember Lisa told me that she always shaves because it's better for

226

flashing guys."

"I've never met an exhibitionist before. Isn't she great?"

"I have never seen a girl show off in public before."

"I've never done that. Well, not since I was a little girl. Let's watch the porn movies. Where are they? I want to pick out a nasty one."

I give Tina a pile of porn DVDs.

"Do you have any other porn movies? We've fucked to all of these a bunch of times."

"I'll get some new ones for next time."

"Are you ready to have sex?"

"Yes."

"Get on your back."

Tina looks me over and sees that I'm already hard. She climbs on top of me, grabs my penis and eases her wet pussy onto it. After a few strokes, she pulls her feet up into a squatting position and does deep knee bends on my boner. Just as I begin to come, Tina pops off to change the position. A stream of semen arches toward my screaming mouth. I turn away just in time and the hot load hits my cheek. Tina bursts into a fit of laughter. I'm frozen by the surprise. Tina controls herself for a moment, looks me in the eye, and explodes into hysterical giggles.

"Ha! Now you know how the girl feels when sperm is flying at her face."

I am stunned, speechless, and covered in semen. Tina looks at me contemplatively and moves slowly toward me, like she's going to kiss me. She passes by my lips and licks the semen off my cheek. I don't move. Tina moves down my neck, licking and sucking the semen off of me. She works her way down to my penis and sucks the semen off of it. I tremble from the stimulation and excitement. Tina swallows and I reach for her. She lies on top of me and I taste my semen in her mouth as she deep-French-kisses me. I fall completely in love with her.

"Let's take a shower together. We're all spermy."

After our shower, I fix us some drinks and Tina grabs one of the porn magazines, pauses a second, and looks at me questioningly.

"I used some of the ladies deodorant that you keep in the bathroom. Do you like the way I smell?"

"Yes, I do. It's just like I remember."

"Are you the one who told me that I should I put it on for you, so you can be reminded of some smell that turns you on while you fuck me?"

"Yes, something like that."

"Oh look. This girl is hot. I'd like to have sex with her. Look at how cute she is."

"Speaking of having sex with a hot girl, I know a sexy girl named Bella and she likes girls. Do you want to see her photos?"

"Is she from around here?"

"No, she's from San Francisco, but she's visiting OC next month."

"Have I seen her pictures before?"

"Yes, I'm pretty sure you have."

"Show them to me. Do you have them? I want to see them before I decide to meet her."

I quickly bring up Bella's photos on my notebook computer while Tina hovers over me impatiently.

"Oh, I remember her pictures now. She's visiting? She likes girls?"

"Yes she is, and yes she does. Should I set up a threesome with her?"

"Yes, definitely set it up! Let me know as soon as she

confirms so I can clear my schedule."

I can tell that Tina is excited and I want to have sex with her while she's turned-on about the pending threesome.

"I've been noticing hot girls at the gym, when I'm at clubs and even out shopping. I've always been aware of cute girls and liked the way they look, but now I look at them and wonder what it would be like to have sex with them."

"Can we have sex now? Can I take pictures of us having sex?"

"Sure, that will be fun. Do you have your camera?"

"I'll get it. How should we shoot?"

"I know, get on your back. I'll get on top and you can shoot a POV penetration."

"Don't make me cum on myself this time."

"OK, you can come inside me this time."

Tina gets on top of me and rides me cowgirl style. Her strong Kegel muscles squeeze my penis while she grinds her snatch on my pelvic bone. I snap several shots and then set the camera on the bed so that I can concentrate on the hot sex. "I can tell that you've been doing your Kegels, it feels great."

"What the hell are Kegels?"

"They're Kegel exercises, they make your pussy strong."

"Oh that's right, those pussy exercises you told me about. I was talking with some girls that told me they do them all the time and that guys love a girl that can hug their cock with their pussy."

Tina stays on top until I squirt my load into her. Tina remains sitting on my penis and gives me an inquisitive look.

"How many girls have you had sex with in your life?"

"That's odd you would ask me that question today

229

because I was just recently trying to calculate that sum. I estimate the figure is well more than one hundred, and it has a high probability of being closer to two hundred."

"How many girls are you trying to have sex with?"

"As many as possible."

"Be sure to invite me to join you with any hot girls you have sex with."

Tina rises up on her knees and my limp penis flops out of her tight vagina. Tina giggles and a slow stream of semen dribbles out of her pussy onto my stomach. I reach for my camera and take a few shots. Tina watches intently until it stops dripping. Tina carefully climbs off of me. She bends over and sucks the semen off of my belly. She swallows and looks at me with an expression of accomplishment.

"That was great. You got to come inside of me and I still got to swallow your sperm. It tasted like my pussy."

"Kiss me pussy-sperm-face!" Tina deep-French-kisses me and then flies off of me like she's weightless.

"Get the magazines out, I'm going to use the bathroom."

I am looking at an old issue of a magazine full of naked eighteen-year-old girls when Tina returns from the bathroom. I point to a model and comment, "This girl looks too young."

"Too young to be legal or too young for you to fuck?"

"Oh, I'd fuck her, but she doesn't look legal."

"How young a girl would you have sex with, if there were no..."

I interrupt Tina to let her know that we've been here before and finish her sentence, "...no social taboos or legal issues."

"Yes, that."

"I have to admit that I have been too inhibited to discuss this topic with you in the past." Tina looks expectantly at me.

"OK, you know the question. So, what's your honest answer?"

My trust in Tina and my confidence in our relationship has grown far beyond my worrying about how she will feel about my answer, so I tell her some of my thoughts this time.

John is stalling. He isn't going to open up to me about this. I can see how hesitant he is. I'm going to get another one of his chicken-shit answers.

"Some girls can catch a man's attention long before they are legal. A man can't fight a few hundred million years of evolution with a few hundred years of culture. Instinct is stronger than social rules."

I'm surprised at John's response, but I'm also pleased that he has finally shared his true feelings with me. I've always wondered what men were thinking when they looked at me intently, back when I was a young girl.

"A civilized man's instinct is always dominated by the need to protect the young, but he may still notice that she is attractive. The truth is that some girls are noticeable when they're still a few years from being of age."

"I've always wanted to ask a man that question."

I want to ask Tina how old she was her first time, but I can't because I don't know if she was molested as a child. I won't stir up any bad memories no matter how curious I am. Maybe if I talk about my youth, and if there are no issues in her history, then she may disclose the age that she got started. Tina is deep in thought for a few seconds, then looks up at me with sincerity.

"I've always wondered how men feel toward young girls. I've always wondered if they want to fuck us at that age."

I want to ask Tina why she is so interested. Her repeated inquires on the subject make me want to ask her how young she was when she got introduced, but I know the rule: a man must never ask a girl how old she was when she first had sex. Even if she repeatedly asks him how young a girl he would fuck. You don't know if she was abused as a child, so you don't go there.

"I'm curious about men and you're the only man that I can ask these questions."

I am beginning to wonder if this is connected to Tina's daddy-complex in some way. How do I segue to asking her for sex from here? "I want us to be able to talk openly about sex. For example, can we have sex now?"

"Sure, I'm not too sore. How do you want me?"

"Lie down in the middle of the bed on your back."

"Talk dirty to me and fuck me hard."

I get on top of Tina in the missionary position and I last forever. I hold her pretty little head in my hands while I pump her hard. Tina gets noisy, so I push her arms above her head and pound her mercilessly. "Fuck me little girl." Tina gets loud.

"Oh yes Daddy, give it to me!"

I get up on my knees and grab Tina's thighs. I pound her so hard that the bed shakes and Tina's body slides back and forth like she's on a carnival ride. I finish and my heart is thumping in my chest as though it's going to burst. I fall beside Tina thinking this is a great way to die. Tina pops out of bed.

"That was a good fuck. Most men can't last that long. I came twice."

Tina looks ravishing and ravaged. "You're the cutest girl I've ever fucked."

"Every guy says the girl he's just fucked is the cutest girl he's ever seen. So, who's the best fuck you've ever had?"

"That's easy, Little Lisa is the best at fucking, however you're a close second."

"I'm going to shower and get dressed now."

I hear Tina in the bathroom laughing hysterically. I get up and run in to see what the problem is. Tina is standing at the mirror admiring herself.

"Good, hard sex on your back."

"I'm sorry, what?"

"Good, hard sex on your back."

"You want to be on top?"

"No silly. Good, hard sex on a girl's back is the only thing that does this."

"Does what?"

"Gives your hair this kind of volume. There isn't any other way to get your hair to do this."

"To do what?"

"You just can't get volume like this any other way."

"Volume?"

"The hair dresser can't get you volume like this. Well, not unless they fucked the shit out of you on your back, and they're all gay, so that can't happen. There's nothing that matches the "JF" look."

"The 'what' look?"

"The 'just-fucked' look, of course. You're so funny."

"What are you going to do about it?"

"I should go out clubbing with my girlfriends and show off my volume. That's what I should do. I'm going to call them and see if anyone can go out later. It's more fun to go out with them after I've had lots of sex because then I'm not trying to get into their pants, like I do when I'm horny."

Tina starts to sing as she admires her big hair. I go to the bar and fix a drink. I prepare Tina's envelope with the two-hour donation plus one, and put it under her purse on the table. My hope is that the unrequested increase in the donation will encourage her to keep seeing me. Tina is still singing when she emerges from the bathroom. She picks up her envelope and gives me a warm smile.

"Thanks for this. I appreciate it. It helps me a lot."

"Thanks for seeing me. It helps me a lot too. Seeing you makes my life worth living."

"You're so sweet. I'm going to go now."

"I hope we can get together again soon."

"Text me and we'll work something out. Bye sweetie."

"Bye gorgeous." Tina slowly saunters out the door in the right direction singing softly to herself.

Chapter 16

You've Turned Me into a Perv

I can't stop thinking about the hot girl that I saw at the store earlier today. I got a tingling feeling in my pussy when she bent over right in front of me to try on a pair of sandals. I was so excited at the store that I bought these hooker heels even though I don't need another pair. I can't believe I reacted like that. I know that I have always noticed and appreciated cute girls, but I have never been sexually aroused by one. Not until now. I remember how I've always liked attractive girls, but I have never obsessed about having sex with them like this. What has happened to me? How did I get this way?

This is all John's fault! That's right, he turned me on to that pointy-butt lesbian, he made me this way. This is all his fault. I was fine before he did this to me. I arrive at the pervert's room just as I decide that he is going to pay for what he's done to me. I pound on the fucker's door.

Holy shit! Something's wrong. There's a ferocious pounding on the door. I jump vertically and fly to the door, wondering what is amiss. I quickly find the situation is

dire. The universe becomes unstable the moment I turn the door handle.

Tina explodes into the room like a detonated bomb. She is fuming with anger. She is cursing at me and pushing me backwards. I gather my feet under me and look up. She is starring me down and moving in. She is exceptionally tall today. Tina's eyebrows narrow at me. I am scared shitless. Her big blue eyes flash with rage. I recoil from her fury and backpedal as quickly as I can. Oh crap, I'm cornered. The ferocious female's nostrils flare as she inhales deeply. She shows her teeth and roars at me.

"YOU'VE TURNED ME INTO A PERV!"

Tina maintains her angry bearing; she takes another breath and screams at me.

"YOU'VE TURNED ME INTO A RAGING LEZBO!"

She's going to kill me. This is how I'm going to die.

"Because of you, every time I see a cute girl, all I can think about is having sex with her. What have you done to me? You've turned me into a complete pervert!"

I am shaking with fear. I am not sure if she is joking or not. She seems genuinely upset and unusually emotional. I am too scared to move. Tina's anger finally gives way to frustration.

"You just don't know how hard it is to meet and pick up a cute young girl!"

Tina plops down on the bed lamenting.

"You just don't know. You don't understand how lucky you are to be a man. You can just walk up to a cute girl and ask her to have sex, and nobody thinks anything of it."

I must have a puzzled look because Tina explains.

"If I walk up to a cute girl and ask her to have sex,

then I'm depraved, but it's OK for a MAN to do that."

I nod silently in agreement.

"I want to find a hot girl to fornicate with, but I don't know how to approach her."

I give Tina an empathetic smile.

"This is all your fault. You've turned me into a sexual deviant! Because of you I'm a butch dyke now."

I am speechless, but I am no longer scared for my life. I am definitely getting aroused, and rapidly. Wow, this is intense. I am startled; however, I believe there must be an opportunity somewhere in this peculiar predicament. I think as fast as I can. Tina seems pretty frustrated about wanting to play with another hot girl and not being able to get one. I'm thinking, "This is pretty cool. Tina is on a cunt-hunt too. This is something else that we have in common now."

"It's so embarrassing that people might think that I'm a wanton carpet muncher. Yesterday I made your lewd little noise at a girl in the locker room at my gym. I can't believe that I made that same disgusting guttural grunt you make when you see me naked. It's hard enough to believe that you do that, and now you've got me doing it. You've turned me into a pussy-obsessed skirt-chaser."

Holy fucking shit! Is this real? Am I dreaming? Is this actually happening?

"You should have seen the look she gave me. She got undressed and when she bent over right in front of me, her tight butt was so hot that your sick pervert's noise just came out of me."

I can't decide if I'm proud of myself, or if I'm ashamed of myself, or if I'm both - simultaneously.

"I seriously wanted to bang her and now she thinks I'm some kind of a pervert. She'll never fuck me now. Sleeping with her was all I could think about. I couldn't even get my regular workout done because I was consumed with lust for her."

Tina certainly has embraced her newly discovered bisexuality. My heart is pounding. I'm getting an erection.

"Earlier today, at the store, I practically came in my pants when an erotic girl bent over. It's like I've got twat-fever or something. What have you done to me?"

I have to admit to feeling a certain twisted satisfaction in the idea that this gorgeous girl knows the frustration of not being able to ask a hot girl for a date. At the same time, I am sympathetic to Tina's dilemma. I want to help her any way that I can. "How about if I lick your pussy and you can fantasize that it's the locker room hotty?"

"I guess if I can't have sex with a hot girl, then the best I'm going to do is have girl-sex with a man."

"I'll do anything for you. What do you want?"

"You better pour me a strong drink and get me high. I am seriously pissed off at you right now. Then you better girl-fuck me as much as I want. That will have to suffice, since this stupid society won't let me fuck a girl."

I hand Tina a drink and she gulps it down in two sips. I make her another and we get high together in complete silence.

Tina looks at me as though she wants my help with something. I suggestively lick my lips. Tina stands up and starts undressing. I do the same. The tall temptress steps down from her six-inch stilettos and returns to her normal height, about two inches taller than me.

Tina tosses her panties absentmindedly at the couch with her other clothes. She doesn't see them fly over the top and fall behind it. Tina jumps in bed and glares at me.

"OK, I'm ready for you to girl-fuck the hell out of me."

I give Tina the longest carpet-cleaning job of my life. My tongue has a cramp by the time she finally has a big orgasm and pushes my head away from her crotch.

I let Tina rest a few minutes, then climb on top of her and shove my dick fully into her pussy in one move. Tina just lies there at first. Slowly she gets involved and by the time I come, I have to hold on to the edge of the bed just to stay on top of her.

"That was a good fuck, thanks. I'm going to rinse off. I can have more sex, and not get as sore, if I rinse off with warm water each time. I'll be right back. Get the porn movies started."

Tina returns to bed and snuggles in next to me. She fondles her breast with one hand and grabs my penis with the other. I reach between her thighs and she spreads her legs for me. Her eyes never leave the screen as I insert my index finger into her vagina.

"This scene with the vibrator reminds me of something I want to try on you. Do you have a vibrator in your satchel of sex toys?"

"Yes."

"Get it for me."

I dig the vibrator out of my pouch of props and hand it to Tina. She has a calculating look in her eyes that makes me somewhat nervous.

"I want to get on top. I'll hold the vibrator against the base of your cock while I ride you."

"Keep it away from my balls, or we'll both hit the ceiling."

"Don't worry, I'll keep it in front of us so your glass balls are safe. A girlfriend of mine suggested it to me. She says that her boyfriend loves it and so does she."

Tina mounts me and applies the vibrator on high speed.

Tina climaxes quickly and I come the moment her powerful Kegel muscles clamp down on my penis. Tina pops off of me, rinses off in the shower, and is back in bed before I catch my breath.

"My girlfriend's right, that is fun. Did you like that? I can tell that you came."

"Yes. Be sure to thank your girlfriend for me. Your pussy is incredibly strong."

"I've been doing Kegel exercises. I looked them up on the internet after you told me about them. They make a girl better at sex; she can give the guy's penis a hug. I've added them to my daily workouts."

"That's why I don't even try to resist falling in love with you."

"Why would you try to resist me?"

"I can't take another broken heart."

"I would never break your heart. I'm not that kind of a girl."

"I know that you wouldn't ever hurt me intentionally, but you'll find your Prince Charming, get married and live happily ever after. Then I'll never see you again."

"I'll still see you."

"How can you be so sure?"

"Because I'm sure that there are no Prince Charmings or happily-ever-afters, but there is a nice dirty old man that feeds my daddy-complex. So, I'm pretty sure that I'll still see you."

"That's why I'm completely in love with you."

"That's sweet. I need to rest. Talk to me. Have you seen our little trucker-flasher?"

"Yes, I've seen her several times in the six long months since you and I were last together. She told me another exhibitionist story-"

"Don't you dare ask me if I want to hear it. Just spit it

out. Don't be a gossip tease! What's our little nympho been up to?"

"This is exactly what she said to me:

I used to live near a little outdoor café where the old men would sit and read their newspapers while they sipped their morning coffee. I would put on a short skirt with no panties and go down there. Across the street from the café was a bridge with a high railing. I would bend over the railing to throw breadcrumbs to the ducks below and flash my butt and pussy. The old men loved it. One time a young guy was there and he was too young and stupid to understand what I was doing there. He must have thought that I was just a slut looking to get laid. He ran across the street and asked me for a date. I slapped him and walked away. I could hear the old men laughing at first and then I heard them cursing at the guy for running off their showgirl.

She tells the best stories."

"That's why I hate young guys. They are so stupid that they always ruin everything."

"Little Lisa doesn't like young guys either."

"Did she really say that? Did she actually tell you this

story?"

"I recounted it verbatim."

"Oh my God, that is fucking hilarious. Lisa is great. She's... our little super hero. I've got an idea. I'll do some exhibitionism for you. I'll put on my hooker heels."

Tina climbs onto her slut-stilts, struts over to me, and strikes a perfect pose. I go over the edge. "I want to fuck you. Bend over."

I try to pound Tina from behind, however her pussy is too far off the ground for me to reach. We cannot properly copulate while she's wearing her super-high-heels. She likes it when I bark orders at her during sex, so I instruct her directly, "Shed the shoes long-legs. Your twat is too tall for me." Tina removes the prostitute pumps and I re-enter. I last only a few strokes once she gets noisy and comes. I ejaculate into her convulsing vagina.

"I'm going to rinse off. I'll be right back. Make me a drink."

Tina returns, we sit with our drinks, and we get high. We look at each other with a grin. We are both waiting for the other to state the obvious.

"Talking about Little Lisa makes us both horny. We should get together with her again."

"Lisa wants to also."

"She does?"

"She always asks if I have seen you. Lisa always says to tell you that she wants to see you again."

"Great. I want to see her again too. Set it up."

"She lives out in the Palm Springs area now. She asked if we could meet her somewhere in between, like San Bernardino or Riverside."

"Sure, I can meet you both there. I want to do this. Set it up and then let me know the time and place to meet. I'm ready to fuck a hot girl."

"Speaking of fucking a hot girl... do you remember about five months ago, we were set up to meet Bella from San Francisco? You confirmed the night before and then you went radio silent."

"Oh, that's right. We haven't talked since then.

"I've been worried about you. You haven't replied to my text messages in months and I didn't know what to do. I didn't know if I should try to contact you some other way or not."

"Let me explain what happened. The morning of our date, I was in a car accident. As you can imagine, I was seriously excited that day. There was heavy traffic as I drove to get my nails done. I wanted to be properly groomed for our sex party that night. The car in front of me stopped abruptly, and I barely bumped it. There was no damage to either of our vehicles.

Everything would have been fine, but my car's stupid air bag exploded in my face and broke my nose. The next thing I know, I'm in an ambulance, in route to the hospital.

The damage to my nose was extensive and surgery was required to fix it. All this time, I have been resting and healing up. I haven't seen anyone since it happened. That's why it's been six months."

"I'm so sorry. Are you all right?"

"I didn't like my old nose anyway, so it worked out for the best. Besides that, I had a deviated septum, and so the septoplasty surgery ended up helping me with that."

"You poor thing."

"My nose surgeon was this cute thirty year old doctor who took a personal interest in my case. He was able to fix my nose while repairing the injury from the airbag. He kept it all under the insured medical coverage. He was good."

Tina liked him. I can tell by the way she talks about him and by the mischievous look in her eye.

John gives me a suspicious look. He thinks I fucked my doctor. I can tell he does. He's jealous. I can tell he is. That's so cute.

I know that Tina fucked him. I can tell that she did by the way she's looking at me. I'm going to be sick.

That is such a typical guy reaction. I'm just going to let him go on thinking that I did. He deserves it for thinking like that. John is completely clueless that no doctor will ever fuck a patient. I would have thrown myself at my cute surgeon, except that several of my gorgeous girlfriends have tried that a zillion times and they have always been embarrassed by it.

I have to stop getting jealous over the other men in Tina's life. If I don't, then she will sense it, and she will never see me again. I need to behave like a good client, not a possessive boyfriend, if I'm going to get to keep seeing her. I try to shake it off and compose myself.

I've never even heard of a story where a girl was able to seduce her doctor. All I hear about is how girls try and try, but never get the time of day. That's the ONE case where a man won't let getting some pussy impact his income.

There is a long, awkward silence that I decide to break, "Your new nose looks great. Did your surgeon change the shape of the bridge of your nose also?"

"You can tell that the little flat spot is gone, can't you?"

Tina is smart enough to know the value of her good looks and how to spend the currency. "I didn't think you could be more beautiful, but somehow you are."

"I like my new nose so much that I posed nude for an adult magazine in LA."

"I'm going to buy five copies."

"Well, they're publishing just a single photo, and it's in black & white. It should be in next month's issue."

"Will you autograph your photo for me?"

"Of course I will. But it doesn't look like me at all. They're going to refer to me by my modeling alias, Chris Morgan. I have always used that alias for my modeling work. Only the paycheck company and the legal department knows my real name. It keeps the stalkers and the freaks away."

I don't tell Tina that I know her real name or that using an alias for escorting won't keep this freak away. I revert back to the topic of her new snout. "I'm glad you're happy with your new nose. You are so cute."

"It not only looks great, it works better. I can breathe more freely through my nose after the surgery than I ever could before. I bet that I can give a great blowjob now because I can breathe while I have a big cock like yours in my mouth."

My expression must be giving away my thoughts. Tina giggles at me.

"Here, I'll show you. Get me the sour candy and I'll give you a porn star blowjob."

Tina goes down on me and doesn't come up for air every few strokes like she used to. She can breathe but I can't. The continuous stimulation drives me quickly to completion. Tina swallows, looks up at me, and smiles proudly.

"See what I mean! Wasn't that splendid?"

"Yes, that was marvelous." I'm out of breath, but she isn't.

"I love my new nose!"

"Me too. I need to rest. I'll make us some drinks, we can get high."

"Where are the magazines?"

I get the magazines out of their envelopes.

"Oooooo, I like this girl. Look at this shot of her butt."

"That reminds me of something I want to show you. I uploaded the photos we took last time. Now we can view them full-size on my computer screen."

"Oooooo. I want to see them!"

I bring up the photos and Tina watches intently.

"Oh, that's right. I remember shooting these now."

Tina's voice takes on a serious and deliberate tone that I rarely hear from her.

"Be careful with these photos... I'm going to be President some day."

"I've promised you that I will keep them private, and I assure you that I will keep that promise." Tina looks at me with trusting eyes.

"I must absolutely love you to let you take photos like these of me."

Tina gives me a long look in the eye.

"Not even my long-time boyfriends were allowed to photograph me nude. I wouldn't let them, and believe me, every boyfriend I've ever had asked me several times to take naked pictures of me. I just didn't trust them. I didn't believe that I could count on them. They were all total jerks when we broke up."

"I think you were smart."

"I trust you John. I trust you more than you realize."

"I will always do everything I can to be worthy of your trust Tina."

"I want copies of these photographs of my butt."

"I'll burn you a CD."

"Great. I don't trust email."

"I want to fuck you. Is that OK?"

"Sure, how do you want me?"

"Get on your back."

246

I barely get into position on the bed before John has his big dick inside me and is pounding me. I just lie there and enjoy how much he wants me. I start to come and don't even notice how sore I am. John gets rough, but I know he won't hurt me, so I submit to his aggression. I have a big orgasm and I can feel that John has come again.

I mount Tina and work hard to squeeze out one more load. I get uncharacteristically vigorous, but Tina accommodates me, and I finish when she climaxes. She's the best lover I've ever had.

"I'm going to shower and get dressed now."

I put the envelope under Tina's purse and see her street clothes tossed all over the couch. I pick up Tina's top and pants and lay them out on the couch for her. I find her hooker heels and set them on the floor in front of her clothes. Tina strolls out the bathroom naked, drying her hair in a towel.

"Where are my clothes? They're not in the bathroom."

I reach down and pull Tina's panties out from behind the couch.

"Oh, that's right. I undressed out here."

Tina looks up and catches me sniffing the crotch of her underwear.

"I see that you found my clothes."

Tina looks at me accusingly and inquires suspiciously.

"You want to keep my underwear don't you?"

I don't answer. I tightly clutch the precious, pussy-perfumed panties to my chest and sniff them again.

"You DO want to keep them. I KNOW you do."

I stare at Tina in silence.

"I can tell that you do. You lecherous lout!"

"Will you wipe them on your pussy before you leave?

That way they'll smell like you. Then later, when I take them out of their sealed plastic bag to jack off to your photos, your scent will help to bring back the memories of our time together."

"That's so sweet. Give them to me and I'll shove them into my twat. That will make them stink like my pussy for you."

Tina shoves the crotch of the panties into her vagina and wiggles them around. She pulls them out and sniffs the crotch like an inspector.

"Ooooo they stink. Here, smell my pussy on them."

Tina shoves the wet panties into my face. I lean into her and the smell of them makes my heart race. I take them reverently from her and lay them out carefully on the table.

"I thought you put them in a plastic bag to seal in the scent?"

"Yes I do, but they need to dry out a little first, or they might get a little too ripe in the bag before I can unpack them."

"Too ripe?"

"Yes, last summer I lost a pair that way, so now I'm more attentive to their moisture content when handling them."

"I'm going get dressed, put on my lip gloss, and leave you to play with your souvenir. Think about me when you're jacking off."

"Don't get dressed yet."

"Why not?"

"I want you to put on your lip gloss at the mirror while you're still naked."

"Why? What are you up to?"

"Just trust me on this one."

"OK, I do trust you, so don't suddenly get weird on me."

While Tina digs her lip-gloss out of her purse, I grab the cash out of the envelope. I move to the mirror and stand right behind her. I rub Tina's pussy with one hand and stuff the cash into her purse with the other. I whisper into her ear, "Daddy loves his little girl."

"Oh Daddy, that feels so good, don't stop."

I bend Tina over and penetrate her in one move. She's wet and I slide right in. Tina climaxes. I climax and release her.

"Ooooo, that was sexy. We've never done that before."

"You asked me to."

"I did?"

"Don't you remember when I told you that I do that to our little flasher? You asked me to do it to you."

"That sounds like something I'd ask for. That reminds me, be sure to set up a sex date with our horny little harlot."

"I'll let you know as soon as I hear from her."

"Yes, text me the minute you get a confirmed date, time, and location. I can be flexible. I'll find a way to work it into my schedule. Now I have to take another ho-bath."

"Another what?"

"When an escort splashes in the tub to wash her pussy after sex, that's called a ho-bath."

"I've never heard of that one."

"I was texting my new girlfriend recently and I wanted some trashy expression to call her. I looked up a street slang dictionary for 'ho' and found the word ho-bath. It described exactly what I do between rounds of sex with you. I draw a short bath and splash around like

249

a little bird. You don't want to shower because that would get your hair wet and you need more than a wet washcloth after sex, so you take a ho-bath like this."

Tina completes her ho-bath, dries off and dresses in front of me. She gives me a hard kiss on the lips, grabs her things, and marches out the door in the right direction. Even after six months, she's still an experienced professional. She's definitely not showing any signs of newbie behavior any more.

Chapter 17

A Raging Lezbo

I knock fast and hard on John's door. Where is he? Hurry up and open the damn door already. I'm out of breath from running to get up here. I'm horny and sexcited to see Little Lisa again. I ask myself silently, "Will it be as good as it was the first time? Does she like me? Do I give good head?" I can't wait to get inside the room and get this date started.

That's not Tina's knock! That sounds like a jackhammer against the door. I peep out the viewer and see only Tina. I wonder if there is someone else out there with her who is knocking like a fucking lumberjack at my door. I throw the door open to confront the asshole. Tina bursts in like a SWAT team and systematically searches the entire room while firing questions at me.

"Is she here yet? Is she coming? Did you hear from her? Is she on her way over? When is she going to be here?"

Once Tina is convinced that Little Lisa is nowhere in the room or the bathroom, she turns to me and explains.

"Sorry I'm late. I couldn't find this hotel. I've never exited the freeway in Riverside before. Is she coming?"

"Lisa called me fifteen minutes ago. She said she was halfway here and was stopping for gas. She said she'd be here in thirty minutes."

"Good, she's on her way over and she'll be here soon. Make me a drink, a strong one. Let's get high while we wait for her."

I pour Tina a strong drink and we get high together.

"Good God! What is taking her so long to get here? I'm so horny I'm going to have to jill off if she doesn't get here soon." I look toward John; I'm expecting him to fix this problem. Why is he just sitting there? Why doesn't he DO something?

My mind races with a twisted pleasure. I am fascinated to see this incredibly cute girl confronted with the same agony that most men know. The frustration of wanting to play with a hot kitten like her, but finding that they're always just out of reach, always on the other side of the glass. Now it's Tina's turn to wait for the knock at the door. I can't help but smile as I observe Tina's anxiety.

"John!"

"What?"

"Check your phone and see if she's texted you."

"Sorry, but the only message I have is the one you sent earlier tonight."

> **From: Tina**
> **Msg: I'm so sexcited 2C**
> **LL again. U have made**
> **me into a Raging Lezbo!**

"Well, I'm going to get undressed now, to save time when our little exhibitionist finally gets here. As I recall,

252

Little Lisa can shed her clothes in a hurry. You can tell she's been a professional stripper."

Tina barely gets into the bathroom and she's back out naked looking around the room in case Lisa arrived. That's the fastest I've ever seen Tina get undressed.

"I'm too horny to wait. Do you want to fuck me? How about if I suck your cock."

Tina blows me harder than usual. She is in such a highly charged sexual state that I come before she even gets started.

I blow-catch John, swallow and chug my drink to wash his sperm down. "Fix me another drink. You're going to have to fuck me now, because I can't wait any longer for our little slut to show up."

"I'm sure that I'm not as good at it as Little Lisa, but I'll lick your pussy if you want me to."

"You're both good at it. Just get busy and give it to me."

I lick Tina's pussy until she comes hard and pushes my head away from her crotch. Tina gives me a strange look.

"Kiss me pussy-face. It seems as though that's as close as I'm going to get to a pussy tonight."

I get on top of Tina in the missionary position and make slow, passionate love to her. She lies there quietly embracing me until I finish. Tina starts asking me questions the moment she feels me come inside her.

"Where do you think she is? What do you think happened to her? Why didn't she come? How did she sound when you talked to her? How long ago was that?"

"I talked to her about an hour ago and she sounded fine when we spoke. I can't imagine what might have happened. I hope she's all right. I wouldn't worry though, this is the kind of thing that happens with Little Lisa."

"Do you think she no-showed because she doesn't like me?"

"No, I'm certain that's not it."

"How can you be so sure?"

"Because Lisa asks me about you every time I see her. She asks how you are doing and if you want to get together with her again."

"She does?"

"Yes, she asks every time. It's the first thing she asks me."

"Can you call her?"

I get my phone and dial Lisa using the speaker so that Tina can hear. There's no answer and the voice-mail box is not set up. Tina looks agitated. I try to console her. "Maybe we should just leave my phone on while we continue with our date and hope for the best."

"Dammit, I wanted to fuck her tonight. I've been horny and looking forward to tonight since you told me this was set up. Why the fuck is it so hard to set up a threesome?"

I look for a way to improve the mood. I pour Tina a drink and give it to her along with a present. "Here's the CD you wanted." Tina frowns at me.

"What CD?"

"You wanted copies of the photos of your butt."

"Oh, that's right. I do."

"So, I burned you a CD with all of the photos we have taken so far."

"Great. Let's look at them on your computer. I want to study the way my butt looks. God, I hope I don't have any cellulite. I'm going straight to the gym if I have so much as one fucking dimple on my ass."

I nervously load Tina's photos onto the viewer and hope she doesn't run off to the gym screaming about some insignificant imperfection in her hot little butt.

Oh shit, did I say that out loud? Now John will be scrutinizing my rear end looking for cellulite! I shouldn't have said anything.

Tina gets quiet and fidgets until the photos load. She quickly studies her photos, concentrating on the shots of her beautiful behind.

"OK. My butt photographed fine, but I see that I need to be more toned in my gluteus maximus. I'm going to increase my squats and lunges in my daily workouts. I want the bottom of my butt to be better sculpted than that."

Holly shit! Now I realize why Tina is such a hotty. She focuses on her appearance like nothing I've ever seen. I guess that's what it takes to be a bikini model. I'm so lucky to know her. "Your butt is so cute that I want to make love to it."

"Lisa said she likes anal, do you know any other girls that like anal?"

"Sure. Lot's of girls like anal sex. Some girls say they come harder from anal sex than from vaginal sex."

"No way, that's bullshit. It hurts too much to butt fuck. It can't be better than regular sex."

"I might have told you about a slim-built girl named Fiona."

"That name doesn't sound familiar to me. What about her?"

"This girl loved anal sex. I asked her if she was open for anal. She answered me, 'Sure you can fuck my ass, that will make me come even harder.' She told me some other interesting things too."

"I remember you telling me that. I didn't believe you at the time, but I believe you now. Give me details. What did she say to you?"

255

"I'll tell you exactly what she said to me:

I wanted to have my own unique talent, you know, a differentiating characteristic or ability as a porn star. I wanted to have a trick to set me apart from all the other girls so I learned how to stretch my holes. I can do fisting in both my pussy and in my butt. A few months ago I went to LA and I shot an entire porn movie in just one weekend. You can play in the back door if you want to, it's OK.

She was a lot of fun."
"Did she really say that?"
"Say what?"
"That she stretched her holes."
"Yes she did, and then she demonstrated it for me. She was incredible in bed. She was so lithe and flexible that I could bend her like a blow-up doll. She loved to be butt fucked."
"I'm not sure if I'm going to like anal sex, but I want to keep trying so that I can say that I did it. Then I will know if I like it or not."
"I can help you with that. I know how to do it the right way, so that it won't hurt."
"I'll think about that. Right now I want to watch the porn movie. Put on the hot lesbian scene and lick my pussy while I watch it."
I do as Tina commands. She comes hard and pulls at my hair but it's too short to grip.

"I can't grab you to pull you against my pussy. Grow your hair longer for me."

I stare silently at Tina. She frowns at me.

"Get on top of me and fuck me hard. Hold me down and rough-fuck me the way I like it."

I mount the bikini model, hold her arms down over her head and pound her shamelessly. Her strong vagina clamps down on my penis and I ejaculate in response. Tina throws me off like a rag doll and bounces out of the bed. "You have strong Kegel muscles."

"I've been working out. I'm going to pee."

"Can I watch you?"

"Watch me do what?"

"Can I watch you pee?"

"Sure, I guess so. But why?"

"I have never seen a girl do it."

"Why not?"

"That's not something I can ask a girlfriend. She'll think I'm a perv."

"Have you ever asked an escort for a golden shower?"

"I've been curious, but I've never had the nerve to ask for one."

"I'll pee on you if you want."

"Thanks for the offer. I'll think about that."

"Well, I have to pee right now, so if you want to watch, then you'd better come with me."

Tina is on the toilet peeing before I arrive. She spreads her legs for me.

"Can you see OK?"

"Yes, and I think you've satisfied my curiosity sufficiently for now. Thanks."

"Fix us some drinks. I'm going to rinse off. Then we can get high and talk before we screw again."

I wash up at the sink, put on my robe, pour some drinks and light up a cigar. Tina bounces in wrapped in a towel, sits next to me and grabs her drink.

"I'm so paranoid now in the locker room at my gym. When a hot girl is in the shower, or when one gets undressed, I'm afraid that I'm going to squeal like a pervert does. You know, like you do. I didn't believe you when you first told me that it happens to you, and shit, now I'm doing it.

I'm girl-horny all the time now. I can't believe what you've done to me. I have... beaver-fever because of you. You've turned me into a total perv!"

"Are you ready to have sex again?"

"Yes."

"How do you want it?"

"I want you to get behind me, and when I tell you to, I want you to pound me hard."

I massage Tina's sphincter and apply lube. I strategically wait for her to orgasm and then fully insert my thumb into her butt. I come in Tina's pussy while I feel my penis with my thumb. I immediately remove my penis and then my thumb. It makes a pop sound and Tina gasps.

"Oh, my poor little butthole. I need to stretch it out. I'm going to rinse off."

I wash my hands, start up the porn movie, and mix us fresh drinks. We will both need to rest before we can screw again. We get high and watch the movie together as casually as long-time lovers. Tina plays with herself until she is aroused. She reaches for my penis and quickly gives me an erection.

"I want to be on top."

"You can get on top of me anytime you want to."

"I like being on top. I like the view. I can see you penetrating me. It's sexy."

Tina bounces energetically on me until she climaxes.

"I'm tired, roll me over like you do... Oh! Yes, like that. Take me Daddy."

I hold Tina's arms down and talk dirty to her. I wait until she's coming and then I reach around behind her. I ease my index finger into her butt while I fuck her pussy. I pull the one finger out. I put two fingers into her anus and shove them in two-knuckles deep. Tina makes a lot of noise. I come in her pussy. I pull out my fingers and penis at the same time.

"Oh fuck that was good!"

I roll off of Tina; she lies limp, panting like a dog on a hot day. I get up and wash my hands at the sink.

"I didn't know that stimulating my butt during sex could feel so good."

"Oh, I almost forgot, will you autograph your photo in the magazine for me?"

"Sure, of course I will. Do you have a copy?"

"I have four copies."

"No you don't."

I don't say anything; I just pull four copies out of my bag. All of them are still in their original wrappers. Tina's eyes get big and she gives me a long look.

"I'm not sure if I'm flattered by you, or if I'm freaked out by you."

"There isn't much difference. Do you want any of these for your friends?"

"If you have an extra one then I'll send it to my little sister. She asked me for one."

"Here, take two copies, in case there is someone else you know who wants one."

"Thanks. What do you want me to write?"

"Anything you want."

"Aren't you afraid your wife will see it."

"I don't care about the consequences. I just want an authentic autograph from an adult magazine model."

"You're cute. I know what to do."

Tina writes a flattering note on her photo, starts to sign below it, and stops abruptly. She hesitates and then quickly scribbles out the remainder of her signature.

"Here you go. I hope you like it."

"Oh my God! I love it. 'Thanks for all the hot times!' You are wonderful. I will brag shamelessly for the rest of my life, even if I never show this to anyone."

"I'm glad you like it."

I study Tina's signature. What name did she start to sign? It certainly isn't Chris Morgan. I conclude that she started to sign her real name. I recognize it from the caller ID that she forgot to block the one time that her mobile phone was discharged and she called me from the phone in her apartment.

I have never told her that I know her real name, or the address of her apartment. I kept her phone number, but I would never call it. That's her private space and I would never violate it. I not only love this girl, I have deep respect and admiration for her. Even though we only have an escort-client relationship, I feel the need to protect her any way that I can.

John is looking at my autograph for too long. Does he see that I started to sign my real name?

"Thank you so much. I will treasure this, always."

"It's not that big of a deal."

"Are you kidding? It's that big of a deal to me. Can I fuck you while I look at your autographed photo?"

"OK, you lascivious miscreant, but I'm only going to fornicate with you again to see if you can legitimately go

260

six times in one night. I didn't believe you before. Tonight I have been counting."

"I'll be gentle."

"I'm pretty sore so if you want to fuck my pussy and it hurts too much, then I'll finish you by hand and you can come on my boobs."

"OK, hand-jobber."

"Bring your cock over here and I'll suck it out of you."

"OK, cocksucker."

"I've warned you not to say anything humorous when I'm trying to give you a blowjob. If I bite you because I'm laughing, then it's your own fault."

Tina blows me like a porn star and I don't make any more jokes. I get close, but I don't finish. "Can I fuck your pussy?"

"If you can come quickly."

"Bend over."

"Ouch, I'm too sore." I get on my knees in front of John and give him a hard hand-job. He grunts but he doesn't come. I give him some head and John makes loud weird noises. I spit on my hand and hand-job him as hard as I can. John grabs my head, and semen squirts all over my neck and breasts. John is trembling. He sits on the bed and falls backward.

"Tell the mortician..."

"You came in me six times!" You DO realize how crazy that is, don't you?"

"Actually, I came IN you only five times, the sixth time I came ON you."

"How is that possible? No man can do that. Are you some kind of mutant sex monster?"

"It's only because you turn me on so much."

"What do girls say to you when you fuck them this much?"

"One time, on the same day, both my boss and an

escort called me 'Superman.' I thought that was a particularly strange coincidence."

"Yes, I'd say that was scary-strange. So how do girls react to your sex drive?"

"Most girls seem surprised when I want to go again, after the second time. Even our little nympho Lisa did at first."

"You must be some kind of freak of nature or something."

"It can't be all that uncommon. Can it?"

"I've never even heard of a story about a man that can fuck like you do."

"I'm sure there must be lots of guys that are multiorgasmic. My sister told me that she knew of at least one guy who was multiorgasmic."

"When I get home I'm going to search the Internet for the existence of sex-crazy men like you."

"Sounds like we're done having sex for today."

"I'm done for the week! I'm going to take a shower and get dressed now, Superman."

I prepare Tina's envelope and put it under her purse on the little table next to her two copies of the magazine. I get fully dressed and put on my shoes in anticipation of walking Tina to her car tonight. This is a bad part of town and I feel the need to protect Tina. It's highly unlikely that anyone who knows either of us would see us at this hour in this neck of the woods.

"I'm going to leave now."

"Do you have everything that you want to take with you?"

"Yes I do. Will you walk me to my car? I don't feel safe in this city. It's kind of late and I'm all the way out in the parking structure. Do you mind?"

"I would be honored to escort you to your vehicle this evening."

"You're the perfect date. Let me give you a proper good bye hug and kiss here, so that we don't have to do that out in the parking structure."

Tina gives me a long warm hug and a deep-French-kiss that makes my knees weak. When she finally lets me up for air, I am speechless. I open the door and Tina automatically walks down the hallway toward the elevators. I follow quickly behind her like a loyal puppy.

Chapter 18

You Just Don't Know

I double-check the room number on my phone as I approach John's door. I find myself wishing that there was a hot girl on the other side waiting for me. I like John, he's a decent enough lover, for a man, but I want to have sex with a girl so bad that it's driving me crazy. He just doesn't know, he doesn't understand how lucky he is to be a man.

I pound on the lucky fucker's door. He owes me. I'm going to make him give me girl-sex tonight. He's going to give me all the girl-sex I want. I know that won't be as much fun as fucking a real girl, but it will help.

I hope Tina found a snatch for some girl-on-girl sex. Maybe then she'd stop blaming me for bringing out her inner lesbian. She scares the shit out of me when she's angry... Oh, fuck! That's Tina's pissed-off knock at the door. Oh shit! What do I do? Should I answer it or hide? Wait. Tina won't kill me. Yes, she'll be ferocious at first, but then she'll be horny as hell and she'll want to get the shit fucked out of her. I run to the door and throw it open.

"YOU LUCKY FUCK! Do you have any idea how hard it is to find a hot girl and pick her up for sex?"

Tina storms into the room ranting something about her lezbo frustration at me. I don't pay attention to the words she is saying, but I know what this means, and I get a boner in response. She's going to be one seriously hot piece of ass tonight.

"You're a MAN. You don't know how hard it is for a GIRL to pick up a girl."

Tina is genuinely upset and my reaction changes from opportunistic, to compassionate, as she laments over her situation.

"You just don't know, you don't understand, how lucky you are to be a man."

"I don't?"

"When I meet a cute girl that I want to screw, I can't hit on her, but it's OK for you!"

"You've got a point."

"You just don't know what it's like for a girl. You just don't understand how hard it is for a girl to hit on another girl. I don't know how she's going to react. She might freak out. What if my girlfriends find out that I'm a closet lezbo? What if they abandon me and won't speak to me because of it? You just don't realize how lucky you are to be a man."

"You're right. I don't know."

"What am I going to do? You've turned me into a lustful lesbian! Every cute girl that I see makes me think about how much fun it would be to have sex with her. All I think about is banging the cute girls at work and at the gym. What have you done to me?"

"Let me pour you a drink." Tina plops down in the chair at the little table and sighs heavily. I bring her a drink and she drains it in one breath. I refill it.

"I need to get high and laid. I hope you're horny tonight. I wish we had a tight teenybopper to fuck."

We drink and get high together. I try to change the conversation to a safe subject to provide Tina a distraction from her problems. "How is work going?"

"Work is great. I've got a good job at a call center for an honest company that treats their employees well."

"Are there any interesting girls working there?"

"I desperately want to have sex with several of the hotties in the phone pool, but I can't hit on my employees. There is a strict 'no fraternization' policy in my supervisor's handbook. If they weren't my subordinates, then I could be fucking those hot little pussies by now. Dammit."

"It sounds like there are some hot girls at work."

"There's this one tight little bitch at work that thinks she's a holy-roller because she's still a virgin at the age of twenty-four. She brags about it like she's better than the other girls. Everyone just smirks and laughs at her behind her back."

"I heard from a psychologist that specializes in teens, that adolescent girls are having anal sex because they can't get pregnant and they'll still be a virgin. Well, they're still a pussy-virgin, but not a butt-virgin."

"I bet this little tramp is a butt-slut, yet she prances around like she is holier than thou."

"I have a story for you about a girl that thought she was 'holier than thou.' Do you want to hear it?"

"Yes, I love your dirty stories, tell me."

"My buddy TJ scoffed at a titty-bar waitress for rejecting him and then he declared, 'She thinks that she's holier than thou.'"

"I chuckled at TJ's reaction and I explained, louder

than necessary, 'I got news for you pal, she legitimately IS holier than thou.' I paused for effect while TJ glared at me with a betrayed expression. Then I added, 'She is holier than thou by exactly ONE HOLE.' The entire bar erupted in laughter."

"That sounds like a bunch of guys at a strip club."

"Can I lick your pussy?"

"I'm going to shave and take a quick shower first."

Tina stands up. I raise my index finger to ask a question. Tina snaps at me.

"No! You can't have me like this. I'm way too hairy and smelly right now, even for a dirty-old-man like you. This is NOT negotiable. Got it?"

Tina steps toward the bathroom and shakes her head mumbling.

"That man is a twisted, debaucherous deviant."

Tina stops in her tracks, turns over her shoulder and commands me.

"Put on the porn movie and find us a hot lesbian scene."

Tina closes the bathroom door. I mutter, "Talk about 'the pot calling the kettle black,' or in this case, the lezbo calling the pervert twisted."

I set up the requested video and smoke a cigar out on the balcony. I brush my teeth and climb into bed. A few minutes later, Tina joins me in bed and watches the movie while I clean her bare floor. I get the mandatory big orgasm out of the way and go to mount her. Tina rolls onto her side toward the movie.

"Do me this way so I can watch these two cute girls going at it."

I put Tina in the scissors position. She watches the porn movie as I pound her pussy shamelessly to completion.

"I'm going to rinse off. Pour me a drink."

Tina returns from the bathroom naked, wiping her crotch with a towel. The sight turns me on and Tina can tell.

"Sorry that I didn't bring any sexy panties or outfits for you today."

"I like you just the way you are. You look great just like that. You're the perfect girlfriend."

"Speaking of girlfriends, nothing is the same now that you've turned me into a salacious squirrel monger."

"What do you mean?"

"Since I can't screw the girls at work, I've started looking at my girlfriends that way."

I can see that I'll have to look up the meaning of 'salacious' later. It sounds dirty. Wow, Tina's vocabulary is on steroids. What kind of girl knows words like that? Wait, what were we talking about?

"Some of my girlfriends are so hot that I have to stop myself from touching them when we're together."

Oh, that's right, we're talking about her hot girlfriends. I'm getting a boner just thinking about it.

"Sometimes we try on clothes together in the same dressing room, if it's one of those big ones. It's fucking torture."

"Do you have any prospects? I understand that it's risky to proposition your girlfriends."

"My hot friend Stacie lost her job, so we've been hanging out together lately. We're best friends, so it's OK for me to buy her lunch and to buy her stuff when she's between jobs. She's been curious about how I can have so much cash and free time during the day. She keeps asking me leading questions. I can't tell her the truth, so I just act vague, like I don't want to talk about it. I can tell that she is suspicious and wants to know more-."

269

A short, strange sound emanates from Tina's purse.

"Was that my phone? Why is it on? I always turn it off in the car, before I come up to the room."

"Why?"

"Because that's just good call girl etiquette, of course. And besides, I don't want to get distracted, or out of character, by getting a call from a girlfriend, or worse yet, from a family member. This is my time away from my real life and I don't want anything to drag me back there before I have to go. It's just a text message. I can check it later."

"You can check it now, if you want to."

"I should turn off the ringer anyway. I'm sorry that I left it on.   I was double-checking the room number before I knocked. I wouldn't want to knock on the wrong door. How embarrassing would THAT be? I would probably bump into some man I know who is seeing his call girl. Can you imagine that? Oh look, it's a message from Stacie!"

From:Stacie
Msg: Thx 4 taking me
shopping 2day and 4
lunch. It was so fun.
We need 2 find new
boyfriends 2 wear
those hot outfits 4.

"The outfits were pretty expensive but that's all right. Stacie is my best friend and she needed to be cheered up. Besides, I wanted to get a new outfit anyway. This weekend I'm seeing my other regular, and he likes to jack off while I parade around in a sexy new outfit. We've never had sex. I've barely even touched him."

My expression must reveal my jealousy, because Tina gives me a sidelong glance and quickly changes the subject

270

back to her girlfriend.

"Anyway, Stacie got pretty hot shopping for sexy lingerie. I was thinking that this is a good way to get into her pants, but then she starts talking about how we both need to find new boyfriends to wear the outfits for. She gave me a long look and then she asked me rather suspiciously, 'Do you need a new boyfriend?' I said, 'Well, I'm not looking for one right now', but I was thinking, 'I already have a client to wear it for.' I can't tell Stacie that. She couldn't handle that yet.

She's so hot. I want to fuck her so bad. You'd like her too, she has that slender build that we both like."

Tina gives me a knowing look and laughs at me.

"Don't worry, I'll share her with you."

"Let's have sex."

"Good idea. I'm horny from talking about Stacie. So, how do you want me?"

"Stand in front of the mirror for me, pretty girl."

"I love to look at myself in the mirror while I'm getting fucked."

Tina submits while I pound her pussy from behind. She is so strong that I climax the moment that she does.

"I'm going to rinse off in the shower. I'll put on some of your jack off deodorant for you."

Tina returns smelling like I remember. I get turned on and she can tell.

"Do you want to try it in my butt?"

"YES!"

"Do you have that numb-butt stuff?"

I rummage around in my bag until I find the anal anesthetic cream. I take it, and the olive oil, to the bed. Tina rolls onto her stomach on top of a pillow. She spreads her legs and presents her cute ass to me. We talk casually while I rub the cream on her anus.

271

"Why do guys want to do anal? What's so great about fucking a girl's butthole?"

"Bella had a good phrase for it. She said, 'I understand why men like anal sex with a girl. It's tight and it's nasty.' I think she said it well." I oil up my index finger and slowly insert it fully into Tina's butt.

"Is she one of the butt fuckers you told me about?"

"Yes, she's one of the girls that I've had anal with every time I've seen her." I slowly pull out my index finger, add more olive oil, and work both my index and middle finger into her tight little shithole. She must be numb to let me do this to her. I ease my fingers out of her. Tina turns and she looks at me with a question in her pretty eyes.

"How many girls have you had anal sex with?"

"I haven't been counting, but it's several dozen, at least."

"What do the girls say while you're doing it?"

"During anal sex most girls yell, 'Ouch!' or they caution me, 'Slow!' and sometimes they just curse at me."

"What do girls say after you're done?"

"After anal sex, most girls want to look at my dick and they'll ask, 'Is it yucky?' or, 'Does it have shit on it?' things like that."

"What does Little Lisa say?"

"Well, of course, I have a story about her."

"I love her stories, tell me."

"It was early in our butt sex relationship. I asked her if I could put it in her butt. She said, 'Yes, you can fuck my ass, but I haven't had an enema, so I don't know if I'm dirty back there. It's OK if you want to butt fuck me, but just know that if my butt's shitty, then it's on you.'"

"Did she say that? Seriously, did she say that to

272

you?"

"Do you need to ask me that?"

"Was it shitty back there?"

"Let's just say that from then on, she has always taken an enema. We start her enema the first thing after she arrives. We do that every time I see her. That's why I always pack enemas in my ho-bag."

"You will have to tell me if my butt is ever shitty. I don't do enemas, not ever. If my butt is shitty, then I'll wash up in the shower. I want to be clean for you, but I don't ever do enemas, so don't ask me to."

"I miss our little butt-fucking nymphomaniac."

"You haven't seen her in a while, have you?"

"No, I don't know what happened to Lisa. I haven't heard anything from her. No email, no text messages, she doesn't answer her phone."

"That explains why you haven't sent me any invitations to a ménage à trois. Keep trying to get in touch with her."

I go back to work on Tina with both hands. With my free hand I put my thumb into Tina's vagina and rub her clit area with my fingers. All the time I have two fingers on my other hand fully inserted into her hot little asshole.

"Oh fuck, I'm going to come. I'm going to come. I'm going to ooooooooooooh yes!"

I try to slowly ease my fingers out of Tina's butt. She gets impatient, reaches behind her and grabs my hand, pulling my fingers out of her tight anus in one swift motion.

"Oh, fuck that hurts!"

"I'm sorry. I didn't mean to hurt you."

"Oh, don't be sorry, the orgasm was great, it's just that my butt is sore. I need more practice so that I can have an intense orgasm from the anal stimulation, but not be distracted by the pain from having my butthole

273

stretched out that much, especially if I'm ever going to get your big cock in my butt. Maybe I'm just too small to take a big cock like yours in my butt."

"You've seen me butt fuck Little Lisa. You know how small she is. I'll show you some other girls."

John shows me photos of several slim-built girls that he's had anal sex with.

"Look at these skinny girls I've done anal with. There's Gina, these are the Twins, this is Fiona, and she's Bella."

Many of the girls are much smaller than I am. I can't help but silently wonder, "How come I can't have anal sex? What's wrong with me?"

"Every one of these hot, slender girls, all in their early twenties, was able to take my XL sized penis fully into their anus, and take a pounding."

"OK, you've inspired me. I'll keep practicing."

"Can we fuck doggy-style?"

"Do you want me like this?"

I get behind Tina and pump her hard. I can still reach the numb-butt cream and olive oil. I rub some cream on Tina's sphincter then lube up my thumb with the olive oil. I ease my cock most of the way out of her vagina and insert my thumb smoothly into her asshole in one motion. I thrust my cock fully into her pussy and feel it against my thumb. Tina comes hard and that makes me climax. She pulls away from me and yelps. My thumb makes a popping sound as it snaps out of her butthole.

"Wash your hands in the sink. I'm going to take a shower and then we can talk some more."

After washing up, I make some drinks. Tina joins me on the couch. We get high and watch porn together. Without saying a word we start making out. We move to the bed. I get on top of her, put it in and pump her.

Except for dirty talk, we don't speak a word to each other until we have both come and rested a few minutes. Tina breaks the silence.

"I'm going to take a shower and get dressed."

I place the envelope under Tina's purse as she emerges from the bathroom. She is fully clothed and drying her long blond hair in a towel. She is deep in thought.

Does John still like the way I look? Why does he have so many photos of those other girls, and he hasn't shot me in so long? I'm going to ask him.

I wait for Tina to formulate her question.

"How come you haven't asked to shoot any photos of me recently?"

"I'd love to take more photos of you. I'll be sure to bring the camera next time."

"OK, I'm going now."

Tina grabs her purse and her envelope.

"Thanks for this."

"Thank you for seeing me. When can we get together again?" Tina pauses a moment to think and then explains.

"I won't be available for a couple of weeks, because I am going back home to Minnesota on vacation. I'm going there for a birthday party. My little sister is turning eighteen next month. She's cute, thin as a rail, and she's always well toned. She is shorter than I am, but she has a much thinner build than I have and she has perky little boobs. She has the kind of body that you like. She wants to be a topless dancer. I am trying to talk her OUT of that and INTO going to college instead. She knows that I was stripping. I told her the last time I was there."

Tina pauses and examines me silently. I want to ask if her sister ever visits Orange County. I want to ask if I could see her in Minnesota when I travel out there. Tina reads me like a book. She frowns at me and her eyes fill with rage.

"Wait. Oh, I know that look, I know what you are thinking, and the answer is NO! Oh you pervert. NO! You cannot see my little sister. Oh, you are a scurrilous scoundrel."

Tina is still calling me names as she exits the door in the right direction. Holy fucking shit! Tina has a hot little sister turning eighteen. Oh my God, what a sight to imagine. I'm going to have to jack off to the thought.

Chapter 19

You Can't Have Too Many Hang-ups

I knock on the door of room 617 wondering to myself, "Why don't more girls have a sugar daddy?"

Why would a girl struggle financially and sexually with young guys when she can easily satisfy both needs with one nice, generous older man? Why doesn't my little sister just get a nice sugar daddy like John? She wastes her time and her pussy on punk assholes and she has nothing to show for it.

I'm looking forward to the uninhibited, open-minded, no-hang-ups sex I enjoy with John. He's got a wicked sense of adventure, which makes him exciting, yet he respects my limits, and because of that, I trust him.

There's Tina's normal knock at the door. Oh my God, I am relieved to hear her normal knock again. I am instantly thrilled that she isn't enraged this time. I'd better look out the peephole just to make sure that it's Tina. I peep and see Tina's pretty smile enticing me. I pull the door open and reach out my arms.

"Hi sweetie, how are you?"

"I'm so happy that you're here. It's so nice to see you

again." Tina gives me a tight embrace and rubs her hard body against me as she kisses me on the lips. I grab her and deep-French-kiss her. She melts in my arms. Tonight is going to be great.

John seems to sense how horny I am and how badly I want to be ravaged.

"I want to have you right now."

"If you want me, then take me."

I grab Tina's arm and lead her to the dresser. I tell her to set her purse down and turn toward the mirror. I stand behind her, looking at her in the mirror. I pull her top off over her head and undo her bra in back. While Tina slides her bra off of her arms, I unfasten her pants and pull them down.

Tina is freshly shaved. I bend her over and she spreads her legs as much as she can with her pants around her ankles. I get down on my knees and spread Tina's cheeks. I stick my tongue as far into her vagina as I can reach. Tina giggles and sticks her butt into my face.

I stand up, spit on my rock hard dick and shove it forcefully into her. Tina gasps and holds onto the dresser as I pound her as hard as I can. Tina makes a lot of noise and I come deep inside her.

"I'm going to waddle into the bathroom and rinse off. Pour me a drink."

Tina returns from the bathroom wrapped in a towel. She plops down on the couch next to me. I hand her a drink.

"Thanks, I need this."

"I hope you don't mind that I attacked you the second you got here. I know you like to visit a few minutes and have a drink first. I promise to lick your pussy to make it up to you."

"As long as you promise to girl-fuck me, then I'll admit that I liked getting taken the moment I arrived. It was sexy and passionate. That was a good fuck."

Tina drains her drink and gives me a serious look. She climbs into bed and arranges the pillows for her head.

"It's time to fulfill your promise. Come here and be my carpet-cleaner."

"OK, but just for the record, it's more like polishing your bare floor."

"Stop talking and get busy... yes, like that, oh that feels so good."

I stay on the job until Tina finishes and pushes me away. She gives me a wonderful compliment as she is gasping for air.

"I wish I had you in my bed at night to lick my pussy, instead of just my stupid vibrator."

"I wish I was in your bed at night too." I get on top of Tina and insert my penis into her vagina. Within a few strokes Tina climaxes, causing me to blow my load inside her.

"I'm going to rinse off. I'll be right back."

Tina is yelling something at me from the bathroom. The door is open, but I can't understand what she is saying. I get up and go to the doorway. Tina has one foot up on the edge of the sink and is toweling off her crotch. The sight is stunning. She doesn't see that I'm right there and yells as she looks up.

"John! Where is my stick of deodorant? Oh, you're here. Good. I want to use the sexy deodorant. I like the way it smells and I love the way you fuck me when I wear it."

Tina is so beautiful and erotic that I can't breathe.

"John!"

"What?"

279

"The sexy deodorant?" John doesn't hear me. He's just staring at my pussy, with his mouth open.

"Yes, it sure is."

I take my foot off the counter so that John can concentrate. "No, you don't understand. Where is it?"

"Where is what?"

"My fucking deodorant you horn-dog."

"Oh, that. I'm sorry; it must still be in my equipment bag. I haven't finished unpacking."

"Well, get it for me so that I can smell sexy for you."

"Right away." I turn and walk over to my bag. Tina follows close behind me, drying her hair with the towel.

"I know it will make you fuck the shit out of me."

Tina watches over my shoulder as I rummage through my ho-bag furiously.

"How much shit do you pack in your lust-luggage when you go to see an escort?"

"I'm not certain, let's see what we have in here. I've got: extra-virgin olive oil; water-based glycerin lube, both packed in sealed plastic bags because the bottles always leak; petroleum jelly; butt numbing cream; saline-based enemas; at least one twelve-count box of XL sized condoms; exam gloves, for fisting; adult magazines, barely-legal-aged girls only; adult DVDs, teenage girls getting anal; notebook computer, for use as a DVD player, for checking escort websites, searching escort reviews and viewing escort photo slide shows; camera; tripod; the same soap, shampoo, tooth paste, and deodorant that I use at home; my toothbrush; several extra brand-new individually wrapped toothbrushes; a ladies razor for the girl to use if she wishes; the ladies deodorant I use for sex; a diet cola when I see you; some bottled water; boner-pills; a deck of playing cards; cigars; lighter; liquor; mixers; and sour candy."

Tina's eyes get wide; she tilts her pretty head and questions me in disbelief.

"You don't bring all of that stuff to every meeting do you?"

"Yes, I always bring this bag."

"Why?"

"Because although I might need only a few of these items at any given meeting, I always bring all of them anyway. I want to be certain that I don't miss out on any opportunity to 'get freaky,' as Little Lisa would say, just because I didn't have one of these items with me?"

Tina gives me a dubious look. I naively ask, "Why, what do you pack?"

"Well, besides my wallet, I make sure that I have my lip gloss, a hair tie, and if I'm seeing anyone other than you, I bring a couple of condoms. When I see you I don't bring condoms, but now I know to bring an extra pair of underwear."

"I appreciate that."

"What's the deck of cards for? Do you play solitaire to pass the time while waiting for the girl to show up?"

"No, the cards are in there in case I get some hot bisexual girls together and we want to play strip poker as a way to get things started."

"Hot bisexual girls?"

Tina's bushy blond eyebrows involuntarily rise in obvious interest.

"Make sure that you invite me to play too."

"Please rest assured that I automatically send you an invitation every time I see another girl. That's those suggestive text messages referring to threesomes that you occasionally get from me."

281

"About the glove... whom did you meet that liked to be fisted?"

"In addition to Fiona that likes to be fisted, I met a squirter-girl in San Diego. She liked to have her pussy stretched out. She put an exam glove on my hand and told me to put my whole hand inside her. It didn't fit all the way in, because I have pretty big hands, and she was a slim girl, but she climaxed and squirted all over the bed.

"Did that really happen?"

"Yes, why? Is that story hard to believe?"

"I'm going to put on the deodorant and then you're going to fuck me. Got it?"

I can't speak. Tina applies the deodorant to her underarms right in front of me. The intimacy is mesmerizing. The moment the scent hits my olfactory organ, my reproductory organ gets erect.

John is excited before I even finish putting on the deodorant. He's like Pavlov's dog, I swear.

Tina gets down on her knees and sucks me a few strokes. She can tell that I'm close to orgasm. She smiles up at me and then climbs on to the edge of the bed doggy-style. I move in behind her and slide right in. I grab her hip bones and pound her to completion. Tina emphatically informs every person within earshot that she has climaxed approvingly.

John is so well trained. I've never had a lover that I could command to do anything I want before. I can't believe he pays me for this. I'm going to keep him, even if I get a regular boyfriend.

Tina nymph-limps into the bathroom and I collapse onto the bed. She is the most wonderful lover on earth. I'm going to do everything I can to keep this relationship going for as long as I can. How did I get so lucky?

I pour two drinks and set them on the table in front of the sofa. Tina strolls in, loosely wearing a towel, and sits down next to me. She seems to be thinking about something. I quietly sip my drink and wait for Tina to formulate her thoughts. Tina reaches for her drink but stops and looks at me like she has something to say. The look in her eye generates unbearable anticipation in me.

"My gorgeous girlfriend Stacie got laid-off from her job a few weeks ago. She and I were talking about it the other day. We were joking about how she needs a sugar daddy, as we were putting it. We were drinking wine and talking all kinds of girl shit. She said she heard that some girls our age have a sugar daddy that pays all their bills. Stacie gave me a long drunken look in the eye and asked me real serious-like, 'Do you know what I mean?'"

"What did you say?"

"I casually told Stacie, 'Well... you know... if you want to make any serious money doing that, then you can't... well, you can't have too many hang-ups.'"

"What did she say?"

"Stacie looked me straight in the eye and replied, 'I'm sure that I don't have any more hang-ups than you do.' I was shocked."

"What did you do?"

"I just giggled at her and calmly replied, 'Well then, I will let you know if I hear of any sugar daddies.'"

"What did she do?"

"I'm not sure if she is even serious, and I'm not going to reveal that I've been escorting to her. Even though we're best friends, I don't think she's mature enough to handle it. She can be a little squirrelly sometimes."

"Is she hot?"

"She's super-thin and toned. She's a gym rat, she works out five or more times a week. She's got long honey-blond hair and a dark tan. She's totally hot. I

283

want to fuck her so bad. I want to get into her pants as a birthday present to myself."

"She sounds great. I'm in. I want to do her. Let me know how I can help. Try to set it up."

"OK, I'll do my best."

"Do you have any photos of her?"

"No I don't, but I can try to get some. You know, regular clothed shots, not nudes. Don't worry, you'll love her."

"That's good enough for me. I brought my camera with me this time. Can I take some photos of you while we fuck?"

"Sure, how do you want to set up? Do you want to be in them?"

"Maybe just some of my body parts."

"You don't want any incriminating evidence?"

"I don't want to ruin hot photos of you by exposing my ugly ass in them."

"I think you look fine."

"You're so kind. Can we do a facial?"

"Sure, that sounds like fun."

I grab the camera; Tina kneels down in front of me and starts sucking my dick. I'm so distracted that I can barely work the damn buttons on the stupid camera. I get set up and start snapping action shots of Tina at work. She is gorgeous.

This shoot has turned into a real blowjob instead of the normal blow-catch. John is lasting a long time. We can't get a facial shot if he doesn't come. Maybe I should shove my finger... .

"Get on your hands and knees." I set down the camera and fuck Tina doggy-style on the floor until I'm close to orgasm. I quickly stand up, grab the camera and tell her to suck the cum out of me. Tina gives me a few hard suck-strokes and I frame up the shot. My grunts must inform Tina of the imminent ejaculation, because she grabs my penis and strikes the perfect porn star pose. I blow my load onto her cheek and snap a couple of photos while Tina holds her pose. "That was great! You are a highly polished professional."

"Excuse me while I go wash off the money shot."

As soon as Tina returns, I steer the conversation to a topic I want to be certain to cover today. "How was your visit to Minnesota?"

"It was fun, I had a great time."

"How's your sister? Is she going to visit you out here any time soon?"

"NO! You are NOT going to see my sister. Got it? I am not going to be responsible for corrupting her."

"Gee, I've never even touched her and you've already got a sister-blister."

"I've got a what?"

"A sister-blister."

"What the fuck is that?"

"A sister-blister is the soreness that develops from having sex with a woman's sister."

"You sound like you have first-hand experience with the subject."

"What makes you think..."

"You do! I know you do. Tell me."

"I don't want to talk about it."

"You debaucherous degenerate. My sister is barely eighteen!"

"That's OK, I like schoolgirls. So do you."

"I'm only twenty-four years old! You are a dirty old man."

"But I need two girls to fuck me at the same time so

that they don't get sore before I'm done."

"You're a libidinous louse. That reminds me of something I want to tell you about. I did some research on the internet and you won't believe what I found."

"What were you looking for?"

"I was looking for you."

"Me?"

"No, not you, sex-freaks like you."

"What did you find?"

"I found a fucking university research study on multiorgasmic males. You are not alone. There actually are other men like you. Some are even worse... well, or better... depending on how you want to look at it."

"Tell me. Details..."

"OK, let me get the copy I printed out. I'll read it to you. It's a research study from Rutgers University titled, Male Multiple Ejaculatory Orgasms. It was published in The Journal of Sex Education and Therapy in 1998."

"Get to the good part."

"A guy came six times in less than one hour."

"Wow! It takes me at least two hours to come six times."

"That's not all."

"What else did you discover?"

"Next I looked up high libido males and found that it is extremely rare, but it does occur. I read the results of a scientific study that found twenty-one multiorgasmic men. They had to search nationwide to find that many, so it's pretty rare. No wonder I've never heard of a guy like you before. You're lucky. Let's have sex Superman."

I certainly do feel lucky as Tina sucks my dick and jumps on top of me cowgirl style. We both come and she lies down on top of me with my penis still in her. I eventually go soft and fall out. Tina is asleep. I feel like her lover.

I lie still, with Tina sleeping on top of me. I shamelessly play with her butthole. I get an erection and put it between her thighs, against her pussy. I play with the tip of my dick against her butthole until it's rock hard. I ease it into Tina's cummy pussy and it slides fully in. I gently rock my pelvis and fuck Tina's pussy while she sleeps. I get unbearably excited and pump her harder. Tina wakes up and I come inside her. She starts laughing at me.

"Have I been sleep-fucking?"

"You were great."

"Thanks for telling me or I wouldn't have known."

"You are such a wonderful lover that you're great even when you're asleep."

"You're sweet, that's a nice thing to say. I'm going to shower and get dressed."

I prepare the envelope and place it under Tina's purse. She has been here more than four hours. I don't have nearly enough money with me to pay her for that much time. Tina has never asked for more money from me, no matter how long she stayed with me. I still worry because almost all the escorts I've ever been with have charged me for every second of their time. I hope Tina will be OK with the regular amount. I don't want her to think I'm chiseling her.

"I'm going to sleep well tonight."

Tina slowly wanders out of the bathroom drying her hair with a towel. She's sleepy. She drops the towel on the floor absentmindedly and reaches for her purse and the envelope.

"Thanks for this."

"It's only the usual amount."

"That's OK."

"It's just that you've been here over twice as long as the rate."

"That's all right, don't worry about that. I had fun."

"You're wonderful. Can I walk you to your car?"

"That's not necessary, I'm parked right out front."

"I hope to see you again soon."

"Text me and we'll work something out."

Tina smiles, I open the door and she slowly saunters the right way down the hallway. I watch her and feel like the luckiest guy on earth.

Chapter 20

A Sugar Daddy

I knock on the door laughing out loud from the joke I played on the uptight office workers downstairs. I continue laughing as I admit to myself that I never imagined I would have a sugar daddy. Then again, I do a lot of things these days that I never thought I would do.

John is a great excuse for me to use to get into Stacie's pants. I will convince John to go along with the idea of seeing my hot girlfriend, but the result will be that I finally get to have sex with her. I'll wait until the middle of our date tonight and then I'll just slip it into the conversation. That way John won't discover how much I want this. I'm so clever.

I'll tell John to book the room at this same hotel. It's a nice place and just a few blocks from where Stacie and I live. John is great, he will do anything I tell him to do. How absurd is it that I'm using my sugar daddy to get my girlfriend into bed? I bust out in laughter.

Tina's knock is fast and early tonight. I swallow my boner-pill and set down the bottle. I fly over to the door to pull it open, but I stop. What's that noise? Tina is laughing. Why is she laughing? Tina never laughs at my door. What the fuck is going on?

I yank open the door and Tina looks surprised. Her big blue eyes flash at me with devilish delight. She's clearly aroused, but I can't understand why. She charges in and turns quickly toward me. She obviously has something on her mind. "What?"

"I have to tell you about what happened with some people downstairs. Do we have a minute to talk, or do you need to throw me down and fuck me right now, like you did last time?"

"We can talk first. That will give my boner-pills some time to work. Have a seat, I'll fix you a drink. What did you do to the people downstairs?"

"I was waiting for the elevator at the lobby level, when I saw a nice display of desserts and a coffee service there. It had been set out for a group that had just concluded a conference in the adjacent meeting rooms. I acted as if I thought it was complimentary, even though that is seldom the case in a business-class hotel like this. I saw that all three elevators were located at upper floors and concluded that it was going to take a while for one to arrive.

I decided that I would pour myself a cup of coffee to entertain myself while I waited. But first, I took a tour of the entire dessert display. I didn't take anything, that stuff has way too many calories and fat. I just looked at each item, I pointed at things, and I made little comments about the selections to myself. Then I took a paper cup and poured myself some coffee. I was talking out loud to myself the entire time. Next I got myself some cream, a sugar, and a stirring stick.

There were some conservative, uptight business-like people milling around. They were looking at me disapprovingly and murmuring to each other about me.

I intentionally took my time. I smiled the whole time but never looked any of them in the eye. I fiddled with all the stuff, and kept making comments out loud like, 'Isn't that pretty?' I could tell they felt intruded upon, and taken advantage of by an outsider. It's great fun to piss-off stuffy assholes like them. I had just finished making my tour with my cup of coffee, when I noticed that several people were pointing at me and seemed to be talking about me in accusing tones. Just then I heard the elevator arrive and I knew it was about to open. I finished stirring my coffee, tossed the stir-stick onto the table, looked up and flashed a big smile at all the people staring at me. Just then, the elevator doors opened. I did a ballerina-style pirouette and made my escape. I am such a brat."

"You are my hero."

"I thought you'd be proud of me. I was thinking of you and wishing you were there to see my exploits. I wanted to tell you about it as soon as I got inside our room."

"That's a wonderful story. You deserve a reward. How can I show you my appreciation?"

"You're a smart guy. Use your head, you'll think of something."

I start undressing. Tina drops her clothes, jumps in bed and arranges her pillows. I give Tina the pussy licking she's earned.

"Kiss me pussy-face."

I Tina's her mouth and penetrate her vagina simultaneously. I come the moment she does. She throws me off and prances into the bathroom panting.

"Fix me a drink and put the porn on. I'll be right back."

I hear the shower start up and Tina singing. By the time I make our drinks and set up the porn movie, Tina appears in a towel.

"I'm sorry that I don't have any panties for your collection today. I'm going to have to buy some more because of you and your underwear hoarding fetish."

"Can you get me a pair of your hot shopping buddy's panties?"

"Are you kidding?"

"I'm sorry, I didn't mean to cross a line-"

"Don't be silly. I'd love to get a pair of her panties for you, but I can't even get a pair of her panties for me! That's why I'm trying to set up this ménage à trois, so that I can get into her pants. You're just the bait and the excuse. I have a plan though. I'll tell her that you want to keep two pair of her panties and that way we can each have a pair to keep."

"Have you talked any further with her about the threesome?"

"I talked to Stacie yesterday. She's still out of work and she wants to do a double with me. She was sober this time, so I think she means it. I would have asked her to join me tonight, but she's visiting her parents to get some money from them. She hates to do that because they ask her a lot of questions and judge her."

"Do you think she will go through with it?"

"She said she needs money bad and wants to get a sugar daddy right away."

"How much money is she expecting?"

"Well, I don't want to break the bank, but at the same time, I had to give her an amount for her to think about."

"What did you tell her?"

"I told her we would each get what works out to be just over half the amount that you have been giving me lately. I hope that's all right."

"Isn't that too little?"

"She thought is was a ton of money for just a few hours time. She's used to slave wages, not call girl rates."

"As long as you think it's enough to motivate her to go ahead with it."

"She's a complete newbie. She doesn't know anything about escorting. We can break her in the way we want her. If this works out, then I want her expected rate to be low enough that we can keep seeing her. We don't want to spoil her!"

"Is she nervous about being turned out?"

"I was expecting her to be, but she wasn't. She doesn't have any idea what escorts do. I asked her how she feels about doing this. She just said that she doesn't have a boyfriend right now and that she needs to make some money until she starts working again."

"What did you tell her about it?"

"I told her I have the situation completely under control and that she can join me on a double to see you. This way I finally get to have sex with her and she won't freak out about it."

"You have planned this carefully. I'm impressed."

"You have to say that you want us to touch each other and then have us kiss. Oh, and you must demand that we have oral sex with each other. If her new sugar daddy insists on it, then she'll do it. She'll have to, she's being paid to do it."

"I'll say anything you want me to say."

"I've been looking for a way to get into her pants and I think this will work. She can get a little squirrelly so be sure that you don't pay us at the beginning like you do me. If she asks, then tell her that we always receive our present at the end of the date and never before."

"I'll do anything you want me to do."

"I can tell that she's getting horny. She isn't getting any these days. She doesn't even want to find a new boyfriend. She broke-up with her old boyfriend over a month ago. That shithead slept with one of her best friends. Can you believe that?"

Tina frowns in deep thought for a second and then blurts a question at me.

"Why do boyfriends cheat on their girlfriends? Why do husbands cheat on their wives?"

"I know a guy that fucked the bridesmaid on his wedding day!"

"Oh my God. You're kidding. Aren't you?"

"We were pretty drunk when he told me the story and I wanted to make certain that I got it right. I asked him, 'Do I have this right? You are exchanging your wedding vows with your bride, and right behind her is the bridesmaid with your semen dripping out of her pussy.' He laughed out loud and said, 'That's a great way to put it.' The story was so beautiful that I almost cried. I shook his hand to congratulate him."

"You're terrible."

"I'm married."

"Men are assholes."

"Most men are insecure and act like assholes to compensate for their insecurities."

"Why are men insecure?"

"I think there are many reasons, but I believe that low self-esteem and poor self-image contribute heavily."

"Why do they act like assholes?"

"Most men are scared of women."

"Why?"

"Because they should be."

"No, tell me the real reason."

"Men are afraid of women because they might fall in love with them."

"Why are they afraid of that?"

"They know that if they fall in love, then they can get hurt badly."

"Did that happen to you?"

"Yes, twice."

"Do you want to talk about it?"

"No, I don't ever talk about it."

"What can I do to make you feel better?"

"You're a smart-"

"OK, you licentious lout, lie down on the bed."

Tina snickers at me at first but then sucks my penis compassionately. As soon as I'm hard she straddles me and inserts my penis into her vagina. She bounces a few times and as soon as she starts to orgasm I shoot my load. Tina keeps bouncing until she is done.

"Feel better? I'll be right back after I rinse off."

What did she call me? Tina is a walking Thesaurus for Christ's sake. I do an internet search for ly-scent-chush. Oh, it's spelled 'licentious' and it means: sexually unrestrained, inappropriate or immoral behavior. Cool! Tina is downright grandiloquent.

Tina appears from the bathroom naked, wiping her crotch with a towel. "How did you develop such a verbose vocabulary for describing grisly geezers like me?"

"One of my roommates had a dirty-old-man's word-of-the-week calendar and we would make jokes about the words and talk about the guys we knew that the word would apply to. I never thought that I would actually use any of those words to describe a man that I know, and that I like."

"Let's do it standing up. Come here." Tina knows the drill. I pound her hard and long. She is panting by the time I finally finish. I pull out and my dick is bloody. Tina must be due in the next few days. "Oh, were you a virgin? Was that your first time?" Tina's eyes flash at me, she reaches between her legs and her hand comes out bloody.

"Oh shit! You've busted my period out of me AGAIN! How do you do that?"

Tina nymph-limps to the bathroom mumbling to herself.

"I'm not supposed to start for several days, I thought I would be safe today from your... period prompting prick."

Tina returns wrapped up in a towel and sits next to me. She grabs her drink and drains it.

"My pussy is sore. How does Little Lisa fuck so many times?"

"Here is how a conversation with Little Lisa went when she returned from the bathroom after our forth or fifth fuck. She sat on the bed with a towel between her legs and casually mentioned in passing, 'I'm bleeding a little from my vagina.' So, I asked, 'Have I started your period?' She says, 'No, it's not that. If you look here you'll see I have a little tear.' I looked closely at her pussy."

"I had literally worn a hole in her pussy meat where the hairy part at the base of my cock rubbed against her pubic bone. She said to me, 'This is bad timing to get a tear in my vagina, I have a gang bang tomorrow.'"

"Although I heard all of the individual words that she voiced, I could not match what I heard with what was possible. I stuttered at her in disbelief, 'You have a gang bang tomorrow?' She just replied to me calmly, 'Yes, I do.'"

"I was in shock. I blurted, 'And just what does that involve?' Lisa gave me a look like I was asking her to explain the obvious. She grudgingly explained, 'Well, a bunch of guys come over and they all fuck me. They take turns.' I asked, 'Is your Daddy there at the time?' Lisa replied mater-of-factly, 'Yes, my Daddy is there the whole time. He holds me in his arms and he tells them when to switch off. He knows how much I can take and he paces them.'"

Tina's eyes widen with wonder as she tries to offer an explanation for Little Lisa's lifestyle.

"I suppose that's just how she... spends her Wednesdays?"

"Do you ever fantasize about a gang bang?"

"Are you kidding! I've never even fantasized about a DP!"

I can't help but smile at Tina's reaction to Lisa's story.

"Oh my God! Did she actually say all of that? She's a fucking gang-banger? She said that?"

"You've met her. She told you some of her stories. You've fucked her. You know her. I wanted you to meet her so that you would believe me when I tell her stories to you."

"Can you believe how unbridled and libertine our little super hero is?"

"Let me put it this way, when I see an escort, I usually feel like I'm a big-shot, a swinging-dick. I usually feel like I'm a playboy. However, when I'm with Little Lisa, she reduces me down to a little boy that is playing with himself as he looks through the bra and panties section of a department store catalog."

Tina stares at me with an uncharacteristically blank expression. I'm turned on from talking about Little Lisa and I'm going to assume that Tina is aroused also. "Can we have sex?"

"As long as you don't tear a hole in my pussy."

Tina sucks me back to life and as soon as I'm hard I ask, "Can we get in the shower and play the virgin game?"

"We had better do it in the shower or the maid will think you popped a virgin's cherry in the bed."

I follow Tina into the shower. I get behind her and insert while she is still fiddling with the faucets. I pound her and bloody water flows freely down the drain. Just before she comes, Tina turns over her shoulder at me and gives me a long look. We both climax. Her look reminds of something I want to ask her.

"I'm going to stay in the shower to clean up."

"There's a question that I want to ask you when you get out."

"What question?"

"My girlfriend and a couple of escorts have turned their heads around while having sex doggy-style, and offered, in a surrendering tone, 'You can do anything you want to me.' They said it like it's some kind of code-phrase and I want to know what it means when a girl says that during sex."

"Have I ever said that?"

"No, not that I can recall."

"Then why ask me? Go ask your girlfriend or one of those other girls."

"I have always wondered what a girl really means when she says that."

"Well, what happened next?"

"I put my thumb in their butts."

"What did the girls do?"

"They turned around again and yelled at me, 'I didn't mean that you could do THAT!'"

"OK, the problem is that you are an extremely literal person and therefore you interpret what the girl is saying literally."

"Huh? Then what did they mean?"

"You are thinking that the girl has given you permission to butt fuck her."

"She hasn't?"

"No, she is just submitting to you sexually and that is a way of voicing her submission."

"I've always wanted to ask a girl that."

"I'm going to finish my shower now and then get dressed."

While Tina sings in the shower, I open my briefcase to prepare her envelope. I see the printouts of the photos from our last visit. I place the photos on the table and slide her envelope under her purse. I look up to see Tina fully dressed.

"I'm going to leave now."

"Do you want to see the prints from our last shoot?"

"Yes I do, let me see."

"The facial shot came out great, look."

"I'm trusting you to be careful with these...."

"Yes, I know, you're going to be President some day."

"Oh, your semen came out great in the facial shots. I want a copy of this one, and these two, and... ."

"I'll make you a new CD with all of your photos on it."

"Put Little Lisa's pics on it too.

"Trust me, I'll put all the photos you want on the CD."

"I do trust you. Why do I trust you so much?"

"Because you instinctively know that I love you too much to ever harm you in any way."

"You're right, I do know that. Thank you for the envelope. I'm going now, bye."

I open the door, Tina steps forward and turns naturally in the right direction toward the elevators. I start to close the door behind her, but she backpedals into me gasping.

"OH, FUCK!"

Tina quietly closes the door and turns toward me. She is completely pale and clearly in shock. Her voice is shaky as she whispers at me.

"Oh fuck me! I think I saw someone I know in the hallway. Oh my fucking God, I hope he didn't see me."

Tina is trembling. Her usually confident eyes have the look of a scared little girl in them. I've never seen Tina like this; she is terrified.

"He had his back to me and he didn't turn around, but I'm sure it's him. I think I'm going to be sick."

"Sit down, I'll get you a glass of water. It's all right, you can stay here as long as you want to."

"That was a harsh reality check. How would I explain being at this hotel at this time of night?"

I try to calm Tina down. She is visibly trembling and looks like she's going to throw up. I nervously bring the little trashcan over and put it by her feet. She doesn't even notice me.

My stomach curdles with the icky thought of getting caught. I envision my entire world crashing down and everyone I know finding out that I've been escorting. I am confronted by the stark fact that I'm in a hotel taking money for sex. I stand up and try to shake the unpleasant feeling off of me the way my dog shakes off water after his bath. I must compose myself and get out of here unnoticed.

Tina stands up sharply and rummages through her bag. She pulls out a huge pair of dark sunglasses and puts them on. She fumbles to the mirror and checks her look.

"Shit, I wish I had a scarf, or a hat, or something."

I can't figure out what she's up to. "You look great."

"I look like me! That's the problem."

"I have a baseball cap in my bag if you want it."

"Let me see it."

I get the hat and hand it to Tina.

"Well shit!"

"What's wrong?"

"I'm a fan of the rival team. Well, if this all you have, then I will take it."

Tina sizes the cap and judges her appearance in the mirror.

"Damn, I still look too much like me."

Tina digs through her purse again and pulls out a hair tie. She quickly makes her hair into a ponytail and tucks it into the back of her shirt. With her glasses on, even her own mother wouldn't recognize her.

"This will have to do. I need to get out of here."

Tina cautiously steps to the peephole and looks out for a long time. She slowly opens the door a tiny crack and peeks out. After a few moments, she slinks out and tip toes down the hallway toward the elevators. I close the door slowly and think aloud, "That was weird."

Chapter 21

Too Many Hang-ups

I knock at the door fuming under my breath, "I am totally pissed off at Stacie for flaking at the last minute. I was so sure that I would get to have sex with her tonight. Dammit! Now I'll never get to fuck her."

I had John set up at this damn hotel so it would be convenient for her and now I'll probably see another person that I know. John opens the door while I'm still knocking. He can see how aggravated I am.

I arrive early to set everything up for the threesome with Tina and her hot girlfriend. Since the girlfriend is a true newbie, I want to be careful to keep her calm. Tina said they would travel together in Tina's car, so I can't scare the newbie or they will both leave. My phone makes a noise. I have a text message.

> **From: Tina**
> **Msg: Stacie flaked**
> **I M on my way now**

Ahhhh shit. No threesome tonight. Dammit, Tina's

going to be extremely disappointed over her girlfriend chickening out on her. I better do something to cheer her up. But what can I offer Tina? I know, we'll figure out a way to make Stacie feel like she missed out on something special, and I'll give Tina the money I brought for Stacie. I rearrange the envelopes and the room to accommodate the change in the cast of characters.

Tina's knock is slow and heavy tonight. I'm at the sink next to the door so I answer right away and Tina bursts in cursing like a lumberjack.

"That flaky little bitch! That fucking little twat-tease!"

Tina stomps back and forth the length of the room. I stay out of her way and quickly fix her a strong drink.

"That God-damned, uptight prissy little cunt. She goes on-and-on to me about how she wants to get a sugar daddy and then when I set it all up for her, she gets cold feet at the last second and bails out on me."

"Here's your drink."

"I exposed myself to her for nothing."

Tina casts an incensed glare around the room.

"She's probably a lousy fuck anyway."

Tina drains her drink and hands me the empty glass. "I'll refresh this for you. Maybe you would like to sit down and if you want to, you can tell me about it."

"I told Stacie last week that there's a sugar daddy that I heard about from a girl that I recently met and that she has seen him a couple of times. I said, 'He's a Professor or a Scientist and he's about forty-five years old.'"

"What did she say?"

"Stacie made a face and then questioned me, 'Is he gross? Is he like... old and fat?'"

"What did you say?"

"I told her, 'No! He's supposed to be in pretty good

304

shape, only average looking, but well groomed, clean, and he's always nice to the girls.' Earlier today I called Stacie and confirmed tonight's appointment. Stacie told me that she hasn't worked in over three months and now desperately needs the money. She said she wants to get a sugar daddy and that she wants to do this double with me tonight."

"What happened then?"

"So just now, I drove over to her place to pick her up and she wasn't ready. She was in her pajamas, no makeup, hair a mess. I asked her, 'What's going on? You said you wanted to get a sugar daddy to pay off your past due bills.'"

"What did she do?"

"Stacie sneered at me and said that she's sort of got a new boyfriend now and that she's probably going to start working again soon."

"How did you react?"

"I couldn't believe it. I wanted to kill her."

"What did you do?"

"I just dropped it and told her that I was going to go and that she could come if she wanted to. What a flaky little pussy-teasing bitch. I spent all that money on her and now she won't put out. Girls can be such bitches. I need another drink."

I make Tina another drink and show her the two gift bags sitting on the nightstand. "Let's arrange her gift bag real nice, the way a girl would like it. I want her to be totally pissed off at herself that she decided to pass on this. I want you to take her envelope for tonight and keep it for yourself."

"I can't do that."

"Please accept it from me as a friend who wants to cheer you up and also to compensate you for what you

305

spent on her."

"You don't have to do that."

"I know, but I'm super-horny from expecting two girls and now I want to screw your ears off, and this way I won't feel so bad about it."

"Well, I'm horny from the anticipation of finally nailing that tight little cunt, so I'll need to get the shit fucked out of me anyway."

"All right then it's settled. You're going to keep both envelops and we're going to hump like rabbits."

"OK, but I'm going to tell her that you paid me double, I kept my clothes on, and that I only gave you a hand-job. Then I'll say I left after fifteen minutes and went shopping. That ought to piss her off."

"I'm glad you're feeling better about it." Tina quickly removes her clothes. I do the same. "Can I lick your pussy?"

"I'm so horny that I'd pay you to lick my pussy right now."

Tina climbs onto the bed and arranges the pillows so that she can watch.

"Oh yes, like that!"

I employ all the acquired knowledge I have to effectively lick Tina's pussy.

"Ohhhhh that feels sooo good."

With her strong thighs, Tina tests the amount of lateral pressure a human skull can withstand.

I wish I could find a cute guy my age that fucks like this. I close my eyes and enjoy the sex.

I stay on the job until she has a big one and pushes my head away. Tina catches her breath and attacks me. She pushes me onto my back, climbs on top, and starts bouncing on top of me. I burn the image into my brain. I make more noise than usual when I come. Tina lies down on top of me with my still-erect penis lodged deep inside her.

We lie in silence for a long time, but I keep my erection.

"You're still hard. Are you going to fuck me some more?"

I roll Tina over and get on top of her while staying inside her. I slowly build up a good rhythm and stroke her for a long time before I finally come.

"Did you come twice? You're amazing."

"Did you bring any underwear for me tonight?"

"No, of course not. I intentionally didn't wear or bring any because I was going to make Stacie bring two extra pair for you and I to keep. She doesn't shave, so she always wears panties. The next time I'm at her apartment I'm going to steal a pair of her dirty panties and start my own collection. If she won't let me taste her cunt then I can at least smell it."

"Do you think you could steal two pair?"

"Pervert."

"Look who's talking."

"That's different, she's my girlfriend. Let's fuck."

"OK, how do you want me?"

"Get me from behind, standing up at the mirror. That way I can at least look at a girl while I fuck."

I get into position, separate Tina's buns, and insert fully into her. I grab onto her hip bones and pound her fast and deep.

"Harder! Oh YES, like that. More! More! More!"

Tina comes and her vaginal contraction makes me come.

"That was good. Make me a drink while I rinse off in the shower."

Tina returns from the bathroom naked and climbs into bed. I bring her drink to her.

"I'm actually glad that flaky-Stacie didn't come tonight. She's cute, but she's so uptight that she would have ruined our night."

"Did you ever get a photo of Stacie?"

"No. She freaked out when I asked her for a photo to show to the sugar daddy. She's just not call girl material. She's not mature enough to be an escort. She's not responsible enough. I'm not sure if she and I can still be friends any more."

Tina seems unusually vulnerable tonight. I will do everything I can to console her, yet I find this change from her normally confident demeanor is exciting.

"I want to find a hot girl that's as big a perv as I am."

"How about the girls at work?"

"I have an interview tomorrow for a job in a different department at the same company. The job pays a lot more and I would work regular office hours."

"You'll be great. If they don't hire you, then it's their loss."

John is more supportive of me than any of my past boyfriends ever were. Why is that? I look into his eyes. I wish I had a boyfriend that was this nice to me.

I look into Tina's beautiful eyes and get lost.

I can tell that John wants to blow at least one more load in me before I leave. I decide to suck it out of him and give my pussy a rest.

I want to have sex with Tina again and she can sense it. She is such a good lover that all I have to do is give her the look, and she puts out for me. I wish I had a girlfriend like her.

"Put on a good porn scene and I'll give you a blowjob."

I start up the movie and Tina starts sucking. I last a long time but she keeps going like a professional. Tina

gives me a hernia check and I come in her pretty little mouth. Tina gags a second, and then she swallows. I get her drink for her and she gulps it down.

"Let's talk, I need to rest."

"Maybe we can find an out-call escort from one of the review websites to play with."

"Sure, if you know how to find one that goes both ways."

"I'll check to see if Little Lisa is available first and if she's not, then I'll look around for an adolescent plaything for us to try out."

"See if you can find one with 'little girl teeth' for us to play with, that would be fun."

"I'm not sure if 'little girl teeth' is one of the searchable criteria."

My pussy is sore and I am secretly hoping that John is done for this session. I tentatively ask, "Are you done or are we going to 'go' again?" John looks at me the way a guy does and quickly orders me into position.

"Lie down on your back, right here in the middle of the bed."

I lie down obediently, "Sure, like this?" John hovers over me and mutters mischievously.

"Yes, I want you just like that."

As he climbs in between my legs on his knees, he looks me over the way a guy ogles a new sports car before taking it for a drive. I prop my head up on a pillow to watch the cunnilingus that I am anticipating, when I see John's raging boner is ready to charge my pussy. Suddenly he grabs me by the knees.

"Slide down this way."

John forcefully drags me toward him and my head plops off of my pillow. I am about to ask about it when he shoves my knees way up by my ears, plants my feet flat against his chest, spreads my cheeks, penetrates my pussy balls-deep, and starts pumping away.

"Fuck your Daddy little girl."

I'm not much in the mood for more sex right now, but I try to be accommodating.

Tina is clearly not engaged in this round of sex.

It seems that he can tell somehow, and that he has some sort of an idea in his eyes.

"I know what to do."

John pauses the action and looks me in the eye a moment. He disengages me and lays my legs down spread around him. Next he orders me.

"Put your arms up over your head."

I do as John asks without understanding why. John pushes my arms tight up against my head, squishing my elbows into my ears. My hands hit the headboard. I take a breath to ask him what the fuck? But he lies down on top of me, grabs both of my wrists and pins my arms down. I know he won't hurt me, so I surrender to his force. John vigorously ravages me. I notice as I submit that it is somehow appealing to me, but only as a new experience.

"Take Daddy's fuck little girl. Be Daddy's little whore. Fuck me little slut."

I don't know why I trust John so much. I trust him a lot more than any boyfriend I've ever had. I always feel safe with him and I feel that he appreciates me more than any boyfriend ever has. He holds me down and finally finishes. I roll him off of me and drag myself to the shower.

Tina is the best girlfriend on earth. This is not an escort-client relationship; this is a romance with a layer of particular constraints. Tina nymph-limps out of the bathroom fully clothed, and gives me a pained look.

"My pussy is so sore that I'm going to have to ice it

down when I get home."

"I'm sorry."

"I'm not, the sex was great, but I've got to go now."

"You're wonderful." Tina gathers her things at the little table.

"Thank you for the double-envelope. This is a huge help to me right now."

"I hope we can get together again soon."

"That might depend on whether I get the job I'm interviewing for tomorrow." I'm not going to tell John that I hope I get the job so that I don't get caught seeing him. I practically panicked when I had to walk in from the parking structure and through the lobby to get to the elevators at this hotel. This place is so close to where I live and went to college that I could run into all kinds of people I know here.

Tina is staring at the door quietly. She seems to be preoccupied with something. "Good luck, I know you'll be great."

"Thanks, I appreciate that. I'm going now. Bye."

Tina looks out the peephole and then through the partly cracked door before she steps gingerly out into the hallway. She looks both ways carefully and then scurries out of sight in the right direction.

Chapter 22

My Butt's a Pussy

I knock at the door wondering why it has been four full months since I last saw John. I know how long it's been because I just had my four-month review for my new position. I remember that I started in my current job the day after I last saw John. That was the night that Stacie flaked on us. That fucking little cunt, I haven't even TALKED to her since that time. I should make her pay me back for the outfit I bought her for that night.

Anyway, it's not like I haven't been trying to set up a time to see John, it just hasn't worked out. Sure, I'm working more hours now, so I don't need the money, and I've had a few regular dates, but seeing an unseasoned guy is not anything like being with John.

John treats me better than my dates treat me. John always contacts me afterward and wants to see me again. He would never make me wait by the phone. He tells me I'm beautiful and he means it. John's admiration gives me more confidence in my appearance when I go on regular dates.

I hope John still wants me. He's been seeing Little Lisa and she always gives him anal. I'm going to get his cock up my ass tonight... the door is opening.

That's Tina's knock. I pop a boner before I get to the door. She's always on time whenever we meet at this hotel, probably because it's located quite close to her apartment. I grab the door handle and jerk the door open to reveal Tina's mischievous smile. She looks great.

"Hi honey, I've missed you."

Tina gives me a long warm embrace and shamelessly rubs her pubic bone against my erection. I almost come in my pants. I peel her off of me and take her by the hand to the little table. She sets down a huge bottle of water and her tiny purse with a question in her eyes.

"What ever happened to Little Lisa? I know that you have seen her a couple of times since I last saw you."

"How do you know that?"

"Did you forget?"

"Forget what?"

"All those text messages you sent inviting me to threesomes with her?"

"Oh, that's right. I send them automatically so I forget. It is such a turn-on to send threesome invitations to you that I don't even care if you receive them. You get them?"

"Yes, of course I do. They make me bust out laughing in the most embarrassing places. My friends and family ask me, 'What's so funny?' and I have to say something like, 'Oh someone sent me a clever message,' and they ask, 'What is it?' and I have to say, 'Oh, it's an inside joke,' then I delete it right away."

"I'm sorry. I'll stop sending you messages."

"No! Don't stop. I love your messages; they crack me up just when I most need a laugh. They are the best part of my day sometimes. Don't you dare stop sending them."

"OK. If that's what you want." Tina confuses me sometimes. I can't figure out what she wants.

"So, what is our little gang-banger been up to? Do you have any new stories from her?"

"Our little super hero always has an interesting story."

"Wait. We were supposed to meet her that night in Riverside, right?"

"Yes, we had a date with her for that night."

"But then she never showed up. What happened to her?"

"Just wait until you hear her story. Can I fix you a drink?"

"That's OK, I've got my water. So, what happened to her?"

"One day, out of the blue, after about a year of no contact, I get a phone call from Little Lisa. As fate would have it, I was in an office full of nosy co-workers when she called. After all this time we had finally reconnected. We spoke briefly and got together a few days later. Here is her story exactly as she told it to me:

> That night, as I was driving out to meet you and Tina, I stopped to get gas. While my car was filling, I called you to get directions and the room number. I was just leaving the gas station when I got pulled over by a cop. He had been waiting for me in the dark. The problem was that my license had been suspended a long time ago, and I meant to take care of it but... . Anyway, I

had gotten a few tickets for driving with a suspended license and so there was a warrant out for my arrest and damn, I got hauled off to jail! It took all night just to go through the booking and the entire inmate processing. I was finally placed in a cell some time the next morning and then a few minutes after that, they came and told me I had been there for a full 24 hours and that I had served my time. So I was released. Due to the overcrowding in the Jails, they let people out early all the time. I went and got my license fixed pretty soon, like the day after that.

That's our little super hero."
"Can you believe the things that happen to her?"
"I would believe anything she tells me."
John has been butt fucking Little Lisa. I know he has. That's why he hasn't been texting me to see him as often. He likes that little butt fucker better than me. I'm going to get his big cock into my butt tonight no matter what it takes.

Tina looks at me with an uncharacteristically determined expression and takes off her clothes. I get undressed as quickly as I can. We are standing naked, looking at each other.

"Do you want to put it in my butt?"
I'm unable to speak. I can't imagine my expression.

Tina looks at me and bursts into giggles.

"Should I lie on my tummy like this? Is this how you and Little Lisa do it?"

"Sure." I carefully calculate my next move in order to optimize this opportunity as I gather the anal anesthetic and the olive oil. I rub the anesthetic cream onto Tina's sphincter and suggest my plan to her, "We'll start with one finger. If you are comfortable with that, then we'll try two fingers. If you can take two fingers then you can probably take my dick."

"But your cock is a lot bigger than your two fingers!"

"Yes, but the idea is to take it in steps, small steps, where possible." I lube up Tina's anus and insert one finger. I gently work it all the way into her tight little butthole. I slowly remove it and explain; "Now we'll try two fingers." Tina barks impatiently at me over her shoulder.

"Don't use your fingers, use your cock! Fingers aren't... exciting."

That's a big step for a butt-virgin, but I'm not going to argue with a hot girl that's telling me to shove my cock into her asshole. I promptly reply, "Good idea." I position the tip of my raging boner against Tina's tight little butthole. She reaches behind her back and grabs it.

"Let me guide it in. OK, now push."

We try repeatedly but she's simply too tight. Tina squeals in pain and pulls away whenever my penis begins to enter her. In a tone of despair and resignation Tina turns around, looks at me sadly, and declares defeat.

"I can't do it. I just can't do it. My butt's... a pussy."

Tina purses her lips and shifts her eyes as she thinks about what she has just said. She looks befuddled as she realizes the hilarious irony of her statement. She shakes it off.

317

"I want to do anal. I am trying to do it."

"It's all right, we'll take it slowly, and we'll only do what you're ready for."

"I'm getting frustrated that I can't take your cock in my butt!"

I am motionless, except for my throbbing erection. Tina reaches behind her back, grabs my erect penis and shoves it into her pussy.

"Just fuck my pussy."

"Good idea." Tina is a fantastic lover, she doesn't get all uptight about butt-to-pussy cross-contamination, like most girls do. I don't last long in her pussy before I come.

"I can feel your wad in my pussy. It feels sexy."

"I love you."

"I can feel it. Or maybe that's just your semen!"

We look at each other for a second and then burst out laughing.

"I'm going to wash up so I don't get sore when we have sex later."

I get up to make myself a drink, and unintentionally step on Tina's panties. I pick them up and sniff the crotch. They smell like Tina's ripe pussy. I want them. I look up to make sure that Tina is still in the bathroom. I can hear the shower running. I sneak the aromatic undies into my attaché of accoutrements. I pick up Tina's remaining clothes, fold them, and lay them on the couch.

Tina returns from the bathroom toweling off and asking me a question. I try to act casually to hide my guilt from snatching her snatch-cloth.

"Why do guy's like anal sex?"

"A girl once told me that guys like to fuck a girl in her butt because 'It's tight and it's nasty'. I think I agree with her."

318

"I remember you saying that. Is my butt tighter than my pussy?"

"Yes, your butt is tighter at the opening where the sphincter is, but when your pussy climaxes, then you are tight everywhere."

"Do you do anal with our little nympho every time you see her?"

"Yes we always do it at least once in her butt and usually two or three times."

"You have seen her several times in the last four months, according to your invitations."

"The last time I saw Lisa, I thought I killed her."

"No kidding? Why, what happened?"

"We were fucking pretty hard, like we always do. She was on her back and I was on top of her. She was coming and her pussy got tight. I had to force-fuck her just to penetrate her pussy. She grimaced, held her breath and then she turned purple. She's done that before, so I just fucked her harder. She bucked and grunted and gritted her teeth. Her cunt got so tight that I had to pin her down and pound as hard as I could to drive all the way in. That's when a big green vein stuck out on Lisa's forehead. It looked like the special effects in a horror movie. It creeped me out, but I figured that I'd already killed her, so I might as well finish and come in her. She would have wanted it that way."

"You are so bad. Then what happened? What did she say?"

"After we both caught our breath, I asked her if she had a big orgasm. She asked me, 'How did you know?' I didn't say anything to her about it."

"Oh my God! You fuck-freak whoremonger. Did she say anything about it?"

"Yes."

"Dammit! What did she say?"

"She said, 'The sex is always good with you.'"

"That sounds like something our little tramp would say after you almost fucked her to death. It always pisses me off that I'm stuck at work and can't get away to join you two. I just stare at your text message and shake my head knowing how much fun I'm missing out on."

"I send you so many text messages that I feel like a fool. Then I don't get any replies for a few months, and I wonder if you've gotten a boyfriend or gotten married."

"Oh, I would definitely tell you if I was going to get married. We're friends, after all. Would you want an invitation? Would you want to come?"

"I would love to come! I'd wear a tux, get you a nice present, and I'd sincerely wish you both health, wealth, and happiness."

"That's so sweet. I'm going to get married when I'm in my late thirties to a man a little older than me who already has his kids and doesn't want any more. I'll marry a divorced man. I'll be friends with his ex-wife and his kids. I've got it all planned out. It's going to be great!"

"I'm an older man that's done having kids. Can I audition to be your husband?"

"You're good in bed now, but in fifteen years you'll be too old to give me all the sex I want."

"Then let's have sex now."

"OK. What do you want to do?"

I lick my lips at Tina and her pretty eyes light up. She jumps onto the bed, arranges the pillows, and lies down with her legs spread.

"OK, I'm ready."

I bring Tina to orgasm and mount her while she's still

catching her breath. I pound her hard in missionary position and come the moment her vagina starts to convulse in orgasm.

"That was fun. Good job."

Tina tosses me aside like a rag doll and bounces toward the bathroom.

"Make me a drink while I wash up. Let's get high."

This girl is incredibly strong for such a thin woman. She's like an endurance athlete, she's as lean as a waif, but she is as strong as an ox.

John has our drinks on the table. I like his obedience. He always behaves like a gentleman.

Tina appears from the bathroom and catches me rummaging around in my bag of goodies. She addresses me in a falsely suspicious tone.

"What kind of nasty knickknacks are you looking for in your carrier of carnal curios?"

"I have a present for you to celebrate our meeting three years ago this week. Happy anniversary."

"An anniversary present? Wait. Did you say 'Three years'? It can't be three years already. Are you sure? What did you get me?"

"I brought the CD I promised to make for you."

"What CD?"

"I promised to put all of our photos and Little Lisa's photos onto one CD for you."

"You did?"

"I'm sorry that I forgot to bring it last time. I was kind of distracted getting prepared last time."

"I want to see."

I hand the CD to Tina and she gives me a bewildered look.

"I want to see the photos silly, not look at the stupid

disk."

"Oh, of course, sorry, I'll load the disk into my computer and bring up the viewer." Tina hovers over me while I bring up the photos.

"These are good. Make sure I remember to take this CD home with me. Let's watch them while we have sex."

I set up the slide show and look over at Tina. "OK, what do you want to do?"

"I'm getting sore down there, I'll give you a blowjob."

I jump into position.

"Can you see the photos?"

"I can see you, that's all I need."

"You are so sweet."

Tina goes to work and I soon come in her pretty little mouth.

"Where's my drink? I need it to wash down your sperm."

I pour another round of drinks for both of us and we get high together.

"I like the way my butt looks in the photograph you took of me in my tiger-striped panties. I bought those with a girlfriend that I want to sleep with. I had hoped to wear them for her, but that didn't happen."

"Did you ever get a pair of Stacie's panties?"

"That bitch! Who'd want her damn underwear? I am totally over her. I haven't hung out with her since she pulled that shit on me."

"How about your other friends and the girls at the gym?"

"I got caught looking at a girl in the locker room at my gym. She seemed both flattered and offended at the same time."

"Did you make the pervert's noise?"

"I almost did when I first saw her. She's a new girl at the gym, and she is much more attractive than Stacie. I want to bang her. I think I'll try to break into her locker, and steal her panties."

"Details please. Describe her to me."

She's super thin, about five-foot seven-inches tall, and incredibly cute. She has smooth alabaster skin, dark blue eyes, straight jet-black hair. She has high firm breasts with huge puffy nipples and she wears black lace thong panties that show off her pointy little butt, just to torture me."

"If you score a pair of her drawers, bring them to our next meeting."

"I know which days and times she's there, because she goes to the aerobics classes. I time my visits to be in the locker room when her class ends so I can be there when she showers. I want to fuck her so bad. I've caught her looking at me too. I would just tell her, if only I had the nerve."

Tina looks at my crotch and her eyes get big. I have been unconsciously playing with myself and I'm fully erect.

"Looks like you're ready to go again."

"Your flirtatious story has aroused me like an aphrodisiac."

"How do you want to do it?"

"I want you on the bed, doggy-style."

"Ruff! Ruff!"

"Oh, you want it rough, do you?"

"You always rough-fuck me."

"You always like it."

"So, stop talking and start fucking."

"I love you."

"You just want to fuck me."

"That too."

"That feels good."

I get in behind Tina and lick her pussy until she warms up. I penetrate her and gently rub her anus with my thumb. Tina's vagina tightens. I pound her fast and hard so that I will come quickly. I last longer that I expected to.

"I don't know how much more my poor pussy can take."

I grab Tina's hips and fuck her as hard as I can. She makes a lot of noise by the time I finish.

"I didn't think I could come again. How did you do that?"

"I'm glad it was good for you too."

"I need to rest a few minutes. Talk to me."

"I meant to ask you about your job."

"For the last four months I've been at a new position at the same company, but at a much higher level. I work in the corporate office with the executives. I can tell that all the men are nervous around me."

"I'm not surprised at all, that you make the men nervous at work."

"Oh, I have a present for you."

Tina digs a pad of paper out of her purse and hands it to me with a mischievous smirk. It is one of those note pads that real estate agents hand out. There is a picture of an attractive woman, about my age, at the top of every sheet.

"That's my Mom! She's a total MILF. She gets hit on all the time. When I meet a guy that I want to keep around, I introduce him to my Mom and tell him, 'See how hot I'm going to be when I'm older.'"

"You will always be hot."

"I'm going to shower and get dressed now."

"I'll get your CD ready for you to take with you."

"Yes, don't let me forget that."

I eject the disk and remove it from my computer. I laugh at the handwritten description I put on it: 'Sales & Marketing'. I wanted a label that will be dismissed as boring school stuff, just in case Tina leaves it out and someone sees it. I put the disk in its case and place it under Tina's purse where she won't forget it.

I see that Tina didn't touch the diet cola today. I wonder if she's changed beverages. I need to pay more attention to her preferences, so that I bring the proper drinks for her. Tina steps into the room.

"I'm ready to go now."

Tina picks up her purse and sees the CD on the table under it.

"Oh, is this for me?"

"Yes, you told me to make sure that I don't let you forget to take it with you."

"What does this say?"

I explain to Tina and she laughs her reply at me.

"You should have just written 'S&M', but then everyone would look at it."

I reach for the door, but Tina wraps her arms around me and gives me a long, deep kiss. My knees get weak, and my brain goes blank.

"I had a nice time tonight. Thank you for my CD."

I open the door. Tina steps forward, but then pauses in the doorway. She tilts her head in thought and turns to me quietly.

"Did you give me the money?"

I whisper, "Oh shit!" and pull Tina back into the room. I close the door as quietly as possible. "I'm so sorry, let me get it for you."

"It seemed like we forgot something."

I dash to my briefcase and produce the envelope. I

run it back to Tina and apologetically hand it to her. "Here you go, I'm so sorry. You know that I would never-"

"Don't worry about it. I just don't want to forget it, that's all. I need it right now. It's all right."

"I'm glad you remembered. I think that I forgot because we're so casual."

"More like, cuz we're so high!"

"Do you have everything now? Do you have your panties?"

"You have all of my panties. You raunchy rascal."

"You say the nicest things."

"I'm going to go now. Bye sweetie."

I visually sweep the room one more time to see if Tina has left anything else and pull the door open. Tina slinks out the door and down the hallway in the right direction. I watch her walk out of sight and close the door. I remove the purloined panties from my tote of trashy trinkets and sniff the crotch. It smells like Tina's pussy. I love her.

Chapter 23

I Want to be Able to Say that I Did

I haven't heard a single word from the guy I dated four days ago. Why hasn't he called me? I spent three hours getting ready for that date. Is he dead? That had better be the reason why he hasn't called me. I know that he's not going to call me, because I didn't sleep with him.

I'm just not all that promiscuous in my real life. If you don't sleep with the guy, then he won't call you. That's the way it always is on regular dates. Maybe I should have slept with him.

I hope he doesn't try to call me during this appointment. I would hate to miss his call. Should I leave my phone on? Maybe not. How would I talk to a date in front of my client? I take a deep breath and blow it out slowly as I knock discreetly on John's door.

I unpack the anal lubricants from my bag and strategically place them on the nightstand just in case Tina indicates that she's got the back door open tonight. I don't want to miss a chance to pop her butt-cherry.

I'm not sure what Tina's favorite beverage is now. I

decided to bring her favorite brands of both diet cola and bottled water for her this time. That should improve my odds of providing her preferred refreshment.

The escort knocking at the door must be Tina, because Jessica doesn't have the room number yet. Does she? She's waiting for me to call her first, isn't she? Yes, that's right, I told her to wait for me to call her.

Upon opening the door I see that Tina looks a little less fit and quite a bit paler than she did two months ago. She looks more like an office worker, and less like a bikini model. I won't say anything about that to her though. She gives me a causal hug on her way in. I make her a drink and we sit down together.

"Have you heard from our little convict lately?"

"Lisa has been out of touch for a while. I didn't want to have to face you again and not have any tangible results, so I've ordered us a nineteen year old out-call named Jessica. She can be here in half an hour, if you want to see her. It's your choice, I don't mind either way. Do you want to see her website photos and her reviews?"

"Yes. Show them to me before I decide."

Tina silently reads Jessica's web ad.

19 year old slut will be your nasty freak.
I will make your dirty fantasy come true.

"Wow, did you see what she wrote in her ad?"

"Yes, why?"

"What the hell is with this girl? Where is she from? Is she from around here? What do you know about her?"

"Her two reviews are fairly positive and claim the photos are authentic and accurate."

"Well the girl in the photographs is cute. I don't recognize her, so it's probably not anyone I know. THAT would be an absolute shit storm. Do you like her? Did you talk to her on the phone? Did she sound normal, or screwy?"

"She sounded reasonably normal when we talked. She said that she can be here in thirty minutes. Do you want to see her?"

"Sure. Do you have a razor?"

My expression must betray my concern as to why Tina is suddenly asking for a razor. She frowns at me and quickly adds an explanation in a scolding tone.

"I'd like to shave my legs, since we're having a guest."

I get the razor from my bag. Tina snatches it from my hand. She gives me an annoyed look, steps into the bathroom, and closes the door. I call Jessica to invite her over.

Thirty minutes later, Tina cautiously steps out of the bathroom. She is fully dressed, and carefully surveys the room.

"Is she coming? Did you talk to her?"

"Yes, I did. She said she'd be here in twenty minutes."

"How long ago was that?"

"About thirty minutes ago, which means she'll be here in about a half an hour."

"How do you tell time?"

"Well, Jessica said twenty 'escort-minutes' which is forty to sixty 'nerd-minutes.'"

"Oh, I see."

"Would you like another drink? Do you want to get high? Can we have sex while we're waiting for Jessica to get here?"

"Let's wait for the other girl. I don't want to get interrupted by someone I don't know. And besides, now

329

I'm a little anxious about meeting a new girl. You can pour me a strong drink though."

"What do you want to do with the other girl?"

"I don't know yet. That depends on if I like her."

"Should I introduce you to her as my girlfriend Tina?"

"Don't use my real name in front of her!"

"But that's not your real name."

"How do you know?"

"Because... escorts never use their real names with clients."

"OK, yes, you're right."

Shit! That was a close one. I need to be more careful. I don't want Tina to realize that I know her real name.

"What name should I call you in front of the other girl?"

I strike a modeling pose for John and suggestively ask, "Which famous person do you think I look like?" He gawks at me and contemplates a few seconds.

"How about... if I call you... Britney?"

"That's fine."

I look at the clock and then at Tina. "This girl will probably be late."

"Don't worry, I will still stay with you for the whole time. Let's talk. I have some questions I've wanted to ask you, but we're always too busy having sex to talk."

I love the questions that Tina asks me. They help me to discover things about her that she would never tell me outright.

"Have you ever met a dominatrix? Do you know any Doms?" John starts to smile before I can even finish the question. I can always count on John to be a complete pervert.

"Yes, I got to know one that I saw as a regular escort. Her name is MJ and she's famous. She dresses men in women's clothing all the time. She told me, 'Usually there isn't even a sex act involved.' She said that some men like the feel of tight fitting bras and pantyhose. At the end of one of our sessions she said to me, 'I've got to go dress people in women's clothing.' She's a lot of fun, we get along great together."

"Is she one of those Goth chicks, with the black makeup and pierced nose and shit?"

"That's what's so great about MJ, she was a marketing executive in business for a few years. She's still clean-cut and professional looking. No one would ever guess that she is a world-class dominatrix. We laugh our asses off talking about how she is probably whipping the same men that used to be her bosses."

"Is she a good lover, or is she a dominatrix only?"

"She's wonderful as a regular escort. That's how I met her. I didn't even know about her dom side for a long time. She's cute and she leaves the backdoor open every time I see her."

"Do you have any pictures of her?"

"She's got a website that shows all her booking options and photographs of her dungeon."

"She has a dungeon?"

"Yes, she does. Pretty cool huh?"

"I'm not sure if that's cool or if that's scary. Show me her website, I've got to see this."

Tina gets engrossed in MJ's website, reading every page and looking at all of the photos. She is startled when there's an escort's knock at the door. I spring up to answer the door. Tina suddenly looks nervous.

I open the door and there stands the girl in the photos. She's wearing tight low-cut blue jeans and a short top that exposes her slim, tight belly. She's hot. I invite her in. Jessica enters the room and immediately locks her eyes onto Tina. "Hi Jessica. I'm John and this is my friend Britney."

"Hi. Nice to meet you both. Do you have something for me?"

I hand Jessica her envelope and she sits down on the edge of the bed. She counts the money in front of us, sets down the empty envelope, and stuffs the cash into her big purse. To break the ice, I ask her, "Would you like a drink?"

"Yes, that would be nice."

Tina stays seated across the room from Jessica and fires questions at her while I mix her drink.

"How old are you?"

"I'm... nineteen."

"How long have you been escorting?"

"Almost six months now."

"How did you get started?"

"I needed to make some fast money and I don't like working at low-wage shit-jobs that are often just as dangerous and humiliating as escorting is."

"How did you decide on your rate?"

"I looked at the other girl's ads and how old they looked and then picked a rate somewhere in the middle."

"Where did you get the photos?"

"They're ones that my boyfriend took a couple of years ago. We broke up, so that's why I started escorting. I need the money."

"Did you write the text in your website ad?"

"Yes, I did."

"How did you decide on what to write?"

"I just thought that's what guys want to see."

"Do you get a lot of good calls?"

"I'm not sure if any call I've had is good."

"How do you get ready for a call, how do you feel?"

"I get dressed and go to the hotel."

"How do you feel after the call? What do you do first?"

"I don't know. I haven't thought about it."

"Have you had a kid?"

"Yes, one, how did you know?"

"You have some old stretch marks. How old is your kid?"

"He's eight."

"Do you tell any of your friends or family that you're escorting? Do they know?"

"I haven't told anyone. Not even my best friend."

"Do people ask you how you have so much money and free time?"

"Nobody has ever asked me that."

"What would your friends and family say if they knew?"

"Oh my God! They would shit their pants."

"How do you go about screening new clients?"

"What's screening?"

"Never mind."

"Are you an escort?"

"I used to be. I made a lot of money for the short time that I was an escort. Then I pulled down my ad and only saw my favorite regulars. Now I pretty much only see John. I have for a long time now."

"How did you get started? What made you do it?"

"I just saw some ads on an escort site, and then one day, I put up mine. That's all."

Tina gives me a look that says she's done asking Jessica questions, and doesn't want to answer any more questions. I nod to Tina.

"OK, John is ready to start now. I'm just going to watch."

"Should I get undressed?"

"Yes." I shed my clothes and get a condom from the nightstand. Tina remains glued in the stuffed chair. When I look up Jessica is standing in front of me completely naked.

Jessica has a hot body, especially for a MILF. I shamelessly play with her in front of Tina. I put on the condom and bend Jessica over. I wipe spit on my fingers and lube her up. I shove in and pound her from behind. Tina watches intently with no reaction. Jessica gets noisy. I finish quickly. I pull out and the condom is bloody. I have started Jessica's period.

"My period shouldn't start for a few days!"

Tina reassures Jessica.

"Don't worry. It's not your fault. John starts girl's periods all the time."

Jessica gives us both a strange look, runs to the bathroom and closes the door. Tina starts looking through the hotel magazine and I mix myself a drink. When Jessica returns, she collects her clothes and dresses quickly. I ask her, "Do you want me to write a review for

334

you?"

"Oh, no, don't say that I started my period during the session."

"I wouldn't ever say that. I start a lot of girl's periods when they aren't due."

"OK then."

Jessica grabs her purse and hurries out the door in the wrong direction. The door slams itself shut behind her before I can get to it.

"Right! She has an eight year old kid and she says she's nineteen. The math doesn't quite work on that. She's not my kind of girl."

"I'm sorry. I should have seen her alone first. Then I would have known."

"Go take a shower and wash thoroughly if you expect me to touch you. Good thing you used a condom on her. I'm having a drink."

I get in the shower and try to think. Shit, that was a fucking disaster. I hope Tina is not too pissed-off at me. I should get a nice present for her the next time we get together. I'll get her something that I know she'll like. I walk into the room not sure what I'm going to find. Tina looks miffed.

"I'll give you a blowjob. Do you want me to get undressed?"

"No, stay clothed. I want to play with your cute butt through your tight pants while you blow me." The idea seems to please Tina.

"Oh yes. Like that." Tina gives me the best head she's ever delivered. Wow! Where did this come from? Tina pauses just before I go over the edge.

"Do you want to take some photos? Did you bring

saying a word.

Tina steps slowly out of the bathroom, meanders over to me at the table and plops down in a chair.

"I need to rest. Can we talk for a while?"

"Sure, is there anything in particular you wish to discuss?"

"It's a shame that you haven't heard from our little Franken-fuck."

"Franken-who?"

"Franken-fuck. That's how I think of Little Lisa since you told me the story of the big green vein popping out of her forehead during sex. I miss her, she makes for a great threesome."

"I'm boggled by how difficult it is to set up a good threesome. I recently tried to set up a threesome with Little Lisa and a girl named Barbie. That's the finger-trap girl that I've told you about. I tried to be careful."

"Be careful about what exactly?"

"I tried to see if Lisa already knew the other girl."

"How did you do that?"

"First I showed Lisa the photos of Barbie and asked if she was acceptable. Lisa said OK. When Barbie arrived, Lisa freaked out, grabbed me by the arm, and insisted, 'Come to the bathroom with me. I know this girl and we don't get along. Get rid of her right now or I'm leaving.'"

"Oh my God! Little Lisa freaked out on you? What did you do?"

"I told Lisa to stay in the bathroom a minute. I gave Barbie a C-note. I told her to go shopping, and to come back in two hours, if she wanted to get the rest of the donation."

"What did she say?"

"I didn't give her a chance to say anything. I hustled

Barbie out the door while Little Lisa stayed in the bathroom with the door shut. Then I apologized to Little Lisa."

"What did Little Lisa say?"

"She told me that she knew that girl by another name, from before, that she's been to some of the same clubs and parties in Long Beach and LA. Lisa didn't recognize her current photos, but the moment the girl spoke, Lisa identified her and hauled me into the bathroom to explain."

"Then what happened? Tell me! This is so exciting."

"Lisa calmed down pretty quickly once I got rid of Barbie. We had a couple of drinks and Lisa screwed the shit out of me."

"Did she know that you'd invited the other girl to come back?"

"I don't know, but she definitely made certain that she fucked me as hard as she could. Jealously is a powerful aphrodisiac."

"Did the other girl return?"

"Yes, exactly two hours after I pushed her out the door she called me. Lisa was still there and naked, but she was done fucking for the night. I didn't want to upset Lisa by rushing her out, so I asked Barbie to wait fifteen minutes before coming up."

"Go on, what did Little Lisa do?"

"She got pissed-off at me, got dressed and was out the door in sixty seconds."

"Did you end up fucking the other girl?"

"A couple of hours later she knocked on my door. It woke me up. She jealous-fucked the shit out of me too. In spite of how bad the evening started out, it ended up being a great night of hot sex."

"Oh, you gluttonous philanderer!"

338

"Tina, you say the nicest things to me."

"That's an interesting story about Little Lisa and the blown threesome that turned out so well for you. I guess you just never know how something's going to work out."

"Speaking of threesomes, that reminds me that I want to tell you about the message I got from Gina."

"Who's she?"

"She's that nice girl with the hot body that you liked the photos of. She's the one from San Francisco."

"What about her?"

"She said she plans to visit Orange County soon."

"So?"

"So I asked her if she wanted to do a threesome with a bikini model and she said sure."

"Show me her photos again."

"She's nice. She's smart, educated, and worldly."

"Tell me something about her. What have you two talked about?"

"There was an interesting observation that Gina made. She said, 'I've met some nice guys that just don't have the time to date. Some of them have become regulars. Several of them are rich, handsome, youthful guys that just want to date and have hot sex with a cute girl, but they are scared to death of all the gold diggers out there, so they see me. These guys say to me, 'You are better in bed than a girlfriend and you don't pressure me to marry you just because we're fucking. In the long run you cost a lot less than a regular girlfriend.' Even though she charges exceptionally high rates, I think her clients have a good point."

"Sounds like she's a... professional girlfriend."

"Pretty much."

"Is she one of those skinny girls that you butt fuck?"

"Yes."

"Set it up. I want to meet this girl."

"OK, I will let you know."

"Do you want to try it in my butt?"

"Yes, I do. I'll get the evoo."

"What the hell is that?"

"Oh, that's just an abbreviation for extra-virgin olive oil. Italian cooks say that all the time."

"Let's try it this way this time."

Tina lies on her side. I lube up her tight little anus, line up my rock-hard boner, and push the tip of my penis inside her butthole in one continuous move. It snaps into her and I hold my position.

"Stop! Oh, shit that hurts. It's so big. Take it out-SLOWLY."

Tina pants and grimaces as I ease my dick out of her asshole.

"OK, now lube it up and let me try to shove it in. Is the head in?"

"Most of the head is in. Are you OK?"

"I have to at least get the head in. I want to be able to say that I did."

I try to push in further and Tina yelps, so I stop. "OK, the head is in, you can say that you got the head in." I can't help but wonder; whom will Tina brag to that she got the head of a penis into her butt?

"Oh, fuck that hurts."

We let it sit in there, neither of us moving, until it starts to get soft. I ease back and let her expel it slowly, like a turd. I can tell that it hurts her.

"I guess I need more practice if I'm ever going to be able to take your big cock in my butt."

I take my half-limp dick in my hand and slap it

repeatedly against Tina's butt cheeks. After a few slaps, it starts to gets hard. Tina reaches behind her butt, grabs my penis and strokes it a few times. Quickly it becomes good and hard. She spreads her cheeks with her other hand and easily shoves my erect penis into her dripping wet pussy. I start pounding her and we both soon orgasm.

"I'm going to shower and get dressed. Do you mind if I go first?"

"No, go ahead, and take your time, I need to rest first anyway." Wow, Tina is even more determined to have anal sex than I am. She is so hot, she is the best girlfriend ever.

I wash up at the sink while Tina showers and I get dressed.

It looks like Tina no longer drinks diet cola, she didn't touch it this time either. Maybe I should just bring her bottled water from now on.

I open my briefcase and pull out Tina's envelope. I had intentionally left it in there because I'd never met Jessica before. Besides that, I didn't want to have two envelopes out at the same time, and risk mixing them up.

I can't help but note the stark difference between the classy manner in which Tina has always handled the donation versus the unprofessional way that Jessica pulled out the money and counted it in front of us. It reminded me of the way a hooker counts her money and then takes off her clothes. Tina and Lisa have spoiled me. They are both professional girlfriends.

I place Tina's envelope under her purse. I don't want to repeat my mistake of forgetting the envelope like I did last time. That was so embarrassing, I can't believe I did that. How could I forget her compensation like that? What happened? She was in the shower like usual, I should have gotten the envelope out of my briefcase at that time. Why didn't I? What was I doing that distracted me? I review the sequence of events. Tina left for the shower and I asked her if she wanted to take her CD with her. It was still in my computer and I had to eject the disk, put it back in its case. Oh shit, then I put the CD under Tina's purse so that she wouldn't forget it. She had told me to make sure she remembered to take it home with her. We both substituted the CD for the envelope. Tina is standing next to me. I didn't see her come over. She picks up her purse and the envelope.

"Thanks for this. I'm going to leave now, but I promise that I'll practice for next time so that we can do anal properly."

"I love you."

"I know."

"I hope it doesn't take another two months for us to get together."

"I'm making a lot of money at my job at the corporate headquarters. The company is super busy right now. I've been working six days a week lately. I don't have any time for appointments or dates. You are the only person that I still see for sex. You have been the only man in my life for a long time now."

"I'm flattered, but do you mind if I ask, why me?"

"Because... we're friends... and I like the sex we have."

Tina gives me a quick kiss on the mouth. "Do you have everything?"

"Yes I do, thanks."

I open the door and Tina strolls confidently out the

342

door toward the elevators.

Chapter 24

Excuse Me...

I knock at John's hotel room door trying to remember what was so weird about the last time I saw him. It was about four months ago. Oh, that's right. It was that Bimbo he invited last time. Wait, there was something else. We tried to set up another threesome about two months ago but that was the night my girlfriend went into seizures and I went to the hospital with her. God it's hard to get a good threesome put together. I'm going to ask John about getting together with our sleazy little slut again.

I arrive at the room early so that I can get set up in advance, before Tina is scheduled to show up. I unpack all the usual goodies for a date with Tina: drinks, pornographic movies, magazines, lubricants, and vibrators. With that chore done, I go out on the balcony and have a cigar. I look through my phone messages to pass the time. I see the exchange of messages from our last failed attempt to meet for a threesome. They are from the night I saw Gina. I read through the text message thread that started just about an hour before Gina showed up.

> **From: Tina**
> **Msg: Sorry, can't come.**
> **My girlfriend just had a**
> **seizure I'm on my way to**
> **the hospital with her now.**

I had immediately replied.

> **To: Tina**
> **Msg: I M so sorry for her.**
> **I hope she is OK. You**
> **must have been so scared.**

The next message had a time stamp a half an hour later.

> **From: Tina**
> **Msg: I was screaming**
> **for ten minuets. She**
> **turned colors, I don't**
> **know if she's OK or**
> **not.**

I tried to send a supportive message.

> **To: Tina**
> **Msg: Let me know if**
> **I can be of help to**
> **either of you.**

Tina is so thoughtful.

> **From: Tina**
> **Msg: Sorry to cancel**
> **like this I m really sorry.**

I replied with the most encouraging message I could think of.

To: Tina
Msg: Don't worry at all.
You need to be there
with your friend.

My thoughts are interrupted. Tina's knocking at the door! I dance over to the door and yank it open to find Tina smiling at me.

"Hi John! It's nice to see you. How are you?"

"I'm OK, I hope your friend is feeling better."

"Oh, thanks, yes she is. It turns out she had a potassium deficiency and that caused the seizures. She got better as soon as they started the treatment and she's been fine since. I have eaten a banana every day since that happened."

Tina pauses. She's thinking about something. I wait for her.

"Oh, what happened with the girl from San Francisco?"

"I had a good time with Gina."

"Which girl is she again?"

"She's the five-foot, six-and-three-quarter inch tall, size zero analist."

"What did you do with her?"

"We spent two hours together at a nice hotel in Anaheim. She was visiting OC tourist attractions with her family."

"What did she tell her family?"

"Well, she was paying for the trip, so they didn't ask any questions when she said that she had a business meeting that night."

347

"She told them she had a business meeting at eight o'clock at night?"

"Yes, she said it was a cocktail party."

"Oh, I get it, 'cock and tail' party. She was being honest."

"She told me that she's never told anyone what she does, or where she goes."

"How long has she been escorting?"

"For at least five years, that I know of."

"How did she get started?"

"I wouldn't know."

"You never asked her?"

"No, I would never ask a girl that."

"Why not?"

"It's against the rules for a guy to ask a girl that question, but it's apparently OK for girls to ask each other about it."

"Why do you say that?"

"Do you remember that you asked Little Lisa how she got started as an escort?"

"No, did I?"

"Yes you did. Also, you and Jessica, the space-case girl, asked each other the same question."

"We did?"

"Yes, you did. Now, have I ever asked you that question?"

"Not that I can recall?"

"There you go."

"How did I reply to Little Lisa and the spacey girl? What did I say?"

"You didn't say much to either one of them. It seems like you don't want to talk about it."

"That's odd. I don't mind talking about it. That is something that I should definitely remember. Let me think about that. How did I get started?"

"Are you sure you don't remember anything?"

"I remember thinking at the time that it was strange that I couldn't reply when that spaced-out hooker asked me how I got started as an escort. I honestly couldn't remember any of the details. That's not like me. I remember everything quite clearly. Nothing is ever fuzzy for me. I wasn't trying to be evasive. I just couldn't recall anything about it. I'll have to think about that."

"In any case, Gina was sorry that she missed you when she was down here visiting with her family."

"Do her friends and family ask her about her work?"

"Yes, they do. She said that she tells them, 'Due to the secret nature of my work, I can not disclose any details.' They all think she's a spy working for the Government."

"That's indicative of how predictable people are as to the conclusions they will draw from limited information. She sounds like she's smart. Do you like seeing her?"

"She's a great girl. I had seen her several times in San Francisco. I thought you would like her. She's nothing like that space cadet I invited over the last time we were together. Sorry about that."

"Don't worry. You never know what you're going to get. That's just the way it is. It's the same when you're dating. This girl from San Francisco sounds like fun. Did you snatch her underwear, the way you take mine?"

"Yes, I've got the pair Gina wore that night. I keep them in the same drawer with yours. Now I have both of your panties together, but I can't get you two together. It's as close as I can get to a threesome with you two." Tina gives me a long look and inquires accusingly.

"Do you rub them together?"

"Yes, I do. I rub them together, crotch-to-crotch,

349

against my dick and fantasize that I'm fucking both of you."

"Bring hers the next time I see you."

"OK." Tina is such a gnarly little pervert. I think that's why I love her.

"I am beginning to think that we will never have another good threesome again."

"It is always difficult to get three people's schedules to match up for a threesome. It's hard enough to see more that one girl in a given night."

"Have you seen multiple girls in one night, one after another? What's the most?"

"One time, I saw five different girls in one night."

"How old were you?"

"I was in my early thirties. I had stamina back then. That was before boner-pills."

"How did you find them?"

"I kept calling the same escort service and after the first girl I saw told them I was a nice guy, they sent their best girls, one after another, through the night."

"I'm going to use the bathroom and get changed now. I need my purse. My little clutch purse is too small to bring a whole outfit, so I just put in an extra pair of sexy underwear. You know, in case some pervert wants to keep them."

A few minutes later, Tina steps out of the bathroom wearing nothing but a pair of sexy underwear. She does a runway-model strut towards me. I get down on my knees. She walks up to me and nudges her pubic bone against my mouth.

"Do you like them?"

I pull the crotch of the panties to one side and start to perform cunnilingus. Tina sighs deeply, presses my face into her crotch, and laments to me.

"I wish I had you in my bed at night instead of just my lousy vibrator."

I never tire of hearing Tina say that to me. "I would love to be in your bed at night."

"Oh, that feels so good."

I lick Tina's pussy until her knees get unsteady. I suggest that she lie down on the bed. I crawl onto the bed next to her. Tina grabs my penis and squeezes it.

"Oh, you're so hard."

I climb on top of Tina and enter her. I climax so quickly that she doesn't get a chance to orgasm while I am still insider her. "I'm sorry that I couldn't wait for you to climax first."

"Why are you sorry? You came. I can feel it down there."

"Well, a gentleman always makes sure that the lady comes first."

"Don't be silly, I came a couple of times in your mouth before you even stuck your cock in me. Trust me, I got mine."

"I'm still hard and horny. Can we fuck again right now?"

"How do you want me?"

"Let's do it standing up, in front of the mirror. You are so beautiful to look at."

John makes me feel wanted. His desire for me turns me on. I want him to take me. I stick my butt out for him.

I get behind Tina and shove my penis into her vagina. She gasps.

"Fuck me hard."

I grab Tina's hips and pound her. The mirror above the low dresser shakes as Tina's head butts against it. Tina climaxes. Her vagina gets so tight that I climax. My knees are shaking. I fall backward onto the bed.

"That was a good fuck. Good job! I'm going to wash up. I'll be just a minute."

Tina returns, sits down and sips her drink. I join her. "I brought you a present. Do you want it now?"

"How sweet of you. Sure. Is it something we can play with in bed?"

"Oh, I hope so."

"How exciting. In that case, I want it right now."

"On the way to our meeting, I bought you some anal-sex anesthetic, and a Butt-plug." I hand them to Tina.

"You bought me anal what?"

"I think you refer to it as 'numb-butt' cream."

"Oh, I remember that stuff. Do the other girls like that stuff? Does it work for them?"

"It's the strongest brand of topical anesthetic that they have at the erotic products store where I shop."

"Tell me about buying it."

"The gay clerk that showed me the butt plugs in the glass display case said, 'This one is curved to reach the prostate.' He said it as though he was commenting from experience. I remarked rather flatly to him, 'Girls don't have a prostate.' He immediately got discouraged. He muttered, 'No, they do not.' He walked away.

The hot lady clerk, that was standing nearby stepped in. She smiled at me and said knowingly, 'I always recommend the glass products to girls. I love my glass.' I was thinking of inviting her to our party."

"That must be a fun store to shop at. Let's give the butt plug a try. Have you washed it?"

"I'll wash it again since we've been handling it. That will warm it up a bit too." Tina takes the anesthetic cream tube and starts reading the directions while I wash her new butt plug.

"This is so much fun! I love to play with new sex toys."

I lube up Tina's butt and the plug. I slowly work the butt plug into Tina's tight anus. Tina impatiently orders me to take a more direct approach.

"Just use your cock."

"OK, good idea." I get positioned and push the tip into her. Tina's butthole is so tight, that I'm afraid I'm hurting her. I slow down, the way Little Lisa asks me to. I shove the tip in, and pause to let Tina get used to it.

"She's a tight little butthole today. Put on lots of lube, put the head in, and then push hard."

I get it fully into her, but the pain is too much. I'm all the way inside her, but I can't stroke, or it will hurt her. The sight of my boner, balls-deep in Tina's asshole, is mesmerizing.

"Ouch. It hurts too much. Pull it out, but pull it out SLOWLY."

I pull out as slowly as I can. Tina flinches and gasps when it pops out of her. She quickly regains her determined expression and announces her plan to me.

"I'll need to practice with my butt plug at home and then we will be able do it next time."

"We're getting closer. I'm proud of you."

"Thanks. I am trying as hard as I can to do it. I want to do it. It's exciting, and it feels good, when it doesn't hurt. I just need to stretch it out more. I'll work on it at home, I promise. I'll give you a blowjob. Go wash off your cock."

"OK, good idea." I wash up quickly, but completely. I return to bed. Tina sucks me and I climax quickly. Tina swallows, rolls onto her back, and looks up at me with a question in her eye.

"Do guys like to wake up to a blowjob?"

"Let me put it this way, when you want a man to fall in love with you and marry you, then do that to him."

"You don't mean that. Is that true?"

"All I can tell you is that I married the woman that did that to me."

"Bullshit! You did not. Did you?" John isn't saying anything. He's just looking me in the eye silently. Wow, he DID marry her. I'd better drop the subject. I'll have to remember that though, in case I ever find Mr. Right, or even Mr. Good-Enough.

"Do you think we could do an overnighter some time?"

"I don't think I can take that much time off from my regular life."

"I'd love to get a wake-up blowjob from you."

"Would you marry me?"

"Girl, I would marry you right now, even without the wake-up blowjob."

"Do you want to lick my pussy?"

"How do you want it?"

"Don't put your finger up my butt, that distracts me. And when I want it hard, then give it to me, don't tease me, that just pisses me off."

I lick Tina the way she likes it, and I don't tease her at all. I thought that girls liked to be teased, for a while at first. Well, most girls I lick do, but Tina doesn't, she likes it hard. Tina fucks like a guy. I love her. Wait, that doesn't make me gay, does it?

Oh, she must be done because she's out of breath and pushing me away. I should let her rest a few minutes, but I'm rock hard and I don't want to miss this hard-on. I climb on top of Tina, but she's incoherent. "Can I fuck

you?"

"You can do anything you want to me."

The moment I enter Tina, she springs to life. She wraps me up while she voices directions and commentary.

"Like that, hard. Faster! Oh, that feels so good. Harder! Oh yes! I'm coming, don't stop. Don't stop. Yes, like that!"

Tina's orgasm is so strong that she makes me climax when I didn't think that I could. I roll off of her and gaze at this wondrous woman.

"That was good. I need to rest. I'm going to just lie here for a while."

"Do you remember that we took photos last time?"

"Yes, I remember. Why? What about them?"

"Oh, it's just that I downloaded the photos from the camera to my computer. Do you want to see them?"

"Yes, show me. Are they good? Do you like them?"

"They came out great. I've been jacking off to them, they're better than my porn."

"I must completely LOVE you to let you take nude pictures of me."

I can't believe that Tina said she loves me. Even though she doesn't mean it, and she only said it as a figure of speech, it still makes my heart melt. Tina gives me a look of confidence.

"I've never let a guy take naked photos of me. Never. Not even my long-time boyfriends were allowed to do that, and believe me, they asked plenty of times. I didn't trust them."

I turn away to hide my involuntary sneer at the thought of Tina's chump boyfriends. I bring up the photos on my notebook computer. Tina takes charge.

"How do I zoom-in with this viewer?"

Tina scrutinizes each photograph.

"Send me a copy of this one, and this one. Oh shit! Look at my butthole, I'm not a butt-virgin anymore!"

I flatter Tina, "You are so hot... that you could... cause a traffic accident." Tina's eyes widen and she blinks shyly. In a confessing tone, Tina slowly admits a story to me.

"As a matter of fact... there was this one time... ."

"Details, give me details. Spill the story."

"Well, it wasn't just me, I was with two other girls. They were tall blonds too. We were walking down the strip in Vegas. We decided to just walk the short distance from our hotel to our hostessing job at a convention for private jets, in the hotel next door.

We were just walking along the sidewalk when some Taxi driver called out to us. We were just kids back then and so we waved back and yelled, 'Hi!' Just then the traffic ahead of him stopped and he plowed into the back of the limo in front of him. He hit the limo hard enough to pop its trunk open. Some guys jumped out of the limo and the cab driver yelled, 'Oh shit!' we laughed and laughed, and just kept walking."

"You're so hot that you're dangerous. You should be required to have a license to be that cute."

"Do you want to have sex again?"

"Do you want to get on top?"

"Lie back. I'll suck you until you're hard."

Tina bounces on me, and then collapses on top of me, after we both orgasm. She lies on top of me much longer than usual. Has she dozed off? I lie still while this wonderful woman catnaps on top of me. I love this girl.

Many minutes pass with Tina slumbering quietly on top of me. My semen drips out of her vagina and onto my leg. I am overcome by my affection for this sweet creature. Slowly she wakes up. She is groggy at first.

"I'm going to get in the shower now. I'm parked

close to the lobby door, so you don't need to walk me to my car tonight. Stay comfortable in bed."

Tina staggers sleepily into the bathroom. I put her presents and her envelope next to her purse on the coffee table. Tina sings in the bathroom and finally emerges fully clothed and smelling like my favorite ladies deodorant.

"I'm going to go now. Thanks for the envelope."

"When can we get together again?"

"I'm sorry that it's been so long. My job keeps me so busy that I don't have any time for fun. Don't worry, I'll find time to see you. I need to, you are my time-off fun."

"Do you want to take any of your presents with you, or should I keep them for you?"

"I want you to keep the rest of the stuff for me, but I'm going to take my butt plug home with me. That way I can practice with it so I'll be ready for next time."

"Aren't you afraid that someone will find out that you have a butt plug?"

"I'm a perv, so it's OK for me to have a butt plug."

"In that case, I'd better get one or two butt plugs of my own."

"I'll just put it in here. Well shit, it barely fits in my little purse. That's what I get for bringing a clutch. Great, I can see it now; I'll probably get pulled over on my way home. 'Oh sure Officer, my driver's license is right here in my purse.' My butt-plug will pop out and land at the cop's feet. I'll casually say, 'Excuse me Officer, could you pick that up for me?'"

We both laugh uncontrollably at Tina's joke. We try to compose ourselves but we're high and still giggling when Tina exits instinctively in the right direction down the hallway.

Chapter 25

I'm So Proud

I am SOOO ready to become a real woman today. I have been practicing all week for this. Today I am finally going to do it. I've been excited for days about this.

I view having successful anal sex as a challenge. I feel that I have not seriously tackled all that many challenges in my life. This has been a particularly exciting challenge for me to work on.

It's wonderful to have John in my life. He is always a gentleman, and yet he'll get shamelessly dirty with me. He's a considerate lover, a generous provider, and a loyal friend. I can't wait to get inside our room, shut out the real world, and play together. I arrive at his door and knock frantically.

I'm obsessed with my desire to fuck Tina's tight little virgin asshole today. I hope she has been practicing with her butt plug like she promised to. She's had three months to practice. Shit, in three months time she could have learned how to play the fucking violin with her asshole if she wanted to. Tina is exceptionally reliable about sexual endeavors. I assign a significant probability of success to achieving anal intercourse today.

An event this important deserves appropriate documentation. I get my camera out of my bag and place it on the nightstand where it will be handy in the heat of passion. I used to worry about shooting photographs of Tina. Now I laugh about my prior fears, because Tina is actually a camera exhibitionist.

There's Tina's knock at the door! Her knock is fast, like a drum roll, today. She must be aroused, or maybe she is merely trying to escape from some business idiots that she pissed-off. I fly to the door and fling it open. Tina jumps into my arms.

"I'm so excited! I want to try anal sex right away, first thing. It's OK if you come right away. Actually that will probably be better. I don't know how much of your big cock I can take in my butt, no matter how much practice I've had."

"OK! Yes, we can definitely try it in your butt when we fuck for the first time today. Would you like a drink first?"

"Yes, make me a strong one. Let's get high before we start attacking my poor little butthole."

"Speaking of little buttholes, do you remember the girl from San Francisco named Gina?"

"Yes. Why?"

"I brought you Gina's underwear."

"Why did you do that?"

"Because you asked me for them."

"I did?"

"Yes, you did."

"Was I serious?"

"How the fuck would I know?"

"Do you have them?"

"Yes, I do."

"Well then show them to me! Don't tease me like that. Show me her photos too."

Wow, Tina is almost as big a pervert as I am. No wonder I like her so much. Tina follows me to my bag and snatches Gina's drawers from me.

"Oooo, they're a sexy design and they're a size zero. Hey! They don't smell! What's wrong with you? Now I'm devastated."

"Well, they're more than six months old. Of course they don't smell any more, but they used to smell great."

"Thanks for teasing me. You're a real shit. Now you've got me in the mood for some pussy. What am I going to do? The only pussy here is mine!"

Tina frowns at me for a second. She seems to have an idea. I wait for her.

"I know what to do."

Tina undresses. I throw my clothes off.

"You are going to lick my pussy and then kiss me with your pussy-face."

I do as instructed and then go back down under to get in a little anilingus, now that she's relaxed. "Your butthole is delightfully accommodating today. My tongue went right in."

"Don't you dare try to kiss me on the mouth now, butt-face."

"Are you ready to try anal sex now?"

"Yes. I want to get your entire cock shoved fully into my butt. I have been stretching it out using my butt-plug for the last few days, because I knew that I was going to see you. Are you ready to try it now?"

"It will be better if we do anal on the second round. I will be able to hold off my orgasm during the insertion. If

361

we do it now, then I will squirt before I get all the way into your butt."

"Fine.   If you're afraid you'll have a premature orgasm, then you can fuck my pussy first."

I look at Tina undecidedly.

"So, how do you want to do it?"

"Get on the bed doggy-style for me." I gently massage Tina's sphincter with my thumb while I pump out the easy first load.   I only last a few strokes thinking about penetrating Tina's hot little butthole. I pull out. Tina sees the camera and remains in position.

"Get a picture of my finger in my butt. This will be the last photo of my virgin butt."

"OK." I get hard again taking photos of Tina playing with her butt.

"I've always wanted a picture like that."

"Can we try it in your butt now?"

"Yes, we should be able to do it this time. I've been practicing.   I took a hot bath earlier and I was able to get three fingers into my butt."

Wow. Tina is more excited about this than I am. How is that even possible?

"I am so ready for this!   What position should we use?"

"Lie down on your side. I'll use some olive oil." I slowly insert one finger, and then two fingers into Tina's tight anus. Tina groans and looks uncomfortable.

"Just use your cock!"

"OK! Good thinking." I give her an olive oil enema and then slather my pulsating penis with the Italian lubricant. I carefully guide the tip of my dick into her anus. I'm shaking from the excitement.   Tina braces herself and pushes her butt onto my penis while she wiggles it into her.

We get my cock most of the way in.

"It's so big."

"Your butt is so tight."

"Give me a second to get used to it."

"Reach inside your pussy and you will feel the head of my dick inside your butt."

"Oh, I can feel you from inside my pussy, that's so nasty."

I reach over for the camera and take a photo of my dick inserted half way into her butt.

"I'm ready now. See if you can fuck my butt.'

I add more olive oil and slowly build up a good stroke. Tina is consumed by the stimulation. As I release my semen into her anus, I am afraid that she'll freak out that I came inside her butt. She seems to have come. I can't tell when I'm in her butt, because her sphincter is always tight. I pull out as slowly as possible. Tina grunts loudly as my still-firm penis pops out of her tight little butthole. She takes a deep breath. Oh no! Here it comes; she's turning to yell at me.

"I did it! I did it! I did it! I've had anal sex. I'm so proud of myself!"

I'm overcome with gratitude for the gift she has given me. Tina is exceptionally pleased with her accomplishment; she celebrates joyously.

"Yeah! Woohoo, I'm a real woman now!"

Tina picks up my camera and takes a smiling self-portrait to capture the moment. I immediately join in her reveling, "Congratulations, you've had anal sex! You were spectacular! That was marvelous."

"I'm so glad that I've finally accomplished it. Shit that hurt. I'm going to go wash up. I'll be right back. We have to commemorate this momentous achievement. Pour me a drink, let's get high."

I wash up at the sink while Tina sings in the shower. I mix up some fancy drinks from the room's mini bar. When Tina returns, she sits down gently.

"Let's talk while my butt rests. Have you heard from our favorite little tramp lately?"

"Little Lisa told me about her trip to a Daddy-Daughter Ball. No shit. It sounded like Sin-derela with black leather and chains. This is exactly how she described it to me:

The Daddy-Daughter Ball was at a private sex club downtown, one that Daddy has taken me to before. Every night they have a different theme. They have gay night, and dyke night, and fetish nights of every kind. We went there one time, and it was the wrong night. The drag queens attending their night got mad at us and told us to leave. The night of the Daddy-Daughter Ball I was dressed in a black leather halter top with openings for my nipples and matching bikini shorts with lots of silver chains. Oh, and I had a black leather choker with fake diamond studs around it. Daddy had a silver chain from my choker to his belt. Lots of the daddies had their daughters on a leash. We got there and made the rounds so that Daddy could meet all the other daddies and show me off. The daughters are not allowed to speak and some of them are gagged or muzzled like a dog. Most of the men are quite old, much older than my daddy, and he's in his sixties. Most of the daughters are overweight women in their late thirties or in their forties. There were some young women there, but not many, and they were all fat. I was the only thin young woman there, so Daddy decided to put me on display for the other daddies to play with. First he put a blindfold on me and handcuffed my hands behind my back. Then he put me in a cage and for the next twenty minutes a bunch of people reached in and fondled my breasts and crotch. It made me super horny. When Daddy took me out of the cage, he removed the cuffs and blindfold. I told him that I wanted to get fucked, but Daddy wasn't in the mood. He's kind of old and doesn't always get an erection, so he picked out a younger guy for me. I got on my knees in front of all the people and gave the guy a blowjob while Daddy encouraged me. The guy came all over my face and the people applauded. I got cleaned up in the ladies room and we went home a little while later. I had to use my vibrator a few times before I could go to sleep that night.

Is she way too sexy or what?"

"That sounds like our little fornicator, she's such a nymphet."

"I think she's a clinical nymphomaniac."

"She's amazing. We need to see her again."

"Can I mix your favorite drink for you? Do you want to try any particular drink? We have a fairly broad selection of intoxicants here."

"Are you drinking from the mini-bar?"

"Yes, I can mix you almost anything."

"Isn't that ridiculously expensive?"

"Yes, but we're on my entertainment expense account tonight."

"Is that why we're meeting at this snotty hotel?"

"I found a great rate at this place by searching last-minute deals online. This is the nicest hotel I could find that is located near your residence. I wanted you to have an elegant environment in which to lose your butt-cherry."

"That's so sweet and considerate of you. In that case, I want a slow comfortable screw against the wall."

"I'm sorry to inform you that I can't do slow or comfortable. Unfortunately, we do not have any sloe gin, or Southern Comfort."

"Well shit! What can you do?"

"I can screw against the wall."

"Then give me a double-screw against the wall."

I look for a topic to chat about while I mix our drinks and we rest between rounds. Tina beats me to it.

"I have taken a different job at the place where I work. I'm doing debt consolidation now."

"Sounds interesting, how do you like it?"

"It's hell! But it's a full-time career position. I make more money, but they want me to work every day. That's because of the terrible economy right now. I can't work every day, I need at least one day off each week to complete my essential errands. I need some time off during the day to attend to my vital tasks, such as: getting my hair and nails done. Those places aren't open late in the evenings. They don't seem to understand that it is imperative that I'm able to go to the gym, and the tanning salon, at least twice a week.

I told them they have to schedule me for a minimum of two mornings off each week. For crying out loud, when will I have time to see you to get my sex?"

"Speaking of sex..."

"Are you ready? How should we do it this time?"

"Let's do it doggy-style again."

"OK."

Tina jumps up on the bed and sticks her cute little rump in the air. I nuzzle in behind her and insert before she's ready.

"Oh, you're inside me already."

I admire Tina's amicable anus. She's not a butt-virgin anymore. I'm still excited from the anal sex. I don't last long once Tina climaxes. I come deep insider her vagina. "Hold still."

I slowly remove my penis from her and put my mouth on her asshole. I grab her hips and push my tongue deep into her butthole trying to taste my semen. She must have washed thoroughly, because there is no evidence of my ejaculation. I release her and she turns around to look at me with wide eyes.

"That was fun, butt-face."

"You're the hottest fuck on earth."

"You're pretty good yourself."

"You are the best fuck I've ever had."

"I thought you said that Little Lisa was."

"Now that you do anal, you're a better fuck than she is."

"Oh, you're so sweet. Make us some more fancy drinks, and we'll get high. I'm going to rinse, I'll be right back."

While Tina splashes in the tub and I make the drinks, I contemplate asking her about her history. Usually that topic is off-limits in the escort-client relationship, but we're way past that. I'm going to ask her, but I'll approach it slowly, so I don't upset her. I look up to see Tina smiling at me. I hand her a drink. We get high.

"That was fun. I like your tongue in my butt, it's nasty. I've never had a guy with a butthole fetish. Be sure to brush your teeth before you kiss me!"

"Do you mind if I ask you about something we talked about last time?"

"That depends on what it is."

"You were telling me that you remember everything."

"I don't remember saying that."

"I'm sorry, I should provide you with a relative context to help associate your cognitive recall."

"Are you high?"

"Yes, but that's not the point."

"Then get to the point."

"Do you remember, two visits ago, when the spaced-out

chick asked you how you got started as an escort?"

"Yes, I remember that. What about it?"

"The last time we met, you said that you didn't remember how you got started, but that you would think about it."

"That's right. I have been thinking about it."

"So?"

"So... what?"

"Can we talk about how you got started?"

"There isn't much to talk about."

"I'm sorry, if you don't want to discuss it, then that's all right, we can drop the subject. I don't want to pry."

"No, you don't understand. I don't mind talking about it, there just isn't anything to say. I haven't ever thought about how I got started. I just did it. I do remember that I was looking at some escort websites one day. I was thinking about how much money they make and how they are their own boss. It sounded like fun."

"Then what happened?"

"It wasn't a significant event, or pivotal moment, in my life. I just saw the escort ads and decided to put up mine. I didn't even think about it, until I started to get email messages from prospective clients asking to be screened."

"How did you decide to go on your first call?"

"One of the men that contacted me seemed like a nice older man. He had excellent references and was a prominent citizen in the community. He easily passed my extensive screening process. We talked a couple of times on the phone and I needed the money, so I set it up to meet him. That's all."

Tina obviously doesn't want to talk about this subject, so I steer the conversation back on-topic. "I'm going to brush my teeth. Can we go again?"

"You have to let my poor little butthole rest. You can fuck my pussy though."

I quickly brush my teeth and return to the bedroom. I look Tina over. She smiles at me.

"How do you want me?"

"Lie down on the bed on your back."

"Can I keep my pillows for my head this time?"

I pump Tina while I deep-French-kiss her. I last a long time. Tina orgasms, but I don't. I feel myself getting close to climax, but if Tina doesn't climax again, then it will be difficult for me to.

I pull my penis out of her vagina, climb up and shove it in her face. Tina laughs at the surprise and then sucks me into her warm mouth. A few strokes later I ejaculate. She takes it all and swallows.

I reposition and re-enter her vagina while I am still hard. I get as many strokes in as I can before I get soft. I deep-French-kiss Tina and tell her that I can taste my semen in her pretty mouth.

"You're such a dirty old man!"

"You're the best girlfriend on earth."

"You're only saying that because you got me for your sperm-shot-trifecta thing. I need to take a shower and use the mouthwash."

"I wish I could make you as happy as you make me." Tina stops at the door to the bathroom, turns and gives me a long knowing look that stops me cold.

"What makes you think that you don't?"

I am speechless. Tina walks slowly toward me, looking me in the eye the whole time. She wraps me up in her arms and kisses me hard on the mouth. My knees get weak.

"I'm going to take a shower and get dressed now."

Tina turns quickly and prances off to the bathroom. I prepare her envelope while I ponder my incredible luck. I am exceptionally fortunate to know this rare and delightful young lady. I hear Tina singing in the bathroom. I place her envelope under her purse, put on a robe, and go out onto the balcony to smoke a cigar.

John is a divine sex partner. I can't believe the outlandish things I'm willing to do with him. I have never trusted a boyfriend the way I trust John. I'm going to go out clubbing with my girlfriends tonight. I won't tell them that my sugar daddy shot a load of semen in all three of my orifices. It will be my nasty little secret. I will just buy them three rounds of drinks to celebrate and say that I got a bonus at work. That will be fun.

Tina joins me on the balcony. She is fully clothed and packed up ready to leave.

"You look happy."

"I love your mischievous little grin."

"I'm going to be wearing a dirty smirk on my face for the rest of the night. I'm an analist now!"

"Can I walk you to your car?"

"You don't need to today. When I pulled in to the front entrance to ask where the self-parking was, the doorman told me I could park right in front and that he'd personally watch my car for me. I like this hotel. You should stay here on the balcony, and finish your cigar. I want to remember you like this."

Tina turns and scoots out the door before I know it. She's a wonderful woman. I can't wait to see her again. I am the luckiest guy on earth.

Chapter 26

I Can't Tell Anyone

I arrive at John's door appreciating that I will get to discuss my recent sexual achievements with the person on the other side. It's been hell not being able to tell anyone that I'm a butt fucker now. I consider this a monumental achievement in my life.

There is NO WAY that I would EVER agree to have anal sex with any guy on a regular date. What would the guy think of me? Besides that, young guys don't know what they're doing in bed. I don't trust them. I have to admit that I've enjoyed going on some regular dates lately. I won't say anything to John about that. I see how he sneers whenever I so much as mention being with another man. That is so typical of the reaction most guys have. Men are such pussies.

It's been a long time since we've met. I have missed having secret sex rendezvous at upscale hotels, with a generous gentleman, even if he is a total pervert. There is no denying that John is an oversexed deviant, but that quality also makes him more interesting. Wait a second. What does that make me? Why is the door opening? I didn't knock. Did I?

I arrive late because I got lost trying to find this business-class hotel that is located quite close to where Tina lives. It is already our scheduled meeting time when I get to the room. I text the room number to Tina and jump in the shower. I come out of the shower to see that Tina sent me a text message a few minutes ago.

From: Tina
Sub: I'm Sexcited
Msg: On my way
now, C U soon.

Great, Tina will be here in twenty to thirty minutes. I put on my robe and start to mix myself a drink, but I am interrupted. That's her! That's definitely Tina's knock at the door. How can she be here already? I answer the door with an empty glass in my hand.

"Hi sweetie! I've missed you. How are you?"

"How did you get here so fast?"

"I live only a few blocks away. I hope that no one I know saw me entering the hotel."

Tina is not as tanned or toned as usual, however she is still arousingly attractive. She no longer has an adolescent look about her. I won't say anything to Tina about that.

"It is great to see you. How have you been? Have you missed me?"

"I've missed you terribly. It's been a long time."

"It hasn't been that long, has it?"

"It's been four months."

"Sorry, I've been working six days a week and they're paying me a lot more money. I just don't have any time for sex. I don't even have time to get to the gym or the tanning salon. I'm going to demand that I get some mornings off during the week. I have to get my hair and nails done and, you know... other vital errands like that."

"Have you hit on any of the girls at work?"

"I almost asked a girl at my gym to go out for a drink with me, but I didn't. I wanted to, and I would have, if only I had the nerve."

Tina plops a gigantic purse on the table. I hand her a drink and she sits down and sips it. Her pants are so tight that she has trouble getting comfortable.

"It's hard for me to get the courage up to ask a girl for a date."

"I want to undress you."

"No, not today. I brought an outfit that I want to change into for you." I think to myself, "You'd never get these pants off of me anyway." I've gained weight and I barely squirmed into them today.

Tina grabs her big purse and announces her opinion over her shoulder as she steps into the bathroom.

"You're going to love it, I'll be right back."

The bathroom door slams shut just as she finishes her sentence. Tina has become more authoritative as she has matured. I like it, but she scares me a little. I drink and get high while I wait for her with wanton anticipation.

I look at my debilitated body in the mirror. I hate not being able to go to the gym and tanning salon as often as I'm used to. I simply must get my regular workouts. I'm never going to become one of those fat-assed, pasty office workers that guys won't hit on.

I dig into my bag. The outfit I brought today is from way back in my late modeling days, when I was fuller figured. It covers up my bulges and pushes my boobs up into a nice cleavage. John will love it. I'll have to hold my breath to fasten it up. He better love it.

The bathroom door opens. Tina struts out wearing a sexy lace-up black and purple corset that flatters her already attractive figure. She looks me in the eye and does a stripper-walk across the room toward me. I turn my chair out from the table like I would at a titty-bar to get a table dance. Tina recognizes the move. She stands between my knees and gives me a performance. I get a raging boner that pops out of my robe. Tina giggles when she sees it, then gets down on her knees and blows my mind.

I blow-catch John and see that he brought new porn. That's always fun.

Tina swallows, wipes her mouth on my robe, sits down next to me and drains her drink. I pour her another drink and look her in the eye as I hand it to her. "I am in love with you."

"Of course you are. Every guy is in love with the girl that has just blown him. Are these new magazines?"

"Yes, I just got those today, on the way here when I got the stuff for our drinks. I always feel like telling the clerk at the store, 'These magazines are not for me, they're for my bikini-model girlfriend.' But no one would believe that anyway."

"Look at the hot body on that girl. I'd like to fuck her. I bet you'd like to fuck her too."

"I've fucked a girl with a hot body like that."

"When? Who? Tell me."

"For a short time, a few years back, I had a super-hot girlfriend with a tight body like that. I fucked her every chance I got. I fucked her five hundred times in the four years we saw each other." Tina looks introspective for a second and then she looks at me with a curious, but serious expression.

"How many times have you fucked me?"

Oh shit! I'm caught. I stammer, "Well, I haven't been

376

counting..."

"Why the hell not? You counted how many times you fucked her!"

Tina looks angry, but only for a second and quickly shakes it off.

"Were you in love with her?"

"I thought I was. We had great chemistry, but because we were incompatible and had unfavorable circumstances, the relationship ended."

"Details! I want details. Don't hold out on me, you know that I love juicy gossip."

"OK, I have a model for relationships." I stroke Tina's thigh suggestively, "You know that I'm exceptionally fond of models."

"Details please."

"My model has three primary factors that determine the quality of the relationship. The first factor is chemistry. Do you turn each other on? Without chemistry, then nothing else usually happens. The second factor is compatibility. How well do you get along when you're not screwing? Can you pay bills together? Do you fight over little shit? The third factor is circumstances. Are you both available? Do you live in the same area? These are the factual matters of your respective situations that affect the relationship."

"What does this have to do with fucking your girlfriend five hundred times?"

"Oh, sorry. So we had great chemistry but we were completely incompatible and the circumstances were... problematic, to say the least."

"So, you loved her, but it wasn't going to last. I bet that as long as you were screwing, then everything was great, but when you weren't, it fell apart?"

"Exactly."

"What were the circumstances that were such a big problem?"

"Well..."

John gets a blank expression and goes completely quiet. He seems to be having difficulty deciding what to say next. What is so unusual about this subject to make him act so strangely?

"I don't think that we should talk about it."

"That's OK. We don't have to discuss it."

"Thanks."

I guess that John is not secure enough in our relationship for him to show me some of the skeletons in his closet. I'm surprised that he is suddenly secretive about this, given all the other private things we talk about. I suppose that since it's about an old girlfriend, then I can understand his reluctance to talk about it.

"In any case, she had an extremely hot body that drove me crazy."

"I can't believe you fucked your girlfriend five hundred times, and that you counted every fuck. You adulterous accumulator."

Tina has a voraciously vulgar vocabulary.

"Let's have sex."

"Can we try anal today? That was so hot the last time, when I came in your ass. I was euphoric for the next several days."

"Me too, I'm so proud of myself! I feel like I've experienced an enormous event in my life, but I can't tell anyone. It's not like I can tell my friends or my family, 'Hey everybody, guess what I did for the first time?' I don't think so."

"Since you can't tell anyone, maybe you should write in a diary, or a journal, like Little Lisa does."

"Little Lisa has a written record of her sexploits?"

"She told me that she has diaries from way back when she first started having sex. She knew she was a nympho even before she knew what that meant."

"She must have a shelf full of books by now."

"She said she has several volumes and that she is still writing in them."

"I'll think about that, but my diary isn't going to be proud of me."

"Well I'm proud of you baby. I'll help you to celebrate attaining this admirable accomplishment. You can be my DP girl now."

"I'm going to need a lot more practice before I can take two cocks in me at the same time."

This girl is too hot to be real. Wait, what were we doing? Oh, that's right, "Are you ready to try anal now? Do you want to take an enema first?"

"NO! I don't ever do enemas. Why would you even ask me that?"

Tina is suddenly angry and defensive. I must have stumbled onto a sore nerve.

"Why do you want me to take an enema? Do you want a... brown shower?"

"Are you serious?"

"I was joking. That was sarcasm you debased delinquent. Why? Do you want one? Do you?"

"I'm not sure. You are so exciting that even your shit turns me on, so I'm not sure."

"Aww, that's a sweet thing to say."

"Yes, I know how to charm a woman, 'Hey girl, your shit is sexy'. That line gets them every time."

"I'm going to use the bathroom. You are going to stay here. You don't want a brown shower, trust me on that one. You wouldn't like it. Besides, I don't think that I can shit on command and I don't EVER take an enema, so ask the cat burglar to shit on you if that's what you're into. She's so nasty that she'd do it, and she'd like doing it."

"I don't know about that. I'm not exactly sure where our little nymphomaniac draws the line. She always closes the bathroom door tight to use the toilet after her enema."

"Are you kidding? If she's nasty enough to break into a boy's locker room to jill off, then she's nasty enough to give you a brown shower. I can't believe how crazy she is. I can't believe that she told you she was going to break into a high school boy's locker room just to masturbate. That is too crazy."

"Uh, she goes to Daddy-Daughter orgies, so I don't consider the locker room thing to be much of a stretch."

"The Daddy-Daughter Ball is just a lifestyle choice, whereas the plan to masturbate in a boy's locker room is a pure perversion, and that shit is just plain deviant. That shit is messed-up big-time."

Tina's rant is so esoteric that I have to turn away to prevent her from seeing me laughing at her antics. Tina strolls to the bathroom and shuts the door. I pour myself a double-strength drink and take a cigar out on the balcony to smoke while I ponder.

It seems to me that Tina has chosen a curious demarcation to draw a distinction on the acceptability of Little Lisa's various behaviors. Tina joins me on the balcony wrapped up in one of the white terrycloth robes. She snuggles up close to me, takes my arm and whispers suggestively into my ear.

"I washed my backside super clean for you. I know how infatuated you are with my butt. If you're going to put your tongue back there, then I try to get it as clean as possible for you."

"You are a wonderful creature."

"You are a depraved degenerate. It's a good thing that I like that about you."

I can't believe how lucky I am to know Tina and to be able to spend time with her like this. I must do everything I can to make Tina feel loved and appreciated. I start to get a boner.

"I can see that you are ready to play. What do you want to do?"

"Can we try anal today?"

"Sure, I've been practicing. Do you think there is a position that works best?"

"Many girls do better having anal on their back. Do you want to try that?"

"Like this?"

"Perfect." I get the anesthetic and the lube out of my bag. I grab the camera and nuzzle in close to Tina's tight little butthole.

"I don't like the numb-butt cream, it stings. Just use the olive oil. I don't need the anesthetic. It's not like I'm a virgin anymore."

I recall that Tina doesn't like it when I put my fingers in her butt, so I lube up my boner, squirt oil on her asshole and push the tip of my dick into her anus.

"Oh fuck you're big! Slowly, go slow until I get used to having that fat cock in my poor little butthole."

Tina rubs her clit fast and hard as I slowly work my penis fully into her asshole. I grab the camera and ease my dick halfway out of her. I snap several shots as she slowly expels my dick. I put down the camera and just barely keep the tip of my cock in her butt. I push it back in and build up a good stroke. Tina makes a lot of noise as I get close to orgasm and pound her. I finish as quickly as possible. The poor girl is panting.

"Oh fuck, that hurt, but I came harder than I usually do. That was fun. I'm going to keep practicing at home so that I can enjoy it more."

I ease out of Tina's shit-hole and she groans.

"Is it all right? Is it messy? Was I dirty? Do you need to shower first?"

"Everything is fine, you can shower first if you want to." I collapse on the bed. I am shaking from the excitement. Tina returns a few minutes later. I wash up in the shower, put on the other robe, and join her at the table.

"I came harder from having your cock in my butt than I do when you're in my pussy!"

"Me too."

"You're a Greek freak."

"I'm so proud of you, now that you are having anal sex!"

"Me too, but like I said, I can't tell anyone."

"Do you want to see the self-portrait you took last time?"

"What are you taking about?"

"I'll show you." I get my computer out and bring up the photograph. "Here's your self portrait from last time."

"I don't remember taking this."

"You were cum-drunk at the time."

"I remember taking this one with my finger in my butt. Look at how good it came out. You've got to send me a copy of this one. I've always wanted a picture like that."

"Speaking of butt photos, I found a picture of our little commando after she suffered an injury in battle."

"What the fuck are you talking about?"

"Oh, the expression, 'going commando' means going without underwear."

"I've never heard that expression."

382

"Anyway, the last time I saw our favorite dirty blond, I asked her to wear panties to our date. I told her to wear them so they'd smell like her. She liked the idea that I wanted a pair to keep for my collection. She put them on and made the long drive from Palm Desert. By the time she got here they had rubbed her butt so bad, that she had a reaction."

"What do you mean by 'she had a reaction'? What happened to her?"

"Here, look at the photo."

"Oh my God! Look at this poor girl's butt. She's so allergic to undergarments that they gave her... a welt on her ass."

"Little Lisa doesn't like clothes all that much in general, and she only wears underwear as a special favor, when one of her daddies asks her to. When I refer to her as a dirty blond, I'm not talking about the color of her hair!"

"Don't ever say that to her face."

"I already told her that I refer to her that way."

"What did she say?"

"She told me I was being devilish and irreverent. She kissed me and said that she liked it. She told me that I should call her my dirty blond from now on."

"I'm horny from talking about our sordid little harlot. Let's have sex now."

"Can we try it in your butt again?

"No, I'm too sore back there to do that again. Lie on your back and I'll get on top."

Tina sucks me a few strokes to get me hard and mounts me. She rides me seductively while I play with her butt. I work my middle finger three knuckles deep into her asshole. By the time she comes, she is screaming and writhing.

"I'm going rinse off in the shower. Wash your hands before you fix my drink."

Tina showers while I wash up at the sink. I mix our drinks and she joins me at the table. Tina clearly wants to take a break from the sex and rest. I wait while she sips her drink and forms her thoughts.

"My butt hurts. Did you have you finger in my butt while we were fucking?"

"Yes, I did. Is that all right?"

"That explains why my butt hurts. You made me come hard though, so I guess it's worth it.

"Our little sex pot says the same thing when I finger her ass during sex."

"Have you heard from our little belle of the Daddy-Daughter ball? Have you talked to her? You haven't sent me any invitations lately. Is she going to play with us or do we need to find another girl for our threesome?"

"No, I've not heard from the caged cat in a few months."

"I almost asked a girl at my gym to go out for a drink with me."

"Which girl?"

"I was in the locker room undressing after my workout when the jet-black-haired alabaster goddess came out of the shower. She just stood there naked, looking at me. I was naked and still sweaty. I wanted to invite her out for a drink so bad. I almost did, but at the last second, I didn't have the nerve."

"What happened?"

"She smiled at me, walked over to her locker and got dressed."

"What did you do?"

"I took a cold shower."

"I'm so sorry. I know how distressing that is."

384

"You would think that if I had the balls to go on out-calls, that I would be bold enough to ask a girl out for a drink."

"I understand that it's not the same thing. But I have confidence in you and I know that, when the time is right, you will find the courage to go through with it."

"Thanks for the encouragement. Oh, I wanted to tell you that I finally remembered how I got started escorting. I've been thinking about it a lot since we last talked, and it eventually came back to me."

"What do you remember? Can you tell me?"

"It's been so long since I've thought about it, that I couldn't remember anything when I first tried to. I have never told anyone about it. Well, except I did tell my sister a little bit one time.

"How much did you tell your little sister?"

"It was last year when I visited her in Minnesota. She wanted to know how I had so much money. I told her that I had been stripping, but that I quit that job and now I have a sugar daddy. I told her that having a sugar daddy is much better than working as a nude model or as a stripper. She was super curious and asked me a lot of questions about what it's like."

"What did you tell her?"

"I told her that stripping and nude modeling is scary and dangerous. She said that she wanted to start stripping. I yelled at her and told her that she needs to go to college, not start stripping."

"You care a lot about your sister, don't you?"

"She has opportunities that I never had. She's a good student. She's got a full scholarship, and she can go directly into a four-year college or university, if she wants to. I don't want her to go down the same path that I did. She has options that I didn't have and I want her to capitalize on her capabilities, not rely on her good-looks, like I have had to."

"She's lucky to have you for a big sister. Is she getting the message?"

"I think so, but she insisted on hearing all about my nude modeling and stripping. She asked me how I got started as an entertainer. I told her that at first, it was only a small step from what I had been doing as a nude model. I don't ever talk to anyone about my days as a nude model. Even though she kept asking me, I wouldn't tell her anything about it. I've never told her that I was an escort for a little while. I just told her that I worked a couple of years as an entertainer."

"Do you mind if I ask you what exactly you were doing when you worked as an entertainer?"

"Oh, I don't mind at all. It actually started when I was working as a hooker-booker."

"I'm sorry, a what?"

"A hooker-booker is the person that sets up the appointments on the phone for an out-call escort or entertainer."

"How did you get that job?"

"I had been working as an out-call stripper, you know, just dancing and getting naked for bachelor's parties. I never once even touched a customer sexually and I never let them touch me in any way."

"Yes, I'm familiar with strippers. I've hired them before."

"The money and drugs were incredible, but the hours and the owners were pure hell. I could see how much easy money there was to be made in the entertainer industry, but I didn't want to be put in compromising positions all the time. I never let customers grope me, but the owners were crazy people."

"What happened?"

"While working as a stripper I had overheard the

owners booking the shows and I saw how that works. Then I learned how to screen customers, how to handle problem callers, that sort of thing. When I quit working as a stripper, I called every stripper agency in Orange County until I found a job at an agency working the phones as a hooker-booker."

"What did you do as a hooker-booker?"

"It was great. I got ten percent of the show fee for every booking. It was easy work. All I had to do was take calls from clients, screen them a little bit, call the girl and confirm the appointment. I was making good money working only a few hours each night. The owner was a nice older lady with a beautiful home in a snotty community in Irvine. I would go there at night in my pajamas and bring my dog. We'd order restaurant food and have it delivered to the door."

"All you did was... talk to people?"

"I just answered the phones along with another girl, then I'd call one of the girls and set up the appointment with her. I would mark the amount and time on my call-sheet. At the end of the night the girls would come by and drop off the agency's split, which was most of the show fee. The girls kept their tips, after they took care of their drivers. My split was ten percent of the show fee, so the money added up fast. I set up anywhere from ten to twenty calls per night, usually working from about seven PM to midnight."

"Did you like that job?"

"It was good money, I got to keep my clothes on, and I did not have to deal directly with the customers in-person. We used our real names because there were no clients there. The out-call girls were making a TON of money. We were carefully screening the clients for them, so they didn't get any weirdos. The owner enforced a strict set of rules. We only sent girls to nice hotels. We always called the hotel to confirm the customer's name, and other shit like that. The girls got good clients and they made a shit-load of money."

"How did you make the transition from Booker to Hooker?"

"OK. So one night, we were short a few girls, due to vacations, their periods, random illnesses, things like that. All the available girls were soon fully booked and then we got calls from some of our better regular clients. There were requests from two nice regulars. They were men that I knew never asked to be touched, and that always tipped well. I asked the owner first, and then I decided that I would go on a couple of calls that night. I carefully selected the clients that I would see, from what the girls had said about them."

"What did you do?"

"I picked a nickname, like the out-call girls do, and then called the clients back. I said we had a new girl named Christy and I described her to them. They agreed to see her, so I essentially booked my own appointments, two of them.

I went home, got changed, and did my makeup real quick. Then I drove to my first out-call escort job. I got to the first client's place and he said he had a second girl coming for a two-girl show. I was surprised, but I had heard of this kind of thing, so I said OK.

The girl that showed up turned out to be a former hooker-booker from my agency that I had worked with previously. She came in and said, 'Hi!' Then she called me by my real name, and said, 'I know you!' I almost died. I couldn't get her to shut up about it either. I screamed at her, 'No you don't know me!' and she says, 'Yes I do!' I yelled right in her face, 'No you're wrong! My name is Christy.'"

"Did she ever catch on?"

"She was too stupid to realize that I was using an alias. I was so pissed-off that I could have strangled her.

388

I quit my job at that agency two weeks later. I never saw that client again."

"Did you make a clean break?"

"I kept seeing a few of the nice regulars that I had met doing shows during those two weeks. I always booked directly with them, not through the agency, so there was no split.

I was independent for the first time. I liked it. I saw some of the men several times after leaving that agency, but I never had sex with any of them. I didn't have sex during any appointment, until I became an independent, full-service, out-call escort. That's when I met you."

Tina stares off into the distance for a long time and then speaks as though she's talking to herself.

"I haven't thought about that period of my life in a long time. You are the only person I have ever told that to. Why does this only come up when I'm with you?"

"Because you know in your heart that I truly love you, and care about you."

"You're right, I do feel that way about you."

"Can I lick your pussy?"

"Sure, let me set up my pillows first."

I get into position and polish Tina's bare floor. After she climaxes, I roll her onto her side, climb on top, and ride her to completion. She pops up out of bed as I roll off of her.

"Put on the porn movie while I wash up."

Tina returns to bed. The porn scene that is playing shows two girls playing with a strap-on. I ask Tina as casually as I can, "Have you ever used a strap-on?"

"No, I never have, but I've always wanted to try one. Every girl wants to have a penis."

Tina sounds like Freud. I mix her a drink. "Do you

389

want to get high?"

"Yes, let's have some more. Can we?"

We drink and get raucously high together.

"How many times can you come in one day?"

"Six times is a good day, and that's happened many times. My record is a dozen times, but that only happened once."

"You do realize how crazy that is, don't you?"

"Can we go again?"

"I'm worn out."

"We don't have to have sex again if you're too tired."

"You can fuck me if you want to, but I'm just going to lie here. I'm too exhausted to get on top, but you can fuck me if you do all the work."

I get on top of Tina in the missionary position and lube up her pussy with spit. I insert and she just lies there. I start up a fast stroke and Tina gets involved. By the time I finish, Tina is screaming and digging her nails into my back. I roll off and Tina pops out of bed. She strolls into the bathroom shaking her head.

"I didn't think I could come again. How did you do that to me?"

"You always turn me on. You ignite me like a solid rocket booster."

"I need to pee. Do you want a golden shower?"

"Are you serious?"

"Do you want one or not? I have to go."

"No, not this time, but thanks for asking me. I'll definitely think about that. I may want one someday."

"I'm going to take a warm bath after I pee and soak my sore pussy."

"Take all the time you want."

After my bath I put on the ever-present ladies deodorant and get dressed. John has my envelope

390

ready for me, right under my purse like always. He is such a gentleman.

"When can I see you again?"

"I'm too tired at night. Let's get together during the day, before my afternoon shift starts. I'm going to have some mornings off starting next week. Text me in a couple of weeks and we'll work it out."

"Can I walk you to your car?"

"No, we're too close to where I live. Someone I know around here might see me. It's not that late and I'm parked pretty close to the front door."

Tina gives me a long wet kiss on the lips.

"Bye sweetie. I had fun."

I open the door for Tina; she tip toes out into the corridor, looks around nervously and scampers down the hallway toward the elevators.

Chapter 27

My Butt Hurts

I am glad I have John as a friend. I feel like I can count on him to always be there for me. He is nothing like the guys that I date. John would never drop me without a word. With John I'd never be left wondering what I did wrong that blew the deal. I'm confident that John will be kind and that he will screw me silly whenever I need it. At the same time, he's never needy or clingy, like the guys my age always are. I knock on his door thinking I should have seen John instead of going on all those regular dates.

It's been six months since Tina last visited me. I wonder if she still likes me? She must have a steady boyfriend, or maybe a steady girlfriend. Oh! That's her knock at the door now.

"Hi John, I've missed you. How are you? You look good!"

"I'm so happy to see you again." Tina looks fabulous. I squeeze her tight when she hugs me, and she practically crushes me in return. She's clearly been going to the gym regularly. I pry her off of me in a reflex of self-preservation. "It's been so long."

"Sorry, my work has been crazy. The debt consolidation business has slowed down. They laid-off a bunch of people, and as a result, I have been working more hours. It's nice to take a break from all that office bullshit and see you. What's new?"

"I have a present for you today"

"Is it a sex toy? Can we play with it?"

"Yes, do you want it now?"

"Of course I want it now!"

"I hope you don't already have one, it's a strap-on."

"Oh my God! You're great. I've always wanted one. Can I play with it now?"

I hand Tina the box and watch her examine it.

"I wonder if Little Lisa will want to use it on me first, or if she'll want me to use it on her?"

"I can't believe you said that!"

"Said what?"

"Our little hussy uttered those exact same words the moment she strapped it on."

"What words?"

"Lisa was wearing it and she started stroking the dildo like a guy jacking off, when she said, 'I wonder if Tina will want to use it on me first, or if she'll want me to use it on her?'"

"That sounds like our little enchantress. We're both nymphos, I think that's why I like her so much. When did you get a strap-on?"

"On my way to see Little Lisa a couple of weeks ago I stopped at a local adult paraphernalia store. I finally settled on the crotch-less, black leather, bikini style strap-on equipped with a big purple detachable dildo."

"Were you embarrassed buying it?"

394

"The clerk at the erotic store says to me, 'I have that dildo in a flesh tone, if you like that better.' I told the saleslady, 'The purple one is perfect. You know, if my girlfriend is going to be wearing this, then I specifically don't want it to look too realistic.'"

"This penis is nice and big. Good job!"

"The sales clerk says to me 'We have dildos in a variety of sizes that will fit in that leather strap-on bikini-bottom.' She showed me an array of seven or eight dildos ranging in size from one that was smaller than your thumb to one that was the size of your forearm."

"I'm glad you didn't get that one."

"I picked the one two sizes from the largest and told the lady, 'I want it to be big enough for my girlfriend to be proud, but not so big that I get shown-up by her.'"

"I want to put it on."

"Sure, open it up." Tina puts it on over her denims and clearly enjoys wearing it. She starts playing with the dildo fondly. She looks at herself in the mirror and strokes her penis the way a guy strokes his dick. Tina looks up longingly and confesses.

"I like it. I've always wanted a penis."

"I think a lot of girls want one of their own."

"I'd love to fuck a cute girl with this"

"Let's get together with Little Lisa so that you can try out your new dick." Tina's pretty eyes get big, and she grins mischievously.

"Yes, definitely. I want to fuck her with this."

"We can DP her."

"Oh, that would be so much fun! I don't know though. She's pretty small and I'm pretty big."

Tina chortles uncontrollably, I feel pleased that the gift is so well received.

"It's fun to have a dick of my own to play with."

"Oh, I want to tell you about what happened when Lisa first put it on. See how the bikini bottoms have fabric fastener straps on both sides? This is convenient, but when it's opened up on both sides, it's kind of hard to tell which end is which. As Lisa attached one side of the bikini bottoms, I could see that it was going to end up backwards on her. I waited until she was pulling it up and was in the process of attaching the second side of the bikini. At that point I got her attention and softly mentioned to her, with a gentle correcting tone that you would use with a child, 'Lisa, honey, the penis goes IN FRONT.'"

"What did she do?"

"Lisa looked up at me confused and then looked behind her. When she saw the dildo pointing out her back side, her jaw dropped and her mouth formed a big "O". She looked embarrassed. She said, 'Oops.' and covered her mouth. It looked like a tail. She quickly reversed the direction of the item and then admired her new look in the mirror."

"What did she say?"

"That's when Lisa started stroking her new penis and thought out loud, 'I wonder if Tina will want to use it on me first, or if she'll want me to use it on her?'"

"That's our little nymphomaniac. She's great. Now I'm horny. I have to leave for work in a little over an hour. I need you to fuck me a couple of times so I don't get in trouble with the cute girls at work. Do you want to fuck now?"

"Yes... but only if you take off the strap-on."

"I'm disappointed in you. You're not nearly as kinky as I hoped you were."

"I'm going to fuck you so hard... your pussy will squirt."

"You better fuck me hard. I'm counting on it."

"You like it hard, don't you?"

"You'll probably start my period."

"When are you due?"

"Not for another two weeks, but your big dick could still bust it out of me."

We stand looking at each other quietly.

Is John going to undress me, or should I just strip? He's looking at my dildo nervously. I tear off the strap-on and undo my pants. John sheds his clothes, so I get naked and lie down on my back in the middle of the bed. John climbs on top of me. I grab his penis and guide it into me. I'm already wet.

I hold Tina down and pound her as hard as I can. She comes hard, looks me deep in the eyes and kisses me. I climax in her. "You're the cutest girl I've ever fucked."

"Every girl that a guy has just screwed is the cutest girl he's ever fucked." Tina throws me off effortlessly and comments, "You need to say that the next morning when she looks like shit. I'm going to wash up."

Tina heads for the bathroom, I head for the balcony to have a cigar. Tina is the hottest girl I've ever met. She is pure poise and class. I'm totally in love with her.

I look at myself in the bathroom mirror. It's nice of John to say that I'm the cutest girl he's ever fucked. That's quite a compliment, considering that he's fucked so many women. He is such a pervert that he's turned me into one. Wait. Oh, shit! That makes me a pervert. This won't do! "John! Hey John!"

Tina flies out of the bathroom shouting my name. I dash into the room from the balcony. "What?"

"Are we perverts?"

"Huh?"

"You heard me. Are we?"

"Are we what?"

"Perverts!"

"Why, what do you want to try now?"

"No, not that, you perv. I want to know if we are perverted or if other people are just... totally repressed sexually?"

"Oh, I see. That depends."

"Depends on what?"

"Your datum."

"What the fuck are you talking about. I'm a model not a nerd. Speak to me in plain fucking English."

"Look at it this way, if 'normal' people are... like the Amish, then we are clearly devils. However, if 'normal' people are like Little Lisa, then we're practically angels."

"Of course, I understand that. Shit, there are prudes out there that would have us arrested, while Little Lisa probably thinks we have no imagination or sense of adventure. What I want to know is, do YOU think we are perverts?"

"I simultaneously hold two opposite feelings in my heart. On the one hand, I am boggled by my fortune of kinky lovers, and on the other hand, I'm disappointed at all the things I haven't tried yet."

"So do you think we are perverts or not?"

"I think we should pursue anything that we fancy, without consideration for any labels or judgment."

"So you think we are perverts."

"I think we should try to be whatever we want to be."

"How do we do that?"

"Can we try it in your butt?"

"Sure, do you have the olive oil? Is it extra-virgin?"

"Yes, it is extra-virgin, just like your butthole." I apply the Italian lubricant to my Italian sausage and to my lover's tight anus. I stand behind her, insert the tip of my penis and push it in.

"Oh shit! You're big. Use more olive oil."

I dribble olive oil down Tina's crack as I slowly stroke her butthole. She relaxes and I pump her ass deeply. Tina gets noisy. "I'm going to give you a semen enema little girl."

"Oh yes, fuck me! Fuck my butt Daddy. Fuck me in my butt."

I grab Tina's hips, penetrate deeply and pump her fast until I climax. We are both breathing hard.

"Go take a shower and wash your dick off real good. I plan to suck it and then kiss you. Get it?"

"I got it."

John jumps in the shower and I lie in bed and wonder. Why do I miss John so much when I don't see him? I'm not in love with him. He's certainly fun and I enjoy his company. He's more than that though. John is respectful, kind, generous, and trustworthy; much more so than any boyfriend I have ever had. He is not the kind of man I would have ever imagined that I would love, but even if we are not 'in love', why not love him?

I return to bed and Tina takes her turn in the bathroom. She wants to rest and talk a while when she returns to the bed. I use the opportunity to ask her something I've been curious about. "Do you mind if I ask you something about your past that you told me about last time?"

"That depends on what it is."

"I was wondering if you would tell me any stories from your days doing out-calls as a hooker-booker?"

"Oh, that was no big deal. There were a few nice regulars that never touched the girls, well, not sexually anyway. Nothing all that interesting ever happened to me when I was doing stripper out-calls. It wasn't traumatic like my earlier nude modeling experiences were."

"We don't need to discuss it if you don't want to."

"That's not it. I just don't remember any of it. I haven't thought about that time of my life since it happened, and I never talk to anyone about it. Let me think about that for a second."

Tina tilts her head and squints in deep thought. She lights up and starts talking fast and excited.

"I had one client that I saw in an expensive hotel in downtown LA. He would pay my full rate for a ninety-minute session and all we would do is dress up in Karate outfits, you know the Gi's that they wear, and we would spar. When I arrived he would already be dressed in his Gi and he had one in my size for me to put on. He didn't even want to watch me get changed. He never got rough with me or hurt me, but he taught me how to throw him and he would ask me to. I could feel his boner when we wrestled, but he never asked for sex, or for me to touch him sexually. I got the feeling that he would jack off after I left, because he was always pretty excited and in a hurry when I would get dressed to leave. I saw him several times over a few months like that."

"Did any of your clients jack off in front of you?"

"I had this one client that would put on women's panty hose and then jack off."

"He never wanted to touch you?"

"He was a total germaphobe, he never touched me or asked me to touch him. We never had sex, even though I saw him a few times. At first I thought he was a weirdo and I considered not seeing him again, but he was nice and he paid my full rate just to dress up with me and then jack off."

"Is that all you ever did with him?"

"One time, he asked me to go shopping with him for

a session. He asked me to meet him at Fashion Island in Newport Beach and told me that he'd pay the full hour's rate for me to go shopping for women's clothing with him. I figured it would be OK, no big deal."

"What happened?"

"I was waiting outside the store we agreed to meet at and I saw his car pull into the parking lot. I recognized it, so I went over to talk to him. I got to his car and he was dressed in DRAG. I couldn't fucking believe it. I screamed at him 'Are you crazy? I can't do this. We'll get fucking arrested if we go into the store! I won't do this.' Then I just walked away and never returned any of his messages again. After a few unreturned messages, he stopped contacting me."

"Wow! You've met some wacky people."

"I had this one client that made a cast of my body. I had to lie on a big table while he covered me with casting plaster from my knees all the way to my neck. I had to roll over then and do my back side too. He made some life-sized rubber-like mannequin dolls with the casting molds. He even gave me one. I couldn't believe how realistic it looked. I put it in the passenger-side seat of my car and thought, 'This is cool, I can use the car-pool lane now.' I even have some posters that he made up showing me standing next to the doll. I think he tried to sell them as love dolls. I still have the posters. I should bring you one."

"My life has been unimaginably dull and boring compared to yours."

"I never think about this except when I'm with you. Nobody has ever gotten these stories out of me. Why do you have this effect on me?"

"Maybe you have never been with anyone who is as interested in you as I am."

"That's probably true. I share things with you that I

401

would never discuss with anyone else. I trust you and I like you."

"I like you too. Can we have sex now?"

"Sure, how do you want to do it?"

"Roll over onto your tummy."

"Why?"

"So I can get on top of you and fuck you."

"Oh, OK. Like this?"

I get on top of Tina and shove my erection between her buns and into her vagina. I dribble olive oil on the crack of her ass and work up a good stroke. I can tell that she's horny today.

"That feels good. Faster, faster."

Tina climaxes but I don't. I pull out of her pussy and oil up her butt. Without warning her or asking her first, I shove my cock balls-deep into her asshole. Tina grunts and tries to buck me off of her. I lie down on top of her and hold her down as I pound her asshole with my boner. I come quickly and Tina is panting when I roll off of her.

"You... dirty-old-man. I need to rest. Get my bottle of water for me. I came so hard that I can't move. Talk to me for a few minutes while I rest."

"You asked me a question last time, and I have calculated an estimate for you."

"What question?"

"You asked me how many times I've fucked you."

"I did?"

"Yes."

"Why."

"How should I know? I told you that I fucked my girlfriend five hundred times and you asked me how many times I've fucked you."

"I asked you that?"

"Yes, you did."

"So?"

"So what?"

"So how many fucking times have you fucked me?"

"I estimate just over one hundred times."

"Seems like more. I'm going to rinse off and then we'll see if you can fuck again."

Tina returns to bed and snuggles next to me.

"We don't have much time so if you want to get me again today, then you better get busy."

"Can we do anal again? I've only fucked your butt twice."

"No, I have to go to work soon and my butt can't be too fucked up. Last time I had to stand up while I talked on the phone because my butt was so sore. The office girls that I supervise teased me about it. I should have written-up those little bitches for insubordination."

"You're a tough supervisor. I'm glad I don't work for you."

"Lick my pussy."

I obediently follow Tina's authoritative instructions.

"Yes, like that. Ohhhh, that feels good."

I climb on top of Tina, insert and pound her. She lies there and takes it. I last forever. I'm afraid that Tina is bored and sore because she is grimacing and squirming to get away from me. I'll finish as quickly as I can and get off of this poor girl. She's a particularly good sport to let me pound her even though she doesn't like it. I better finish soon or she's going to throw me off of her. I wrap my arms around her shoulders and force-fuck her as hard as I can. Her vagina clenches and I can barely keep penetrating her. I fuck her harder and Tina grunts and convulses in spasms. Is she fighting me off or is she coming? Tina grabs my butt and digs her fingernails into my flesh. I ejaculate. Tina gives me a long deep kiss.

"I love the way you fuck me John."

"I love the way you fuck me Tina." We lie silently in each other's arms for a long time. Abruptly, Tina throws me off of her and springs out of bed.

"That was fun. I'm going to shower and get dressed for work now. I've got a new part-time job. I'm answering phones for a big home mortgage lender and I have to dress better than I did when I worked at my last job. It's in a nice office and everyone is quite professional there. I'm making good money too."

I prepare the envelope and put it under Tina's purse. She emerges from the bathroom looking sharp.

"Thanks for this."

"Thanks for seeing me. I hope we can get together again soon."

"I've arranged to work the late shift two days each week now. I don't have to be at work until four PM. We can meet at one o'clock and still have two hours before I need to get ready to leave for work. The men I work with in this new company are young finance executives and they are all nervous around me."

"I know you're busy, so I'll try not to bother you with text messages."

"I love to get your messages. I'll let you know when we can meet again."

Tina transfers her just-applied lip-gloss from her lips to mine.

"I've got to go to work now. Bye."

Tina flies out the door in the right direction and the door slams shut behind her. I have a drink, a smoke, and a snack. Then I doze off for a while.

Two hours after Tina departed from our tryst, I receive

a text message from her.

From: Tina
Msg: my butt hurts

Maybe some comedy is called for.

To: Tina
Msg: Sorry butt,
not really

Before I can set my phone down, it chimes.

From: Tina
Msg: Im going to die
laughing. I asked a
caller RU the
home-boner?

I reply back to her:

To: Tina
Msg: Maybe you have
"boner on the brain"
because you wore one
today!

A few seconds later she replies:

From: Tina
Msg: U R 2 funny
LMAO

I wonder what the hell 'LMAO' means?

Chapter 28

If Only I Had the Nerve

I knock on John's hotel room door with a sense of nostalgia and a dirty smirk. Even though it's been fun meeting him like this, I know that this is probably the last time.

I won't tell John this is the last time. I remember him saying that he would be too sad, and he has that fear of never seeing me again. Besides, who knows?

I must be ovulating because I'm unbearably horny. Good thing that Greg is out of town this week so I don't have to worry about using contraception with him. John is definitely infertile or I'd have gotten pregnant by now. I finally have a good enough job that my medical insurance pays for my contraception patches. By the end of this month I'll get my medical exam and have my patch in place. It will be a huge relief when I don't have to worry about getting pregnant anymore. I am NEVER having kids.

It seems like I send Tina fifty messages before I hear back from her. I'm certain that it's only a matter of time until Tina changes her phone number and her email, and then I'll never hear from her again. That knowledge makes what little time I get with her even more precious, but the fear of it ending is always on my mind.

That's Tina's knock. Even though it's been six months, I recognize it immediately. I swing the door fully open. Tina flashes her cover-girl smile at me. She looks great. Even though she looks more mature, it's a great look on her. I can't stop looking her up-and-down. Tina laughs at me, flings herself on me and wraps me up in a hug that is suitable for long lost lovers reunited. I whisper into her ear, "It's our five year anniversary of when we first met!"

"No way. It can't possibly have been five years. Can it? Wait. Was I still in college? Was I still modeling? Are you sure that it's been five years?"

"Yes, I'm sure. I found my old print out copy of your website and your first review. The date is five years ago this week. I remember that you told me you were in school and that you were modeling at the time."

"How old was I?"

"You said you were twenty-two at the time."

"Oh, shit. It has been five years. I'm twenty-seven now."

"I'm so glad that we met, you're my favorite person in the world. Let's have some champagne to celebrate."

"Are you kidding?"

I give Tina a suggestive look while I pull a premium-brand bottle of champagne from the little refrigerator. Tina gives me an incredulous look. I smile at Tina and then produce two chilled crystal champagne glasses from the tiny freezer compartment.

"You brought expensive champagne and glass flutes to this crummy hotel?"

"This is an important anniversary and it deserves to be

celebrated in style."

"OK, but I can only have one glass or I'll get sloppy at work later."

"That's too bad. I love you even more when you're sloppy drunk."

I can't believe how debonair John is. He gracefully pours our drinks, presents mine to me, and then delivers a suave toast to our half-decade of decadence. He is literally charming my pants off of me.

I forgot to take my boner-pills until just before Tina arrived. I'll make some conversation to give them time to work. "Do you mind if I ask you about how you made the leap from doing no-sex out-calls to doing full-service out-calls like you were doing when we first met?"

"No, I don't mind talking about it with you. It didn't feel like any leap at all. At the time it seemed like it was just a small step, to go from what I had been doing, to escorting. Being an escort to gentlemen clients is much nicer, and safer, than many of the weirdo nude modeling casting calls I went on when I was younger. While I was stripping, I had seen first-hand how much easy money there was to be made in the entertainer business; that is, if you knew what you were doing and if you were independent."

"How did you approach it?"

"I analyzed the situation and figured that I could make good money, but that I also needed to be independent. I had to be the person in charge. No more working for some asshole, or with some stupid bitch."

"What did you do first?"

"I remember looking at the OC escort ads and thinking: I already know how to screen for good clients. I know how to set up appointments. I decided to set my screening standards and my rate super-high. I was going to be careful to be super selective about who I'd see and where I'd agree to see them."

"What happened next?"

"That's when I decided to set up as an independent escort. I set up a separate email address. I got a new, separate mobile phone and number. I found a photo, wrote the text, and posted my own ad on one of the popular call girl ad websites for OC. I liked being in control of my ad, my photos, my information and I especially liked that I controlled the screening. I could decide what level of screening I wanted to do and who I would agree to see."

"How did it go?"

"I only saw the very best clients. I was very picky. I would agree to see only the clients that I liked after talking to them on the phone and after they passed all of my screening criteria. I said, "Sorry" to a lot of guys that called and emailed me. My screening process was super strict. If anything was flaky, then I dropped the guy, blocked his calls and emails, and went on to the next guy. I ended up approving only about one out of every ten guys that gave me the full information I requested. Of the men that I screened and approved of, I ended up seeing only about half of them."

"That must have been about the time that I called you for the first time."

"I don't remember, shit, I got so many calls after my ad went up. Then after my first review, I started getting a lot of calls from older gentlemen that didn't blink at my rate, but wanted to know how old I was."

"That's when I called you. After your first posted review. We met at this hotel on our first date."

"Is that true? I don't remember that, it's been so long ago."

"You didn't have your ad up for very long."

"I only saw a total of about five or six different clients in OC as an independent escort. Three of them, including you, live locally and became instant regulars."

"Did you get a lot of inquiries?"

"I was able to get as many appointments as I wanted, whenever I wanted them. I was also working some occasional hostess jobs as well. It was fun to travel to Vegas, or Miami, to do a hostess show and it paid well. You and one other regular client started buying two-hour sessions and that meant that I didn't have to work as much. After only a couple of months I saw only my favorite regulars, and that easily paid my bills each month."

"I'm glad we have gotten to know each other."

"Me too! Why is there a guitar case on the bed? Do you have some kind of weird new fetish that I don't know about?"

"I wrote a song for you. It's your present for our five-year anniversary. Do you mind if I play if for you?"

"You wrote a song for me? No you didn't. Did you? What kind of song? When did you start writing songs?"

"It's a love song. I need you to pretend that you are the one singing it, because it's written from your point of view." Tina gives me a wide-eyed look as I get my guitar out of its case and tune it. She acts like we're in uncharted territory as I tell her, "The title of your song is, 'If Only I Had the Nerve'. You should recognize the lyrics, since you essentially wrote them." I play some basic chords and sing the tune as best I can.

I would tell her how I long to touch her gentle curve, I would tell her, if only I had the nerve.

I would tell her of the affection I hold in reserve, yes I would tell her, if only I had the nerve.

I don't tell her 'cause she might think I'm a total perv, but it'd be worth the risk, if only I had the nerve.

Ya know that lez don't match the image I try to preserve but it'd be worth the risk, if only I had the nerve.

I know I'll find her, but I hope I find her soon, 'cause I could use a friend, who knows what I'm going through.

I know out there's the best-friend-lover I deserve, and I will find her, if only I have the nerve.

I'll go shop'n 'n club'n with my secret fellow perv, and I will find her, if only I have the nerve.

Now I want the cute young girl who's standing right here, I'm going to tell her, as soon as I've got the nerve.

Oh, I want to feel the touch of her gentle curve, I start to tell her, but do I still have the nerve?

Oh... oh! ...dammit!... If only... I had... the nerve.

"Oh John... that's lovely. That is a beautiful song."

Tina is looking at me seriously. She must be upset or disturbed. She is frowning in deep thought. She is glaring at me with ferocious eyes. I'm scared.

"You are going to fuck me right now, and don't fuck me gentle, fuck me hard. You know, HARD, the way I like it."

We undress quickly and I do as instructed. I struggle just to hang on and stay on top of her. She is bucking like one of those rodeo horses and her fingernails are dug deeply into my buttocks. A vein on Tina's forehead starts to bulge. She's screaming.

"Harder, harder! Faster! More! More! More!"

Tina climaxes loud and hard. She throws me off like a rag doll, springs up from the bed, and announces her opinion approvingly.

"That was a good fuck! Good job."

Tina steps toward the bathroom and politely informs

412

me what's going to happen next.

"I'm going to wash up a little bit and then you are going to lick my pussy."

Tina has certainly changed in the five years I have known her. The wide-eyed little girl is gone and a fierce sex goddess has taken her place. Tina has grown into a beautiful woman, both physically and psychologically.

I jump in bed and order John to lick my pussy. I suppose that I could ask him to, but I know that he wants to and this way saves time. Wait, there is something that I wanted to remind him to do. As soon as John grabs my cheeks and pulls them apart I remember. I warn him, "Don't lick my butt yet. After you make me come I want you to kiss me with your pussy-face." John follows my orders precisely.

John is sensual, but at the same time, he's also dirty. He fucks like a girl. I have a big orgasm and push John's head out of my crotch. He kisses me when I order him to and then he asks me to get up on my hands and knees. John gets behind me and we do it doggy-style with John's thumb in my butt. We both come hard and collapse in a heap.

John rolls away from me. He knows that I don't like to cuddle with him after sex. I'd like to cuddle, but he always gets a boner and jumps me. I appreciate that he accommodates my preferences. I am going to miss having a dutiful sex slave at my beck and call.

I give Tina a carpet cleaning and then we walk the dog. I put my thumb in her tight little butthole and she takes it. I've been afraid to ask her for anal sex, because I'm not sure if she still likes it. I can tell that it hurts her. Even though it makes her come hard, she often complains about the pain after. I don't want to pressure her for it, because I want to keep seeing her. She orgasms, which makes me climax. I ease my thumb from her anus as she pulls away. After we have rested, I get in the shower to clean up. I return to bed and climb in next to Tina, but not touching her.

John is the only man I will have anal sex with and I want to get butt fucked one last time. I suck his penis until he is hard and then ask, "Do you want to put it in my butt?" John's jaw is too slack to speak, but he nods. I explain, "Before I came over I took a hot bath and practiced with my butt plug so we can do anal." I lie on my stomach as John gets the olive oil. He takes his time and gets me ready.

I barely get into the bed before Tina goes down on me and sucks my dick. I love this girl. I am watching her take me to heaven, when she blows my mind by asking me for anal sex. I totally love this girl.

I reach back for John's penis and it is rock hard. I stick my butt up in the air and tell him to put his cock in me. He shoves the tip in and waits for me to adjust to it. John gives me a few slow strokes with just the tip to get me used to it. When I am relaxed, John penetrates me fully, and then gradually builds up the stroke. He fucks my butt harder and harder until he is pounding me. He lasts forever. It hurts, but I don't want to stop. John grunts and talks dirty to me. He calls me his 'horny little girl' and I whisper, "Fuck my little butt Daddy." I start coming and John pumps me fast, deep and hard. I am out of breath when he finally comes. I feel his hot semen squirt inside me.

I butt fuck Tina harder than I ever have before. We both climax vigorously and then go limp.

I am too exhausted to get up. I don't know if I have ever come that hard before.

I regain consciousness and see that Tina is motionless, but she's breathing. I figure that I'll clean up first this

414

time and let her rest. When I return, Tina asks me to hold her and kiss her. I'm surprised because Tina doesn't like to cuddle after sex. She fucks like a guy.

I am going to miss John, but I can't tell him that, so we just cuddle a while. It's better this way, no sad goodbyes. He'll probably get another boner if we cuddle, but that's OK, since this is the last time.

We lie in bed together for a long time. Eventually Tina gets up and walks slowly to the bathroom. She leaves the door wide open and I can hear her singing in the shower. She returns with a towel wrapped around her and lies down on the bed.

"Oh, my butt hurts. Can we talk for a little while, so I can rest?"

"Good idea. I need a break too."

"Remember when we first met. I never let anyone even touch my butt back then. Now I look forward to anal sex. Then you turned me into a raging lezbo. I have to be careful in the girl's locker room at the gym so I don't get caught looking at the cute girls, or making your perverted little noise. That reminds me, I have to tell you about the cute girls at work."

"You mean the hotties you aren't allowed to hit on?"

"Yes, them. I transferred to a new job at work. Now I work in a different department on a different floor. That means that I can date the girls in the phone pool, because I'm not their supervisor any more. We've been going out for drinks after work, and there's three of them that I think I might be able to play with."

"I'm so happy for you."

"You've turned me into a twisted pervert."

"Speaking of a twisted pervert, I want to give you my honest answer to a question that you have asked me several times before."

"What question? Why? Do I keep asking you the same question?"

"You have asked me a couple of times, 'How young a girl I would I have sex with.'"

"Oh, THAT question. I've always wanted to ask a man that."

"In the past, I have been too inhibited to give you much of an answer, but now I want to tell you how I feel, even if you're going to think that I'm a total perv."

"Well, I already think that, so you aren't risking anything. Besides, I like that about you."

I look Tina in the eye, "I would have wanted to be your first lover, when you decided to try it."

"I wish I had known a man like you when I was a teenager. At that age I wanted a daddy-figure to touch me and to make me feel like a grown-up girl."

"Yes, well, it's a good thing we didn't meet then because I would just now be getting out of jail."

"Speaking of jail, have you seen our little fugitive lately? You would have sent me a text message invitation, right?"

"I haven't seen or heard from Little Lisa in over six months. I think she has a new daddy now. She even took down her escort web site."

I am enjoying John's company. I always do, but I have to leave soon. I should have already left. I am going to be late to meet my boyfriend's parents, but I don't care. This is my last few minutes with this man that means so much to me. I can't leave just yet.

Tina looks at the clock and pauses deep in thought. I wait for her to finish processing whatever she's thinking about. I want her.

I will miss John, but I can't say that to him. I press myself against him and suggest, "We have time for one more, if you're up for it." John answers me with his devilish grin.

I suck John's penis and he gets hard again right away. I wish my new boyfriend could fuck like this. Maybe I can teach Greg some of John's tricks. I lie on my back and tell John to get on top and kiss me while he fucks me. I am getting just what I want and it feels so good. We come simultaneously. We kiss long and hard. We stare into each other's eyes for a long time. Without thinking, I say, "I love you John." He replies immediately.

"I love you too Tina."

I throw John off of me and turn away. I am afraid that he will get upset if he sees me crying. I hide my face in my hands and run to the bathroom. I close the door. I don't want him to see me like this. I flush the toilet to cover the sound of my sobs.

We have sex for what will undoubtedly be the last time during this meeting. Tina comes hard and that makes me come too. In the heat of passion, Tina accidentally says that she loves me. She meant to say that she loved the orgasm, but I said it back to her. She's too polite to correct her mistake and hurt my feelings. Tina runs to the bathroom with her face in her hands and closes the door. She is laughing at my foolishness, but that's all right. I know that an attractive young woman like her is never going to love an old fart like me. I do appreciate how incredibly nice she always is to me.

I don't have an envelope today so I just put the C-notes in a pile under Tina's phone on the table. I feel sleepy. Tina is still in the bathroom with the door shut. I lie down on the bed to rest.

I open the bathroom door and hear John snoring. I make enough noise to wake him up without letting him know that I caught him sleeping.

417

I must have fallen asleep. Tina is coming out of the bathroom fully clothed and toweling off her hair.

"Can I take this stick of ladies deodorant?"

"It's almost empty."

"It's completely empty."

"Then, why do you want it? That's a goofy souvenir, isn't it?"

"Ha! A question like that from the man that keeps my underwear as souvenirs."

"We have already established the fact that I am a complete pervert. What's your excuse?"

"I want to get the same brand and scent so that I can remember our sex when I'm with someone else."

Dammit! I knew it. Tina has a boyfriend, or worse yet, a fiancé. Now I know for certain that I will never see her again. Well, that is, not until she's been married for at least six months.

John just looks at me and blinks, so I say 'thanks' and shove the empty ladies deodorant into my purse along with the money under my phone. I thank John for the donation and for my song. I tell him that I have to leave now.

"Will I ever see you again?"

"I'm sorry that it's been so long. It seems like a year."

"This is only the second time we've been together in a full year."

I can't tell John that I have a boyfriend now. Even though he would be happy for me, I see how he always sneers whenever I talk about another man. That is such a typical guy response. I'll give him an acceptable excuse for his fragile little ego to cling to.

Tina is taking a long time to respond. Her tone of voice is different from usual. She is hiding something, I'm sure that she is.

"I just don't have the time to see you anymore. My new job pays a lot more; it's enough to cover all my bills. I have to stay after-hours for training, but I'm meeting nice professional men my age there. Some have college degrees and careers in finance. I'm taking my job much more seriously than I used to. I guess I'm growing up. I've got to go now."

Tina DOES have a new boyfriend. I KNOW she does. I'll definitely never see her again. I didn't realize how much I love her. I hope she leaves before I start crying.

"Don't get up, you look comfortable. I will see myself out." I sit on the bed next to John, give him a kiss and tell him goodbye. I hope he doesn't see me crying.

Tina is anxious to leave and gives me an unusually long and deep kiss goodbye. She must have hay fever or an allergy, because her eyes are watery and she sniffles as she exits the room. I hope I get to see her again, but most of all, I hope she finds happiness. I want all her dreams to come true, because I love her, and because she deserves to be happy.

Chapter 29

A Knock at the Door

$\mathbf{I}$ enter room number 609 and set down my bag and briefcase. I am certain that I'm forgetting something. What is it? Normally I would text the room number to the girl at this point, but there's something different about the protocol this time, because it's our first date. Oh, that's right, the new girl instructed me to call her from the hotel room after I check in and give her the hotel phone number. That way she can call the front desk and ask for me by name. Every girl has her own screening method. Well, at least any girl that I would want to see has some kind of security procedure that she uses. It's a good thing that this newbie didn't require any provider references from me. It has been so long since I have seen a girl that advertises that I don't think I could come up with any references she could contact. Where's her phone number? What's her name?

I pull out an unmarked manila file folder where I keep all of my escort website and review printouts. The folder catches on the edge of my briefcase and the pages spill all over the floor. At my feet is a mosaic of suggestive photos with client ratings, does/doesn't check marks, and my handwritten notes.

I gather up the pages and see Tina's old web ad on top. I smile as I read my scribbled note from the first time I called her: Sounds like a newbie, extensive screening, allow a week for new clients to get cleared.

I haven't seriously shopped for a new girl since I met Tina. I haven't wanted to. But now I have to find a new girl. I haven't heard from Tina since I last saw her eight full months ago. I bet she got married to a rich, handsome banker that's her age and she's pregnant with his kid. I bet I never hear from her again. In addition to that, Lisa has a new daddy now, so she isn't available any more. The situation is clear; it's time to find a new girl. I look up and see myself in the mirror. My hair has turned completely sliver. I sure hope this new girl has a daddy-complex.

I locate the newbie's review and web ad. Her name is Kristen. With any luck, she's waiting for my call.

I call the number to leave her the requested message. "Hi Kristen, this is John Smith, I have just checked-in at the hotel. The phone number for the hotel is 555-0169 and you can ask for me by name. I hope to hear from you soon, I'm looking forward to seeing you today."

I need to pass some time, so I unpack my bag of goodies. I made sure I brought the XL's today since a newbie will require them, but she will probably not have any XL's with her. At first I leave them out, like I always do, but then I remember that I'm seeing a new girl. I hide the porn, lube, and condoms in the nightstand. I don't want to scare the newbie. It's been a long time since I've seen a new girl and I've forgotten my usual protocol. I don't want her to think that I'm some kind of a pervert. That reminds me, I need to be sure to ask Kristen if she likes girls. I wonder if she's one of those girls that likes porn.

What else do I do for a newbie? Oh, I need to get her envelope ready before she gets here. I get it out and double-check the required donation amount against my handwritten notes on her review print out.

The hotel phone rings loudly and it startles me. I'm not used to the house phone ringing, but this is how who's-her-fuzz wants to do this. "Hello."

"Hi, John?"

"Yes, it's me." I smile as Kristen speaks to me in a nervous little girl's voice.

"Hi, it's Kristen. What's your room number? Are you ready for me to come over?"

"Hi Kristen, we're in room 609, that's room six, zero, nine. Are you familiar with this hotel?"

"I know where it is."

"Have you been here before?"

"No, I haven't. Why?"

"Oh, it's just that if you don't want to go through the lobby to get to the elevators, then you can drive past the main entrance, around to the right, and into the parking structure."

"Wait, I need to write this down. Around to the right... OK, then what?"

"Drive up one level and look for a big sign that says 'To The Lobby'. This time of day there are usually some parking spaces right next to the double glass doors that lead from the parking structure to the Lobby."

"Doors to the lobby. Got it. What's next?"

"Just inside the glass doors you will see the elevators to your left."

"That's good, go on."

"Exit the elevator on the sixth floor. Go to your left down the hallway to the end where room 609 is."

"This is great. It can be so hard to locate a room at a hotel."

"I'm ready for you as soon as you can get here."

"I'll be there in fifteen minutes."

She sounds anxious and excited. She sounds like she's pretty green. You can always tell when the girl's a newbie. I have to keep myself busy while I wait for her to get here. She'll be at least forty minutes. How am I going to keep my mind occupied when I'm this horny?

I text the room number to Kristen's cell phone. Just in case she loses her notes, she'll have it on her phone and then she doesn't have to call me for it.

To: Kristen
Msg: Room 609 c u
soon.

She's clearly a complete newbie, so I have no idea what to expect this afternoon. Looking through my papers I see old photos of my favorite girls. I fondly remember Tina and Lisa as newbies. They were so fresh and cute.

Oh, I almost forgot something. I always send a text message to Tina whenever I am going to see Little Lisa or, in this case, when I see a new girl.

424

To: Tina
Msg: Hi Tina, I'm
meating a newbie!
Do U wanna cum?

I never know if Tina might reply, and besides that, I just like the idea of sending an invitation for a threesome to a bikini model. I don't care if she even receives it. It feels good just to send it.

I look at my collection of Tina's photos. I say out loud, "You never know when it will be the last time that you'll ever see her. At the same time, you never know when you will get to see her again." I turn to the photo and review of the newbie that is currently running only thirty minutes late. I mumble aloud, "Kristen's website photo is hot. Her only review characterizes her as a super-cute newbie. Most importantly, she's on her way over. But what if she's not the girl in the photo? The image on her website isn't all that revealing. It may not be her photo anyway..."

My phone chimes. It's a reply message from Tina!

From: Tina
Msg: hiiiiii, well the
reason you haven't
heard from me is that
I'm 8 months pregnant!
*****shocked face*****
hahaha, how's that for
juicy gossip? miss ya!
Xxxoooxxxooo

My mind reels, "What the f... ." My thoughts and the silence shatter. There's a knock at the door.

THE END

425

This concludes the first Book of the Stories of Orange County Girls Trilogy.

You can find the continuation of this story in the second Book of the Stories of Orange County Girls Trilogy, titled:

MILFs

The True Stories of Hot Orange County Mothers

You can find the conclusion of this story in the final Book of the Stories of Orange County Girls Trilogy, titled:

DADDY, I'm Your Daughter

The Story of an Orange County Love Child

Acknowledgments

The authors are gratefully indebted to the many generous persons who have contributed to this story and made this work possible.

Aliases have been employed to maintain the anonymity of all contributors who wish to remain so.

Glossary:

69: mutual, simultaneous oral sex.

Analist: a person that performs anal sex.

Anilingus (or Analingus): oral sex with the tongue in the anus, also know as rimming.

Ass To Mouth: pulling a penis out of a girl's ass and putting it directly into her mouth, or another girl's mouth.

ATM: Ass To Mouth common abbreviation.

Back door: anal sex.

Ben Franklins: $100 bills.

BJ: blowjob, oral sex, man's penis in woman's mouth.

BBBJ: bare back blowjob (no condom).

Bermuda Triangle: a 69 involving three people.

Boner-meds, boner-pills: erectile dysfunction medication.

C-notes: $100 bills.

Call Girl: a woman that provides companionship to clients.

CIM: come in mouth.

Client: a person that hires an escort.

Cum-drunk: euphoria induced by sexual climax.

Cunnilingus: oral sex, a tongue on a woman's vagina.

DFK: deep French kiss(ing).

Dick check: the inspection of a client's penis for STDs.

Dildo: an artificial penis.

Doggy-style: sex position similar to dogs.

Donation: the money a client gives an escort.

431

Double: two escorts that know each other seeing a client together.

Double-anal: two penises in one anus.

DP: double-penetration: one penis in the woman's vagina and another penis in the woman's anus simultaneously.

Escort: a person that provides companionship to clients.

EVOO: extra-virgin olive oil.

Facial: ejaculating on the girl's face.

Finger-trap: two guys and one girl configured with one penis in the girl's mouth and one penis in the girl's pussy (or butt) simultaneously.

Fisting: inserting a fist into the vagina or anus.

Full Service (FS): the escort provides penile-vaginal sexual intercourse.

Greek: anal sex.

Hand-jobber: an escort that provides only hand stimulation to the client's penis and does not provide bj or Full service.

Ho-bag: a bag brought to an appointment that contains a collection of items that may be useful.

Hobbyist: a person that enjoys the hobby of engaging with escorts.

GFE: girlfriend experience: a provider that offers conversation, friendly attitude, kissing with tongue, BBBJ, and other services that resemble a date with a girlfriend.

Hooker-Booker: a person who makes appointments for an escort.

Hooker heels: super high-heels that scream, "Fuck me."

In-call: the client meets at the escort's location.

Jilling off: the female version of Jacking off.

Kegel: muscle of the female pelvic floor.

Lezbo: a Lesbian, a girl that has sex with girls.

LMAO: laughing my ass off.

Magic square: a 69 involving four people.

Ménage à trois (French for threesome): sex involving three people.

Menu: a list of services that a given provider offers.

MILF: a mother I'd like to fuck.

Mish: missionary position, a sexual intercourse position where the woman is lying on her back and the man lies on top facing her.

Newbie: a call girl, or client, with little or no experience.

Nymph-limp: the abnormal gait of a person sore from sex.

OC: Orange County, California, USA.

Off-the-grid Call Girl: a girl that never advertises, who only sees clients after her escort-friend has approved them and often only does 'doubles' with her escort-friend.

Oralgasm: climax resulting from oral stimulation, either BJ or cunnilingus.

Out-call: the escort meets at the client's location.

Overnighter: the escort stays the night with the client.

PITA: Pain In The Ass, typically a spouse or significant other.

POV: point of view, filming from the man's-eye-view.

Privates: porn stars providing escort services at private parties.

Provider: an escort service provider, an escort.

Regular: a client that sees a given escort repeatedly.

Rim: anilingus.

Safe: using a condom.

Screening: verification of a client prior to meeting.

STD: a sexually transmitted disease.

Session: an appointment with an escort and a client.

Sexcited: sexually excited.

Sexploits: sexual exploits.

Spank bank: memories of particularly pleasurable sexual experiences to be recalled later, especially to enhance masturbation.

Spits: CIM, but doesn't swallow, goes and spits it out.

Speak directly into the microphone: bbbj.

Swallows: CIM and swallowing the semen.

Walk the dog: intercourse doggy-style

References:

A Research Study from Rutgers University titled, "Male Multiple Ejaculatory Orgasms: A Case Study". Published in The Journal of Sex Education and Therapy, Volume 23, Number 2, (C) Copyright 1998"